Thre...
se...

AU...

Billionaires

Exciting new romances from reader
favourites Margaret Way, Amy Andrews
and Jennie Adams

AUSTRALIAN
Billionaires

MARGARET WAY
AMY ANDREWS
JENNIE ADAMS

All the characters in this book have no existence outside the imagination
of the author, and have no relation whatsoever to anyone bearing the
same name or names. They are not even distantly inspired by any
individual known or unknown to the author, and all the incidents are
pure invention.

M&B™ and M&B™ with the Rose Device
are trademarks of the publisher.
Harlequin Mills & Boon Limited, Eton House,
18-24 Paradise Road, Richmond, Surrey TW9 1SR

AUSTRALIAN BILLIONAIRES
© by Harlequin Enterprises II B.V./S.à.r.l. 2009

The Wealthy Australian's Proposal © Margaret Way PTY., Ltd 2009
The Billionaire Claims His Wife © Amy Andrews 2009
Inherited by the Billionaire © Jennifer Ann Ryan 2009

ISBN: 978 0 263 87543 0

009-0909

Harlequin Mills & Boon policy is to use papers that are
natural, renewable and recyclable products and made from
wood grown in sustainable forests. The logging and
manufacturing processes conform to the legal environmental
regulations of the country of origin.

Printed and bound in Spain
by Litografia Rosés S.A., Barcelona

The Wealthy Australian's Proposal

MARGARET WAY

Margaret Way, a definite Leo, was born and raised in the sub-tropical River City of Brisbane, capital of the Sunshine State of Queensland. A Conservatorium-trained pianist, teacher, accompanist and vocal coach, her musical career came to an unexpected end when she took up writing, initially as a fun thing to do. She currently lives in a harbourside apartment at beautiful Raby Bay, a thirty-minute drive from the state capital, where she loves dining alfresco on her plant-filled balcony that overlooks a translucent green marina filled with all manner of pleasure craft, from motor cruisers costing millions of dollars, big graceful yachts with carved masts standing tall against the cloudless blue sky to little bay runabouts. No one and nothing is in a mad rush so she finds the laid-back village atmosphere very conducive to her writing. With well over one hundred books to her credit she still believes her best is yet to come.

Don't miss Margaret Way's exciting new book, *Cattle Baron: Nanny Needed*, coming in August 2009 from Mills & Boon® Romance.

CHAPTER ONE

NYREE had been up at the crack of dawn. Her great friend and benefactor Miss Em, also known as Professor Emilia Scott, was coming home after a month spent in beautiful New Zealand with her sister, Louisa. The two sisters were very close. Nyree had not been so blessed. She had no sister to share her joys and pains, let alone the agony of sudden and violent family bereavement.

Six years before, when she was just into her teens, her parents had been travelling home from a piano recital. Her mother had been driving—unusual when her husband was with her. They had been very happy that night. Her parents had been soul mates and great music lovers. But, as fate would have it, the night that had begun so happily had ended in disaster. Speeding towards them had been a young man who, despite the law, was using his mobile phone to have a half-hearted argument with his girlfriend about where to go for a weekend away.

The police investigation had concluded that the young man had been so preoccupied with his conversation he had momentarily lost control of the vehicle and swerved onto the wrong side of the road—right into the path of the oncoming car.

Fate moved the players. Man was but a pawn.

Two vehicles taken out. Three deaths. Shattered lives for all who were left.

Those were the days when Nyree had felt her loss so starkly she literally hadn't been able to speak. Not even when her grandmother, Jessica, had told her to "get a grip". She had been taken in, albeit reluctantly, by her father's parents, the only relatives to hand. No matter what pain she'd been in, her grandmother had never let up telling her to "get a grip". It had become a familiar mantra. Never had her grandmother said, *I'm here for you, Nyree. We share our pain.*

That had never happened. Not then. Not now.

When she was small Nyree had sensed her grandmother didn't much like her, and hadn't liked or approved of her beautiful mother, who'd been of Italian descent. That had been considered a serious drawback. Her grandmother was stuck with an old Anglo-Celt mindset at a time when the nation embraced multiculturalism. Jessica had been so certain her son had made a disastrous marriage, a clairvoyant might have told her.

The bliss of her parents' marriage had proved her wrong.

Nyree almost hated her grandmother, but couldn't quite make it. Maybe hate had been left out of her nature, but it had got pretty bad. Almost overnight she'd gone from being a day student at the prestigious school she had attended since Grade One to being a boarder.

Her parents, who had been so proud of their little girl, had wanted her to have the best of everything. Swinton College *was* the best. The college was just down the road, not halfway across the country, but Jessica had dived on the idea of Nyree's becoming a boarder. The truth was, Jessica was actually unfit to be a grandmother.

"Your grandmother means well." Her grandfather, Alan, a far more kindly person, had tried to explain away the decision. He'd known for sure his wife didn't mean well. He'd been married to her for over forty years.

"The child is the spitting image of her mother. I can't handle that. She'd be better off at boarding school. Don't we keep hearing how bright she is?"

To heap tragedy upon tragedy—didn't it always go in threes?—Alan Allcott had died of a heart attack little more than a year later. Fourteen by then, Nyree had been done with being shocked by anything.

"Heartbreak!" her grandmother had pronounced, placing the blame. *"That mother of yours is the cause of all this. She was the one driving that night. Not my beloved Martin. My son! He would have known how to take evasive action."*

So Grandfather Allcott had made his departure without a lot of fuss. Maybe he had had too much of married life. Another funeral to attend. There she had met her grandfather's brother, Howard, for the first and only time. Howard was "the black sheep of the family", according to Jessica—based on the fact her great-uncle Howard had abandoned the family business over thirty years ago to join an artists' colony in Far North

Queensland. She'd made it sound the height of decadence. Great-Uncle Howard had appeared very different from his brother. But then Great-Uncle Howard didn't have a wife like Jessica to sour his system. Despite that, Nyree had persisted in searching for some redeeming feature in her grandmother.

She'd found none.

It had been Miss Em—Professor Emilia Scott, Principal of Swinton College for Girls—who'd kept a keen compassionate eye on Nyree Allcott, one of her star pupils. She'd known all about Nyree's sad home situation and had applauded the girl's strength of character. It had been Miss Em who'd come to Nyree's rescue when her grandmother had more or less kicked her out a month after her school graduation.

"I've done my duty by you, Nyree. You've been given a first-class education. Now you must stand on your own two feet."

Where was she supposed to go? She was after all only seventeen years old.

Miss Em had risen to the occasion—though Nyree's grandmother had been quite beyond her understanding—offering Nyree the comfortable guest flat built underneath her graceful old colonial mansion that looked out over the deep broad river. The older woman had suggested, as Nyree was no longer at school, she should call her Emilia, but Nyree had thought it inappropriate to address her former principal and mentor in such an informal way. It wasn't as though they were level pegging. Miss Em was a woman of stature. She was the greatly respected, always approachable

Professor Scott. Miss Em had been Nyree's compromise, and Emilia had let it go at that.

Those days had been very hectic. Then her first year university exams had been over. Nyree had studied child psychology. God knew she had enough insight into the lives of sad and lonely, love-deprived children. She had done well, though it had been no easy thing finding the time to study, often into the early hours, while still maintaining two part-time jobs.

In the years since she had left Swinton College she and Miss Em had become great friends. A good deal of her time had been spent in the main house, enjoying Miss Em's stimulating company—and, as Miss Em had always reassured her, *"I'm enjoying every minute, Nyree. Your company is delightful."*

It made a nice change from, *"Goodbye—good riddance!"*

Out on a hillside walk one day, among the yellow blossoming wattles, Nyree had shouted it to the heavens. *"Thank you, God, for Miss Em."*

She had no idea if He was up there, but she'd said it all the same. When in doubt, any port in a storm! Either way, Nyree Allcott, a true orphan of the storm, had been saved by the generosity and compassion of a wonderful woman.

Barely a year later Fate, over which no one had control, had stepped in again. While Nyree and two of her university friends—ex-Swinton girls—had been enjoying a companionable cup of tea with "Prof Scott". Emilia, with hardly a sick day behind her, had tipped her head back against her wing-backed chair and calmly exhaled a single out breath. It had been her last. That splendid heart had simply given out.

Nyree couldn't even begin to ask herself why. What was the point? She had lost her best friend in the world. Given her history, what could she expect?

Later, when the heavily attended funeral and wake was over, Miss Em's sister Louisa had taken Nyree's trembling hand, telling her she was the granddaughter Emilia had never had. *"She loved you, Nyree. She fully intended to change her will, never thinking she would go so quickly. Did any of us, dear girl? I've made out a cheque, which you must take. It will help you through until you get on your feet. It's what Emilia intended."*

Everything had been wrapped up quickly after that. Louisa had returned to her family in New Zealand. The Scott family home had been put on the market and sold within a week. Nyree, numb with grief, had moved into a rented house with her university friends.

About ten days ago a letter had arrived with the name of a well-known law firm stamped on the lower left hand corner. Nyree had stood in the hallway, weighing the letter in her hand. She hadn't been able to begin to guess what it contained.

"Open it. Open it!" advised her friend Michelle, peering over the upstairs banister.

"I don't have the heart to open it."

"Let me do it." Michelle raced down the steps. "Maybe your old witch of a grandmother wants to settle some money on you."

"When hell freezes over!" Her grandmother was still

hale and hearty. Nyree expected she would leave her entire estate to her chihuahua, Miranda.

Michelle ripped open the letter excitedly, while Nyree stood holding her breath.

"You'd better read this, Nyree. It looks like something *good*!"

And so it had proved. At a time when Nyree had believed nothing good was going to happen to her, something had.

Miss Em had indeed been a woman to reckon with. In the last six months of her life she had tracked down Nyree's great-uncle, Howard Allcott. She had not met him in person, but they had exchanged letters and spoken on the phone. During that time Miss Em had managed to instil in Howard Allcott a much-needed sense of family. The evidence was right there in front of Nyree's stunned eyes. Howard had died at seventy-nine, making Nyree the sole beneficiary of his estate. Nyree had been requested to make an appointment to see a Mr Morris Brockway, an associate of the firm, who was handling Howard Allcott's estate.

CHAPTER TWO

A FEW days later Nyree had found out that, although there was no money to speak of, there was the greatest gift in the world:

A house!

She hadn't been able to believe it. Her heart had leapt with gratitude. She owned a home of her own, with paintings lining every wall.

"You like art, eh?" the solicitor asked with an indulgent smile.

He had never seen a more beautiful young girl in his life. The combination of large lustrous dark eyes, their beauty emphasised by arching black brows and long black eyelashes, flawless olive skin and a rioting mane of caramel coloured hair sun streaked with gold, was breathtaking. He wondered if that remarkable hair was dyed—it was so startling against the big, velvety dark eyes.

"I like the idea of a home of my own more." Nyree's excitement was just barely held in check.

"Don't get me wrong here," the solicitor warned. "My understanding is it's no mansion. It was the homestead for an old sugar plantation. Most of the land has been sold off, but there's quite a bit remaining and the land has become valuable. Word is DHH has plans to build a big eco-friendly tourist resort up there."

"DHH?" Nyree felt the first shiver of premonition.

"Surely you've heard of it? It's huge—although they operate mainly in the North. David Hollister is a billionaire many times over. DHH is David Hollister Holdings. He owns great chunks of everything. Builder, developer, air and road freight, pastoral interests, a chain of resorts. His son and heir, Brant, is a chip off the old block, I believe. He's very much in the news these days, with his dad handing more and more over to him. I shouldn't be a bit surprised if you hear from the son. He's an architect as well an engineer; his father's right-hand man. Good for you to know in advance. I'm certain if you hang out you'll get an excellent price."

"Except I won't be selling, Mr Brockway." There was a determined gleam in Nyree's eyes. "DHH will have to look elsewhere."

She took the train from the state capital, Brisbane, to tropical North Queensland, travelling along more than a thousand miles of incredibly lush coastline to get to her destination—the town of Hollister. No question it had been named after the illustrious billionaire or his buccaneering forefathers. Another thousand miles of coastline remained if one wanted to explore the prodigal wilderness of Cape York. No train line had been constructed to go up there. It was still frontier country.

Extremely remote, the entire region was covered with rainforest that was becoming of great botanical interest.

She had never fully realised just how big her home state was—667,000 miles of it. It was enough to swallow up Western Europe and still leave the long Pacific coastline and hundreds of offshore islands. She was so looking forward to visiting the Great Barrier Reef—one of the wonders of the world. It would be right on her doorstep. The entire journey was giving her such a thrill. She wondered if Miss Em knew about it all? If there really was a Heaven, Miss Em surely had been whizzed up first-class.

Glorious country rolled past her window, gilded by the sun. It was a lyrical landscape, with a sky a dense cloudless blue above a shimmering membrane of silver heat.

The great numbers of farms astonished her. She saw peanut farms, citrus farms, banana plantations, sugar plantations—an eternal presence in the tropics—lush cattle-fattening properties with humped Brahmins cooling off in blue lotus-filled ponds. As the train passed, they lazily lifted their heads to gaze at the spectacle. It was a panorama of endless *green*, with the rich red earth smothered in vegetation and ranks of palm trees waving their fronds in the breeze.

A great wealth of mineral resources lay further inland and to the north-west. Mount Isa, with its enormous deposits of copper, lead, zinc and silver; Weipa with its bauxite over the larkspur Great Dividing Range on the distant skyline. Great crimson pioncianas were in bloom everywhere—beside the track, in the fields; there were mango trees laden with fruit, coral trees, tulip trees in

orange flower, cascaras with yellow blooms, the ubiqui-
tous coconut palms, bougainvillaea—that brilliant
parasite—running wild over abandoned fences, water
tanks and the roofs of old timber homesteads left empty
and neglected in the all powerful sun. She was going to
need a camera to capture this prodigal world.

Along the way they pulled into stations made re-
splendent with displays of staghorns, elkhorns, palms,
a staggering variety of cascading ferns and the state
emblem—the purple Cooktown orchid in butterfly
abundance. It made the trip even more spectacular. She
had done well choosing the Sunlander train over taking
a plane. Now she knew so much of the countryside. She
wanted to know so much more.

But it was hot! *Very* hot. The instant she stood out on
the platform at her destination, clutching her capacious
tote, she felt the humidity on her skin. She had been
wearing a short lime-green bolero over an amethyst
singlet top; now she took the bolero off and tucked it
into her bag. Her hair was curling riotously in the humid
heat. Time to twist it into a knot. Maybe she would have
to get her hair cut?

All around her, faces were baked brown. Everyone
was very casually dressed—the young women in skimpy
tank tops and really short shorts, the young men in much
the same. Older people were a little more on the conser-
vative side. Not much. Lots of colourful tropical shirts.
A mix of races. Really good-looking people.

Curly strands were flying everywhere like cork-
screws. She brushed them back impatiently, aware her
whole body was dewed with sweat. Another fumble

in her bag for her sunglasses. The glare was fantastic! She had never seen such light, even in sub-tropical Brisbane. No wonder artists headed up here. What she had to do now was find a cab. It would probably cost an arm and a leg—unless there was a bus to her destination. Somehow she doubted it. Her house—what elation to be able to say that!—was on the outskirts of the town.

She watched as the luggage came off. She had marked her suitcase with a length of red ribbon for easy identification. The only problem was quite a few other people had not only had the same idea, but the same choice of colour. Luggage collected, she looked left and right. The passengers and the people who had come to greet them had all but melted away. Time for her to set off. She was all revved up without knowing exactly where to go. Ask someone. The obvious answer. Only the street outside looked deserted. Where the heck had they all gone? Life was full of profound questions. Like where had all the frogs of her childhood gone? Where did the flies go in winter? They had to go somewhere.

Frangipani trees were in prolific flower, their luscious perfume rising in the hot air like incense. The train station was just outside of this very pretty town's business centre. Should she head there to catch a cab? In the distance, towards the glittering Coral Sea, she could see cranes and hoardings with "DHH" on them.

DHH had better not trouble *her*. She was a woman in possession. No amount of money would induce her to give up her new home. University wouldn't start up

again until late February–early March. She was even
thinking of finishing her degree at Cook University in
Townsville. Not that far away. It offered a broad range
of disciplines, even enjoying world leadership in
subjects of special importance to the tropics—health,
environment, tropical diseases, bio-medical work. She
had looked up the full list of faculties, bachelor, post
graduate and masters programs on the website. Cook
University would suit her very well.

Nyree stood upright, though it wasn't easy when she
had to hold on to her heavy suitcase with one arm and
keep her tote firmly over her shoulder with the other. All
of a sudden the town centre seemed a long way off. She
could see the importance of acclimatization. The sun
was burning a hole in the top of her head.

She had scarcely crossed one road, heading for the
main street, when a big silver Mercedes pulled up alongside her. Temporarily defeated, she dropped her bag,
watching with bated breath as the driver swung out of
the car, rounded the bonnet and came towards her.

In those precise moments she experienced the same
panic she'd felt as a child that instant before she fell off
her bike. This would be a life-changing encounter. She
was sure of it. Maybe there was something of the witch
in her? Her grandmother, Jessica, still claimed Nyree's
mother had bewitched her son.

The man moving so lithely towards her was lean,
sleek and strongly muscled. He brought to mind the
image of a graceful black leopard. To top that he was
impressively tall—inches over six feet. Turquoise eyes
glittered in his darkly tanned face. He had very distinc-

tive, very precise features. In fact, the definite planes and angles and the high chiselled cheekbones gave him a decidedly exotic look. Some famous guy had had cheekbones like that. Who was it? A name popped up. Rudolf Nureyev. But Nureyev had been Russian. Nevertheless this guy had that kind of face. One you wouldn't forget in a hurry.

At any rate, the sight of him was as good as paralysing her. Such a phenomenon did exist. She clasped her tote tighter to her chest. The feeling of panic didn't subside. If anything it increased, sweeping like brushfire from her head to her toes. The feeling was too powerful to be anything *good*. She knew it in the primitive depths of her female psyche.

"Where on earth are *you* heading?"

Her ears picked up like radar. The commanding voice, along with the looks and the manner—that did it! Her reaction was instantaneous. Here was the living, breathing, epitome of the supremely self-assured alpha male. It put her on the warpath.

"Into town," she answered, in a cool, clipped voice. "No law against it, is there?" She had only just arrived and was already into a skirmish.

"You didn't see one written up on the signpost, did you?"

Nyree swallowed a ready retort. Obviously he was a *personage* in this one-horse town. "So what now? Why have you stopped me?" She was demanding an answer. Was aggression an antidote to panic?

"Maybe because it seemed to me you were about to fall over," he said, studying her petite figure with those extraordinary eyes. "That looks like a heavy suitcase you're lugging."

"Tell me about it!" she burst out in irritation and frustration.

"Stay calm, Rapunzel," he said dryly.

"I beg your pardon!" To her horror, involuntary tears sprang to her eyes. No one was allowed to call her Rapunzel. Her father had used to call her Rapunzel when she was a child, with a long tumble of fair hair—much blonder than it was now.

He was taken aback by the sudden glitter of tears. They got under his skin much like an injection from a needle. "Sometimes the sun can get to you if you're new up here," he offered in a kinder tone. "You *are* new, aren't you?"

"Does it matter?" She gave him a no-nonsense, challenging look.

"Of course it does." He moved nearer.

Her heart jumped and she fell back a pace. "You like to keep tabs on everyone, do you?" She was obliged to tilt her chin because he was so tall. "Maybe you'd be so kind as to tell me where I can find a cab?"

"Where do you want to go?" He stood still, studying her. Head to toe. Nothing sexual in it. More as he would study a recalcitrant child.

"I wasn't asking *you*." She knew she was being very ungracious. But this man offered a threat to her psyche, if his powerful effect on her was anything to go by.

"You'd better accept my help if you want to get out of here," he suggested in a crisper tone.

"What about some information instead? Who are you?"

"This is so *sad*." He gave a mock groan. "You don't know me."

"I don't know if I *want* to know you," Nyree snapped, wondering where this was heading. She was acting *so* out of character. She was usually a pleasant person. What was the matter with her? A touch of sunstroke?

"Brant Hollister," he introduced himself. "And you are?"

She gave a gasp, her real shock hidden under irony. "*Brant Hollister!* Give me a minute to take that in. Tell me, do I genuflect?"

"You can skip it for today." His eyes narrowed. "What say you get in the car? Your cheeks are all flushed. I can drive you wherever you want to go."

She needed to have her head examined—because she made a move towards the big Mercedes. "What if I said Alice Springs?" she asked facetiously. Alice Springs was dead centre of the huge continent.

"You don't want to go to Alice Springs this time of year. You'd bake." He held the door for her. "I'll put your suitcase in the boot."

"Shouldn't I ask for some ID?" She looked up at him. God, he was stunning—in his forceful male way. She recognised it, but she was quite prepared to leave it at that. She definitely didn't feel at ease with him—though just from looking at him she recognised the fact he was unquestionably a *gentleman*.

"Too late!" he said mildly, and closed the door.

As soon as he started the car, state-of-the-art air conditioning kicked in.

"Oh, that's lovely!" she burst out in an ecstasy of

coolness, putting her two hands under the damp hair at her nape.

"At least something's good," he returned dryly. "So where to, Ms—?" He shot her a glance that held more than a touch of intrigue.

"Allcott," she said. "Nyree Allcott."

It was his turn to startle her. He gave a disbelieving laugh. "Not Howie Allcott's great-niece?"

She swung her head, her neck at a haughty angle. "Howie was a buddy of yours?" She objected to the quality of his laugh.

"Howie was *everyone's* buddy," he said dryly. "Especially at the pub. Don't, for the love of God, tell me he left you the farm?"

There was a pain in her chest a bit like heartburn. "I'm delighted you didn't already know."

"Especially as he made me a promise he would sell out to us," he shot back.

That kept her silent for all of two seconds. "All hearsay," she remarked. "He's dead, so he can't confirm or deny it. The farm is mine, Mr Hollister. His will says so."

"You're going to work it?" he asked, with obvious sarcasm. "You surely don't want me to take you *there*?"

"Yes. Unless it would take all day and all night," she replied sweetly. "How far away is it?"

"It's not a question of how far." His answer was short. "It's more a question of dropping you off at a derelict old farmhouse that only rampant vegetation is propping up."

"You want to nab it all the same," she pointed out, with swift malice.

"We want to knock it down," he corrected, with a clash of his fine white teeth.

"Well, *I* don't!" she came back at him sternly.

"That's great—terrific!" he said in disgust. "How old are you anyway? Sixteen? Seventeen?"

"I'm nineteen, if you must know," she corrected him wrathfully.

"Really?" He didn't look impressed. "You knew the old codger?"

"I met *the old codger* once, at my grandfather's funeral," she told him in a fever of hostility. "It seems as though my grandmother was right. He *was* the black sheep of the family."

"Oh, I wouldn't rate Howie as that. He liked the drink too much, and it was his ruination. Somewhere along the line life for Howie took a dark turn. But he was a very fine painter."

"Just not good at looking after houses," she said, unable to stifle the note of regret.

"No. I can safely say Howie never lifted a finger to do anything around the place. As you will see. No mowing. No slashing. No gardening. No maintenance. Once in a while he got one of his ladies in to do a bit of washing up, Hoovering—that kind of thing. So you'll have lots of tall thick grass. Lots of sna es. You seem such a polished little miss I don't know hat you could possibly cope."

"A polished, *stubborn* little miss," she amended, perversely pleased with the "polished". "Anyway, I'm not so little. I'm five-four."

"Maybe when you're standing on a box. I'd say five-three at the outside, and I'm spot-on with measurements. So, what do you do for a living, Nyree? Obviously I can't use the name Rapunzel for fear of reprisals."

"No, you can't." She looked steadily out of the window at the lush green landscape. Cuban Royal palms were lining the roadway with many coloured oleanders—pink, white, yellow, apricot and all shades of red. The air conditioning was picking up the delicious perfume.

"I think it makes you sad."

"I'm surprised you noticed." And she was. Very much. He was a bit of a mix. Arrogant, mocking, but perceptive, maybe even kind.

"Don't want to tell me?" He shot her another look, noting the swan's neck and the riot of curls. She must have been the prettiest baby in the world. She still looked little more than a child if not for the knock-out sexy punch—and he wasn't blind.

"No. I don't expect you to understand."

"How can I when you won't try me?" He employed a reasonable tone.

"What is it you want, Mr Hollister?" She hated the faint tremor in her voice. "Friendship? To get me on side? Talk me into selling the farm?"

"I think the state of the farm will do that, Nyree. In fact, I'm damned if I'll take you there."

To her shock he pulled off the road, then switched off the engine.

"Where are your parents?" His strongly marked brows drew together.

She threw up her head, readying herself for defiance.

"None of your business." He was making her uncharacteristically aggressive, but she couldn't seem to stop it.

"Are they dead?"

God! Could he see her tragic chaotic past in her eyes? "I don't need any pity, much less comfort, thank you very much, Mr Hollister."

"Come off it. Brant will do. So who *do* you have? What about this grandmother?"

Nyree was surprised into a moan. "*She* doesn't want me. Never did. My parents were killed in a car crash coming home from a concert when I was thirteen. After that I went to live with my paternal grandparents. My grandfather died a year later. Just gave up the ghost. Can't say I blame him. My grandmother shoved me off to boarding school just down the road. She didn't want a child ruining her day."

"So you've got issues?" he said quietly.

"Haven't you?" she retaliated.

"Hey, what about dropping the hostile tone?" This was one imperious young lady.

Suddenly Nyree was ashamed. "I swear it's not like me. Maybe you're rubbing me up the wrong way?"

"Maybe we're doing it to each other. What if I take you back to *my* house?"

She laughed. "Are you serious? You're inviting me to stay with you?"

"I'm single, but it's not a bachelor pad," he told her dryly.

"You're still single? A catch like you?" She opened her lustrous eyes wide. "I'm amazed."

"You were expecting I had a dozen kids?"

"Not impossible. Turn the car back on, Mr Hollister. I'm not a party girl."

Now he gave a genuine laugh. "I have to tell you, Ms Allcott, you sure don't look it."

"Oh. How *do* I look?" She touched her hot cheek. What a fool thing to ask. It had just popped out.

"Hardly more than a schoolgirl," he told her repressively. Wiser to think of her that way.

"Well, I have to tell you I'm at university. I intend to become a child psychologist. A good one."

"So you're going for the big picture? But all in good time. So you'll be going back to Brisbane?"

"Don't sound so hopeful. I'm going to put the farm to rights. Then I might enroll at Cook to finish my degree."

"I admire your ambition." He switched on the ignition. "Let me take you back home with me. My grandmother is there. My mother and father have been divorced for years now. My mother has remarried. She couldn't take the way Dad is—never at home. He has a frenetic lifestyle, and of course he's a workaholic. He's in Singapore at the moment, on business, then Beijing. We might see him for Christmas."

His right-hand flicker indicated he was about to make a U-turn. Heart pounding, she laid an urgent hand on his. *"Stop."*

Skin on skin. Yet she might have been stripped to the bone! Unnerved, she made a soft, involuntary mewing sound that might have come out of a frightened kitten. Nothing in her nineteen years had prepared her for an electrical charge on contact. Her whole body was flashing sparks.

"I want to go to the farm." She made her tone even more combatant, fearing she was losing all connection with her former safe world. "If you don't want to take me, I'll wait for a cab."

He raised his brows. "What—here? Right here?"

She looked about. They appeared to have left civilisation behind. The stupidity of it made her flush deeper. "Take me back into town."

"You're making a big mistake, Ms Nyree Allcott."

She didn't cave in. "So? I'm perfectly within my rights. Have you any idea how much this means to me? *Have* you?" She was betrayed into showing high emotion. "Of course you don't. You've led a charmed life. I expect everyone dotes on you. Apple of your grandmother's eye. Your father's heir and right-hand man."

"You've been reading up on me." He looked directly into her brilliant eyes.

"I've been reading up on your *father*," she said scornfully. She certainly wasn't going to tell him that he, the son, had received serious mention.

It didn't appear to bother him in the least. "Look, if it will make you happy I'll run you out to the farm. Let you see what condition it's in. Then I'll take you home with me. You can stay for a few days while I get someone in to do some heavy slashing. Do you know anything about snakes?"

"I've never met one," she said facetiously, pleased he had given in.

"You'll see your first in under a minute, once we arrive at the farm."

That shut her up like a clam.

CHAPTER THREE

HE DROVE slowly down an unsealed road which continued for about half a mile before turning off at a fork.
Nyree peered around her. Huge trees were trailing some
kind of epiphyte: long curly plants like moss. It was
growing so thickly she thought in a fading light it would
look quite ghostly. It was gothic enough now, in broad
daylight. Surely this sort of stuff decorated trees in the
Southern States of America?

"Gosh, what is this? Frog's Hollow?" she asked.

"Not far off. Starting to get cold feet?"

"You wish!" As though she'd admit it. "What's the
name of the farm? Does it have one?"

"Hey, you hit it in one. It's Frog's Hollow."

"It *isn't*."

"Why so astonished? Actually, it's Belguardo. The
original owners of the sugar plantation—the farm has
lost a lot of land since then—were the Pascolis.
They're long gone. The two sons left when the sugar
industry hit big reversals. The homestead was quite
splendid in its day, I believe. There are photographs.

But Great-Uncle Howie let it fall down around his ears."

"How tragic!" she mourned. Just what sort of a man had Great-Uncle Howie been?

"It is, in its way," he said. "On the other hand, who needs a mansion way off in the wilds?"

"I do," she proclaimed flatly.

He shot her mutinous profile a glance. "Then you're asking for trouble."

"From you?"

"Fiery little thing, aren't you?"

"I have Italian blood," she said, proud of it. Secretly she was thrilled with the farm's Italian connection.

"So that's it," he said. "The golden skin and the dark eyes. I'm not sure if I'm game to ask if you bleach your hair." He was certain she didn't, but he wanted to see her take the bait.

She did. "Suppose you just check these roots." She tipped her head sideways for his inspection. "You've checked everything else."

"I have to say not much escapes me," he laughed. "Actually, though your tawny colouring is fairly rare, I have seen it before—in northern Italy. I've seen a lot of the world."

"I bet!" She spoke as if it marked him as a pleasure-seeking, self-indulgent globetrotter. "I haven't even seen the Great Barrier Reef."

"If you're especially good I can fix that." He gave her a smile that was all sardonic dazzle and danger.

"Why? Have you got a big yacht?"

"Big enough to take you sailing." He realised he was

deliberately trying to provoke her, just for the reaction. "Of course if you can't swim there's always the *Lady Ashlee II*, named after my mother. It's the family speed yacht. Australian-built, like a lot of the world's top yachts. A hundred and forty-eight footer. She can travel at twenty-nine knots."

"How modest," she said sweetly.

"Well, I guess there are *some* modest billionaires, but not my dad. The *Lady Ashlee* is a great boat. Great lines. Tons of space. We've had wonderful times aboard her."

"You take your girlfriends?" He was sure to have women falling over themselves for him.

"Not one of them doesn't love it. Now, what about your boyfriends?"

"*Friends*, thank you. I don't have a particular boy-friend."

"Now, how could that be, young Nyree?" He slanted her a mocking glance.

"I wish you wouldn't patronise me. I told you I'm nineteen."

"And that's an answer?"

"Oh, shut up."

On the fork road it got a whole lot bumpier. She guessed in the wet season, which was due to begin, the track would become hazardous.

"And Great-Uncle Howard lived out here?" she mar-velled.

"When he wasn't dossing down in town. You realise when the rains come you'd need a four-wheel drive to get in and out? Any little cheap car and you'd do the back end in. Even a four-wheel drive wouldn't have a chance in a flood."

"I can see that. I'm not stupid," she said severely.

"Just foolhardy. Tell me, do you consider yourself a good driver?"

"I think I am." Though she wasn't so hot on reverse parking.

He made a jeering little sound. "You've barely had time to find out."

That infuriated her. Never in her life had she met anyone who could so get under her skin. Worse, it had been immediate.

"What the heck are those grey veils hanging off the trees?' she asked, twisting her head.

"Don't you know? Spanish moss."

"Thought it was. I wasn't expecting it around here. More *Gone with the Wind* sort of stuff."

"Lots of it grows in the district. Someone must have brought it in. It thrives in a tropical climate with high humidity. It gets its nutrients from the air and from rainfall. Actually, it's not really a moss at all. It's part of the bromeliad family. My grandmother is something of an authority on tropical plants and flowers. Very well known in her circle. She's had a number of books published. Though that was years back."

"Really?" She approved of the note of pride in his voice. "How interesting. What's her name? I might know of her. I'm very interested in tropical plants and flowers myself. I lived with—" She broke off, afraid to speak of Miss Em without becoming emotional.

"Go on. You lived with—?" She'd said she didn't

have a boyfriend, but did she? A lover? She might look very young and virginal, but she was extremely beautiful, with a sexual aura she hadn't a hope in hell of hiding.

"A great lady who was very kind to me," Nyree managed after a pause. "We shared that great interest. She had many books on flowers, tropical flora, and flower paintings all over the house. She passed away recently. I can't bear to speak of it just yet."

"I understand. I'm sorry."

The dark flow of his voice soothed her. He sounded sincere. "Does your grandmother write under Hollister, or does she use her maiden name?" She quickly changed the subject.

"As a matter of fact she does. Alena—"

"I know," Nyree burst out, delighted. "Don't tell me. Alena Kalenin?"

He nodded. "She's at home. Want to meet her?"

"I'd be honoured to meet her," Nyree said, stunned by the connection. "That's amazing! I've always had an idea she was Russian?" That would explain his cheekbones and the exotic look. Genetics.

"Russian descent," he said. "Her father, Andrei— my great-grandfather—was a Russian aristocrat in the employ of the last tragic Czar, Nicholas II. Andrei just managed to get his family out before the Bolshevik revolution. They had to leave everything, including their estates. They arrived in Paris penniless. Over the years they moved from Paris to London. My Hollister grandfather actually met my grandmother in Hong Kong. They were married within a month. The rest is history."

"But that's fascinating!" She was much intrigued. "And Grandfather Hollister?"

"He died several years ago," he said briefly. "He and Alena had a good life together." He too changed the subject. "So, who was your 'great lady'?"

"Professor Emilia Scott. Miss Em." She swallowed the hard lump in her throat. "She was Principal of Swinton College for Girls. I went there from age five to seventeen. Does that clarify things for you?"

"Now, now!" He tutted. "No need to get your back up again. Could I ask if you're expecting any boyfriends—excuse me—male *friends* to come visiting?"

"Listen, I have enough on my plate without complicating life."

"You must have a hard time beating want-to-be boyfriends off," he remarked dryly. "Or perhaps you freeze them out?"

She knew he was trying to take the mickey out of her. "Well, freezing *you* out would be a pleasure."

"Wishful thinking, young Nyree." He laughed. "You sound like you crave your own company?"

"I like my own space, yes."

A self-immured Rapunzel, perhaps? "So, what's hiding behind the defences?" He shot her a searching glance.

"Nothing that need matter to you," she returned tartly, and looked away.

Her new home was *jungle*. He hadn't been exaggerating. The homestead was almost invisible beneath an incredible burden of tropical vegetation gone mad. Parasitic tropical plants had taken over, revelling in their

undisputed ownership: figs, bougainvillaea, ferns great
and small, pandanus, heliconias, gingers, crepe myrtles,
hibiscus. Real mosses clung to the rising front steps
and adhered to timber balustrades covered in a gorgeous
display of flowering vines.

"Gosh!' she said in an awed trance, raising her eyes
to the corrugated iron roof.

Beautiful orchids were bursting out of the broken
guttering, white with golden throats. On the ground,
cymbidiums ruled the roost. She had never seen a
display so magnificent. Certainly not in the open
ground. Generally they were grown in pots. Cascading
down the massive fig that acted as a flying buttress for
the house were purple dendrobiums, the state flower,
hardier than she had imagined possible. She had often
bought a small bunch of them, four or five stems with
a little bit of fern, for over six dollars. In this one place
alone there was enough to stock a dozen florists.

"Well, are you game to get out?" He had been
watching her carefully, attracted by the picture she pre-
sented. She was like a flower herself. But, boy, did she
have her prickly little thorns!

"I am if you are," she said hardily. "Do you think
those steps will hold us?"

"Difficult to tell. Come on, then. Let's get it over."
Outside the car, he bent to pick up a small fallen branch,
beating the grass with it before pitching it into a great
thicket of Bird of Paradise which had spread out all over.
"Don't stand there looking bewitched with your strange
deserted house. I guess you can take one look inside."

"Thank you so much." She joined him, looking

around almost furtively. Her first impression was of a
haunted house, or the witch's abode in a fairytale. Her
second was of massive neglect. Lots of windowpanes
were cracked, some missing altogether. The air was a
luminous light green. Like incense. Spooky. She was
almost afraid to call out, *Anyone at home?* Someone
might answer.

Brave as she tried to be, she found herself almost
shrinking against him. Now she could fully appreciate
his height and strength. "It's a wonder Great-Uncle
Howie didn't get strangled by all the plants as he slept.
Oh, look—*look*!" Before their eyes fluttered an
enormous blue butterfly, its upper wings a marvellous
iridescent blue with black margins. It was *huge*!

"Ulysses," he said casually. "You'll see plenty of
butterflies up here. They love the lantana. Come along,
now. Shall I hold your hand?"

She was determined not to touch him again and set
off the fire crackers. "I'm sure I can manage without,"
she said, putting on a spurt of pace and bravado. She
danced up the rickety steps, grateful they held beneath
her weight. At the top she gave a shriek. "Oh, my gosh!"

He was with her in seconds, sweeping her off her feet.

Brant didn't find it difficult. She was a featherweight.
"Relax. That's a common ordinary garden snake."

"You've checked, have you?" she asked shakily. "It's
disappeared."

He laughed. He was really enjoying himself. "Like
me to carry you over the threshold?"

"Don't be an idiot." Her heart was pounding so hard
in her chest she thought it might jump into her throat.

"Don't say that to your groom," he warned.

Something about her appearance had been teasing him. Now he knew what it was. His grandmother had a very valuable oil painting hanging in her bedroom—an Alma Tadema. It was in his famous classical style. Ms Nyree Allcott might have posed for him, with her masses of light hair, small classic features, great dark eyes and all. The thought made him smile into her face, dark eyes wary, cheeks aglow.

Just a smile, but it pierced Nyree like an arrow. She was terrified. It wasn't as though for all her talk she hadn't enjoyed many a mild flirtation. She hadn't as yet broken her vow—no sex before marriage—but she knew what it was to be hotly desired. Now she was feeling pretty darn *hot* herself. It simply wouldn't do. It was foolish and embarrassing. And he was *the enemy*. Most probably he was prepared to do anything to get her to sell up and get out. Who knew what was in anyone's mind? Who knew their real intent?

While she was speculating, he pushed open the front door, holding her all the while. She might have been a neatly wrapped package.

"No key?" Her voice sounded as agitated as she felt.

"No key," he confirmed. "Hard to keep anything out. Nothing worth stealing." Taking his time about it, he lowered her to her feet. "You won't have any electricity. It will have been turned off."

"Haven't you ever heard of candles?" she asked, doing another impersonation of her grandmother.

"I dread to think of a fire."

So did she. "So, can we look around?"

"Why ask me, Ms Allcott? You're the owner."

"Indeed I am," she said, with the greatest satisfaction. "There's no future whatever in your trying to get rid of me. I'm here to stay."

He lifted a mocking brow. "I'll be amazed if you stay one night." As he spoke he began walking before her, to check things out. "Would you like to wait here a minute?"

"No, I wouldn't!" She was keeping the powerful friction between them going. "You must know some very timid women?"

"I'd say they all know how to protect themselves better than you," he returned crisply.

"On the contrary, Miss Em was proud of me." She stalked after him. "She said I have all the brains, the commitment and the backbone that's needed to make a success of my life."

"I'm sorry I didn't meet Miss Em." He caught sight of an enormous but harmless spider. Even as he looked, it disappeared into the woodwork. "But she doesn't know what you're taking on now."

"Miss Em would be disgusted you're trying to take this house from me," she said wrathfully, instinctively following his gaze upward. "What are you looking at?" Just as she said it something snaked around her leg. "Oh, my God!' she moaned, her whole body freezing.

He spun, his dynamic face showing a flash of real concern. It swiftly abated. "For crying out loud! It's not a lion. It's a *cat*."

She exhaled noisily, glancing down at the ugliest, most battered moggie she had ever seen. "You poor old thing!" she cried, reaching down to lift the piteously meowing cat into her arms. "Poor old girl!" she crooned, then her head flew up as she gazed accusingly at Brant Hollister. "Is this Great-Uncle Howie's cat?"

He held up defensive hands. "Forgive me, Ms Allcott, I wouldn't know. It's obviously not feral. It knows the house, so I would have to guess, yes. Don't think it will have starved." He moved close in to make his own inspection, gently scratching behind the cat's ear. "Plenty of things for a cat to eat. There must be hundreds if not thousands of mice."

"Do you *mind*?"

"Frightened of mice too?" His turquoise eyes sparkled with outright mischief.

"Most women are. I'd sooner face a Doberman than a mouse."

"Don't worry. A Doberman might just turn up." He knew of two to fit the bill. Jupiter and Juno—splendid guard dogs.

There was a rustling noise from the top of the timber staircase. The both looked up—Nyree, it had to be admitted, on the fearful side. Not so the cat. It sprang abruptly out of her arms and sped up the stairs towards the sound.

"Probably birds," Brant said, thinking Ms Nyree Allcott was too young to be on her own in the world. Young, but gallant. Feisty too. What *was* her story? Plenty of tragedy, by the sounds of it.

"It's not going to kill a bird, is it?" she asked, staring back at him, her heart in her eyes.

"Cats *do*, young Nyree."

"So they do," she lamented—then fired up, as he'd

expected. "Listen, I'm a *woman*, not a kid. Certainly not *young Nyree*."

"Great. Terrific. You're a woman." The hell of it was, she *was*! A God-sent beautiful young woman. Brant's will-power gave way. He shot an arm around her waist, pulling her towards him.

"Don't you *dare* touch me!" she said, fire in her eyes.

"I *am* touching you." There was amusement not lust in his gaze.

"Kiss me, I meant," she clarified sternly.

"My dear Ms Allcott, I'd rather kiss the cat."

She never did get a word of disgust out, because he did something truly astounding. He cupped her face with one hand, fingers closing around her chin, then lowered his dark head...

She was swamped—temporarily at sea....

It was just the fiercest, *sweetest*, most terrifying kiss of her life. A chastening, not to say punishing kiss. And it *burned* her. It burned her mouth. It boiled her blood. It sent bright sparks and shooting sizzles along the network of her veins. An enormous lassitude came over her. She was losing all strength in her limbs. She thought she clutched at him. She wasn't sure. The momentum of excitement had reduced her to a captive.

One kiss to open a Pandora's box! One kiss to make a woman *burn*!

When he finally released her she shook her head violently to clear it. Curly tendrils of hair sprang Medusa-like to frame her dazed and dazzled face. "How could you *do* such a thing?" she gasped.

"Don't be silly." He tucked a long curl behind her ear. "I'm absolutely certain that wasn't your first kiss."

"I don't remember inviting it!" A rosy blush mantled her cheeks.

He gave that a moment's consideration. "I'm not sure that's true, Nyree. Think about it. You've been provoking me from the first minute.'

"Provoking you, is it?" She was all the more furious because the charge was true. She had known all along she was pushing the boundaries.

He nodded. "Anyway, don't worry about it. You never know—it might change your attitude."

"Which is what?" She was feeling *so* shaky and strange.

"Hostile, antagonistic, wary. Want me to go on?'

"And you wonder why?" She swept on, not waiting for his answer. "I'm not afraid of you, Brant Hollister. I can stand up to you. No matter what you do."

He saw the determination in her face, the strength of character that no doubt had helped her survive tragedy and emotional deprivation. "What I'm *thinking* of doing, God help me, is quite weird. In fact it's only just occurred to me. I could build you a brand new house some place else. Somewhere you'd be safe. I'm sure we could arrive at some agreement."

"And wouldn't that suit you?" she scoffed. "I don't need a brand-new house. I have this."

The atmosphere between them from the word go had been charged with an edgy tension that was, at its core, sexual. Brant was forced to confront the fact. Ms Nyree Allcott had arrived without warning out of nowhere! How much easier it would be to deal with an older woman. Not this beautiful displaced nineteen-year-old girl. It shocked him, but he realised he was battling to keep his hard head above water.

You shouldn't have kissed her. No excuses.

He could only cite a sudden storm of desire. That was the reality of it.

There was a ten-year gap between Ms Nyree Allcott and himself. He had packed a lot of living into those ten years, whereas—let's face it—she wasn't all that long out of the classroom.

You shouldn't have kissed her, his inner voice repeated.

Except she had an aura unlike any other young woman he had ever met.

"So you're serious about staying up here?" he said, glancing over to where she was standing.

Was she? Great-Uncle Howard's legacy offered her independence.

Take him up on the offer. Nyree's voice of caution spoke up. *You can't stay here by yourself. It's too isolated. Too lonely. It's probably haunted. And it's falling down.*

"I *am* serious about staying, Mr Hollister—" The decision was made.

He broke in, an edge to his tone. "If you call me Mr Hollister again, I'll throw all caution to the wind and kiss you again."

Her heart shook. "No way!" She was weak under the bravado.

"Better think again."

Her chaotic feelings were making her so nervous. The ambivalence! He fascinated her—irritating her one

minute, seducing her the next. "I am staying—Brant."
She didn't think of it as caving in. More as good
common sense. "You can't know what owning a house
of my own feels like. I'm going to fix this place up."

She gazed about her, ignoring all the horrendous
things. The rooms were big and light and airy. The
hallway ran from back to front, which would allow
every available breeze to flow through the house. The
woodwork appeared to be in reasonably good condition,
although the parquet of the entrance hall was severely
damaged in places. The ceilings were ornately plastered. There were rather elaborate architraves and
moulded cornices. A chandelier that once would have
been splendid was dark grey, caked with dust.

"Howie leave you a fortune, did he?" he was asking
sardonically.

"How do you know he didn't keep his money under
the bed?" she retorted, not about to tell him of Miss Em's
additional legacy. "But then, I suppose you checked?"

"God forbid! You do rave on, don't you?"

She dropped her eyes, so he wouldn't see her flurry
of emotions. "Only with *some* people."

"Let's keep moving."

When she could catch her breath. *Why* had he kissed
her? To dominate her? Subdue her? Exploit her? God,
she wanted to *hit* him. This man was a threat to her. She
wasn't going to allow him to jeopardise her chances of
making a good life for herself here in this magical place.
Her own private wild kingdom.

She realised she would have to fight hard. He was
enormously charismatic, and far too rich. His sexual

aura alone exerted a powerful grip. It was a terrible thing for a man to be so sexy. The merest physical contact caused considerable emotional turbulence. She was still pumping adrenalin.

Best to *hate* him, she decided. In a light-hearted kind of way. So much safer.

See you stick to it! said the voice in her head.

CHAPTER FOUR

THEY couldn't find the cat when it was time to leave, so Nyree left a bowl of long-life milk and another of dry cat food. She had found them in the pantry. At least Great-Uncle Howie had been feeding his cat.

It wasn't until they were well on their way back into town that she remembered the paintings. "What happened to Howie's paintings?" She sounded so suspicious it was as if Brant might have been responsible for spiriting them away.

"Search me!" He flicked her a glance. "You might ask his Number One girlfriend. He had an entourage. But Dolly led the pack. Dolly Dryer. She's quite a character, is Dolly. She owns and runs the Hibiscus Hut. It's a small but surprisingly good restaurant on the edge of town."

"The plot thickens. I suppose she fed Howie occasionally, or he would have died a whole lot sooner. But Dolly? What sort of name is that? I only know of Dolly Parton."

"I'm not sure what Dolly is short for," he said lazily. "Maybe it's not short for anything."

"What the heck *was* Great-Uncle Howie?" Nyree

asked. "All these women. He sounds like a sultan with his harem."

"The Sultan of Hollister!" Brant gave an enigmatic laugh. "He would have been a very handsome man in his time. He was a great talker. Extremely well read. A cultured man. A lot going on under the surface, but he never spoke of it. Loneliness—guilt, possibly. Who knows? He was a great drinker, of course. Again a way of forgetting. He was forever falling off his stool at the pub. Mostly he did it as a joke. He liked to play the clown—which he most decidedly was not."

"You sound as though you liked him?" She swung her head in surprise.

"I did. Very much when he was sober. The tragedy was Howard Allcott ruined his life. He had a real gift, but he was self-destructive. He rarely spoke about his family until very recently. We knew he had a brother who died years back. Then all of a sudden there was talk of a great-niece. Obviously you. He never kept in touch?"

She shook her head regretfully. "Harems were in. Great-nieces were out."

"So your inheritance came right out of the blue?"

"Yes." She stared out at the glorious blue sky with never a cloud. "I think blue is the right colour. Blue is for happiness." His eyes were an extraordinary mix of blue and green—a genuine turquoise. "What happened to the furniture? Presumably there was more than we saw? At least at one stage. And the paintings, of course. Paintings first. I *love* paintings," she exclaimed passionately.

He already knew to scrape the surface and see her passions run deep. "You could have stepped out of one yourself." He knew his grandmother would be as intrigued as he was by her wonderfully *paintable* appearance, and her resemblance to the toga-clad young woman in the Alma Tadema. Not to mention her connection to Howard Allcott, a figure from his grandmother's past.

"No point in buttering me up, Mr Holl—I mean Brant." Nyree fell back on a strict tone. "Great-Uncle Howard really did make you a promise he'd sell to you?"

There was a half-smile on his face. "Well, the project wouldn't have gone up in smoke if he hadn't—but, yes, he did."

"So I'm in the way?"

"To an extent," he agreed. "I should warn you Dolly had expectations too. We bought up all the other old farms."

"Dolly did?" She swung her head, dismayed.

He nodded.

"Maybe he treated her badly, then?" Nyree started to worry.

"Never!" Brant shook his head emphatically, certain Dolly had taken the paintings off the wall. "The only person Howie treated badly was himself."

"Thank God for that!" Nyree released a pent-up breath. "No doubt DHH offered a good price to the others?" She made it sound like a challenge.

"That goes without saying. We *live* here, young Nyree. We operate mostly in the North. Our reputation for fair dealing is very important to us."

"I expected you to say that. This project, then, it must be enormous?"

"It will be big—and the best."

"The biggest and the bestest! So, hypothetically speaking, where would you relocate *me*?" she asked sweetly.

"A stone's throw away." His reply was terse. "Then I can keep an eye on you."

"But how extraordinary! I don't *need* you to keep an eye on me." Automatically she bridled. "Anyone would think you've appointed yourself my minder."

"Well, you're here with me *now*," he countered. "You got in the car of your own free will. You've graciously consented to coming back to my house. You *do* need to keep me on-side."

Her cheeks flushed. *True.* "Only because you own the town. And probably the whole damned district, plus a few of the offshore islands."

"I'm afraid so," he said, and laughed. "You don't really want to go back there, do you, Nyree?"

Now his voice had sunk to *the* most beguiling level. "Don't waste your valuable time trying to charm me. I'm determined to stay at the farm. You can help. You have legions in your employ. Get a few people in to help me clean the house. Groundsmen to take care of a fair section of the grounds. I promise you, you won't know the place by the time I'm finished."

He stretched out a hand to tap her shoulder. More sparks flew. "Well, you'd better finish before the cyclone hits," he warned. "You saw the state of the roof."

"So? It can be repaired." Roof? Cyclone? That was demoralising.

"Certainly. But you'll be in thrall to the workmen for a very long time."

Nyree swallowed. "You're not really expecting a cyclone. *Are* you?"

"Matter of fact, we are. We haven't had a good one in quite a while. We're about due. They go in cycles."

"I didn't know there *was* a good cyclone," she said. "You're just trying to frighten me."

His eyes gleamed. "Be afraid. Be *very* afraid, young Nyree," he mocked. "Though I guess it's useless trying to frighten feisty ole you. I am, however, giving you the facts. Tropical cyclones are a fact of life. The cyclone season is coming up. Sometimes the anticipation of one can be unbearable. The humidity and the heat. You've heard of going troppo? It happens. The electrical storms alone would be enough to make you jump out of your skin."

"We do have them in Brisbane," she pointed out loftily. "Anyway, I'm not the type to hide under the bed in a storm."

"Our storms are a whole lot *meaner*," he said. "Remember you've crossed the Tropic of Capricorn. I'd hate to think of you alone at the farm."

"Now, *that's* a comfort! Don't think I don't appreciate it. Are you going to ring ahead to let your grandmother know you're bringing me back with you? I don't really rate as a guest."

The smile was seductive. "My dear Ms Allcott, I'll ensure they run out the red carpet. But first I'm going to feed you." He slanted a glance over her petite frame. "You must be hungry. I just hope you're not anorexic."

"That's ridiculous. I eat well. I don't *look* anorexic, do I?" Once more she was trapped into begging a response.

"Just joking. Actually, you *glow* with health."

"I got lucky! A compliment."

Then he spoilt it. "It's not *all* good. You must have hollow legs, because you're no weight at all. I hope you're hungry?"

"I think I can swallow something," she said, turning her face away. "And I really want to meet Great-Uncle Howie's paramour. She must be a good age?"

"Sex appeal is ageless," he said. "Didn't you know?"

"I haven't exactly *seen* too many sexy septuagenarians,' she said, from the lofty plateau of her nineteen years.

"I'm not sure you understand what sexy means. It doesn't just mean being young and gorgeous." He aimed a brilliant glance at her.

"You can't mean *me*!" She offered a laughing disclaimer. "Not the gorgeous bit, anyway. My grandmother couldn't abide my looks."

So she had grown up totally without vanity? "I *do* mean you," he clipped off. She wasn't fishing for a compliment. At some stage young Nyree Allcott's life must have been hell.

"Well, I know I don't look *ordinary*," she amended, surprised by his sharpened tone. "No more than you do. My father and mother thought I was the most beautiful child in the whole wide world. I'm just saying my grandmother as good as threw me out of the house largely because of my looks. I'm the image of my mother."

Brant couldn't control a hot flash of anger at this grandmother. "And this is bad?"

She turned her head. "I don't want to talk about it.

My grandmother adored her only son. She hated the woman he married."

"Now, that, Nyree, is seriously *sick*!'

"It happens." She shrugged. "I didn't take after my father. I'm my mother."

"Then you're a very lucky girl. I wouldn't worry myself with anything your grandmother might have thought or said in the past, Nyree. I'm only glad you got lucky with Miss Em. What was the Em short for again? Don't tell me—Emilia?"

"She wanted me to call her that, but I thought it wasn't respectful enough. I hit on Miss Em and we left it at that."

"So Miss Em's gain was your grandmother's loss?"

"Bitterness defined my grandmother," Nyree said, her voice full of sad regret. "Nothing I ever did pleased her. I was much better off at boarding school. Afterwards Miss Em took me in. I miss her terribly."

"Of course you do," he said. "But all the good times will return, and you have the happy memories. The love you felt for Miss Em will survive."

Nyree couldn't reply. She was afraid of bursting into tears. Nevertheless a wave of comfort swept her. Sometimes he *could* say the right thing!

There was a single parking spot right outside the Hibiscus Hut. He nosed the big Mercedes into it and then turned off the ignition. Nyree put her hand to her rioting hair. "I'd like to freshen up first. I can't have a skerrick of lipstick left." She flashed him a glance that clearly allotted him the blame.

"Do you really need it?" Her full mouth was beautiful, a natural rose.

"Of course I do. Men didn't know anything about anything. Without a bit of make-up I really do look like a kid."

"But a very pretty one. The powder room is at the rear. To the left. I'll organise a table. See if Dolly is in today."

From the outside the Hibiscus Hut looked amazingly attractive. A beautifully designed retractable awning in a deep emerald and white striped canvas stretched out over the footpath and offered shade. To either side of the glass-doored entrance glazed green pots with a magnificent display of orchids spilling out of them were ranged.

Inside, the air-conditioning came as a welcome relief from the humid heat. Dolly, if she had done the decorating herself, had a real eye for style. The palette she had selected suited the tropical North perfectly: lime, aqua, turquoise, plenty of white. The glass-topped tables were surrounded by finely woven rattan chairs, with the fabric on the cushions picking up the colour scheme. But what took Nyree's attention after an initial sweeping glance were the beautiful paintings hanging on the wall. Paintings she immediately fell in love with.

Fiercely she clutched Brant's arm. "You have to believe me—I'm a bit psychic—but I know some of those paintings are Great-Uncle Howie's work."

He took her hand and held it tight. "I can't claim to be psychic, Nyree, not even a bit but, yes, a good few *are* Howie's work. They stand out. Dolly probably took them for safekeeping." *Like hell she did*, he thought, knowing he would have to do something about it.

"And put them up on her wall?" Her eyes had gone huge.

"It looks that way. Go tidy yourself up. I'll see if she's here."

She frowned at him and snatched away her hand. "Only my *hair* isn't tidy," she pointed out angrily, then stalked off. He wasn't some older cousin she had hero-worshipped since childhood. Hero-worship meant some lack in oneself. He was Brant Hollister. The enemy.

And don't you forget it!

Gosh, she was lucky to have that voice in her head.

In the well-appointed powder room she combed her hair, then arranged it in the classic knot that suited her to a tee. Several splashes of cold water on her face, then a touch of lipgloss. Staring into the mirror, she realised she looked good. Full of a lust for life! This really was an adventure. It was exciting, but a bit of a torture to know she would be seeing a lot of Brant Hollister. Under different circumstances she would have liked to have him on-side as a good and powerful friend. Heck, it was even looking that way right now.

When she returned to the main room she saw him standing in conversation with a tall, striking brunette, a little on the lush side. A silky waterfall of hair spilled down her back. Nyree couldn't yet see the colour of her eyes, but the young woman was immaculately dressed in a white linen sleeveless shirt and skirt.

Their conversation appeared so intent the voice in her head started up again: *Maybe they're madly in love with each other?*

Oh, shut up. Very oddly, some of her confidence evaporated.

But you know nothing about him. He's much older than you. An experienced man of the world. He's probably had dozens of women by now. She looks like she's known him her whole life.

She did. It was there in the body language. Now the woman's hand, wrist encircled by two splendid gold bracelets, had moved to his arm, clung.

Don't interrupt them.

Why not?

Just a word of warning.

She couldn't hang around there. Other diners had broken off their murmured conversations to look up and smile at her. At the same time they were taking her in. Very likely wondering who she was. She had come in with Brant Hollister. That alone would ensure attention. Still, the locals seemed a friendly lot.

Nyree threaded her way to Brant Hollister's side, conscious her outfit was way too casual, especially if seen beside the statuesque brunette's. Of course he *would* be attracted to a tall woman—not a pint-sizer like her.

"Ah, Nyree. There you are!"

Sure enough, he extended his arm fully to shepherd her in.

The brunette turned about with a practised smile on her face. Nyree, intuitive to the nth degree, saw she had to fight to keep it in place.

She hates you on sight. Not good, Nyree girl.

Brant made introductions, his tone suggesting Nyree might well be a visiting relative of whom he was fond.

Lana Bennett scrutinised her closely. Tip to foot. "So here you are!" she exclaimed brightly, for all the change that had overtaken her expression. Up close she was even more attractive, with fine poreless skin, even features, and marked black brows over light blue eyes.

"We'd just about ruled out the possibility your great-uncle had any family to speak of."

"As you say, here I am." Nyree gave Brant's woman a sunny smile. "And I'm here to *stay*."

"Surely not?" Lana Bennett's expression said, *Oh, my God!* "A young girl like you? You couldn't possibly live at that derelict farmhouse. Certainly not by yourself."

"Why not?" Nyree kept a charming smile in place. "I'm looking on this as a great adventure. I intend to do the farmhouse up. And I'm going to get myself two big guard dogs," she confided. "Rottweilers, maybe. Or German Shepherds—Dobermans, that kind of thing. Good company."

"She's joking, isn't she?" Lana, who appeared to be breathing a little harder, turned to Brant for confirmation.

"Don't ask *him*," Nyree insisted. "His name is Hollister."

Lana's blue eyes turned to ice. "I beg your pardon?"

"He may be the most splendid person in the world to you, Ms Bennett, but we both know he wants the farm. *My* farm."

"And you think trying to make a home for yourself out there is better?" Lana asked incredulously, a disapproving frown in position.

"You don't have to answer that, Nyree," Brant broke in smoothly. "Why don't you sit down?" He pulled out a chair for her. It was a wonder he didn't press her into it. "We won't keep you now, Lana." He turned back to his friend. "You told me you had many things to do. So, see you tonight." He bent his dark head to brush the cheek she proffered.

A token kiss, Nyree decided, watching. Just an air peck, really. *Was* she his girlfriend? Lana Bennett definitely thought so. And they were meeting up that night!

"Nice to meet you," Nyree piped up from her chair, playing the good just-out-of schoolgirl role he seemed determined to cast her in.

"If you need any help, call me," Lana Bennett told her crisply. "Brant will give you my phone number."

"Thank you so much," Nyree responded, knowing she wasn't going to be calling Ms Bennett any time soon.

"Your girlfriend doesn't like me," Nyree leaned across the table to whisper.

"What's *not* to like?" he answered nonchalantly. "Lana is a close friend. I've known her all my life. She's not my girlfriend."

"But you're *close*? You can tell me how close. I won't tell anyone else."

"What are you going to have?" He ignored her question, picking up the menu. "The seafood is local. Always superb."

"Let's talk about the paintings," she said, still whispering. So many people had smiled and waved to him. He was the North's Crown Prince. "Where's Dolly?"

"She hasn't come in yet," he said. "Why don't you let me handle this for you?"

"You don't think I can handle it myself?"

"You should watch that temper of yours," he told her, busy checking the menu.

"I didn't know I had one until I met you."

"Which is only today." His eyes glittered, mocking. She sat back in wonderment. "You're right! Now, isn't that *strange*?" She realised she was behaving as though he had always been in her life. So, for that matter, was he.

"Strange indeed," he agreed, pinning her startled gaze. He wasn't about to tell her he had been drawn to her at first sight. "Now, what about some seared scallops in the white truffle sauce to start. Then I recommend the barramundi. Can't do better. Or maybe the Red Emperor. Both superb reef fish."

"Don't encourage me unless you're paying," she said, picking up her own menu. "I'm not some little cousin from Brisbane."

"You might as well be. I'm so enjoying your company." He gave her a lazy smile, though she swore she saw something flare at the back of those turquoise eyes.

"You don't have to pretend you like me," she warned.

"Why should I pretend?"

A waitress zoomed in on them, an infatuated smile on her pretty face. And why not? "I'm awake to your wicked wiles. I know what you're playing at."

"Then you know a damned sight more than I do," he returned bluntly.

They had finished a delicious meal and were drinking coffee—amazingly good—when…enter a gypsy woman! A bodacious woman. She really should have been heralded by a ripple of flamenco music, Nyree thought. She was maybe on the wrong side of sixty, but she was amazingly colourful, with real presence. A silk scarf was arranged gypsy fashion over her forehead and tied back over a plethora of dyed ebony waves and curls. Big gold hoops swung from her ears. Real gold, judging from their lustre. She wore a scarlet blouse tucked into a skirt printed with brilliant tropical flowers gone wild. Lots of baubles that picked up the various colours were draped over her exuberant chest, tumbling into her still remarkable cleavage.

Maybe that was how she came by her name, Nyree thought, dazzled by the theatrical entrance. It couldn't be anyone else but Dolly—her late great-uncle's long-term lover. What a woman! She had swept in like the Queen of the Gypsies, and she was heading directly for them. Brant stood up as she sailed majestically towards their table.

"Brant, my darling, how lovely to see you!" The voice was a lush contralto. The words were more sung than spoken. She planted a kiss fair and square on his handsome mouth. "And this beautiful little lady is…?" Black kohl-enhanced eyes surveyed Nyree with extreme interest. "Isn't she a little young?" She gave Brant a hard nudge in the ribs, laughing with real enjoyment.

When she finds out she'll tell you to go away. Go on. Beat it!

"A little surprise in store for you, Dolly," Brant said, looking very much as if he wanted to laugh right back. "This is Nyree Allcott—Howard's great-niece."

Dolly gaped at him as if he'd gone crazy, then back at Nyree. "It *can't* be."

Nyree came respectfully to her feet. "It is, Ms—" God, she'd nearly said *Parton*. "Great-Uncle Howard left me the farm. He left me his paintings too. I see you've very kindly looked after them for me by hanging them on your walls. Thank you so much."

That astute but diplomatic little speech gave Dolly no cheer. Her attitude turned confrontational. She swung her head Brant's way, setting the gold hoops in motion. He pulled out a chair for her. "I hung them on the wall, my dear," Dolly announced when she was settled, "because they're *mine*. Howard owed me."

C'mon!

Brant eyed her. "Unfortunately, Dolly, he didn't put them in your name before he died. You've only just hung them up, surely? They weren't there a fortnight ago, when I was last in."

Nyree, with her tender heart, interrupted. "You wanted the room to look beautiful, didn't you, Ms Dryer?" Miraculously she dredged up the name. "I had no idea he was such a wonderful artist."

Dolly covered eyes black as night with such a heavily be-ringed hand Nyree started to count them. "He could have been a big name!" she burst out in an operatic lament. "He was in so much pain. His only way of letting it out was his painting. Poor Howie!"

Nyree quickly shifted to the adjoining chair. "You loved him, didn't you?" she said very gently, taking Dolly's hand.

Dolly lifted her head, her be-ringed fingers curling around and cutting into Nyree's with long painted nails. "You're a nice child," she crooned. "I *did* love Howard. But he didn't love me. He didn't love anyone. It wasn't that he was cruel. He wasn't. Some woman had stolen his heart. Left him bereaved and without one. Maybe someone who looked like you?" Black brows knotted, she stared intently into Nyree's face. "You have the sort of face a man never forgets. The sort to launch a thousand ships. Maybe your grandmother?" Dolly's hand tightened, as though she could wring the answer out of her.

"Not *my* grandmother, Dolly," Nyree said, vaguely shocked. "Take my word for it. Not even my grandad loved her."

"But you've got *two* grandmothers, child," Dolly persisted. It was as if at long last she had set foot on a hitherto undiscovered track.

"Please—I didn't know the other one, Dolly," Nyree said, looking anxiously to Brant for support. Slowly she managed to remove her crushed hand.

"How can that be?" Dolly demanded, rolling her kohl-lined eyes to the ceiling.

Brant intervened. "Nyree hasn't had an easy life, Dolly," he said. "She lost her parents not all that many years ago. I'm sure when you two get to know one another she'll tell you more. But for now, what about the paintings? They *are* Nyree's. Howie left them to her. It's all legal. And Nyree loves paintings."

"Why wouldn't she? Look at her. She's a Donatello angel!" Dolly cried, throwing up her hands.

"I would love to *give* you one, Dolly." Nyree hit on a solution, lured in by this strange, bold woman. "The one you love best. Or two, if you can't decide between one and the other."

Knowing Dolly, a tough-nosed businesswoman, Brant had been expecting the mother of all histrionic displays. Instead young Nyree appeared to be reeling her in.

Dolly scrunched up eyes that were working sure and

fast. "Do you think I could have the big canvas on the back wall?" she asked, reaching for Nyree's hand. "I would miss it dreadfully if you took it away. Howard painted it during our best year together."

Nyree flashed a glance at Brant. His striking face gave nothing away. No help there. "You mean the big island landscape between the silver leaf sconces?"

Dolly nodded. "I was lying naked beside him when he painted it," she lied. "Of course I was in better shape then."

Brant laughed. He couldn't help himself. To counteract that, Nyree answered Dolly kindly. "Of course you may have it, Dolly. I *may* call you Dolly?"

"It's really Delilah," Dolly confided, lying yet again. She smiled, showing one gold-capped tooth. "I was very beautiful when I was young. I stopped being Delilah around forty-five, when I started to lose the first flush of youth. Sure enough Howie took it upon himself to rename me Dolly. So Dolly I became." Her black eyes made a full circuit of the dining room. "If you could find it in your kind sensitive heart—one so young—I'd also like the abstract—*Pearl in the Ocean*."

Now Brant chose his moment to speak up. *Pearl in the Ocean* was arguably Howard Allcott's finest abstract work. "I'm sorry, Dolly, but the abstract spoke to Nyree the minute we walked in. Didn't it, Nyree?" He slanted a speaking glance at her, daring her to deny it.

He was spot-on. "I really *love* it, Dolly," Nyree said, enormously grateful Dolly hadn't settled on it as her first choice. "Can you not choose another?"

"I believe Dolly will be very happy with the Orchid

Island landscape," Brant said, leaning back comfortably in his rattan chair.

Even Nyree could see that his brilliant turquoise eyes said, *And that's all you're going to get!*

Brant knew, if Nyree didn't, that Dolly had amassed quite a few of Howie's paintings over the years, without really asking. She wasn't about to take the pick of them from Howie's young heiress.

Day one and he had squared up perfectly as Ms Nyree Allcott's protector. Clearly her youth and inexperience had got to him. He didn't want to think about her other kind of impact on him. This tremendous urge to *touch*. Hell, he wasn't a vulnerable man. He managed his emotions extremely well. But this young woman's sexual aura, innocent or not, was both dizzying and disarming. Add to that, he really *liked* her. It was a whole combination of things he had never experienced before.

CHAPTER FIVE

BACK on the leaf-canopied street, with the tropical sun blazing down on them and troops of tourists jamming the sidewalks, he walked towards a tall timber hat stand that had been strategically placed outside a gift shop. The stand was decorated with an amazing display of straw hats, caps and hand-printed scarves—clearly for the tourists to buy.

"Come along. Come along," he said, as Nyree dawdled. "You'll be needing one of these."

"Yes, Cousin Brant." She matched her tone to a goofy expression.

He laughed, then after a moment's hesitation picked one out. "Try this on."

"You've got good taste," she said. She would have picked that one herself.

"Of course I have. Brilliant taste. Here—take it."

"I do *have* hats, you know." She took the ultra-wide-brimmed straw hat, soft and floppy, from him, twirling it with pleasure. One side was weighed down with silk hibiscus in burnished shades of yellow and orange. She knew it would suit her and her colouring.

"I'm sure you could do with another one," he said. "Put it on."

"You know what? You're a bully." She settled the enormously flattering straw hat on her head, then gave him a smile. "How do I look?" She tipped her head this way and that, an unconscious coquette.

A man could go to hell and back for a smile like that, he thought, experiencing a solid jab to the heart. It was the first *real* smile she had given him.

"Brant?" she said uncertainly. He had such a strange expression his face.

"That's fine. You'll do," he said briskly. "Wait here while I pay for it."

"Don't you dare!" She began to rummage in her tote.

"Pay me later," he said, moving away from her into the shop.

They'd turned in to Coral Fields Estate. Obviously an estate at the very top end of the market. And why not? Spectacular luxury homes sat facing a sea of incredible blue, the water glittering crystal-clear in the shallows so one could see the white sand.

"To think people like me don't have to pay a penny to enjoy such a glorious view!" she exclaimed, staring out enraptured as the Mercedes cruised the long upward drive. "Do you have a beach?" Excitedly she turned her head.

Everything about her was getting to him. They weren't easing into some kind of friendship. They had made an instant powerful connection. Mysterious were the ways of a man with a woman.

"Of course we have a beach—very private. You'll

love it. It's a good thing you have olive skin. Not that you'll be able to go without sunblock at any time."

"You're going to make a great hands-on dad," she said, going back to staring out. "No need to tell me which house is yours."

"They're all mine, in a way," he said casually. "I designed the lot of them. I'm an architect."

"So you are!" She applauded him. "*And* an engineer. I'm very impressed."

"As you should be. It took infinite hours of hard work, study and work experience from the bottom up. I needed to have an overall view of operations."

"Well, I have to say you look like you have limitless reserves of energy," she told him sweetly, peering ahead. "That's your place right at the top, isn't it?"

A splendid house stood on a promontory between two pristine secluded bays. She could see the shimmering white sand, fringed with magnificent tree ferns, and coconut palms growing at extraordinary angles, a host of cabbage tree palms.

"It looks *enormous*! Napoleon and his army could lose themselves there."

"Napoleon *who*?" he joked. "The house was built with many functions in mind. My grandmother lives with us. She has what is virtually her own house. As do I. As does my dad—when he's home. We're together but apart. If you know what I mean. It's the way we all like it. We're a very close-knit family, but Dad and I don't need to have Alena right under our nose."

"Just like me?" she scoffed cheekily. "Your much-loved grandmother must be in her seventies." How lucky,

lucky, *lucky* he was to have one! "Would she have known Great-Uncle Howard?" She swung her caramel head, nursing her new hat in her lap as if it were precious.

"Alena knows everyone," he responded without expression. "She knew Howard Allcott quite well. He painted her portrait."

"Wh-a-t?" That piece of information floored her.

"And did a wonderful job of it," he said, ignoring her little screech. "My grandfather commissioned it. Alena was at the height of her beauty."

"I don't believe this," she said with immense disgust. "Why didn't you tell me before? There's a connection."

"So there is," he said flatly.

It was more like a great enclave than a house, Nyree thought, studying the front façade. It appeared as more a series of sculptural interlocking villas than one house, each villa standing three storeys high, each complementing the other marvellously. Nyree was speechless. She had never seen anything like it. No wonder he thought the farmhouse was only fit to be knocked down.

"I've used a reinforced concrete construction everywhere," he said, amused by her ever-changing expressions. "The house will withstand the fiercest cyclone."

"I bet!" Instantly her brain conjured up a great hurricane of unbridled ferocity, the storm lashing the sea at the foot of the great bulwark of a house to a fury. "You must be very proud of it," she said in an awed voice. "You're so clever!"

"Now, there's a surprise! Something about me you like."

She flushed. "I admire your *gifts*. I didn't say I liked *you* personally. No, wait. That's very ungracious. I do appreciate what you're doing."

"Which is?"

"Why, taking me in, of course. Just a night or two—until we can get people in to tidy up the farm," she added hastily. "This is an extraordinary place. It suits you. Just like the farm suits *me*. It's *mine*!"

"It's really scheduled for demolition."

"No way!" She shook her head. "It's like I said. Having a place of my own means a great deal to me."

"It might come as a shock to you, but I do understand. Now, come inside."

He stretched out a hand. Excitement started up again. Wonder of wonders, she gave herself up to it. Life, she was finding, had become a real adventure.

"Where are you going to put me?" she asked as they walked through massive double doors giving on to a marble-floored space large enough to hold a ball. "I'm sure your broom closet is bigger than the farmhouse."

"What broom closet?" he said. "We have guest suites. People are always staying with us. Many overseas visitors, friends, business associates. I have a suite in mind for you."

"That's what's so interesting about you." She stared up at him. "You're always a step ahead. Make that a mile. When do I get to meet your grandmother? I'd like to look better than this." She gazed down at herself, not happy with her casual outfit. Miss Em, always beautifully turned out, had liked her to look pretty. "Clearly she's a great lady."

"That she is," Brant confirmed. "She actually has a

title, if she cared to use it—which she never has. Not that I can remember anyway. She's the Countess Alena."

"Gosh, there must be a story in that!" Nyree gasped.

"A very sad story in parts, Nyree," he said. "She may tell you one day. She has her own personal maid who's been with her for twenty years. Her name's Jasmin—part-Chinese, part-Malaysian. You'll like her. As for you, you'll do fine. You'll meet Alena pre-dinner. She's not as strong as she used to be. She has a heart condition—not major, but her health is carefully monitored. Dad and I don't want to lose her. She said she's not going anywhere until I'm happily married."

"Then you'd better get a move on, hadn't you?" Nyree responded sweetly.

"How do you know I haven't got the right woman in mind?" he asked, focusing his attention on her.

"Gee, I bet she loves you to bits."

"We'll just have to wait it out and see. By the way, we'll be having a few other people to dinner."

Nyree showed her dismay. "*Now* you tell me! I'll eat in the kitchen." She already had confirmation that Lana Bennett was going to be one of them.

"Joke, is it?" he asked.

She angled a glance at him, throwing back her head to do so. "If I'm around you a day longer I'll have to invest in some killer heels."

He made a jeering sound. "Wouldn't you be a tiny bit scared you'd topple over? Anyway, you must have packed a pretty dress?"

Nyree stared at him. "Give me a break. I came up here to work. I only brought rags."

"As if I believe that. The outfit you've got on is kind of chic. Or you make it chic. I don't mean *really* dress up, like Cinderella at the ball. Just a pretty dress, okay?"

She surprised herself by closing her fingers tightly around his wrist. "Listen, I don't really want to join your little dinner party, Brant. I don't know anyone."

"You want to meet people, don't you?" he countered.

"Sure. I've met the adorable Lana. Is *she* the woman you're waiting for?"

"It's really not your business, Ms Allcott." He looked down at her delicate hand with its tapering fingers, an enigmatic smile on his face.

"How right you are!" She took her hand away, hopefully without blushing. "I just can't help being curious."

"I'll tell you what I'll do. You try to pick out something nice and—"

"Well, I do have... I only meant..."

"Kindly allow me to get in a word. I *want* you to join us. My grandmother will be expecting you. Ten people in all. Not a crowd. And when I've settled on the right woman I promise I'll let you know. That's if you don't sell up before Christmas and head back home."

Her dark eyes flashed. "I'm *not* selling, Brant Hollister. Let's be very clear about that. I dare say your path has been strewn with successes, but you're going to fail with me."

"Am I?" he softly mocked.

"I've given you notice." She spoke haughtily.

"What you lack in inches you make up for in voice projection. I can only ask who taught you that particular tone? The grandmother, right?"

It took Nyree a full minute before she could answer.

"My grandmother makes *me* sound like Mother Teresa. Now and again I do employ her tone…"

"Well, I never!"

"And don't laugh," she said sternly. "I'm one serious person. I do Miss Em as well. But Miss Em was a true lady."

"And you're a great mimic," he said, looking entertained. "Think you can amuse yourself this afternoon? I have appointments to keep."

"Of course I can," she retorted, vexed. "I'll go down to the beach."

"Take sunblock, and don't go in far in the sea, though the bay is safe. You *can* swim?"

"Do you know anyone who *can't*?" she asked caustically.

"Lana can't," he answered mildly. "Not well, anyway. She's strangely averse to getting her hair wet. But don't say anything. She might get upset."

Immediately Nyree adopted the lotus flower position, bending her tawny head. "Your wish is my command, O Lord and Master!"

She had fully expected Brant would travel to his appointments in the Mercedes, or maybe the Range Rover she had spotted. Instead he took off in a Bell helicopter from a helipad in the grounds.

"Gadzooks!" she cried—one of Miss Em's expressions. She stared upwards as the helicopter lifted into the intense blue sky, rotors whirring. A helicopter. A yacht. Surely there was a Lear jet tucked away somewhere? Maybe his dad had taken it on his business trip.

Her own accommodation was far more luxurious than the best five-star hotel. Brant had settled her in what was called the Topaz Suite. Apparently there was an Emerald Suite, a Turquoise Suite and an Amethyst Suite, which he said he would show her when he had time. There were servants. He called them household staff. A major-domo—Vincent—a very pleasant man, and his equally pleasant and attractive wife Gina, fiftyish, who was in charge of running the household. Both were obviously of Italian extraction. Gina had her own staff too, who all appeared to be Asian—probably Vietnamese. So, a league of nations.

Everyone smiled. Everyone appeared happy. Why wouldn't they in such a splendid house set like a jewel in its glorious environment?

The Topaz Suite was huge—the topaz coming from the colour of the silk bedspread, the cushions and the upholstery on the day-bed. The colour was picked up again in the South East Asian rugs that were scattered across the golden polished timber floor. There were no curtains, only white shutters that could be folded away or adjusted as required. The adjoining bathroom was fantastic. It had a huge picture window that looked directly out over the bay, the view framed by golden timber cupboards with open shelving that held lovely thick towels, bath mats, and all manner of bath salts, lotions, potions, body creams, fragrant soaps.

But what captured her attention way beyond the beauty, the space and the luxury of the suite was the painting in the bedroom that could be best viewed from the bed. It was a large oil on canvas, depicting a remarkable profusion of tropical flowers, giant leaves and ferns. The flowers dominated the canvas, but to the left was a view of a turquoise sea with a coral island rising out of it. To her stunned eye it was a *tour de force*.

She adored flower paintings. They were irresistible. They spoke a universal language. Her eye moved to the explosion of tropical orchids, lilies and liliums, hibiscus of incredible size, Torch Gingers, Strelitzias, some gorgeous flower she didn't yet know, giant banana leaves, philodendron leaves. As specimens, they all looked so *real* she found herself putting out her hand as if she could touch them, inhale their heady scent. In the bottom right hand corner was a signature, in a small but beautiful script.

Howard Allcott.

That stopped her short. What on earth was going on here? Brant hadn't been honest with her. Or not honest enough. What did it all mean? Her great-uncle had painted a portrait of his grandmother? She'd had no idea he had painted portraits. That was a very special skill.

And now this. She remained gazing at the painting for quite a while, her expression tender and sad, then she turned away, resolutely hunting out her bikinis. She had brought several—all nylon-Lycra. She might be petite, but she had just the right figure for a bikin She intended going for a swim. The mysteries would ave to wait.

Hair in a plait, she pulled on a cover-up, caught up her beach bag and her new hat, then made her way down through the house, across a grassy promontory to steps cut into the cliff face. The steps were topped with granite blocks, and there was a hand rail to hold on to for safety.

Great buoyancy in her every movement, she jumped the last step onto the broad crescent of white sand that lay between her and the sea, that was glowing with a near neon luminosity and the tropical fluorescence. She stood still for a moment, filling her lungs with pure salt air. She couldn't remember a time when she had felt so wonderfully carefree. This was heaven, and she didn't have to pay for any of it. When some of the jungle was cleared at the farmhouse she might have her own view of the sea.

Halleluiah! She had lived through hard times. Bring on the good!

That unforgettable afternoon she frolicked in the crystalline shallows. Exhilarated, she swam out until she couldn't touch the sea floor. Afterwards she did a little sunbathing, careful to apply lotion liberally beforehand. She could just imagine the comments she would have to endure should she acquire a pink peeling nose. Later she ambled along the foaming water's edge, exploring right down to the next bay, picking up some exquisite shells. The only footprints on the sand were hers and the sea gulls'. Hours slipped by before she began to think of collecting her things and making her leisurely return to the house.

The spirit of the place welcomed her. She could feel it in her bones. For the first time since she had lost Miss Em her spirits were soaring. Miss Em would approve. Miss Em had loved her.

By the time she reached the top of the cliff the wind was whipping at her hair, pulling it out of its plait, nearly stripping her cover-up from her. She had been on the beach for hours. It was almost sunset. She turned one more time to stare out over the sea. Less than an hour ago it had been the colour of precious stones: emerald, sapphire and sparkling aquamarine. Now it had turned to indigo. Layers upon layers of colour were invading the western sky. Mauves, yellows, pinks, lime-greens, and an unbelievable palette of crimsons, with the dipping sun blazing in all its glory on its journey down the horizon.

Never had the world seemed so clean and bright. It was wonderful to be at one with nature, with the heavens and the sea. She dropped her beach bag, careful to weigh down her hat, which had somehow become precious to her, while she stood in a near mystical trance. In front of her dazzled eyes it was as if the western sky caught fire! A conflagration of red and orange, rose and gold. Such beauty would lift anyone's mood.

"We call it the miracle hour," Brant's voice said from behind her.

Sexuality in sound waves. She spun like a dancer. It was staggering how familiar he seemed. How did one explain that? Their lives had barely touched, yet they had formed a connection that held a powerful physical component.

"Oh, you're home!" she exclaimed.

"Twenty minutes ago."

Brant allowed his eyes to move over her. She had at once the most innocent and the most seductive body he had ever seen. Small beautiful breasts, lovely limbs, glorious skin. In a matter of hours she had turned a sun-kissed pale gold.

"Enjoy yourself?" He kept his tone casual.

Did he really need to ask? She looked radiant. He had a mad impulse to fling out his arm and draw her into his embrace. Keep her there. He had never felt like that about a woman. Come to that, he had never really known what it was to be intoxicated by a woman's beauty and bright, endearing personality. Now Ms Nyree Allcott, all of nineteen, had entered his life, instantly altering it.

You're letting your senses get the upper hand.

God, yes. Hadn't he wanted her in two minutes flat? What was even more extraordinary, it felt perfectly *natural*. As if it was meant to be. It was enough to take a man's breath away.

"I've had a perfectly beautiful afternoon," she answered him, in a soft reverent voice. "This is my kind of place. A dream of paradise! No wonder artists are attracted to the tropics. I've never see a more magnificent sunset. The sun is way down on the horizon, but it's so glorious, so dazzling, it's lighting up the entire sky."

He spoke gently. "Stay with me and you'll see many more." He couldn't retrieve the words. They had sprung from the depths of him. In their way, dynamite stuff.

"Aren't you sweet?" She managed to answer calmly enough, even though something inside her began to ache to *belong*. To really belong! It was her dream. "When the jungle is cleared I'll have my own view at the farm," she said, trying to cover a moment of high emotion. "I know it can't possibly match this—this is an absolutely *perfect* uninterrupted view of the sea and the not so distant islands—but only billionaires can afford this little lot."

"We're aware how fortunate we are." He smiled, and the smile stayed in his brilliant turquoise eyes. "So, what have you chosen to wear this evening?" An arm around her shoulder, he turned her back towards the house.

"I don't think I'll tell you." All of a sudden she wanted to hold on to him for dear life. Never let him go. Just being with him felt tremendously *good*. "I'll make it a surprise."

She had known him a day. She had known him all her life.

Nyree was making her way downstairs when she saw Brant hastening towards her. He was wearing a very stylish beige linen suit and an open-necked navy shirt with a cream stripe.

"You look beautiful." He kept his tone light. In actual fact she looked exquisite, in a light-as-a-breeze floral dress that hung from spaghetti straps. The bodice cupped her small breasts, flowed close to her body to her ankles, showing off high-heeled gold sandals. All that beautiful skin on show. The dress was amazingly pretty, yet he guessed it would have been inexpensive. She had style. One either had it or didn't. Money couldn't buy it. Obviously she had shampooed the salt out of her hair. It sprang up and away from her small face in a gleaming, sinuous mane.

"Pass muster, then, do I?" There was challenge in her lustrous dark eyes.

"Okay—you look ravishing," he conceded.

"And *you* look madly, dashingly attractive—even if we are on opposite sides of the fence. Come to escort me down to dinner? That's a surprise."

"I love it when you're nice to me." He slanted her an amused glance. "It so happens Alena wants to meet you before the others arrive."

"Oh, my gosh!" Nyree looked down at herself. Her outfit was pretty—it was a great pattern—but no way would it hold up against what she guessed the Countess and the female guests would be wearing. Always needing to give people labels, she had already secretly identified Brant's grandmother in her mind as the Contessa.

"There's absolutely no need to be nervous," he said. "Come along." He held out his hand.

Quiet fell over her.

Alena Kalenin—Hollister—was nothing like Nyree had expected. She had imagined from Brant's height that the Countess would be a tall woman, rather like Miss Em. Spare, elegant, commanding.

The lady that confronted her, seated in an armchair more like a throne which dwarfed her, was *tiny*!

Nyree thought when standing even she would easily top her. Probably she had diminished with age. Which wasn't to say she wasn't immensely regal. She was. Her silver hair had been set to form a halo around a remarkably unlined parchment-textured face. She wore a long midnight-blue *moiré* silk dress and a glorious necklet of large pearls that sat perfectly within the high neckline. Her eyes were as dark as Nyree's own. Dark and piercing beneath artfully tended high-arching black brows.

Her voice, when it came, was firm and precise—no sign of age—with an accent after long years still in place.

"Please, my dear, let me have a look at you—Howard's great-niece."

In such a presence—and the suite was mind-bogglingly Old World opulent as well—Nyree found herself dipping into a spontaneous little bob. "Good evening, Contessa," she said, moving forward. "It's an honour to meet you."

There was nothing whatsoever studied about her, Brant decided, standing quietly in the background. It was obvious their young guest had spoken from the heart. Indeed, she had shown for the first time in his hearing an accent of her own in saying *contessa*. Of course—she had Italian blood. He wondered if she spoke the language, as he did.

"Eyes—the windows of the soul!" Alena pronounced, leaning forward in her chair and offering Nyree a tiny be-ringed hand, the wrist encircled by a magnificent diamond cuff. Diamond and sapphire pendants swung from the lobes of her ears. "Yours are so beautiful and so pure. You have come to the right people, Nyree. A lovely name. It suits you. I well remember a beautiful New Zealand actress called Nyree Dawn Porter. She played Irene in the *Forsyte Saga*. But that was way before your time. Whatever you wish to do, child, we will help you. Be assured of that. I see no trace of Howard in you. Your Italian blood is uppermost."

"On my mother's side, Contessa. My mother was very beautiful."

"As are *you*!" The Contessa threw up her tiny hands. "I wanted Brant to bring you to me so we could meet for the first time in private. We will talk later at length, if you would like that?"

"I would indeed." Nyree blushed. "Your grandson has been very kind to me, when he could easily have been otherwise."

"Not so!" The Contessa flashed her grandson such a spirited, loving, mischievous smile that Nyree immediately caught a glimpse of the great beauty of the Contessa's youth. The cheekbones were still there. The arched brows and the brilliant eyes.

"You see the resemblance to the girl in the Alma Tadema?" Brant asked.

"But of course!" his grandmother exclaimed. "Nyree's beauty is classic. And that hair! You may not believe this, Nyree," she confided, "but I once had hair to my waist. And such hair! Not all those wonderful waves and curls like yours, but straight—very thick and lustrous. My hair was as dark as my eyes. Tomorrow, perhaps, I'll show you the Alma Tadema."

"And my great-uncle's portrait of you?" Nyree begged. "I would love to see it. To see *you*!" The sincerity rang genuine.

"I'll think about it," Alena said slowly. "Now, I suppose we must go down to the guests. Nyree—I'll take your hand."

"Of course, Contessa." Nyree sprang to the Contessa's aid. In a very strange way it was like seeing Miss Em's ghost. The two women couldn't have been more dissimilar in appearance, but it seemed to Nyree they cast over her a similar mantle of womanly protectiveness.

His grandmother had made no move to correct Nyree over using her title, Brant observed, watching the two of them bond so easily. Alena Hollister she might be to the rest of the world, Alena Kalenin for her books, but his grandmother had accepted Nyree's "Contessa" as her due. Of course his grandfather had often called her Countess if she sounded especially regal. It had been playful. But no one else outside of Nyree had attempted the same. Yet his grandmother seemed more than happy with Nyree's use of her long relinquished title.

CHAPTER SIX

"I THINK that'll do for today!" Dolly whipped out a huge red handkerchief and mopped her sweating brow. "Come on, ducky, stop now before you drop."

"I'm sorry I told you my nickname, Dolly," Nyree said, going to the back door and emptying her bucket into the ferns. Afterwards she washed her hands at the shining kitchen sink, dried them, then slumped wearily into a chair opposite Dolly.

They had been working all day, and now the two of them were spent. The "Big Heat" was mounting. The Weather Bureau was monitoring a cyclone off the coast of Fiji. The cyclone season was underway, with the town and the entire district making preparations for any possible onslaught.

"At least we're getting there," Nyree breathed with satisfaction. "I can't thank you enough, Dolly, for being so supportive."

"You're Howie's great-niece, aren't you?" Dolly said, pouring them both home-made lemonade and adding chunks of ice. "Besides, you're a real lovely kid."

"I'm a *woman*, Dolly," Nyree stressed. Would anyone see her as that? Was it her *height*? Or lack of it? Even the Contessa called her "child", though she must seem a child when the Contessa was approaching eighty.

"Not yet, sweetheart," Dolly said slyly. " I know a little virgin when I see one. Pure as the driven snow."

Well, even Dolly had been a virgin once. "That obvious, is it?" Nyree moaned.

"No greater allure for a man," Dolly pronounced in her lascivious contralto. "Brant has been taking a far more than kindly interest in you. Look at all the help he's given you. Staying at the big house. Meeting Alena. I've always been terribly, terribly jealous of her, you know," Dolly abruptly confided. "Haven't seen her for years. Is she still beautiful? Couldn't be. She must be eighty. Years older than me."

"Why would you be jealous, Dolly?" Nyree frowned her puzzlement.

"I was jealous of every woman Howie looked at," Dolly said, fixing Nyree with an intense gaze. "Especially in the early days. He was a very handsome man. The women fell for him in droves."

"Isn't that what hippies did? Fell for one another in droves? I've read about the big love-ins. But what does that have to do with the Contessa?" Nyree couldn't disguise her curiosity.

Dolly looked away guiltily, as though she'd been caught off guard. "Nothing. Nothing at all. He painted her portrait, you know."

Dolly had clearly decided to back off. "I haven't seen it as yet." Although she and the Contessa *had* become amazingly close over the past month, Nyree still hadn't been invited to see the portrait—and she hadn't had the temerity to ask again. She had, however, been shown the Alma Tadema in the Contessa's sumptuous bedroom, and noted the resemblance to herself.

"I only saw it the once. Even then I wasn't meant to." Dolly's painted red mouth stretched into a wry grimace. "I had to steal a look."

"So what are you implying? Great-Uncle Howard was in love with the Contessa?" Nyree's voice rose a full couple of tones.

"You and this Contessa bit!" Dolly retorted, looking incensed. "*No one* calls her that. Not even Howie. How did you get into it?"

"She *is* a Russian Countess, Dolly. That's why. She looks and acts like the true aristocrat she is. She's been in this country God knows how many years, yet she still retains a Russian accent. Brant has quite a look of her— those cheekbones that give him such an exotic air."

"Oh, he's exotic, all right!' Dolly cried, tempestous feelings unleashed. "If I was only thirty years younger I'd give that Lana Bennett a run for her money."

Nyree felt actual pain in her chest. "Brant says she's only a friend."

Dolly broke into a rich cackle. "Listen up, kiddo," she snorted. "Lana Bennett has gone most of her life believing one day she'll be Brant's wife. Struth, they were an item not all that long back. She told me herself."

"Maybe she was fantasising." Nyree clung tightly to the idea. "I've seen them together. Brant doesn't *act* in the least lover-like around her."

"It's *money*, my girl," Dolly said. "Money marries money. Don't you get that? Lana's dad has been in partnership with Brant's father on many a project. He's on the board of DHH. You're in the wrong dream, my darling, if you've got a hankering for Brant Hollister. You're too young and innocent for Brant. He likes a sophisticated woman."

"I don't think Lana is all that sophisticated," Nyree returned with spirit. "She's not terribly well read. She didn't even know the heroine's name in *War and Peace*. The last time I saw her—it was at a dinner party at the house—she told me I looked like a shampoo ad. Laughed while she said it. I thought her very rude."

Dolly twirled at the hair curling wildly around her ears. "Jealous." As she spoke, Dolly glanced at her watch. "You have a magnificent head of hair. As do I." She tossed back the rest of the lemonade, then rose to her feet, straightening her off-the-shoulder blouse. "Now, ducky, I'm off. I'm due at the restaurant tonight. A special fiftieth wedding anniversary dinner for old friends of mine. You're going to be all right here by yourself? I do wish you wouldn't do it, but all my efforts to stop you have failed."

Nyree pulled herself to her feet. "Stop worrying, Dolly. I have the dogs. They'd *eat* anyone who tried to do me harm."

"I'm sure glad *I'm* a friend." Dolly, who normally wasn't the least nervous around dogs, rolled her eyes.

They walked out onto the verandah and Juno and Jupiter, sleek Dobermans, rose to accompany them out to Dolly's four-wheel drive. Quarrelling lorikeets with their gorgeous display of plumage were bursting in and out of the grevillea blossom in an orgy of feeding.

Brant had insisted on bringing Juno and Jupiter over to act as Nyree's guard dogs. She had been powerless to stop him. It had appeared to be a condition of her staying at the farmhouse on her own. It had worked well. An animal lover, she was beginning to really enjoy their company. Though ferocious when on guard, they were proving affectionate companions.

She waved Dolly off—noticing she had a rather painful blister on her right forefinger—then stayed out on the verandah, surveying her wild kingdom. She loved it here—especially since miracles had been wrought. And it was all due to Brant. He gave the orders. Things happened. Not in due course. Right away. She knew in her heart he was only humouring her until such time as she chucked it in. But for now he was allowing her to have her little adventure. He had so much money it really didn't matter.

A great sweep of grass had been slashed and mown right around the house, protecting it from snakes. The rampant climbing morning glories had been pulled off the tall tank stands. The jungle was subdued, except for the wonderful bank upon bank of day lilies she absolutely loved. Brant had even sent a man to cut some of the branches of the great coral trees so she could have her view of the sea. The corrugated iron roof had been fixed, the orchids relocated in the pots and hanging baskets she kept on the verandah. The weatherboards had been repainted a soft moss-green, and most of its timber boards had been renewed, as had all the broken windowpanes and the timber shutters on the French doors, repainted pristine white, fixed securely in place.

The temperature hadn't dropped. It looked very much as if they were in for an electrical storm, although the sky was still a dense but sultry blue. She rather liked thunderstorms. She had lived through plenty of them in sub-tropical Brisbane.

Towards dusk, she heard the sound of a vehicle coming down the private road. Quickly she bound her freshly washed hair in the delicate hair ornament the Contessa had given her: four fine gold loops encrusted with crystals that fitted over her head. It was quite beautiful, classical in design. Nyree treasured it because it had been a gift.

"Much like what the young girl in my Alma Tadema paintings is wearing," the Contessa had said. *"I'd like you to have it."*

It suited her so well Nyree had taken to wearing it much of the time, unaware the sparkling crystals were actually diamonds. It kept her hair bound, and away from her neck.

She wasn't expecting visitors—Brant was in Cairns for a few days on business, and it had made such a difference to her world—so she had pulled on a short blue and yellow patterned smock, not bothering with a bra in the humid heat.

The dogs gave the identity of the driver away. They went mad but in a welcoming way. It was *Brant* in the Range Rover! Excitement took wing. She had thought to set herself against him, yet in no time at all he had undermined all her defences.

*You've got a job in front of you, girl. Brant Hollister
is the last man in the world to fall in love with.*

Why wasn't she listening to the voice of common
sense?

She saw he was heading for the double car port at the
sheltered side of the house. Since she had been under
the shower the sky had changed to an extraordinary
glittery gunmetal. Flocks of birds were flying overhead,
homing in to their resting place, their screeching clear
warning of the storm to come. The palm trees that had
been waving their fronds stood motionless in the strange
lull. It was like being in the eye of a storm. For the first
time she got an inkling of the terrible power of storms
this far north of Capricorn.

Swiftly she ran about, turning on a few lights. The
interior of the house had turned gloomy, and she wanted
him to see all the improvements she and Dolly had made.

He came up the short flight of front steps accompanied by the dogs, calling her name.

"I'm here—here," she announced, quickly running to
the open doorway. "I thought you'd still be in Cairns?"

God, wasn't it wonderful to have him back? Not only
was he part of her waking life, he had become part of
her dreams. It was as though she was on the edge of
some great revelation. Whether good or bad she had yet
to find out.

"I'm here now," he retorted crisply. "I thought you
told me you knew all about tropical storms? Your
shutters should be closed."

"So, okay, I was about to shut them. And I'm well.
Thanks for asking."

"First things first," he clipped out. "Put the dogs in the laundry. They hate storms. Then get cracking inside the house." He turned about and went back onto the verandah. "It'll be on us in another few minutes."

How right he was!

It began with dramatic suddenness. One minute there was an odd waiting silence, then hell broke loose.

"Oh, my God!" She rushed to his side and caught hold of his arm.

He put his arm around her waist and drew her close to him. "I hate you being out here in this isolated place," he said with a subdued rage. "*I* hate it. *Alena* hates it."

"Well, I love it!" Despite herself, her voice was shaky. The wind was *roaring* outside, as if monstrous howling wolves were trying to blow the house over. Its primal voice was rattling the strongly built shutters. The rain was coming down in a ferocious torrent, slanting in to the front of the house, crashing down like Victoria Falls on the iron roof. A flash of lightning, truly terrifying, lit up the interior like a film set. Brant had turned off the electricity. If the worst came to the worst she would have to rely on candles. There were stacks of them in the pantry.

Moments after the lightning came the thunder. It was loud enough to wake the dead. Nyree actually jumped, and his arm tightened around her.

"It's okay. I've seen a lot worse." He had to shout to be heard.

"How long will it last?" she shouted back, lifting her head to him, immensely grateful he was with her. She had seen plenty of storms, even the odd violent storm, but nothing to compare with the velocity and the sheer power of *this*! It was actually making her feel ill.

Just as Brant had feared, down came the hail. As they were later to find out, much of it was as large as golf balls, providing a temporary snow field. Hail smashed its way across the verandah, striking at the shutters. They held. The windows on one side of the house were still unprotected. Sure enough they heard a crack, sharp as a rifle shot, then the sound of breaking glass.

"Stay there," Brant ordered. The safest spot was the core of the house.

"I'm coming with you."

"Not in bare feet, you're not."

"I am too." In all truth she didn't want to be separated from him. Not for a moment. It was like being under fire on a field of battle.

The broken window was in the smallest bedroom, the one least sheltered by the great mango tree. The curtains were sopping wet, blown back and torn. Glass fragments, glittering like diamond squares and triangles, lay all over the polished floor and the rug.

"Back to the other room," Brant waved her away, noting her pallor. "This will have to wait."

The romance of her wild kingdom had shown its turbulent face.

Fifteen minutes later it was all over. Just like that! Great arrows of sunlight were piercing the mushroomed cumulus clouds that were shot through with iridescent veins of silver, livid green and gold. Brant had gone out onto the verandah to open the shutters. Now a glorious blast of air heavily perfumed by mountains of crushed blossom—jasmin, gardenia, ginger, frangipani and oleander—rushed into the house.

Nyree didn't venture out. She stood framed in the open doorway, brushing damp strands of hair away from her heated face. The grass was covered in hailstones, and there was shredded blossom everywhere, lying in rainbows against the ice. One of the palm trees had taken a lightning strike. The trunk was snapped off at an angle of forty-five degrees. There were circles of blue forming in the grey sky.

She put a finger into her ear. "I think I'm deaf."

"That was nothing," he said, returning to her, glad her bright colour had come back—although she was warily watching him, as though expecting a lecture. She had tried to remain stoic but she hadn't fooled him one bit. Not with his arm around her trembling body. The storm had frightened her—as well it might.

"Let's have a cup of coffee," he said.

"Good idea. My nerves are shot."

"I didn't think you'd admit to it."

"Pretending wouldn't work," she answered wryly.

"Not with my arm around you."

"Well, it *was* scary," she flashed.

"Give me a broom and I'll clean up the broken glass. The window will have to be patched up with a piece of plywood for the time being."

She took the broom out of the closet, then passed it to him. "There's plenty of unused timber out in the car port."

"I know."

To her infatuated eyes his stunning bone structure seemed more prominent than usual. Even his expression was a bit on the daunting side. "I'll make the coffee," she said, her nerves at an exquisite pitch.

"Let the dogs out first."

"Very well, Mr Hollister."

Later they sat in the living room, freshly painted her favourite yellow, with a high-gloss white trim. Great-Uncle Howard's *Pearl in the Ocean* took pride of place, dominating the room and adding tremendous panache to what was now a very inviting space.

"You've done wonders," he said, more tersely than he'd intended.

He knew she had style. She had done a great job turning much of the abandoned farm house back into an attractive home. But being with her, having his arm around her during the storm, holding her to him, conscious she was wearing very little under the pretty smock, was making even *his* iron control falter. Her attraction was so powerful it was all he could do to keep his hands off her. He knew he was judged by everyone—those who knew him, those who only knew *of* him as David Hollister's heir—to have everything he wanted. What he wanted was right here. He didn't want anything else as long as she stayed near. This was a rare moment for him—a moment of acute revelation.

Nyree set her coffee cup down, unnerved by his manner. "But you're angry, aren't you? Not pleased at all."

"What do you expect, Nyree?" He frowned. "First and foremost you're living a dream. An unsustainable dream."

Of course she was. But she wasn't ready to admit it. "Don't start, Brant," she said in quick defiance. "Please don't. I'm a bit on edge." *A bit* hardly said it. The atmosphere inside the house was as electric as any storm.

"You're not the only one," he felt forced to say. "What about me? I feel responsible for you."

She jumped up in a temper. "I don't *need* you to be responsible for me."

"That's ridiculous and you know it. I'm happy to do whatever you want."

"Anything to indulge me, you mean. You have so much money you don't care one way or the other. You think I'm just some poor deprived kid who should be allowed to play house."

"Well, aren't you?" He was acutely aware of the danger that was flying all around them. Hot passions mixed up with a supercharged sexual hostility. "You lost the parents you adored at a very vulnerable age. You had years with your ghastly grandmother until Miss Em stepped in to save you."

"Pop psychology!" she cried out in scorn.

He ignored her. "Then you lost your mentor. Howard's legacy has set you free—but only if you sell the damned place. Surely you can see that? We expected to acquire it when Howard died. You're right," he admitted tautly. "You've got me all confused—and I'm a guy who doesn't confuse easily. I *am* letting you play house. You know why? You and your history have got to me. Does that make you happy? It would have been so much easier to deal with an older woman, a settled person. These days I find myself ready to do *anything* you want, even though I know it's a kind of madness. I'm indulging you in what I know to be a fantasy."

He ran his fingers through his thick dark hair, betraying his agitation.

"What if I give you the villa that will be eventually built on this spot? It's going to happen. Some part of you must know that. The thing is, Nyree, you shouldn't be way out here on your own. Even with the dogs it's a tremendous worry. Word goes out. You've been seen in the town. Everyone is talking about Howie's beautiful great-niece. How long do you think it will take before you have uninvited callers?"

"Then they can clear off!" she cried with perverse fury, knowing he was absolutely right. "I'm quite safe with the dogs."

"Oh, yeah, you're a real Superwoman!" he snapped. "There are ways to subdue dogs," he added grimly.

So many drifters passed through the tourist towns. Men without ties, without women, without scruple. A beautiful young woman alone, unprotected. He couldn't live with it. Alena wanted it all to come to a halt. She had grown very fond of Nyree, often commenting on Nyree's broad range of interests—unusual in a young girl. Interests no doubt encouraged by her beloved Miss Em.

"You're paranoid, as far as I can see," Nyree announced wrathfully. It was all an act. Her heart was pumping away madly. She *knew* her position was untenable, but she'd be damned if she'd give in to him without a fight. "Absolutely paranoid!" She covered the living room with her arms crossed.

"Well, you can't see very far," he retorted bluntly, tracking her progress with his eyes. "You're not giving enough thought to this, Nyree. I don't want you here. It would be bad enough if Howie had left you a house in the town. But way out here… It's too isolated."

"Who says I have to have *your* p-permission?" She was so angry she was stuttering.

"I do," he said. "You wouldn't want me for an enemy."

"Is that a threat?" She looked at him, aghast.

"You know damned well it's not." He shot to his feet, uncharacteristically off balance. Her eyes were huge. Overbright. "You take all my help—"

"I've thanked you, haven't I?" she flung at him. "I'm tremendously grateful. What are you trying to do to me, Brant? Send me away? Because I'm telling you now, *I'm not going!*" She even stamped her foot.

"And I have no intention of leaving you here," he countered, moving towards her, a towering male figure. "Alena is worried about you. She told me to tell you to pack a bag and come back to the house," he said, in a quieter tone. "Cyclone Callie is forming in the Coral Sea. We're all on alert. It could live for as long as two or three weeks, and if it comes in it will come at great speed. If you think this afternoon's storm was bad, you won't want to be out here on your own during cyclonic weather—even if a cyclone doesn't hit."

The rational part of her was aware of all this, but she was beyond reason—at the mercy of her ungovernable emotions. She had never felt remotely like this in her life. "You want to control me utterly, don't you. *Why?*"

"Don't play the little fool," he ground out, feeling himself being pushed beyond his limits.

His vision was filled with her. His nostrils were inhaling with tortured delight the extraordinary *scent* of her. He had to gulp in air. Finally, out of all patience, he reached for her, hauling her into his arms.

"You've known what was on my mind since the very first day."

She flushed, the vivid memory of their first meeting streaking before her eyes. She was ready to faint with the yearning that threatened to engulf her. He filled up her whole field of vision.

"So you want me?" she cried. "You think I don't know? I'm all sorts of a fool, according to you, and yet you want me. What as? Some tawdry little affair? I'm not wife material. I'm too inexperienced—too stupid for you. No, I take that back. I'm far from stupid. I'm clever. I'm just not clever about *you*. That's where Lana Bennett comes in. It's the talk of the town."

"The hell it is!" He dismissed that in a fury. "*You're* the talk of the town. You know so much and yet you know *nothing*!"

"So *tell* me!" she shouted. A primitive rage, driven by this torrent of unresolved yearning, had taken hold of her. She was so agitated her whole body was throbbing.

"Why don't I just *show* you?" he ground out, his tone unbearably harsh.

In a blaze of action Brant swept her off her feet, knowing she was so shell shocked she could offer no resistance. She was such a featherweight he could have walked halfway across the world with her in his arms.

They were on the sofa… Her warm body was draped across his knees, her beautiful curly head tipped back into the crook of his shoulder, arching her throat. God, he *adored* her. How had it happened?

"Bravado one minute, silence the next." He spoke tersely. "You're a very complicated person, aren't you?"

"And you're *not*?" She tried to raise her head to defy him, only he swooped…

His first kiss literally sizzled across her mouth, leaving a trail of fire.

An experiment? Whatever had been intended, it had a galvanic effect. Her heart was beating inside and out, sensation expanding at such a rate she felt her whole body go into meltdown. His strong hands actually seemed to be melting through her skin to her bones. She went limp and alarmingly languorous. She couldn't have stood up even if she'd wanted to. All she *could* do was fall back with a helpless moan.

The next time he kissed her it went so deep she began to drown in a sea of sensation. She thought she locked her hand around his neck. She wasn't sure. She wasn't sure of anything. What did she know about sex and passion? He was taking her some place she had never been before… His hand moved down over the soft fabric of her smock, caressing her breasts through it, bringing her sensitive nipples to tight painful life. She couldn't disengage…her longing for this to continue was too fierce…it was wonderful and it was terrifying…like the effects of a dangerous stimulant.

His hand moved lower, down over her stomach, which quivered under the pressure, then abruptly he stopped—even though her knees were spreading in a movement that was totally involuntary. She wanted his fingers to enter her…she *wanted* it…*longed* for it… She had never known a lover, but more than anything in the world she wanted her first lover, her only lover, to be *him*.

Even so, she knew she was panicking... There was a good chance she would lose not only her virginity but her reason. Her reactions were astonishing to her... She wasn't herself at all. She was *woman* with *man*. Her first man. She was going to *live* the experience. Maybe die of sheer excitement.

"There's nothing to panic about." Brant's voice came in a swift undertone. "I'm only making love to you. A little."

A little?

Dear God, if this was a *little*, how would she withstand the real thing? Her whole body had flamed into life beneath his hands. Nothing could save her. She was losing herself, despite the very real worry that fluttered like a moth at the back of her mind. How far were they going? She wasn't prepared for sex. Yet his every kiss was taking her down deeper and deeper into a sensual whirlpool.

This was how it happened. Blind passion. Emotions out of control. Ecstasy mixed with fear.

You love him.

The voice in her head did nothing to soothe her extreme agitation. How was it possible she could love so deeply, so madly, a man she really didn't know? How could she abandon herself like this to his voluptuous lovemaking? She had curled herself into his aroused body, fitting herself to him, a sure manifestation of his power over her.

Brant drew in his breath sharply, wrenched himself sober, though his heart was banging painfully against his ribs and his powerful arousal was an agony. He was desperate to pick her up and carry her to her bedroom. Slam the door. Lock it. Make love to her for hours and hours. Leave his imprint. Make it so she would never forget him.

Only…only… He tried desperately to regain control… His *body* was demanding he take her—his sex drive sizzling its way along his arteries. But his *mind* told him he could never hurt her. Never, never, *never*! She was wise to trust him. He didn't know if that made him feel better or worse. His desire for her had grown with every passing minute of every passing day. Today that desire had all but brought him to his knees. His life, which for the most part had been all about business, was now focused on a woman. She didn't just arouse him sexually. Her well-being had come to mean everything to him.

He looked down at her, shaking his head a little from side to side in an effort to bounce away his driving desires. Her beautiful dark eyes were brimming with the tears of high emotion, breaking his heart and in the end reining him in.

"I'm sorry, Nyree." He picked up her hand and kissed it like some knight of old. "I'm sorry I frightened you. I'd never hurt you. You must know that."

"I do," she gasped. Her breasts were rising and falling in agitation. "I'm a virgin, Brant." She had to tell him. Warn him?

"I know. Girl into woman." He bent and took silvery teardrops into his mouth, willing his heartbeat to stabilise. "Come back to the house with me. Say you will. Put me out of my misery."

She stared into his eyes, seeing tiny flecks of gold in the brilliant turquoise. "I can't refuse you," she murmured finally.

She truly couldn't.

CHAPTER SEVEN

CYCLONE CALLIE, initiated as a cluster of thunderstorms over the Coral Sea, continued to hover out to sea. Either it would die there or it would cross the coast, bringing destructive winds and flooding. The region was on cyclone watch. Everyone hoped it wouldn't be upgraded to a cyclone warning. Either way, people were being given plenty of updates, through radio, television and the Weather Bureau in six different languages: English, four Asian, Italian.

Nyree had settled back into the big house, treated by everyone from the Contessa down as though she were family. It was the most marvellous feeling. She was being made truly welcome. In a sense, it felt to her like a coming *home*. She certainly wasn't drawing back from the affection she was being shown. In fact she was revelling in it. The death of one parent profoundly isolates a child. The death of both parents places an insupportable and terrifying burden on such a child.

She had been a *lone* teenager. No brothers and sisters to share the burden of her grief. All she'd had was a grandmother who had been horrible to her. God knew which way her life would have gone without Miss Em. Miss Em had fixed a vulnerable young girl's mind not on the distress of her life but on the challenges that lay ahead. Miss Em had cast her as an achiever. She wasn't going to fail her.

In a near magical way the Contessa had taken up from where Miss Em had left off. To Nyree's mind, both women shared the same wonderfully endearing personality traits. They had warmth, humour, spirit, charm, and a serious and abiding interest in intellectual pursuits. She and the Contessa got on so famously it seemed to Nyree they were well on the way to a powerful attachment. There had been no settling in period. They had *clicked* from the start. It helped that because of the circumstances of her life she had grown used to and greatly valued the company of women at the culmination of their life— accomplished women who had so much wisdom to offer.

She was enjoying every minute of her new life. Of course she knew everyone ultimately stood alone, but her great wish for *family*, a profound human need, was finding expression within Brant's family. Such was the sheer unexpectedness of life. Her journey towards becoming a *woman*, a real woman, was well underway. Had she known it, she was positively *blooming* in this glorious tropical landscape, living an existence that had been offered to her like some precious gift. She wasn't lost. Brant had found her. A divine mystery at work?

Brant, who was often busy from early morning to mid-evening, told her she had given his grandmother a new lease on life.

"She's wonderfully at ease with you, Nyree," he reported back, clearly delighted about the whole thing.

That meant so much to the thriving Nyree. Even Jasmin, the Contessa's devoted maid and companion, was glad of her many extra breaks, so she could go into town and meet up with her friends.

Nyree had finally been shown the Contessa's portrait, painted by her great-uncle. It had been put away in storage as the Contessa's late husband had taken an inexplicable dislike to it.

Not inexplicable at all! As Nyree had found out.

She'd stood in front of the large portrait that had been placed on a decorative easel, her heart in her mouth. The style was reminiscent of the famous American portrait painter John Singer Sargent— bravura in concept.

The Contessa when younger—she would have been perhaps in her early thirties at the time—had been stunningly beautiful. In the portrait she was seated in a high-backed Louis chair, covered in ivory silk with tiny sprigs of blue flowers. The exact same chair was still in her bedroom. One hand lay on her lap; the other was draped over the gilded side of the chair. Her copious raven hair was drawn back from her face and arranged in a coil on her neck. She wore no jewellery except for a great engagement ring and her wedding ring. Her silk morning gown was ice-blue, with a wide sash in a deep sapphire, the ends trailing over her gown. The Louis chair had been placed in front of a magnificent Chinese screen— also still in her bedroom—as a background.

It was a knockout portrait of a beautiful and sexy

woman. A countess who'd reigned over men's hearts. In this case her husband's—Brant's grandfather—and also, without a shadow of a doubt her ill-fated Great-Uncle Howard.

Here was his *femme fatale*. His *Dark Lady*. His *downfall*.

Nyree had stood transfixed, hardly knowing what to say.

"You can see he was in love with me, can't you?" the Contessa said very softly, from behind her. By now she knew Nyree was very intuitive.

"Anyone with eyes to see could," Nyree answered, just as gently. "Not that I could blame him."

"Let me tell you I was attracted to him," the Contessa confessed. "But that was all it was or could be for me. Afterwards, when the portrait was finished, Howard was like a lost soul. I tried to counter the attraction with coldness. Previously I had been very kind to him, not fully realising what I was setting in train. Howard sent me a letter full of torment that my late husband—a wonderful man—found quite by accident. He thought I had really fallen in love with Howard, but I convinced him Howard was only living a dream. My husband took care of matters. Howard never bothered me again. This portrait, that had held pride of place, came down. Your great-uncle very sadly took to drink as a solace. The depth of his connection to me was *not* reciprocated, Nyree. Unfortunately Howard let his feelings consume him. He had women. Plenty of women. Maybe he only fixated on me because I was not to be had. Who would know? It's a sad story. You know it now, child. We won't speak of it again."

"But the portrait is so beautiful!" Nyree cried in dismay. "*You* are so beautiful. What are you going to do with it? It should be seen."

"Not in this house, my child." The Contessa shook her head.

"Then may I have it?" Nyree begged. "I'll treasure it always."

The Contessa took only seconds to decide. "Of course you may," she said, clasping Nyree's face and planting a kiss on her forehead. "I would give it to no one else."

Nyree continued to keep a check on the farm, airing the house as though she were coming back to it, walking dreamily around the empty rooms, reliving the sublime moments when Brant had made love to her. Had it actually happened? These days she had reason to doubt it. He was acting more and more like an older cousin, with his mind firmly on more important matters.

Dolly had taken Howard's cat—simply called "Cat"—to live with her. The guard dogs had been returned to their minder—one of DHH's employees. In the sultry heat and the intermittent heavy downpours the grounds were quickly reverting to jungle. No wonder her great-uncle had gone mad trying to maintain the place. He should have sold. Probably would have, only Miss Em had convinced him to leave his entire estate to her. If she did sell she would ask top price. DHH would have to cough up. Her darling Miss Em had ensured she would be comfortably placed. When her children came along—and Nyree fervently wanted children—one of the girls would be called Emilia.

For now she was her own woman. Only months ago that would have been the ultimate status. But these days she had to confront the fact that she wanted above anything to be Brant's woman. The woman in his life. He'd sparred with her, comforted her, put his brand on her, mended her. If one believed in Cupid, his arrow had hit the vital spot.

Don't let him smash up your life like the Contessa smashed up Great-Uncle Howard's. A cautionary voice fought for her attention.

She wasn't frightened any more. Another thing was certain. Whichever way things went she wouldn't, like Great-Uncle Howie, take to the bottle.

On her way back from the farm one day, she called into town to see her friend Dolly. Dolly wasn't at the Hibiscus Hut, as it transpired, but as Nyree was returning to the runabout Brant had put at her disposal a woman shouted, "Hold on, there, Nyree."

Nyree turned with a sinking heart. She recognised the voice as Lana Bennett's. Lana Bennett wasn't a friend. Never would be. Lana Bennett had marked her down from the beginning as Trouble.

"How nice to see you!" Lana confounded her by smiling brightly. "I hope you have time for an iced coffee?" She grasped Nyree's arm in the friendliest possible manner. "Terrible weather we're having, isn't it? The only consolation is it lasts such a short time. Most of the year is perfect."

What could she do? Had Lana undergone a much-needed sea change? She had heard of such things.

They went back to Dolly's, where Lana ordered iced coffee for both of them, and two "slivers" of orange-almond cake. "My shout!"

"Please let me pay for myself." Nyree wanted to.

"Won't hear of it!" Lana smiled, showing beautiful white teeth, perfectly straight.

Their order arrived. It took Lana only two minutes more to get down to the real business of the day. "When are you moving out of the big house?" she asked, giving Nyree an encouraging look. "You can't stay there for ever, you know."

"I'm aware of that, Lana," Nyree answered. "It's scarcely my intention anyway. Only the cyclone threat has brought it about. Brant and the Contessa didn't want me at the farmhouse. It was worrying them. They've been very kind to me."

"Why wouldn't it worry them, silly girl?" Lana exclaimed. "Foolhardy in the extreme! Good heavens, you could get raped."

Nyree set down her long spoon. The iced coffee was very good. "I don't think anything like that was ever going to befall me. Obviously you haven't heard I had two big Dobermans standing guard."

"And that made you feel safe?" Lana's brows shot up superciliously.

"Why wouldn't it? They would have *eaten* anyone who posed me a threat. Even Cat would have gone for them with her claws. I was perfectly safe. But I didn't like the idea of worrying the Contessa at this particular time."

"Ingratiated yourself with her, have you?" Lana laughed with open contempt.

That clarified matters. The gloves were off. "What is it you want to say, Lana?" Nyree called on her grandmother's tone. She could do it at will. "Spit it out before it chokes you."

It clearly wasn't what Lana had expected her to say, or said in the way she'd thought. "Hey, drop the tone!" she exclaimed in shock. "Cheeky little thing, aren't you?" She kept her voice low. "What I want to say is this. Don't turn those big brown eyes on Brant. It will bring you no good, only heartache. Brant is *mine*. He knows it. I know it. Everyone approves. He *will* marry me. He will only trifle with you. Who are you, anyway? A no one—the great-niece of the town drunk. What a pedigree! I know Brant feels responsible for you. You *are* young. But for your own self-respect, my dear, you have to move on. Sell the farm. You'll get a good price. After that, go as far away as you can. There's nothing for you here."

"Really?" Nyree began to delve into her tote for her wallet. "It's a free country. It follows I can roam freely. Is there a threat mixed up somewhere in there, may I ask?"

"Are you serious?" Lana looked taken aback. "I'm not threatening you. I suppose I'm doing Brant's job for him. He's confessed he doesn't have the heart to tell you himself. That's men for you. You've charmed his grandmother, but you haven't charmed Brant to the point where he doesn't want you off his hands. He does. More importantly, he wants the farm. One no-account person and you're holding up the whole project. It will be marvellous for the town—and the whole of the North." She leaned further across the table, her expression earnest.

"If you'd like to borrow some money until such time as the farm is sold I can lend it to you. It would be strictly between the two of us. I feel for you. I want to help."

"If that's the case, you'll help by shutting up," Nyree responded, laying money on the table. "If Brant wants me gone, he'll tell me. He doesn't need you or anyone else to do his dirty work. I'd say he'd be very angry if I told him what you've had to say today." She stood up, hoisting her tote over her shoulder.

"You're in love with him, aren't you?" Lana flashed, a kind of violence in her eyes.

Nyree leaned down, perhaps risking scratches. "No way I'd tell you. And no way I'll tell him what you've had to say. So you're safe."

She could see, deep down, that Lana Bennett was a very unhappy person. She wasn't about to add to it. If Brant loved Lana Bennett so be it. There was nothing Nyree could do.

Except *mourn*.

Maybe Great-Uncle Howard's unhappy experience had put a hex on her?

Cyclone Callie swept in from the sea. Driven westward by the easterly trade winds, it struck the town of Laguna, some forty miles north of Hollister, right on midnight. Torrential rain was falling all over a vast area. A natural occurrence in all tropical areas of the world, cyclones, hurricanes, typhoons brought with them wild destructive winds, damage to life and property, as well as major flooding. The continuing monitoring of the status of Laguna said it was not as severe as had been expected.

Though badly affected, the town and the surrounding district were not damaged at the level everyone had feared, the reason being Cyclone Callie had been downgraded from a Category Five to a Four, weakening to Three.

Buildings had lost roofs, power lines were down, and the electricity supply was cut in some areas. There was widespread flooding, with many roads impassable. Mercifully none were dead, none missing—a few non-life-threatening injuries. The town had been well prepared, but they still needed help from the emergency services as well as from trained volunteers.

Brant had long since made his decision to go. He would take the helicopter and land it on any section of the highway or the town that had been left high and dry, taking medical supplies, food and bottled water. He was guaranteed to be met by emergency personnel in one of their Land Rovers.

"I'll come with you," Nyree said, determination and willingness to help visible in every line of her. "I can be of service. People need looking after—the old, the children. I can be there for them, even if it's only minding the kids or making tea and sandwiches."

Brant shook his head, dismissing the idea out of hand. "It won't be any picnic," he told her, too adamantly for her liking.

"Who's expecting a picnic?" Nyree was nearly dancing up and down in frustration. "I'm coming, Brant. Stop treating me like I'm a child."

His brows met. "I'm not, Nyree. Honestly I'm not. It's just—" He was so damned protective of her. Over-protective, perhaps?

"Let her go, my darling," the Contessa intervened, laying a hand on her grandson's arm. "You're concerned, I know, but Nyree is a very capable young woman." The whole household had learned that.

"There—you see!" Gratitude to the Contessa flashed from Nyree's dark eyes. "I'm no *child*. I'm a capable *woman*. The Contessa has said so. What more do you want?"

"Dear Lord!" Brant groaned, putting a hand momentarily to his temple. "Women!"

"You can't wrap me up in cotton wool!" Nyree cried, confronting the issue head-on. It was something he had done from the day he had met her. Her mind had to scurry away from what that meant. No time to explore now. She was still feeling raw from her confrontation with Lana Bennett.

The Contessa was laughing quietly, her still brilliant eyes moving between the two of them "My feelings exactly. Your grandfather adopted the same attitude with me, Brant. It was *infuriating*." She turned to speak directly to Nyree. "You have got to be well wrapped up, though. Oddly, it can turn very cold with the rain. You'll need a raincoat and gumboots, of course, and a good tight cap that will come down over your head."

"Thanks for supporting me, Alena," Brant said, very dryly indeed. "If things worsen it could turn into bedlam, you know."

"Have you forgotten all the young women who served so bravely and competently at the front line?" replied the Contessa, who had seen many sad and tragic things in her life.

"No, I haven't," Brant conceded with a sigh. "But I don't want to take Nyree into any kind of danger."

"Where you go, I go," Nyree said, as though that settled it.

She turned on her heel before he could say another word. She needed to hunt up the necessary gear. She already knew where it was kept. Something was bound to fit her.

They were met, as promised, and driven into town, flood waters gushing away in a rippling tide from the tyres of the big four-wheel drive.

"If you want to be helpful, go to the town hall," Brant instructed, already in the thick of it. This wasn't his first rescue mission by any means. He had been at it since his teens. The town hall was where those evacuated from their homes had gathered, as pre-planned.

"I'll take you." Managing a smile, an exhausted-looking woman in her forties came forward to take hold of Nyree's arm. "Good of you to come. We need all the help we can get. The name of Hollister is revered around here. Are you family, dear?"

Nyree shook her head. "Family friend." She *was*— no matter what Lana Bennett had said.

The size of the crowd of displaced people, and the howling of the frightened children brought tears to Nyree's eyes.

"I'll get right in there and see to the kids," she said promptly. "They look like they desperately need comfort."

The woman nodded her approval. "Their dads will be out helping. Their mums are already flat out trying to feed everyone. I'm Heather, by the way."

"Nyree."

The two women shook hands. "I'll go and join the tea and sandwiches brigade," Heather said. "You see what you can do for the kids. It would be good if you could find a way to keep them entertained. There are story books, paper, crayons—all that sort of stuff. The library is right alongside, with easy access between the two buildings."

It was almost like being back at school again, with Nyree Allcott, Head Girl, organising all the lower grades for Sports Day. In no time at all she decided to set up a kids army—a stroke of luck, because the idea immediately took hold. Howling stopped in sheer surprise as the children were organised into grades. Responsibilities were handed down the line. Older, more capable-looking boys and girls acted as group captains, answerable to Nyree, who elected herself Commander. That brought lots of giggles. She had taken off the beanie so her hair sprang around her lovely face and down her back in a wildly curling glory. This added immeasurably to her success—and to the piquancy of her title.

There was no shortage of food and drink: muesli bars, sandwiches, fruit, biscuits, bottled water, and chocolate to keep spirits up. Quizzes were held—Nyree making sure they were all questions adapted to the age group—then art competitions, sing-songs. The sound of young voices soaring soothed the nerves of the townswomen, all close to exhaustion point. Knowing their children were safe and happy in Nyree's care allowed them to get on with their more pressing workload.

* * *

By the afternoon of the following day Nyree too had reached exhaustion point. The ferocious winds had died away. Rain was still falling—but nothing to compare with the great deluge of two nights before. Everyone inside the town hall was safe. The men out in the thick of it—coming in relays for the quick restorative of a cup of tea and something to eat—were all accounted for.

Nyree hadn't caught a single glimpse of Brant, though she had been assured many times he was safe. Clearly she had her anxiety written large on her face.

"He's a real hero to us folk in the North," the Mayor's wife told her with a kindly, curious eye. "A real man of the people. A great guy. He'd be a darn good Prime Minister. We'd all be behind him."

With the worst of it over, the children who had been behaving so well started to get noisy. They wanted to get *out*! Out into the fresh air.

"I'll take over from you, Commander." A fourteen-year-old boy, a born leader, elected Group Captain, came to her side, carrying sandwiches and a pot of tea on a tray. "You've done a great job. You must be clean out of puff."

"Just a little, Ian," Nyree drew a shaky breath. "Thanks for this." She had dossed down with the children, but found herself unable to sleep. For most of the night she'd kept looking towards the entrances, hoping Brant's tall figure would move into the main hall.

All she wanted now was to sight him. She wanted to put her arms around him. Hug him. Tell him she was so proud of him—like everyone else.

She was returning her tray to Heather when Heather's

husband, covered in thick streaks of mud and slime, made his way towards his wife, grasping her shoulder as though about to fall down. It was clear he was in a state of shock.

Something had happened. For a minute Nyree crouched over like a woman in pain. She was assaulted by anxiety, but determined to find out the cause of it. She set the tray down, then nimble-footed made her way out onto the street, staggering a little with tiredness. The rain was coming down heavily, but she cared nothing for that. She wore only a yellow tank top and jeans, trainers on her feet. She'd been hot and sticky in the hall, but now her hair and clothing were already sopping wet. She saw a man coming towards her—a volunteer worker, a big, tough-looking man in easily identifiable orange gear. As she got close he appeared to be on the verge of tears.

"Is something wrong?" She caught hold of his arm, staring into a blackened, oil streaked, strained face. "Please tell me. I came with Brant Hollister."

"Right!" The man made a huge effort to pull himself together. "You shouldn't be out here, miss. I'm sure Mr Hollister is all right. He's been a tower of strength. One of our mates has been killed. Right at the *end*!" he exclaimed bitterly. "He lost his footing and fell back against a power line. A dreadful accident. He's got a wife and kids."

Most probably among the children she had sought to entertain, Nyree thought with real grief. "I'm sorry. *So* sorry. But I have to find Brant."

"Go back into the hall, love," the man advised, his voice breaking. "Nothing you can do."

"Thank you." Her hand went out to him, trying to offer some comfort. "But I have to find Brant."

"Then look for the ambulance," the man told her, re-alising she was dead set on her task. "They're taking the body away. You'll most likely find Mr Hollister there."

The minute she saw him Nyree felt such relief. If some-thing had happened to Brant...! It didn't bear thinking about. She didn't think she could survive such a tragedy. She rushed forward to meet him—only one of the men had caught sight of her and immediately told Brant. Instantly he turned, tall and powerful, moving with cat-like grace and purpose amid the mayhem. They met up halfway, and Brant caught hold of her and whirled her about.

"I want you to go back to the hall," he ordered, undoing his yellow oilskin and fitting her under it. "I'm all right. Poor devil lost his life. A hell of a thing to happen. We're moving him now. A tragedy. He lost his footing through sheer exhaustion. We were all aware of the fallen power line."

"I'm so, so sorry!" She held on to him for dear life. "Promise me you'll take good care, Brant? *Promise!*"

"With a reception like this?" Her words reverber-ated in his very soul. Turquoise eyes ablaze, he hugged her rain-soaked body to him. "Ask one of the women to find you some dry clothes. I'm here for at least another night, but I'm pretty sure I can get you out. A lot of people will be able to go back to their homes. The water is subsiding fast. The lucky families will rally around their neighbours. Mercifully the sand bags held. It's not nearly as bad as was first feared. No arguments now," he said, as she went to protest. "Just do what I ask, Nyree. I've heard all about your splendid efforts with the kids, but I can see you've used up your strength."

They were back under cover of the town hall building. Brant released her from her cocoon, only to pull her back into his arms "Hang in there, Commander," he said, half teasing, wholly proud. "You've been very brave."

"Of course I haven't." Her teeth began to chatter. Every muscle in her legs and back ached from fatigue and sleeping on the hard floor of the hall.

"Oh, Nyree!" With a groan he lifted her clean off her feet, planting a long, deep, possessive kiss directly on her mouth.

Plenty of people would have seen it, would be ready to pass the news on. But Brant either didn't give a damn or actually wanted people to see them together. A couple. No one could possibly kiss a relative or family friend like *that*!

"Get changed," he ordered. Then he turned and disappeared again into the rain.

"The long wait's over!" Heather touched Nyree lightly on the shoulder. "You'd better come along with me and get dry, dear," she said, with understanding and kindness. "I know what it's like to wait for your man."

CHAPTER EIGHT

HE'D BEEN told to frighten her. Just that. Not to touch her. That had been made very plain. Just give the little fool a good fright, then get the hell out of there. The money was too good to refuse. He'd get it when the job was done. He hadn't had work—hadn't tried all that hard—for a good eighteen months. The stash on offer would tide him over Christmas and the New Year. He'd been just long enough in the town to know the score. He'd even seen his little victim. Hell, what a beauty! He licked his lips. It was going to be very hard for him to get close to her, albeit wearing a balaclava, and then switch off. But he knew if he disobeyed orders he would be hunted down like a rogue dingo. His client was one of the North's mega-rich. A good-looking bitch, but he thought her appalling. Jealousy was such a curse. And women were the worst of all...

The moment Brant was inside the house, he went in search of his grandmother. They weren't expecting him until the following day, but the emergency services had the situation well in hand.

Alena drew him into a loving embrace. "So good to have you home again, my darling. Nyree has been like a cat on a hot tin roof."

Instantly he felt the quickening in his body. "Where is she?" He didn't look in the least worn out, as well he might, but brimming over with life.

"She went into town." Alena smiled, reading him well. "A few little errands for me. So considerate! I have *two* grandchildren these days. She was heading out to the farmhouse afterwards."

"Oh, no!" Brant groaned. "I wanted her *here*. Safe. Not at the farmhouse. Not without the dogs."

"Don't overdo the protectiveness, my darling," Alena warned. "Nyree won't sit still for it. She's a young woman of spirit. She's at the farmhouse to say goodbye." Alena reached up to pat his shoulder. "I don't blame you for feeling so protective. Just ease up a little. She's young, but she's up to whatever you want of her. Why don't you take a run out there when you're ready?"

"I'm ready now," Brant said. He gave Alena a parting kiss on the cheek.

Nyree had to admit it was with a faint air of melancholy that she moved through the farmhouse. Great-Uncle Howard's paintings had already been packed up and put into storage. Brant had said it was a precaution in case Cyclone Callie hit their part of the coast. She even shed a few tears. How unhappy poor Howie must have been. It sounded as if there had been plenty of women for him to pick from, only he'd settled on the Contessa. A love that was truly taboo. Even then her great-uncle hadn't been able to let go. Now he was dead. She was greatly saddened by his loss of direction. It *couldn't* be allowed to happen to her.

Surely she could take Brant's kiss at Laguna's town hall as a clear message? Lord knew it had been a clear enough message for a lot of people. Rumour had spread like wildfire. When she had all but run into Lana Bennett outside the town pharmacy Lana hadn't uttered a word, her dark head held high, but the expression in her eyes had been so malignant it had made her shudder. Lana Bennett *hated* her—which was a clear indicator that Lana held real fears. But no matter Lana's feelings—and Nyree could see they were extremely intense—Lana was a civilised woman. She had a name, a reputation.

Somewhere in the house a board creaked. That was odd. She stood perfectly still while the house settled around her into a listening silence. Nothing! She drew a long breath. For the very first time she felt the farm's isolation. She could have done with Juno and Jupiter right now. Her heart was beating so hard she could scarcely breathe.

The creak came again. There *was* someone in the house. She didn't want to believe it but her senses told her it was so. The last thing she could do was allow her strength to drain out of her. She moved a few feet to pick up a solid brass candlestick, taking long, deep breaths to steady herself.

"Is anyone there?" she called, ashamed when her voice sounded shaky and near desolate.

That wouldn't do. She had to summon her courage, her spirit.

"Show yourself!" She tried again, forcing not her grandmother's but Miss Em's indomitable tones.

To her horror, the intruder did. He was tall and thin, his head covered by a black balaclava except for his eyes—a washed-out blue—and a thin-lipped mouth. His voice was coarse, lowered to a mere whisper.

"Hi there, little lady! Give you a fright, did I? No wonder…way out here on your own."

Nyree heard the gloating satisfaction. "Don't come a step closer," she said. It was as though Miss Em had *really* stepped in. "You need to get out of here. And fast. Or you could finish up in jail."

"*You're* the one who needs to get out, girlie," he grunted. "You're not wanted here."

Nyree gripped the candlestick tighter. "Who sent you?" she demanded, seizing on a hunch. "Someone did. I bet you'd rather not say. How much did she pay you?"

The intruder made a sharp dismissive gesture, as though he didn't want her to continue. "I bet you're scared when you're all tucked up at night," he muttered. "I bet you're scared now."

He moved closer, wanting to come into physical contact with her despite the fact he'd been warned not to. He'd never seen such a beautiful woman. What harm would there be in touching her? Her skin was so flawless he would love to stroke it. She was completely at his mercy. The hand that held the candlestick was trembling, though he didn't doubt she fully intended to use it.

Plucky little thing! He had to admire it. Full of fight. He'd really love to—

Wow! He moved forward a pace, then paused

abruptly, seeing her whole expression change. It had gone from ready-for-anything valiant to thrilled within seconds. It was as though her guardian angel had suddenly materialised, great wings spread, gloriously male and all-powerful. It didn't make sense.

It did to Nyree. "The man I love is right behind you," she said.

The intruder tried to run and was blocked.

"Hell, man, I meant no harm," he wailed. "Back off."

Brant did no such thing. His turquoise eyes flashed in a killing rage. He ripped off the balaclava, grateful when he didn't recognise the face. He wasn't anyone from the town. Putting his considerable strength behind it, Brant unleashed a punch that connected with the man's jaw. The brutal contact gave him enormous satisfaction.

The intruder went down for the count, slumping heavily to the floor. Brant stood over him, knowing he was perilously close to giving the intruder the beating of his life.

"No, Brant. *No!*" Nyree ran to him, afraid of what might happen. "Someone sent him. He was supposed to frighten me off."

Brant's daunting expression didn't alter. "I couldn't care less who sent him right at the moment." His tone lashed. "First things first."

"No!" She put herself between Brant and the moaning man on the floor, pressing her hands against Brant's chest. Rage was coming off his body in heat waves. "He didn't touch me. I'm begging you to stop. It's *you* I care about. Not him."

It was a highly precarious situation. And no one was

more conscious of it than the groaning intruder. This was *Hollister*. He was supposed to be out of town. That bitch had her information wrong. He stayed put, nursing his jaw and his broken nose. He needed an emergency medical department. Would that be before or after he was taken in by the police? The operation—supposed to be an easy in-and-out—had gone terribly wrong. And he wasn't finished with.

It was taking time for Brant to wind down his rage. Nyree still clung fast. "You're in a bit of pain, my friend," Brant said, a twisted smile on his mouth.

"You've broken me nose," the man whimpered pathetically.

"Ah—my sympathies. Who sent you?" The demand came, gut-low. "Who gave you the job?"

"I want to explain." The intruder started to sob. "It was that bitch in town—the Bennett woman. Lana. She put me up to it. 'Just frighten her', she said."

"But you couldn't stop there, could you?" Brant couldn't control what he did next. He sank his boot in the man's ribs.

"It was just a job," the man groaned. "I'm broke. Your little lady would have killed me before she let me touch her. I wasn't going to. *Swear.*"

"Was it your old car I saw pulled off at the side of the road?" Brant rasped.

"After I'd done it and got paid I was heading off," the man said. "I'm gonna try for a job at Mount Isa." God knew he felt the urgency. Mount Isa was well over six hundred miles away.

"Well, then, you'd better get going." Brant's voice

was very cold. "It will be quite a drive. And I'll be checking on your arrival."

"Ya goin' to let me go?" There was relief and astonishment in the man's tone.

"Get out of Hollister or pay the price," Brant told him grimly, still exerting massive control. "Now, get up off the floor and get the hell out of here. Don't attempt to go near the town. Don't try to contact Lana Bennett. I'll deal with her."

"She put me up to it," the man repeated, as though that was a point in his favour. "Nothin' worse than a jealous woman."

"Don't go back for any worldly possessions either," Brant warned. "Though I guess they're already in your car."

"I'm on my way, mate!" The man staggered to his feet, mopping at his bloody nose with a filthy rag from his trouser pocket. The sheer exhilarating relief! For a moment there he'd thought he wouldn't get out of the house alive.

Some time later Brant came in from the verandah, having watched the intruder make off down the drive. He had wanted to call the police, have the deadbeat slung in jail, but the story would have come out and there would have been a scandal. There was to be no scandal attached to Nyree. He would deal with Lana, and with her family. He had known Lana all his life but he hadn't seen this coming. He felt as if he had failed Nyree when he knew with every fibre of his being she was the love of his life.

"You'd better put some antiseptic on your hand," Nyree suggested, very quietly, going towards him with a swab and a bottle of antiseptic. "The skin is broken."

"I'd like to have killed him!" There was anguish on Brant's striking face. "He might have been sent only to frighten you, but the sight of you was too much for him. It was all there in his body language. God knows what would have happened if I hadn't arrived."

"I'd have thumped him over the head with the candlestick," Nyree maintained stoutly, gently taking his uninjured hand and leading him to the kitchen.

"You mean you would have *tried*."

Nyree looked up quickly into his face. She could see he was suffering. All because of her. After her life of emotional deprivation and unresolved grief the knowledge that he loved her—really loved her—made up for the pain. Love had the power to heal all wounds.

"It's over, Brant," she said gently, though her face was radiant. "You came. You were here when I desperately needed you. Let's just dump all thoughts of Lana Bennett and that pathetic character. You broke his nose, you know," she concluded, with a little wry laugh.

"Pity that's all!" Brant went to the sink, washed his hands, dried them, allowing Nyree to apply antiseptic to his bruised and scraped knuckles.

"I'm so glad you're here," she said, her voice and face alive with emotion. "So glad I cou—"

He hauled her to him, his longing such that he had no use for words. He wanted her crushed against him. He wanted her safe. Safe for ever. His mouth came down hard, stayed like that, devouring her, until she gave an involuntary little whimper. It wasn't his mouth—she adored the passionate pressure—it was his strong hands, clenched around her lightweight body.

"I'm sorry!" Immediately he relaxed his hold. "You make me so afraid." His voice vibrated with niggling worry.

She was so young, and she'd had little time to experience life. *No* experience of sex. He couldn't help it, but that made him furiously glad. She hadn't even finished her education. Of course she could. He would help in every way possible. But was she ready to marry? Was she ready to marry *him*?

Unknowingly, she would be taking on a huge load. One day he would succeed his billionaire father, with all that entailed. It was a lifestyle greatly to be desired, but with it came lots of hazards ordinary people would never know or wish to contend with. His parents' marriage had been destroyed along the way. It *couldn't* happen to him. He needed Nyree. He would never let her run away.

Nyree rose on her tiptoes to stare into his blazing eyes. "How can I make you afraid? I *love* you!" It came out in a breathless rush. "I'll always love you. You've changed my life. You've changed *me*. Do you not want me in the same way?"

Brant shook his head dazedly. He wanted her so much he was in pain. "Nyree, my love, I want you *more*. I want all of you. Body, soul and mind. I'm prepared to do anything to keep you. I want to love and protect you. Alena has told me to lighten up. She knows the strength of my feelings for you. I guess my grandad was the same about her. But we're one-woman men. Even Dad hasn't got over my mother. He lost her. I could never lose you. I want to marry you. I want to marry you the moment you're ready. But I beg of you—put me out of my misery and make it soon. You can have your own life. You must finish your degree. You can become a child psycholo—"

No doubts crippled Nyree. The past was history. Brant was her future. This time she took the initiative. She pulled his dark head down to her and began covering his face in burning little kisses, casting off every last little inhibition along the way. This man was her life, her love, her soon-to-be husband. This was her homecoming. She knew she possessed powers only he could unleash. They would forge a wonderful marriage—a wonderful partnership.

Brant responded by lifting her up onto the counter to make their lovemaking easier. She was a creature of air and fire. His woman. Core of his heart.

"I'll only ask one thing." Nyree broke off their hungered kissing, her beautiful face flushed and enormously excited. "One of our girls must be called Emilia, okay?"

If a man was allowed to weep, he would. Weep with gratitude and triumph. *One of our girls! Their children.* "Emilia it is!" he declared, in a deep, exultant tone. "After all, Miss Em sent you to me."

* * * * *

The Billionaire Claims
His Wife

AMY ANDREWS

Amy Andrews has always loved writing and still can't quite believe that she gets to do it for a living. Creating wonderful heroines and gorgeous heroes and telling their stories is an amazing way to pass the day. Sometimes they don't always act as she'd like them to, but then, neither do her kids, so she's kind of used to it. Amy lives in the very beautiful Samford Valley with her husband and aforementioned children, along with six brown chooks and two black dogs. She loves to hear from her readers. Drop her a line at www.amyandrews.com.au

**Don't miss Amy Andrews's new book,
A Doctor, A Nurse: A Christmas Baby,
coming in November 2009 from
Medical™ romance.**

Dear Reader,

When my editor asked me to be part of this anthology I balked. Me? Write a billionaire? But who could resist being in an anthology with two other fabulous Aussie writers, Margaret Way and Jennie Adams? So, always up for a challenge, I decided to give it a whirl.

Almost straight away, before I even knew the names of the characters, I knew they were going to be total opposites. She was going to be a free-spirited hippy-chick to his uber-wealthy, driven business man. I knew that they'd once loved each other very deeply but their different life philosophies had eventually driven them apart. And I knew that I wanted to take Mr Rich-List and pull him out of his comfort zone, making him utterly dependent on another human being – to start with anyway. There's nothing sexier than a powerful man having to be nursed back to health by a woman. Particularly if that woman happens to be his ex-wife.

As you can tell, I had some fun with my hero, Nathan. Yes, we authors can be downright evil from time to time :-) But to be fair, I also throw Jacqueline into Nathan's world – the glamorous multi-billion-dollar strip that makes up the famous Gold Coast.

I hope you enjoy their story and their gradual realisation that some people are just meant to be together.

Amy

To Mandi Carr, veterinarian, for her
invaluable assistance with this book and her
unflappability when faced with a barrage of
strange "what if" questions.

CHAPTER ONE

DR NATHAN TRENT felt like hell. He trudged through the downpour, his Italian leather shoes squelching as he pulled his saturated jacket closer to his body. Another set of chills skated across his hot, soaked skin. His fever and the rain were making his teeth chatter. He sneezed, and the razorblades in his throat cut a little deeper. His joints ached, making each footfall feel like a step up Mount Everest in the middle of a blizzard.

He thought about his sleek new Porsche, covered in mud and abandoned a kilometre away, bogged down deep in roadside slush. He should have waited it out. At least it was warm and dry inside his latest toy. But he'd been driving in torrential rain for hours with no let-up, and Jacqui's place hadn't seemed that far. And he needed to get horizontal—an impossibility in the confines of a car that was built for show not practicality.

The thought of throttling his estranged wife sustained him as the rain belted down around him. He couldn't even hear the roar of the ocean somewhere to his left over the noise from the heavens.

Why couldn't she live in civilisation? In a city? Or a town? Or at least on a highway somewhere, instead of this narrow pot-holed excuse for a road that strung together a series of communities collectively known as Serendipity.

His fingers shook as he checked his mobile phone for reception, shoving it back in his jacket pocket in disgust at the barless signal. No mobile towers out here to ruin the pristine, free-range, organic air. No chemicals or satellite dishes—or anything that was remotely useful to civilisation!

'Damn it, Jacqui!'

Twenty minutes later not even the faint glimmer of lights up ahead could rouse an ounce of glee. The flu that had started as a vague sore throat and sniffle this morning now had him fully in its grip. Water from his hair and his forehead dripped onto his lashes and he blinked, half expecting the lights to be gone—an illusive mirage summonsed by a fever-addled brain.

Nope. They were still there. He forced his legs to walk faster, his joints protesting at the increased demand on his flagging reserves. When he finally drew level with a darkened row of shops, one solitary light shone from an illuminated sign mounted on a pole near the front door of the middle building.

It had seen better days. The light blinked on and off in some kind of electrical death throe, and between his delirium and the pouring rain he could just make out the letters. *Veterinarian.*

It took all his determination to lift his arm, make a fist and rap against the heavy wooden door. He shivered as he waited, feeling desperately ill and frustratingly weak.

'Come on, Jacqui, answer the bloody door!'

His curse was drowned out by the deafening drumming of rain and the pounding of his fist against the wood. The effort to be heard strained his inflamed vocal cords, ripped through his sore throat and hammered through his throbbing temples. He leaned his forehead against the door and contemplated death.

His own this time.

Dr Jacqueline Callaghan woke with a start and looked at the red illuminated figures on her bedside clock. One a.m. Her heart was pounding almost as loudly as the storm outside, and her eyes fluttered shut as she realised it was just the continuing heavy rain on the tin roof that had woken her. Shep, lying stretched out at the end of her bed, hadn't moved a muscle.

Her eyes flew open when the noise came again a few seconds later. Shep even lifted his head. That wasn't Mother Nature knocking at her door. She groaned as she dragged herself out of bed. Being woken in the middle of the night wasn't unusual in her line of work, but what pet crisis could there possibly be in this God-awful weather?

She stumbled into the red cotton robe she kept by the bed for emergencies such as these, desperately trying to clear the fog from her brain. She'd been up most of last night with a sick horse from one of the nearby properties. She was dog tired, her body craving the restorative powers of good, solid sleep.

The pounding came again. 'Yeah, yeah,' she muttered as she descended the internal stairs as fast as her groggy brain allowed, Shep by her side. She flicked the outside light on and opened the door.

It took a moment or two for Jacqui's brain to compute who the cursing, dishevelled-looking man standing on her doorstep actually was. He was dripping—literally—his hair plastered in dark wet strips against his forehead, droplets running down his face and clinging to his eyelashes. His suit was completely soaked.

She peered closer, something primal inside her knowing who it was despite her sensible side rejecting such a preposterous supposition. *It couldn't be.* 'Nathan?'

Had he been well, his keen wit intact, he would have said something ironic, like *Hi, honey, I'm home*, but at the moment it was taking all his strength just to stay upright. 'Jacqueline.'

She stared at him askance. Nathan Trent—richer-than-sin fertility specialist, maker of a thousand babies, darling of the business community—was standing on her doorstep.

'What…what are you doing here?'

Nathan shivered as icy fingers stroked his skin. He felt like a popsicle, even though he knew somewhere deep in the recesses of his brain that he was burning up.

'I'm sorry, Jacqui,' he said, ignoring her question. He needed to get dry. He needed to crawl under ten blankets and sleep. 'I feel like h…h…hell.' His teeth chattered uncontrollably. 'Do you th…think I could c…come in?'

Jacqui blinked, the enormity of seeing him again so completely out of the blue too much for her sleep-deprived brain. But the croak of his voice and the alarming sway as he let go of the doorjamb at last penetrated through to the doctor in her.

'Whoa!' she said, reaching for him, steadying him. 'What's wrong?' she asked, ushering him in and shutting the door.

Nathan closed his eyes and luxuriated briefly in relative silence as the heavy door muffled the storm. It was dry and warm inside, and he'd never been more pleased to be anywhere than he was right now to be inside Jacqui's house.

'Nate?'

His eyes fluttered open and he frowned down into her concerned face. 'Flu,' he muttered, attempting to shrug out of the jacket that suddenly felt as if it weighed a ton against his aching shoulders. 'Feel like crap.'

Jacqui helped him off with the sodden garment, putting her arm around his waist as he swayed again. His long-sleeved business shirt was soaked, but it was hot against her arm—not cool as she had expected. She reached up and felt his forehead.

His skin was flushed and practically scorched her palm. 'Come on,' she said. 'Let's get you dry.'

Nathan eyed the steps and groaned. They might as well have been the Alps. He could barely keep his head up, let alone master a flight of stairs. He was tired. So tired. Deep down in his bones weary. 'I can't.'

'Hold on to me,' Jacqui murmured, 'I'll help.'

She was no dainty, fragile female. Most of her practice consisted of puppies, parrots and goldfish, but some of it was large animal work, and that required the strength and stamina which her statuesque frame coped with easily. But still, as he put his arm around her shoulders and leaned into her, she staggered under his bulk.

She'd always appreciated how his superior height and broad male shoulders had made her feel more feminine, and she was surprised to feel a familiar stirring deep down low at the solidness of muscle beneath her hands, the bound of his heart against her palm and the way her be-ringed fingers looked with his shirt splayed beneath them. She quashed it, bracing herself for the slow trip up the stairs.

At the top she guided him to the lounge room. 'Sit,' she instructed him.

A hundred questions vied for front-line attention in her head as she scurried off to the linen cupboard. She pushed them aside. Nate was obviously unwell. Why he'd turned up on her doorstep after a decade could be discussed when he was better.

Nathan sneezed as his shaking fingers attempted to undo the buttons of his shirt. The warmth of the house was a welcome haven, but he needed to get out of his wet clothes. He cursed as he fumbled the job, the buttons refusing to budge.

'Towels and blankets,' Jacqueline announced, re-entering the room with an armful of linen. She stopped in front of him, watching his feeble attempts at undressing himself.

Nathan looked up at her. Backlit by the light, her crazy ringlet hair of russet and gold looked almost angelic. Was he hallucinating? 'I'm sorry. I can't do it.'

Jacqueline gazed down at the whole lot of man sitting

in her lounge, looking like a drowned rat and helpless as a kitten. It was an admission she knew wouldn't have been easy for him. She sighed and knelt. 'Let me.'

She briskly undid the buttons, ignoring the chest she'd known like the back of her hand ten years ago, and pushed the wet shirt off his shoulders and down his arms. She grabbed one of her towels and threw it around his shoulders, cocooning him in it while she attacked his dripping hair with another.

Nathan drew the soft fluffy towel closer. It smelt like soap and sunshine and Jacqui, and he closed his eyes, hunching into it, absorbing its warmth. The fabric rasped against his heated flesh, goosing his skin. A wet nose nudged his hand and he opened his eyes.

'You still have Shep,' he said, stroking the dog's head. He'd given her the golden retriever as an anniversary gift years before.

Jacqui's heart skipped a beat. 'Yes,' she said briskly, continuing the job.

He sat placidly, his hand on Shep's back, as she towelled his hair, incapable of offering any assistance. A shard of a memory from their past undulated through the fevered quagmire of his brain.

His eyes fluttered open. 'You used to like to play with my hair,' he murmured.

Jacqueline's hands stilled, and she looked into his amazing green eyes. They were glazed with fever, and she could see the lights were on but no one was home. She ignored him, taking his shoes off. 'You're going to have to stand so I can get your pants off.'

Nathan heard the words come towards him from far

away. They sounded disconnected, and he gave a goofy laugh. 'You used to like to get my pants off, too.'

Jacqueline gritted her teeth, reminding herself it was the delirium talking. 'Up you get.'

He rose slowly and leaned against her as she reached for his fly. He gave another juvenile laugh, and she rolled her eyes as she dispensed with his soaked trousers and underwear, trying to channel a mother superior–like indifference.

He stood still while she briskly rubbed him down, drying his legs with as much clinical detachment as she could muster, ignoring another part of his anatomy she'd once known like the back of her hand.

He swayed again, and she held on to him with one hand while the other arranged some bedding on the couch. 'You can sit now,' she murmured.

Nathan collapsed back onto the couch. He felt icy cold all over and he shivered, tucking his legs up towards his chest. 'Freezing,' he murmured, wrapping his arms around his knees.

He looked incredibly vulnerable, naked on her couch in the foetal position, the overhead light bathing his superbly tanned body in a soft golden hue. He almost looked like the boy she had met at uni, not one of the most influential men in the country, and she threw a one-hundred-percent-duck-down duvet over him to block the image from her sight and her mind.

She looked down at him for a long time. 'What are you doing here, Nathan Trent?' she whispered.

Jacqui placed Nate's clothes into the washing machine, ignoring the 'dry clean only' advice next to the designer label. She hung his jacket up and parked his equally expensive-looking shoes near the front door.

She crept back into the lounge. Shep had taken up position on the floor near the couch, and thumped his tail as he spotted her. She switched off the overhead light and reached across Nathan's supine form to snap on the nearby lamp.

He looked totally out of it, his cheeks flushed, his full lips slack with slumber. She stroked the back of her hand against his roughened jaw. He was hot. So hot. He murmured something unintelligible, shifting slightly, and she withdrew her hand abruptly, scuttling away to the couch opposite.

Her heart drummed a crazy beat, matching the inclement weather in its ferocity, and she held her breath. Fortunately Nathan settled quickly—which couldn't be said for her pulse—and she sank gratefully into the leather cushions, pulling her feet up under her.

God, how she'd used to love watching him sleep. Of course his hair had been longer then. A curly mop that she had loved to push her fingers into, rub her face against. It was shorter now, cropped closer to his head, its tendency to curl severely denied.

He had slept naked then too. They both had. Clothes had seemed such an inconvenience when neither of them had been able to get enough of each other. Even at the end, when they had drifted apart, their desire had still been a potent force, keeping them bound to a marriage that no longer worked.

Jacqui shut her eyes against the memories. There was no point dredging up the past. The man lying on her couch might be the man she'd married all those years ago—was still technically married to—but he was as much a stranger to her now as he had been at the end. And wishing things had been different didn't make it so.

It was five a.m. when Jacqui next awoke, her neck stiff from falling asleep in a semi-upright position. The rain still pelted against the roof like a platoon of tap-dancing soldiers, and a grey watery dawn was breaking through the window. And Nathan Trent still slept on her couch.

Except the duvet no longer covered him. At some stage he had moved onto his back, pushed the blanket down to his hips, exposing his smooth, bare chest and only just covering what lay a little further south. The long leg closest to the edge of the couch jutted out too, escaping its covering, its foot flat on the floor. The opposite arm was thrown up over his head, his face turned away from her, pressing into the bulk of his bicep.

Dear God, he was gorgeous. She'd tried not to look before, as she'd been undressing him, but now she couldn't stop. Maturity had given his body an edge, a hardness that youth hadn't. He'd always had a good body, but now he looked…fit. More honed. As if he worked at it now instead of relying on a God-given gift.

He murmured and turned his head, and she held her breath. His eyes fluttered open. The clocks stopped. The rain faded. Her breath stuttered to a halt. It took a second or two for those incredible jade eyes to focus on her.

'Thirsty,' he croaked.

It took another beat or two for her functions to return. She sucked in a breath. 'Right. Okay. Be right back.'

Nathan watched her leave, trying to figure out where he was and why Jacqui was here. But his head felt as if it was stuffed with cotton wool, and it hurt too much to think anyway. He sat up and the room shifted. He vaguely felt Shep lick his calf as he buried his forehead in his hands and waited for everything to stop moving.

Jacqueline entered the room and paused momentarily. He looked even more imposing sitting upright, his back and chest and both legs exposed, the duvet bunched around his hips.

'Take these,' she said, injecting a businesslike note into her voice, forcing herself closer. She nudged his hand with the glass, two pills on the flat of her palm.

'What are they?' he asked, looking at them.

'Cold and flu tablets.'

Nathan reached for them as they swam out of focus. He located them through sheer force of will. He felt as if someone had been lighting spot fires in his joints, and would have taken any pill she'd given him to extinguish the flames. He pushed them past his lips, into a mouth that tasted sour and furry, and gulped the whole glass down.

'Thanks,' he murmured, collapsing back against his makeshift bed as a coughing spasm took hold. The aches intensified, pulsing in protest as each cough tore through his spine, his chest, his head.

Jacqueline frowned. The cough sounded nasty. Maybe it was more than the flu? Maybe he'd managed to give himself bilateral pneumonia in the pouring rain last night? She left him for a moment and retrieved her medical bag from the clinic downstairs.

His eyes were shut when she returned. She opened her bag, pulled out her stethoscope, and perched herself on the edge of his couch. She rubbed the stethoscope in her hands to warm it, and then placed it on his still exposed chest.

Nathan opened his eyes. *Jacqui.* Jacqui was still here. 'What are you doing?' he murmured.

'That cough sounds nasty. Just checking your lung fields,' she said briskly. 'Sit up.' She grabbed his arm and pulled.

Nathan couldn't muster the energy to resist. 'It's just the flu,' he protested. He was a doctor, damn it. He knew flu when it had the audacity to invade his usually impenetrable immune system.

Her long fingers felt heavenly against his skin, the wide bands of her rings like icicles. He studied the chunky jewellery adorning her fingers. The intertwined strands of metal set with earthy stones took him way back, to days when they'd eaten spaghetti straight from the tin before crashing together in a tangle of limbs after night duty. When they'd stayed up late eating honey toast and watching old black and white horror films in bed.

'I could have given you diamonds,' he muttered.

But even his feverish brain recalled she hadn't given a damn about diamonds. It had been her funky eclectic style, sourced from garage sales and op shops, that had attracted him all those years ago. And cheap and cheerful still looked better on her than any diamond on any woman he'd ever seen.

Jacqui heard his voice rumble through her earpieces as she moved the stethoscope around his back, but his eyes were shut and she dismissed the odd statement as his temperature talking. His skin was warm under her touch, and the urge to rub her cheek against his oh-so-close shoulder was surprisingly powerful.

'It sounds clear,' she murmured, pushing him gently back and out of reach.

Nathan shut his eyes, the effort to sit up rendering him completely exhausted. He was drifting off when something was pushed into his ear canal. 'Hey,' he protested, opening his eyes.

'Shh. It's just a thermometer,' Jacqueline said, pulling the tympanic device out of his ear and looking at the digital display. 'Thirty-eight point nine degrees.'

Nathan looked at her for a long moment, trying to work out why his wife was here. *Jacqui was here?* 'I s'pose I should be grateful you only stuck it in my ear,' he murmured, before the effort to keep his eyes open became too much again.

Jacqueline rolled her eyes at the old vet joke she'd heard a thousand times. She looked down at him. His stubble was heavier now, but no less fascinating. She sighed. He'd drifted off again. He was bound to do that for probably most of the day—maybe even tomorrow as well. So she'd better get used to him lying on her couch looking all shaggy and fascinating. It was going to be a very long weekend indeed.

Saturday evening, after a slow, rainy day in her clinic, and multiple trips up the stairs to check on Nathan, Jacqueline put an Enya CD on low, collapsed on the couch opposite a still sleeping Nathan and an ever-present Shep, and opened her book. Not that she could get into it. Her gaze kept flicking to his face, checking on him. His lashes, so long they cast shadows she could see from across the room on his cheekbones, were endlessly fascinating.

An hour later she realised she'd read the same page over and over. The clock said eight and the evening stretched ahead of her. She looked at him again, and was startled to find him looking back at her.

'Hi,' he said.

'Hi.' Neither of them said anything for a moment. 'Are you feeling better?' His gaze was clearer; the fevered glitter it had been sporting since he'd landed on her doorstep had dulled.

Nathan shook his head, and winced as his neck protested the sudden movement. 'Marginally.'

'Are you hungry? I can make you something. Some toast, maybe?'

He gave a weak smile. 'Ah, toast. Jacqui's cure for everything.' He knew she would have been happy to eat tea and toast the rest of her life. It was like the sixth food group to her. His stomach turned at the mere thought of food. 'Pass.'

She ignored his dig. 'You're due a couple more tablets.'

Good. His sore throat had settled, and he didn't think his head was in imminent danger of exploding from his shoulders, but he did feel as if he'd gone ten rounds with a giant. 'Where's your bathroom?' he asked.

'Out the door to the left.'

Nathan sat gingerly. He took a moment to gather his energy and stood, his legs disgustingly weak. A wave of dizziness hit him square in the solar plexus, distracting him momentarily from the sudden realisation that he was naked. And then Jacqui was there, holding him around the waist, the thin multi-coloured bangles adorning her wrists jangling, the metal of her rings cool against his heated flesh. He figured it wasn't anything she hadn't already seen a thousand times before.

'Sorry.' He grimaced.

Jacqui swallowed, her face hot. Was he apologising for needing her, or for his full-frontal nudity? 'It's fine. Just hold on to me.'

He allowed her to lead him to the toilet, and while he was taking care of business she placed his clean underwear and a spare toothbrush on the vanity. She hovered outside the bathroom, waiting for him to finish, relieved to see him slightly less exposed for the return trip. She handed him the tablets and water as he climbed back under the covers.

'Thanks,' he said, swallowing the entire contents of the glass, grateful beyond words for her help, just too exhausted to convey it adequately.

He shut his eyes and felt instant relief. But a strange nagging sixth sense pulled at his leaden lids and he looked up to find her watching him.

'What?' he croaked.

He'd been here for less than twenty-four hours, but already her house was filled with him. After he left she'd never be able to sit on that couch again without thinking of him laying there buck naked. 'Why are you here, Nate?'

Good question. If only it didn't hurt his head so much to think. He shut his eyes. And then he remembered.

He fixed her with an intense stare. 'I need my wife back.'

CHAPTER TWO

NATHAN woke to the smell of frying bacon and toast and his stomach grumbled. He was starving. His mouth watered. He rubbed at the stubble on his jaw, momentarily wondering where the hell he was. The ceiling didn't look familiar and he wasn't in his bed.

He turned his head and saw a half-drunk glass of water on a coffee table and Shep dozing nearby. Then it returned. Driving to see Jacqui. The Porsche getting bogged. Walking in the rain. The flu.

He stretched, feeling only a vague ache now, but malaise sat heavily in his bones. He thought about sitting for a few moments before he attempted it, and was surprised how weak he felt as he levered himself up. The duvet bunched around his waist and he pushed it aside.

Shep woke and lurched slowly up off the floor. 'Hey, boy,' he murmured, ruffling the dog's ears.

He'd missed Shep in the beginning. Terribly. Almost as much as he'd missed Jacqui. Then all too soon life had consumed him and he hadn't thought about Shep for years. Maybe that was what he was missing from his life now? Maybe a dog, a pet, would help fill up this strange emptiness that afflicted him from time to time? Give him something to come home to? He made a mental note to check into it when he returned home.

Nathan stood, feeling vaguely light-headed, leaning heavily against the arm of the couch for a few seconds before pushing off and following his nose. He wasn't sure what day it was, but his stomach felt as if it had contracted down to the size of a walnut, so it had to have been a couple of days since he'd eaten.

He passed a window filtering grey light and vaguely acknowledged the continuing rain. He could hear the sounds of cooking and singing coming from the room ahead, and forced his wooden legs to take bigger strides.

Nathan reached the doorway and stopped abruptly. Jacqui had her back to the door, standing in front of the stove, singing in a fake falsetto and dancing along barefoot to a song from a battered-looking radio nearby.

She was wearing some loose pants that sat low on her hips—probably that hemp stuff she loved so much—and a white strappy singlet that had ridden up to reveal the small of her back.

Her bottom was swaying, and she was clicking her fingers to the beat above her head. The bangles on her arms jingled and the metal of her rings blurred as her fingers wiggled and her corkscrew curls bounced in time.

He smiled at the scene before him. 'You haven't changed, I see.'

Jacqui nearly had a heart attack as his voice broke into her tuneless singing. She whirled around abruptly, her heart thundering. He was lounging in her doorway in nothing but his underwear and his stubble as if he belonged there. He had that just-rolled-out-of-bed look she'd always found utterly irresistible, and she was overwhelmed with a surge of lust she hadn't felt in a decade.

Oh, God! No, no, no. She would *not* make this easy for him. He couldn't show up at her door on a dark and stormy night, collapse on her couch for two days, tell her he needed his wife back before lapsing into unconsciousness, and then just expect her to melt into a puddle of desire at his feet.

'*You* have.'

And he had. Even with next to nothing on, with his body essentially the same—familiar on so many levels—the changes were undeniable. He wasn't the boy she'd lain naked with, spinning happy dreams on endless nights. Who'd been content eating cold spaghetti and drinking wine from a cardboard box. Who had thrived under killer shifts and arrogant consultants because he'd loved his job.

That boy was long gone. He was a man now. Successful beyond his wildest dreams. Aside from the designer threads, it was in the way he held himself, the proud tilt of his head, the commanding angle of his jaw. Even knocked flat by the flu, lying naked and vulnerable on her couch, there had been an undeniable authority, a tangible aura of power about him.

Nathan's gaze was drawn to Jacqueline's bare midriff, where the top had ridden up. Her belly button was as fascinating as it had always been. He moved higher. As usual she was braless, and he could see that despite her life-long aversion to supportive measures her breasts were still firm, her nipples just visible through the white fabric.

He shrugged. 'We all change, Jacqui. Evolve.' His gaze dropped to her chest again. 'Well, most of us anyway.'

Jacqui placed a hand on her hip and raised an eyebrow. 'Evolve, Nate? Or sell out?'

Nathan laughed, and regretted it as the dull ache behind his eyes gave a vicious pulse. 'Evolve.'

Jacqui gave him a silky smile. 'You say potato. I say po-*tar*-toe.' She preferred cold-spaghetti-boy to medical-tycoon any day.

The toast popped behind her and she turned away, grateful for the reprieve from the gorgeous stranger in her husband's skin.

'You're obviously better,' she said, slathering butter onto the toast. 'Hungry?'

Nathan's stomach growled as he watched her, the sway of her hips as mesmerising as it had always been. 'Ravenous.'

Jacqui gripped the knife hard as his voice, still a little husky from his flu, carried an entirely different meaning towards her altogether. She was conscious of him watching her every move as she bent and pulled the perfectly crisped bacon from the oven, adding it to the tray of goodies. She took a calming breath before lifting the tray and turning to face him, still unprepared for the familiar kick down low as his jade gaze slid over her.

'Why are you really here, Nate?'

Because he needed his wife back. That was what he'd said. Needed. Not wanted. He *needed* her back. His choice of words had been curious. Very curious. And she'd turned them over in her mind a hundred times since he'd uttered them. Had he said he wanted her back she would have dismissed it as a flight of fancy issued from the depths of a flu-ravaged brain. But need. Need indicated necessity rather than desire. Need was an entirely different word altogether. It was more…calculated.

'I told you. I want a reconciliation.' And this time it wasn't fever that glinted in his eyes but stone-cold purpose.

There was a moment of silence. Jacqui's head spun and she gripped the tray so hard she was surprised it stayed in one piece. He just stood there, looking at her, his expression deadly serious. *Oh, God!* He hadn't been delirious that night.

She swallowed. She couldn't do this. Not on an empty stomach. Her gaze dropped to his naked chest. Not with him in his underwear. She moved forward, tossing her hair, praying her tremulous legs would carry her to her destination.

'For God's sake, Nate,' she said as she passed by him, injecting as much bored-with-the-view into her voice as possible. 'Put some clothes on.'

Nathan smiled as she strutted by, her nonchalance not fooling him for a moment. Her perfume embraced him in a hundred rekindled memories, and none of them involved her asking him to get dressed. In fact he doubted she'd ever uttered those words to him. 'I remember a time when you would have asked me to take my clothes *off*,' he said to her back.

Hell, he remembered a time when she would have ripped them off for him.

Jacqui almost stumbled with the tray as she set it

down on the table. She took a moment fussing with the plates before she raised her face and looked him square in the eye. 'Those times are long gone.'

Nathan noticed the determined jut of her chin and the hardening of her toffee eyes. *Yes, they were. They seemed about a million years ago now.* He pushed away from the doorframe. 'I'll be right back.'

He climbed into his trousers and his business shirt, doing up three buttons, rolling up the sleeves, not bothering to tuck it in. He joined Jacqui in her braless singlet and hemp pants, feeling way overdressed.

He smiled to himself as she swiped at some egg yolk that had dripped down her chin. 'You are a disgrace to hippies everywhere—you know that, don't you?' he said as he took a seat opposite.

'Not all hippies are veggies,' she protested.

'Just as well.' He grinned, enjoying how she devoured her food. He'd used to love watching her eat. Like everything else, she did it with gusto. 'They would have revoked your card years ago.'

Jacqui savoured the salty flavour of the free-range bacon and the warm squelch of locally churned butter, ignoring Nate's familiar patter. He'd always teased her about her lackadaisical approach to the alternate lifestyle she'd embraced in her teens. A 'hybrid hippy', he had affectionately called her.

'Mmm, but it tastes *sooooo* good,' she said shutting her eyes in rapture. At the moment eating was preferable to thinking. Eating gave her a focus other than Nate's preposterous statement.

Nathan shook his head and smiled at the look of bliss

on her face. The corner of her mouth glistened with a smear of butter that in another time and place he would have taken great pleasure in removing with his tongue. Her corkscrew russet curls framed her face in the same wild abandon they had a decade ago, and she looked so happy, so sated. Like a goddess.

The hippy goddess of abundance.

'How did I end up with you?' he mused.

Jacqui opened her eyes and stared into his puzzled gaze. His beautifully sculpted lips sported a Mona Lisa smile. Their gazes locked, and for a moment neither of them said anything, contemplating their wild glory days when neither of them had needed anything but each other.

'I don't know, Nate. I don't know.'

Nathan's stomach grumbled and he broke their eye contact, helping himself to some toast and placing an egg on top. As hungry as he was, he didn't think it wise to pile up his plate after two days of starvation. Jacqui was right, though, it did taste good. *Damn* good. He could feel the residual weakness from the flu virtually disappearing as he ate, the restorative effects of protein, carbohydrates and coffee making him feel bulletproof again. Preparing him for the verbal sparring to come.

'So, I take it that's your Porsche bogged down the road a bit?' Everyone who had come into the clinic on Saturday had reported the unusual sighting.

He looked up at her and nodded. 'Is it okay?'

Jacqui frowned. 'Of course. Why wouldn't it be?'

'Sports cars attract attention.'

She laughed. 'Isn't that the point?'

'Sometimes not the good kind.'

'This is hardly the Bronx, Nate. Don't worry, your mid-life-crisis toy is safe here.'

Nathan chuckled, well used to her disdain for the trappings of wealth. 'What makes you think my car represents a mid-life crisis?'

Jacqui shrugged. 'You're forty-two and you're here.'

He laughed again. 'Sorry to disappoint. I'm crisis-free.'

Although that wasn't entirely true. He did have a problem or two. One she could help him with. The other…that odd, restless feeling that kept rearing its ugly head…that was best left undefined. Best left well alone.

'Well, the car certainly doesn't represent option number two.'

'Oh?'

'Yes—you know. The I'm-compensating-for-a-lack-of-what-I-have-in-my-shorts toy.' God knew she'd been reminded of that too often this weekend.

This time Nate roared laughing. 'No. Nothing Freudian about it.'

Jacqui had forgotten how magnificent his laugh was, and she felt goosebumps feather her skin and her nipples tighten in blatant response to his sexy baritone. She watched over the rim of her coffee mug as the crinkles around his eyes and mouth relaxed. But the amusement still sparkled in his jade gaze.

God, she'd missed this. Sharing a meal with him.

She placed her coffee mug down on the table. Time to lay their cards on the table. Her stomach was full and he was dressed. She couldn't bear the suspense any longer.

'Okay, Nate. Spill. Why the bizarre request?'

Nathan watched her watching him, her gaze wary.

Would she listen to him? Would she hear him out? Would she agree? 'I have a...problem only you can help me with.'

Jacqui's heart started drumming in her chest. It seemed so loud in the intense silence that followed his statement it was real competition for the rain on the roof. Surely he could hear it? 'Go on.'

'You ever heard of a guy called Vince Slater?'

Jacqui frowned, the name vaguely familiar. 'Some rich old guy who's on to wife number six?'

Nathan chuckled. Good summation. Except he was also a world-renowned financial genius, with razor-sharp business acumen and the Midas touch. And a friend.

'That's the guy. He's agreed to join the executive of TrentFertility, which will put us in a very strong position for the float.' He looked at Jacqui, looking at him as if he was speaking in tongues. 'You *do* know about the float?'

Jacqui nodded. Her mother kept her up to date with all Nate's goings on. She received regular clippings from the nation's newspapers, all featuring Nate's very commanding presence.

TrentFertility was about to go public.

'Of course. We do have TV and newspapers out here, you know.'

He ignored her sarcasm. 'This is big for me. Bigger than anything else I've done.' She needed to understand that he wasn't asking anything of her lightly.

Jacqui heard the hard edge in his voice. He wanted this badly. 'I don't understand. Why do you need Vince? Surely you have enough money of your own? Why do you need his financial backing?'

Nathan shook his head. 'It's not about his money. It's about confidence. Market confidence. Vince is a seasoned executive. He's known and well thought of in all the right business and financial sectors. He has experience, and a reputation for shrewd fiscal choices. Stockmarkets, particularly in the last few years, are notoriously jittery. Having him on board will be a ringing endorsement for TrentFertility.'

Jacqui listened to Nathan's clinical assessment of Vince Slater's attributes and felt chilled by how detached he sounded. 'So billionaire doctor, top of the rich list isn't enough for you?'

Nathan stalled. She didn't get it. She'd never got it. A nerve jumped at the angle of his jaw. 'Like I said, it's not about the money, Jacqueline.'

She sighed at his stiff response. She, more intimately than anyone, knew that. She understood the demons that had driven him to push himself beyond just a career in medicine. She had been party to all his young-man dreams, his drive to make something of himself beyond just plain Dr Nathan Trent.

The hand-to-mouth existence of his childhood, when he'd been forced to live out of the family car for a while after his father's bankruptcy and subsequent suicide, working three jobs to put himself through med school, had hand-tooled him to build the medical empire he resided over today.

Twenty fertility clinics responsible for a thousand babies—several to high-profile couples. He'd gone global five years ago, with clinics expanding into the Asian and European markets. Three research facilities.

He'd come a long way and become a force to be reckoned with—both in medicine and in business. More importantly, he'd built something that no one could take from him. Because underneath it all Nathan Trent— fertility guru, medical magnate—craved security.

She sighed. 'What's this got to do with me, Nate?'

'Vince's wife.'

Jacqui saw the slight flicker in his gaze, the way he couldn't quite meet her eyes. He looked guilty as hell. She shut her eyes. Had money totally corrupted him?

'Oh, Nate…you haven't?'

Nathan blinked, his gaze settling back on hers. He drew his brows together, annoyed that she would think what she was obviously thinking. 'No,' he denied icily, his jade gaze chilly. 'I bloody well haven't.'

'Nate…' He could deny it as much as he liked, but something had happened between the two of them. She could read him like a book. 'Tell me.'

'Abigail's taken a…a shine to me.'

Jacqui raised an eyebrow. 'And you haven't encouraged her?'

'No.' His denial was as emphatic as he could make it. 'She's young enough to be my daughter. And married. To a close business associate and dear friend. You know me better than that.'

Did she? Truth was, she didn't know him any more. She hadn't even known who he was for the last couple of years of their marriage. Perhaps she never had? Perhaps she'd only ever seen what she'd wanted to see?

But he hadn't exactly been a monk during the decade they'd been apart. Her mother made sure she had a copy of every picture of every woman who had ever been photographed gracing Nathan's arm.

'She's got the wrong idea,' Nathan supplied.

'And how would she have got that, Nate?'

'Not through anything *I've* ever said or done,' he said firmly. Infidelity had always been abhorrent to him. Jacqui knew that. At least she'd used to. 'But she's persistent. She thinks I'm playing hard to get.'

'So tell Vince.'

Nathan shook his head. 'Vince may be a financial genius, but he's dumb as a rock when it comes to matters of the heart. He loves her. You know what they say—there's no fool like an old fool. It'd break him.'

Jacqui was taken by the softening of Nathan's voice as he spoke about Vince, given his earlier businesslike summation of the man. Seeing Nate bordering on sentimental took her back to the old days—when he'd been nothing like the man who had looked at her from the kitchen doorway with cold purpose less than thirty minutes ago.

It was clear that while Vince was a means to an end, Nathan held obvious affection for the older man. But she had a feeling that the worst was yet to come, and hardened her heart. 'I don't suppose it'd help the float any either?'

Nathan lips flattened into a grim line. 'Vince would resign. It'd cause a big scandal. A newly floated company might not survive the backlash. Vince is TrentFertility's greatest asset for legitimacy in this new frontier we're embarking on.'

'Aren't *you* its greatest asset?'

Nathan returned her gaze, feeling curiously flat-tered. 'Not this time. This is a whole new ballgame and I need him.'

She turned her attention to the murky contents of her coffee mug, formulating the question she didn't want to hear the answer to. 'And I fit in to this how?'

'Cover. If we reconcile, she'll back off.'

Jacqui shrugged. 'You don't need a wife for cover. Get a girlfriend.'

Nathan shook his head. 'Tried that. Hasn't worked.'

'So what makes you think she'll respect the sanctity of marriage? It seems she has no problem cheating on her own husband—why would bagging someone else's be a no-go for her?'

He shrugged. 'I don't pretend to know what goes on inside the head of a twenty-two-year-old girl who's been spoilt rotten all her life. All I know is that happily married men are a no-no for her. I suppose even princesses have *some* moral codes.'

Jacqui suppressed a laugh at the distaste in his voice. Poor Nate. Things were obviously on top of him. Fending off a determined female and chasing the almighty dollar even higher into the stratosphere had obviously run his immune system into the ground.

'So why now? So close to the float? Why not take evasive action months ago?'

Nate ran a hand through his hair and placed his coffee mug against the throb that had started in his temple at thinking about it again. 'I underestimated her determination. I came home Friday evening and walked into my bedroom to find Abigail naked on my bed. Vince was in the other room.'

'Oh, no.' Jacqui laughed, covering her hand with her mouth to stifle further merriment. 'That's awful.' She pictured the scenario and bit her cheek to stop herself laughing again. It wasn't funny, she knew, but she'd have loved to be a fly on the wall.

Nathan pierced her with a steely glare. 'It's not funny, Jacqui.'

Jacqui nodded, muffling her mouth. 'No.' She shook her head vigorously. 'I know.'

But it was obvious to Nathan it was still tickling her fancy. She was sitting with her arms folded, a hand clamped across her delectable mouth, her body practically shaking with suppressed laughter, her curls vibrating around her face.

'So, after I got rid of Vince, I told her you and I were reconciling. She's invited us to dinner at their place on Monday night.'

It was Nathan's turn to smile as he laid his trump card on the table. Jacqui stilled, her hand dropping from her face, a gasp escaping from her mouth. 'You told her *what*?'

'She's dying to meet you.'

'But… But…'

Nathan chuckled.

Jacqui fixed him with a glare. 'This isn't funny, Nathan.'

'No,' he said with mock contrition. 'I know.'

But still, he meant it. This was no joke. She could tell he was absolutely serious. She shook her head. 'No.'

'It won't be for long. The float's in a month, then maybe a couple of weeks after that. Just enough to convince Abigail that we're happily reconciled.'

Jacqueline pushed her chair back and started collecting their dishes. She had to do something—anything to get out from under his compelling gaze. She needed to think. She couldn't process information when he was looking at her as if they hadn't been apart for a decade. She reached for his plate.

'Jacqui.' He put a stilling hand over hers.

She dropped the plate and it rattled against the wood. 'I can't just pick up and leave, Nate, even if I wanted to. Which I don't. I have a life here. Work.'

'I've arranged for someone to cover your practice.'

She blinked, his arrogance sucking her breath away. Of course he had. Why let a little thing like her objections get in the way of another billion or two?

'We're done, Nate. We were done a long time ago—maybe even from the start. We always had different dreams, and no good can come from pretending otherwise.'

She pushed away from the table, turning her back on him, stalking into the kitchen, dropping the crockery into the sink. She pushed the plug into its hole and flicked the taps on, concentrating on the gushing water and not on the man who had come to her house with the most ridiculous suggestion she'd ever heard.

'You owe me, Jacqueline.'

Even over the gush of the tap, the drum of the rain and the gallop of her heart his quiet but unflinching statement snaked towards her, pregnant with purpose. She squeezed eco-friendly detergent into the water and stared at the frothy bubbles in the sink for a moment, before slowly reaching for the taps and shutting them off.

'You said you wouldn't collect.'

Six years ago Jacqui had stumbled across this, her beloved vet practice, nestled right near the ocean smack in the middle of a series of small communities that shared her life philosophy. It had been serendipitous indeed—she'd fallen in love, and it had been for sale. And she'd wanted it.

Wanted it with an intensity that had surprised her. Wanted it more than she'd wanted anything in the preceding four years. She'd been functioning on autopilot since her split with Nathan, and the practice had been the first spark of life—true, grab-you-by-the-guts life— she'd experienced.

But she'd been skint.

After every bank manger in Australia had turned her down, she'd swallowed her pride and rung Nathan. Nathan her ex. Nathan whom she'd walked away from when it had finally dawned on her that he was never going to change. Nathan who'd never wanted the babies and white picket fence that meant so much to her.

Much to her surprise, he hadn't batted an eyelid. He hadn't questioned her or lorded it over her, just deposited the sum of money into her stipulated bank account. Almost as if he'd been doing a favour to a distant relative. Maybe a crazy old aunt he was slightly embarrassed to have as a branch in his family tree. As if by doing so he could finally wipe his hands of her—discharge his duty.

And that had hurt. It shouldn't have. It had already been four years and she was over him. But it had. To be dismissed so resoundingly. Like a bug on his windscreen or a piece of lint on his expensively cut jacket. A mild annoyance.

So she had worked like a demon to pay him back. And she had—in two years. But deep down, even though he'd assured her in their one and only phone conversation there wouldn't be any strings, she'd always felt she still owed him. And now he was calling in his debt.

His stringless debt.

Looking at his face, the rigid set to his jaw, the steely determination flinting his gaze, she marvelled that Abigail would even dare pull such a stunt on such a ruthless man. She shivered. Where was the Nathan she'd fallen in love with? Surely he was there somewhere?

He shrugged. 'You're forcing my hand.'

Nathan felt about as low as he'd ever felt. But he wasn't going to let Abigail ruin things for him. Owning a publicly listed company on the stock exchange was the pinnacle, his father's ultimate dream realised, and he hadn't come this far to stall so close to the top. So what if he had to play on her sense of obligation? This was business, and if Jacqui was collateral damage then so be it.

'You could be less superior about it,' she snapped.

'Hey. I did ask nicely.'

Jacqui shook her head at his calmly neutral delivery. This was just business to him. 'Not this, Nate. You can't ask me for this.'

Nathan moved forward into the kitchen. He stopped in front of her, excruciatingly aware that some errant part of him wanted to move closer.

'It won't be for long. I promise. Just do this one little

thing for me. Then you can come back here and get on with your life.'

Jacqui could feel herself wavering. This close, his charisma was suffocating. Compelling. Which was precisely what she was worried about.

It wasn't just uprooting her life and the hundreds of inconveniences that would cause. Having him back in her world for two days—even semi-comatose— had been curiously fulfilling. Living with him? For weeks? Now he'd given her a teaser, the temptation was intoxicating.

But she had to remember that they were still two different people, living two completely different lifestyles. He was still chasing success and she still wanted to settle down with a tribe of kids, that white picket fence and a dog or two.

But she *did* owe him. She knew it. Her conscience knew it. Her highly developed sense of fairness knew it. He'd help make her dream possible. Who was she to stand in the way of his? Just because she didn't approve and it wasn't her dream didn't negate it for him.

Nathan could see the indecision in her toffee gaze. He raised his hand and placed it on her bare shoulder. 'Please, Jacq. I need you.'

Her pelvic floor muscles shivered as his pet name for her rolled off his tongue as if they'd never parted. The years fell away. He was again the boy-man she'd fallen in love with.

She shut her eyes to block out the appeal in his earnest green gaze. She only wished she could also shut out the memories and the warmth of his breath against her face. Tendrils of desire, real and remembered, wrapped her in their addictive embrace.

Jacqui took a mental machete and hacked them back. She opened her eyes and looked him straight in the eye. 'With one proviso.'

Nathan nodded, prepared for bargaining. 'Name it.'

'I want a divorce.' Seconds ticked by. Nathan looked at her blankly, and she continued. 'When all this is done—I want a divorce. I think we've dragged this out long enough.'

It was time to move on. Way past time.

Nathan couldn't have been more surprised had she slapped him in the face. Divorce had always been one of those things on his to-do list. But life had been insanely busy. He'd been building an empire and everything else had fallen by the wayside. At the back of his mind he'd always assumed she'd initiate proceedings, and he knew he would never have held them up. He would have signed what was needed. But she hadn't, and life, his empire, had taken precedence.

Now, standing here in front of her, looking at her for the first time in a decade, it seemed so…final. He knew legally severing their connection was merely a formality—apart from the loan, they'd not had a thing to do with each other in a decade—and he knew without a doubt that she wouldn't want a single thing from him. But suddenly it didn't seem so clear cut. Did he want to live in a world where Jacqui wasn't at the end of an invisible string? Even if it had taken him until now to give it a good hard tug?

He shook his head. This was crazy. He was close to

his dream. And that was paramount. He wasn't going to let two days back in her company derail his purpose. A divorce was a cheap price to pay for what he wanted. He should be Mexican waving.

The nerve jumped in his rigid jaw again. 'I'll see to it.'

The heavy finality of his words was like the bells of doom heralding a tragedy, and Jacqui couldn't believe she was even considering a fake reconciliation.

'We won't be able to make dinner tomorrow anyway, Nate,' she said, staring directly into his eyes for one last appeal. 'The whole area is flooded. The rivers won't be down again for days. We're not going anywhere.'

Nathan smiled at her. He'd won. 'Lucky for me, I own a helicopter.'

CHAPTER THREE

JACQUELINE stood staring at the Gold Coast panorama before her as the last of the sunset's orange hues turned to a blushing crimson in the evening sky and lights twinkled on up and down the coast. Nathan's sixtieth floor penthouse in Q1, the world's tallest residential building, towered over all the other skyscrapers, and dwarfed Surfers Paradise beach far below.

Was it only this morning she'd been tucked up safely in her sleepy little hollow, in another state, living her life her way? In a few short hours she'd not only crossed state borders but surrendered control of her life to Nathan.

For now.

She placed her hand against the floor-to-ceiling glass, feeling the cool against her palm. She shut her eyes and then opened them. The stunning view greeted her again. She gave another quick blink.

Nope. Still there.

She wasn't sure if it was vertigo or the enormity of being back in Nathan's world, but she suddenly felt dizzy.

She placed her other palm on the glass, reaching for an anchor amidst the unexpected turbulence in her life.

Nathan walked into the massive open plan lounge and spotted her by the windows, stopping to stare at her silhouetted figure. She'd barely spoken to him since breakfast. She hadn't been sullen, merely…resigned— packing and making her own locum arrangements while he organised their transport.

Which had made him feel worse. Spitting-mad-angry he could handle—hell, he was used to it from volatile Jacqui—but this subtle duty-under-sufferance routine was tapping his guilt reservoirs and milking them for all they were worth. The fact that he was totally beat, the dying remnants of the flu still maintaining a foothold in his system, left him more susceptible to her silent censure.

Maybe it was his lowered resistance, but watching her as she admired the view he couldn't help but think she looked good here. Which was a stupid thought. Pointless. She was here for such a short time, and then she'd be gone. Here to play her part and then disappear, with their signatures on a dry legal document.

But he couldn't deny the unsettling feeling he'd had of late that something was missing from his life. Back at Jacqui's house, having Shep around again, he'd thought maybe it was animal companionship he'd been lacking. But now, having Jacqui here, he wasn't so sure. Maybe it was her? Or at least a woman to share his life with.

Her shape called him from across the room. Even after ten years of not seeing her, her body was as familiar to him as his own, and his fingers curled into his palms in primal recognition. From her height, to the rich glory of her russet curls, to the strength of the muscles in her arms, thighs, calves and stomach—every detail was imprinted into his fingertips.

Silhouetted like this, he could see the angle of her shoulderblades, the arc of her spine, the curve of her waist, the dip of her back, the rise of her bottom. He remembered those places vividly despite the years. He remembered how she liked to be kissed, where she liked to be touched, and how she sounded when she came apart in his arms.

In fact there wasn't anything he didn't remember. And, flu or not, he wanted to touch her again so badly desire sucker-punched him hard in the solar plexus and fogged his vision. He grabbed the back of a chair, his fingers biting into the fabric as he fought for control.

He hadn't expected this. He hadn't expected to feel such a potent rekindling of the lust that had enthralled him in the earlier years, blinded him to their differences. Sure, he'd expected to feel some attraction—Jacqui was still a damn fine-looking woman—but he'd thought it would be gentler, mellowed somehow, more nostalgic.

Not like this. This powerful surge of possession that had him in its grip. This urge to brand her as his own again if only for a few weeks. He'd fooled himself into thinking he could see her again, and have some *faux* platonic reconciliation and it would all be terribly civilised. But he wasn't feeling remotely civilised at the moment. He was feeling very, very primal.

He blinked to dissipate the haze of longing, and took a deep breath before releasing his grip on the chair and moving towards her with sudden clarity. 'I'll put your bag in the master bedroom.'

Jacqui had felt his presence behind her long before he'd spoken. She didn't turn around. 'You don't have to give up your bed for me.' Her warm breath fogged the glass.

Nathan kept his voice deliberately neutral. 'I'm not.'

It took a beat or two for his meaning to become clear. She turned slowly, her heart skittering madly in her chest like the gait of a new-born foal. 'I'm not sharing a bed with you.'

Nathan felt his own pulse-rate kick up a notch as she bathed him in her unwavering toffee gaze. 'What did you think reconciliation meant, Jacqueline?'

Jacqui clenched her hands. 'Not that—and you know it.'

'It's necessary.'

'I beg to differ.'

Nathan moved closer, crowding her towards the glass. This near he could smell her skin, hear the not so steady timbre of her breath. She swallowed, and his attention was drawn to the length of her neck. He raised his hand and placed two fingers on the pulse at the base of her throat. It fluttered madly at his touch and her pupils dilated.

He smiled. 'Are you afraid, Jacqueline?'

Her heart thundered through her chest and reverberated in her head. She could feel it pulse against his fingers.

'Of you?'

Nathan shook his head. 'Of wanting things. Wanting to get back a little of the old magic.'

Jacqui fought for control while the air in her lungs stuttered to a halt.

They had been soooo good.

Damn him. If he thought he could play her, that she was still the old, easy Jacqueline who could deny him nothing, then he was wrong. She raised an eyebrow with as much indifference as she could muster, and forced a cool smile to her lips.

'I think you're transferring, Nate.'

He chuckled, and then sobered, the pads of his fingers stroking light circles around the pulse beneath them. 'I think you want this as much as I do.'

His overwhelming certainty and the intoxication of his body heat pinned her to the glass, and she was grateful for its frostiness. God, he smelt so good.

She shrugged, desperate for control. 'Denial is good for the soul.'

Nathan snorted. He didn't believe in any of that Zen hippy claptrap. And her body, her mouth, was so close. One more step and he'd be pressed against all that yielding feminine warmth. Blood was rushing everywhere. His temples pounded, his skin burned, his groin tightened.

'We're adults, Jacqui. Technically still married. And we're sharing an apartment, pretending to be reconciled. It's a natural step.'

Jacqui shut her eyes against his hushed seductive tones. He might as well have been the serpent himself. Her eyes fluttered open. Had he moved closer?

'Isn't that taking the charade a little too far?'

Nathan shrugged. 'It'll be more authentic if we're really lovers again.'

It sounded so reasonable when he said it like that.

No, no, no. She shut her eyes again, blocking out the curve of his sexy mouth. She'd be stupid to travel down this path. It had taken years for her to walk away last time, despite knowing they weren't good for each other.

Nathan Trent just wasn't a guy you left.

She opened her eyes. 'I can do authentic.'

Nathan shook his head. 'No. At the moment your eyes say…' He slid his palms up her neck slowly, cupping her face. His thumbs applied gentle pressure beneath her chin, tilting her head back slightly. He inspected her gaze for a long, lingering moment. *'Reluctantly reconciled.* But if I do this…'

He stopped for few seconds, searched her gaze for resistance, and then lowered his head. His intention was to stroke, tease, tantalise and then stop. But the second her lips touched his all his good intentions were swept away on a tidal wave of lust, and he opened his mouth, greedy for more, welcoming the maelstrom.

Her moan tickled his lips, and he sucked in a harsh breath through his nose, inhaling her taste, absorbing her flavour, wanting more. He pushed her back hard against the glass, imprisoning her with his body, revelling in the feel of her around him infusing his senses. He stroked her neck, plundered her mouth as if they'd never been apart.

God, he'd missed this. Her mouth was sweet, and it fitted his just right. Her tongue was stroking his and her hands were twisted in his hair, her bangles cool against his face, her breasts squashed into his chest. Just like old times.

Dangerous. Very dangerous waters. He had much to achieve in the next few years, and letting himself be seduced back into the past wasn't on the agenda. This kiss was merely trying to prove a point. It took all his will-power to wrench his lips from hers.

Jacqueline gasped, and mewed at his departure—she couldn't help it. The noise had been dragged from her as he deprived her of his mouth. Their breathing was loud in the silence between them, ragged with unfinished business. She couldn't think, couldn't talk. She could barely see.

Nathan placed his forehead against hers, fighting for control of his breath, his pulse. Her warm brown gaze had turned molten with undiluted desire. He placed his hands on either side of her face and looked deeply into her eyes. 'Now they say *reconciled and loving it.*'

Jacqueline closed her eyes, fighting to regain control of her breathing. She placed a hand over his and gently removed it. She pushed off the glass and stepped away from him on shaky legs.

'Forget it. I'm not sleeping with you, Nate.'

It was his turn to press his face to the glass, cooling his fevered brow. 'Your body tells me a different story.'

Jacqueline gave a harsh laugh, suddenly feeling as cold as the sheet glass deep in her chest. She felt for a nearby chair and sank into its plush leather depths. 'Lucky for me my brain doesn't reside in my pants, then.'

Nathan felt too destabilised to give a snappy comeback, or even defend his sex. He turned to face her. 'Jacq—'

'No, Nate.' She shook her head vigorously and held out her hand to ward him off as he reached for her. 'I'm here. And I'll play my role. But this reconciliation is only an act. If you kiss me again like that I'm leaving. Debt or no debt. Divorce or no divorce.'

Nathan watched as her heated gaze hardened. He'd seen that look before and knew it brooked no argument. 'If you insist.'

Jacqui nodded and stood. 'Thank you.'

Nathan watched her back as she moved away from him. 'We *are* going to need to be convincing.'

His voice pulled her up short, and she gave a soft snort as she twisted to face him. 'Oh, I'll be convincing.'

He didn't move as she turned away, slowly retreating. And despite her earlier warning a worm of naked lust trilled through him at the promise in her words.

Surprisingly, Jacqueline slept like a baby in Nathan's guestroom's king-sized bed. One night up with a sick horse followed by two more up with a sick naked man, had taken their toll. Not even the memory of that steamy kiss, burnt as indelibly into her lips as the memory of him into her DNA, was enough to keep her awake.

It was, however, the first thing she thought about when she woke the next morning. She stretched, and sighed at the futility of her erotic reminiscence as the luxury of the eight-hundred-thread-count sheets caressed her skin. He could kiss her like that every minute of every day, do that thing he did in bed that sent her into the stratosphere, and it still wouldn't erase the fundamental differences in their lifestyles. They were walking a different path now. Maybe she'd been kidding herself that they'd ever walked side by side?

Jacqueline arose, pulling on her gown, and wandered

out to the lounge area, her stomach growling. She padded into the kitchen to find a note propped against a chrome wire fruit basket laden with fat red apples. Nathan's bold, slashing hieroglyphs—as if he had scored the paper with a sword dipped in ink—stood stark against the thick quality stationery.

Fresh croissants on the table. Dinner at 7:30.
Nathan.

Jacqui picked it up and ran her fingertips over the commanding strokes of black print. The card felt opulent in her grasp, rich and plush, and she remembered with fondness the smutty notes he'd used to leave her anchored on the fridge door via a cheap magnet souvenir from a pharmaceutical rep.

Except he'd signed those, 'Nate'. And there'd always been 'X's and 'O's.

For a crazy second she held the note to her nose and inhaled. But then her stomach growled, and another scent called to her. She found the croissants through smell alone. The fluffy pastry melted on her tongue. Damn the man for remembering her weakness for flaky breakfast treats! It reminded her of their honeymoon in Paris at a seedy hostel, and of how very far away she currently lived from any kind of patisserie.

She was shocked to discover it was ten o'clock when she'd eaten her fill. She stood at the huge glassed wall, looking across at the panoramic display of multi-million-dollar, multi-storey coastal real estate and the magnificent ocean vista.

She supposed she should have been impressed, but the day stretched ahead of her. A whole day with nothing to do but think about Nate and that kiss.

No, no, no. She would not let him monopolise her thoughts. She'd proved over the last ten years that she could push him to the outer, and she would not let sentiment and hormones hijack her Zen-like attitude to their failed relationship.

Fifteen minutes later the cloud-like lift had delivered her to the foyer, and she walked the short distance to wriggle her toes in the warm sand of Surfers Paradise beach. A brisk stroll restored some equilibrium to her being. She and Shep walked on the beach every morning at home, and she was grateful that Nate's address allowed her to be near the regenerating calm of the ocean.

The pounding of the surf was like music to her suddenly troubled soul, and she lingered on the beach, letting the water lap her ankles. Far out beyond the bobbing heads of eager swimmers a row of surfers waited for the next big wave. Scantily clad sunbathers lazed about, despite the bite of the blazing morning sun. Children squealed as the waves caught them unawares, and lovers took full advantage of bare skin.

It *was* paradise. The broad arc of perfect white powdery sand was breathtaking. The high-rise skyline, as much a part of the vista before her as the beach, was somehow almost beautiful in its grandness, the landscape somehow co-existing peacefully with the sun and the surf.

A breeze blew her hair behind her, and even the knowledge that it would be tangled beyond belief wasn't enough to make her secure it. There was just something about the sea breeze on her scalp that was enriching and, despite her russet colouring and tendency to freckle, Jacqueline raised her face to the ball of solar energy above in silent worship.

'Thought I'd find you here.'

Jacqui allowed her eyes to slowly drift open and focus on the man beside her. He was in a business shirt and tie, his trousers rolled up, his jacket slung over one arm and his shoes held in the opposite hand. He should have looked like a pimple on a pumpkin, and yet somehow he managed to look as if he belonged here. Poseidon risen from the sea in the guise of a modern-day businessman.

He certainly out-manned every other male on the beach. A dangerous observation with the memory of his kiss still fluttering through her mind like the tail of a kite in a fresh breeze. Her heart thudded a little harder.

'Interesting beachwear.'

Nathan shrugged. 'When in Rome.'

Jacqui studied the horizon for a few moments, then the waves lapping at her feet, excruciatingly aware of the occasional brush of Nathan's shirt against her bare arm. Her earlier sense of calm was disappearing fast.

'Did you want something, Nathan?' she prompted.

'I forgot to mention that tonight is quite dressy.' He dragged his gaze from the ocean and juggled his shoes while he reached into his jacket. He pulled out his credit card and passed it to her. 'Buy yourself something amazing.'

Jacqui looked at the piece of plastic he was pushing at her, and then up into his face as a cold hand gripped her heart. She felt as if every system in her body had just ground to a crashing halt.

'Why is it that I feel like Julia Roberts to your Richard Gere?'

Nathan rolled his eyes. 'Don't be melodramatic, Jacqui. It's a prop, that's all. I'm asking you to go out and buy a very expensive prop. I don't expect you to pay for it.'

Jacqui sucked in a deep breath. In through her nose, out through her mouth. In through her nose, out through her mouth. She'd been back in his world for less than twenty-four hours and he was already making her nuts. First a kiss, then an insult.

She pushed his hand away, searching for some of that Zen. 'I'm going to pretend we didn't have this conversation. We're on the beach and the sun's shining and it's a beautiful day.' She shut her eyes and took another cleansing breath.

'Abigail will be dressed to kill.'

Jacqui opened her eyes, assessing the cool jade chips in his flinty gaze as she pinned him with one of her own. 'So will I.'

A brush against her leg distracted her from the sudden heat in his eyes and the flare of his pupils, and she looked down. A small child clung to her calf for dear life. She swayed and tottered, trying to find purchase in the shallows as the outbound waves eroded the sand from beneath her feet, before finally landing with a hard plonk on her bottom. She started to cry.

'Hey, there, baby girl,' Jacqueline crooned, crouching beside the chubby toddler.

She looked around for a concerned mother, and when

none seemed to be forthcoming picked her up to comfort her. She was wearing navy bikini pants with frills adorning the seat, and a matching sun shirt. A floppy yellow hat, the rim wet, completed the picture.

The little girl grasped Jacqueline's arm, her pouty lips turned down, her forehead crinkled, her blue eyes full of fat tears. Her whole face, from the strawberry-blonde fringe plastered to her forehead to her dimpled chin, was a picture of such tragic wounded toddlerhood it was hard not to laugh.

She looked at Jacqui, and then at Nathan, and pointed a fat sandy finger at him.

'I know,' Jacqui soothed, swaying slightly. 'It's all his fault, isn't it?'

'Hey,' Nathan protested.

The little girl stopped crying then, and just as abruptly shot him a gappy smile.

Nathan laughed. 'Still have a way with the babes.'

Jacqueline would have rolled her eyes, had she been capable. But her heart had banged to a halt for a brief second as the familiar ache roared to life with a brutal stab.

'Where's your mummy?' Nathan asked, looking around. He could see a harried young woman looking around frantically further down the beach, and he waved at her to attract her attention.

It was easier to do that than watch the way the toddler's hand squished into Jacqui's breast. Or see the way she looked so at home with a child on her hip. Or the sudden stricken look in her eyes as she stared down into the toddler's face.

'Oh, thank you! I'm so sorry,' the woman apologised, whisking the toddler out of Jacqui's arms and squeezing the child to her in a boa-constrictor-like embrace. 'She's *so* quick these days.'

Nathan smiled and waited for Jacqui to say something, but she was looking kind of dazed. 'No problem,' he assured her .

Jacqueline watched their retreat, unable to move, barely able to breathe, already bereft at the loss of contact with the chubby baby hands. The little girl waggled her pudgy fingers, and Jacqui couldn't drag her gaze away as the yellow hat disappeared into the crowd.

'Are you okay?'

She took a deep breath. And then another. The pain in her chest pulled viciously with each expansion of her lungs. She turned her attention to the horizon again, desperate for the earth to right itself, for the pain to go away, for calm to return. She tuned into the steady, soothing rhythm of the ocean.

In through the nose, out through the mouth. In through the nose, out through the mouth.

Nathan waited a few minutes. 'Jacq?'

She nodded. 'I'm fine.'

He waited another minute. 'You never did have that baby?'

Jacqui gave a brittle laugh to fend off another twinge in her chest. 'Nope.'

'There must have been other men, Jacqui.'

She looked up at him. 'Why? Because there's been other women for you?'

He shook his head. 'Because you're a sexy woman

who, from what I can remember, has a very a healthy libido.'

He seemed so calm and collected, while inside her a hundred emotions swirled around in seething disquiet like a giant bubbling cauldron. She wanted to lash out, wanted to hurt him. 'Oh, there have been others.'

Nathan flinched, surprised to find her admission didn't sit very comfortably with him. He'd suggested it because ten years was a long time, but now it was out there the thought of another man being with her really grated.

'Nobody I wanted to have a baby with, Nate.'

His irritation evaporated as her wounded eyes sucked him back into the past. To the monthly disappointment when her period arrived, and how devastated she'd been to find out about the PCOD which complicated her endometriosis and further blighted her fertility.

'Not that *you* wanted to have a baby with *me*.'

Her quiet statement slapped him across the face hard. The sounds of the beach faded and he became very still. 'That's not true.'

Jacqui shook her head on a half-laugh, half-snort, and blinked to clear a sudden welling of tears. 'Oh, come on, Nathan. It's been ten years. At least be honest with yourself now. You only went along with it in that last year to placate me, and because you knew we were falling apart and it was a way to hang on. But if you think I couldn't see the relief in your eyes each month, then you're wrong.'

Nathan regarded her quietly for a moment. Jacqui had always possessed an uncanny knack of seeing straight through him. She was right—he had been relieved. And simultaneously guilty. 'It just wasn't the right time for me.'

Jacqui nodded. He'd been busy working his way to the top. He hadn't wanted the distraction of a child.

'You know,' he said hesitantly, not sure how his next suggestion would be met, 'it's not too late. Plenty of women whose circumstances have never been advantageous are using fertility specialists to fulfil their life-long dream of having a child.'

Jacqui blinked. She dragged her gaze away from the horizon as it pitched out of kilter. She felt as if her head was going to spin off her shoulders. If her feet hadn't been grounded in wet, heavy sand she might well have levitated. This truly was surreal.

She opened her mouth to speak, but nothing came out. She cleared her throat and tried again. 'It's been a decade,' she spluttered. 'What makes you think I still want that? God, Nate, I'm thirty-eight. I gave up on that dream years ago. I'm not the same person I was back then.'

Nathan took a moment to study her. He had noticed the changes. Ten years ago she would have flayed him for offering his credit card to her. She certainly would have told him to stick his pseudo-blackmail attempt. And she would definitely have jumped at the opportunity to have a baby by any means.

'Just a suggestion. From someone in the field.'

Jacqui shook her head at him. 'You still don't get me, do you? Do you think I would bring a child into the world without the benefit of a family? A mother and a father? I wanted to be a family with you, Nate. Not just the mother of your child.'

Nathan looked down at her, surprised at how her words clawed at his gut. *A family.* Something he'd always taken for granted until his father had done the unthinkable and smashed their family bond to smithereens.

The wind blew strands of russet curls across her face, and as much as he itched to tuck them behind her ear he didn't dare touch her. She was pretty ticked off. And then his mobile rang, and he almost kissed it as he removed it from his belt. A business crisis he could handle—a difficult delivery, no worries. But his ex-wife looking at him with her toffee eyes and talking about family was too confrontational.

'I have to go,' he said, flipping his phone shut a few moments later.

'Then go.'

He'd been resoundingly dismissed, but for the first time in a long time Nathan was torn. He didn't want to be here, but he didn't want to leave either.

'For God's sake, Nathan,' Jacqui said, barely holding it together. 'Go!'

Nathan gave a terse nod. 'See you tonight.'

Jacqui stood for an age, staring into the vast blue yonder, before plonking herself down in the shallows. The waves sucked at her, soaking her skirt and hollowing the sand beneath her. She didn't care.

Their conversation played like a cracked record over and over in her head. Damn Nate. Damn him for pushing his way back into her life and making her want things again that she couldn't have.

CHAPTER FOUR

Nate got home from the office with half an hour to spare before dinner. 'Jacqui?'

Silence greeted him and he frowned. The stillness was ominous, and a trickle of doubt slithered up his spine. Had she bolted? She'd been upset on the beach. Angry. Maybe she'd decided it wasn't worth the hassle. *He* wasn't worth the hassle.

He clenched his fists as the thought undermined his usual unwavering confidence. He needed her. But, more than that, after a few days in her company he was actually looking forward to seeing her again. His day at work had dragged, and he couldn't remember the last time he'd been so unproductive.

Yes, he'd been fighting a vague sense of disquiet for a while now, the usual thrill of walking into his office at TrentFertility having been annoyingly absent, but it had never interfered with his productivity. Until now. All he'd done today was stare at the wall and think about her damn lips. About that kiss.

And then, after the beach incident, he hadn't been

able to rid himself of the vision of her with a child on her hip. Or the way she had looked at him with her big toffee eyes and told him she'd never wanted a baby with anyone else.

He hadn't been sure how he was going to be greeted, and his pulse had thudded in anticipation the entire way up in the lift like some teenager on a first date.

But he *had* expected her to still be here.

'Jacqui?' he called again.

He moved through the living area, calling her name and checking the deck before ending up in her bedroom. He could hear the shower spray coming from the open *en suite* bathroom door and, despite knowing he should turn around and leave, his relief that she was still here was so overwhelming it banished all caution.

He sauntered across the room until he was standing in the doorway. The frosted glass of the shower stall gave away no details, just a blur of flesh, but knowing she was here, naked and near, gave him a sense of satisfaction he doubted he'd felt in a long time.

The desire to open the door and join her, take up where he'd left off last night, was surprising in its intensity. It had been a long time since he'd held her naked body, and hearing her splashing around was setting fire to his libido. He grasped the doorjamb to prevent the impulse becoming a reality.

'Thirty minutes, Jacq.'

Jacqueline's hands stilled in her hair, shampoo suds streaming down her face. 'Nathan?'

'Were you expecting another man to come visit you in the shower?'

Her pulse tripled at the flirty edge to his voice. She was excruciatingly aware that she was naked and wet, and that only a thin panel of glass separated them. She covered her breasts, turning away from the door. 'Get out of here,' she spluttered, ducking her head under the shower spray.

'It's okay. I can't see anything much.'

The fact that he could see anything at all had her nipples growing hard beneath her palms. 'Nate!'

He grinned, holding up his hands. 'I'm going, I'm going…'

Jacqui sagged against the tiles. How did he do that? Still do that? After all this time? Turn her on with just a few words? Especially when she was still mad at him over their conversation on the beach. How could her body betray her in that way?

She finished the shower in record time, threw on some clothes and partially dried her hair with the dryer, scrunching it with her hands to keep the glorious curls that corkscrewed around her head in order.

She sauntered into the lounge with ten minutes to spare, determined to put what had happened at the beach aside and forget that he'd been watching her for who knew how long while she showered. She wasn't here to rehash old hurts or rekindle passions. She was here to smile, look pretty, act devoted and leave with her divorce papers.

Nathan was waiting, his back to her, admiring the view, and her stomach did a little flop at the broadness of his shoulders and the sculpted contours of his butt, displayed perfectly in tailored trousers.

'I'm ready,' she said, annoyed at the husky tremor in her usually rock-steady voice.

Nathan turned, and despite the distance between them his thorough head-to-toe left her feeling as if he had touched her. He had the top two buttons of his shirt undone and the sleeves rolled up to his elbows, and she was gripped by the urge to do a little touching of her own.

'And worth the wait,' he murmured.

And she was. Jacqui's individual flair for fashion was in full swing. Her kaftan-type dress somehow combined tie-dye with geometrical patterns, and with her height it gave her an Aztec priestess vibe. She wore large hoop earrings and no make-up. The V neckline hinted at a cleavage, and an intricate belt made from loops of fine gold chain and a network of what looked like coins cinched the garment in at the waist.

'Great belt.'

Jacqui looked down. 'Thanks. I bought it at an antique market in Turkey years ago.' She fingered the elaborate piece. 'I loved it so much I took up belly dancing.'

Nathan had a mental image of a veiled Jacqui dressed in harem pants, gyrating her hips and undulating her belly. He wanted to cancel dinner and eat her instead.

He cleared his suddenly dry throat, forcing his legs to walk to the drinks cabinet and pick up her cocktail. 'Martini?'

Jacqueline shook her head as he advanced towards her, the drink already mixed, complete with the olive he knew she loved. 'Are you trying to get me drunk, Nate?'

Nathan chuckled as he drew close enough to lean in and kiss her. He smiled and handed it to her. 'Dirty,' he said. 'Just the way you like it.'

Jacqui swallowed and took the proffered drink—mainly for something to do with her hands other than yanking him closer. There was a charge in the air between them tonight, a vibe, and that wasn't why she was here. Even if he did look so good she wanted to smash the drink against his giant glass window and drag him to the floor.

Martinis weren't the only thing she liked dirty.

She took a gulp of the clear liquid. A great big one. The gin kicked in immediately. She picked up the olive and sucked on it, barely noticing the bite of vermouth as his heated gaze zeroed in on her mouth, skewering her to the spot more effectively than the toothpick through the olive.

Oh, God. She'd told him she wasn't going to sleep with him. And she meant it. But if they kept this up—this pseudo-sexual dance—then she was kidding herself that this night was going to end anywhere else but in his bed. If they even got that far. This had to stop.

She placed the empty toothpick back in the glass and threw the rest of the martini back in one shot. 'Shall we go?' she asked, handing him the glass and moving away. *Well* away.

He blinked. It took a beat or two for the mists of lust to clear from his vision. Great—they hadn't even left yet, and he was so hard for her he was light-headed. If he kept this up—literally—he'd be brain-damaged by the end of the night.

Nathan took a deep calming breath. 'Sure,' he said.

They left the apartment and entered the lift. It ascended and dinged shortly after, and he gestured for her to precede him. 'Now, remember, we're newly reconciled,' he said, moving down the hallway with her. 'Are you sure you can carry that off?'

He had to ask that after the olive? 'I'll be fine.' She nodded.

'Really?' He stopped at Vince's door. She was surprised to hear the sudden edge of tension lacing his voice. 'I don't think I can stress how important this is, Jacq.'

That much was obvious. 'Relax. Trust me.'

She knew she could keep her end of the bargain. Memories of loving Nate came easily. But he was suddenly looking too tense. Too serious. She frowned. Where was Mr Sure-of-Himself? Shouldn't *she* be the nervous one? If he went in there looking like this he would be the one to blow their cover, not her.

Nathan looked at her for confirmation, his gaze falling straight down into the deep V of her cleavage and the unfettered splendour beneath. Oh, God, how was he supposed to concentrate on pulling this off when she was braless? 'Jesus, Jacqui. Couldn't you have at least worn a bra?'

Jacqueline arched a brow, unsure who this uptight man before her was. What the hell was the matter with him? She had to do something. Fast. She smiled and casually pushed the doorbell, turning to him. 'That's nothing.' Jacqui took a step closer, so their bodies were touching, and raised herself slightly on her toes, pressing her mouth against his ear. 'I'm not wearing any underwear at all.'

Nathan felt the breath stutter to a halt in his lungs as a surge of pure, high-octane lust zinged at warp speed through his system. He pulled away slightly. 'Jacqui…'

His husky warning curved her lips further. She pulled his head down and slammed a kiss against his lips that she hoped would live with him way after the ink was dry on their divorce papers. His greedy response, the plunder of his tongue and the harsh sucking of his breath, told her it just might.

Jacqueline pulled away, satisfied with the result even if naked need roared in her head, urging her to continue. Now he looked like a man who'd been in bed for a week with his lover. She turned in time for the door opening and slipped into her role.

A maid ushered them in and Jacqui smiled to herself, dragging an unmoving Nathan in with her by the arm. *Nice to know she could still bring him to his knees.*

And then it was action stations.

There were introductions, and Jacqueline finally came face to face with Abigail Slater. The woman who wanted her husband. Abigail shook her hand politely and gave Nathan a kiss on the cheek. As her lips lingered Jacqui was hit by the sudden overwhelming urge to scratch the younger woman's eyes out. How blatant! The impulse to snap, *Back off, bimbo,* rose on a tidal wave of white-hot jealousy, and she clamped her mouth shut lest it spew out unchecked.

What the—? She'd seen a hundred pictures of beautiful women gracing Nathan's arm—neatly clipped out by good old Mum—and none of them had roused such instant bile. Sure, she'd drawn moustaches on all of them, and then used them to line the bottoms of the cages in her surgery, but she hadn't wished any of them obliterated from the earth.

'Well, now,' Vince said. 'I can see why Nathan's been keeping you a secret. No wonder he looks so smitten.'

Jacqueline laughed. She could see Abigail's pout in her peripheral vision, and her smile widened further. 'I'm afraid the feeling's entirely mutual,' she admitted, and blasted Nathan with her best hot-for-you look as she ran her palm up over his abs to the flat of his pectoral muscle.

Nathan blinked, his brain still stuck in the no-underwear rut. His hand slid down her back and ran across her rump, searching for a telltale line. Nope. Nothing. He had a picture in his mind of her *sans* dress, wearing nothing but the damn belt that jingled with every movement. *Dear God!*

'Isn't that right, Nate?'

A slight edge in her voice brought his wandering mind back. She was staring at him with parted lips, and with a large dash of snap-the-hell-out-of-it swirling in her toffee gaze.

Right. They had a show to put on.

He smiled down at her and bent his head to place a loving kiss on her mouth. 'Absolutely.'

'It just seemed so sudden—didn't it, Vince? We were only just saying that last night.'

Jacqueline watched as Vince nodded adoringly at his wife. Abigail—pretty in a plastic gym-bunny kind of way—gave her a hard look that demanded an explanation. Luckily they'd spent some time in the chopper yesterday getting their story straight.

Jacqui shrugged. 'We didn't want to put any pressure on ourselves by going public too soon. We've been working on this for a couple of months.'

'But we didn't want to keep it secret any longer,' Nathan added. 'It's time to shout it to the world.'

Vince laughed a great booming laugh and clapped Nathan on the back. 'Well, then,' he said. 'This definitely calls for a celebration. A toast.'

'Yes,' Abigail murmured. 'I'll go fix us some drinks.'

It was one of several toasts they made over the course of the evening. They dined on the balcony, overlooking a glorious ocean crowned in moonbeams by a large full moon. Waiters served them freshly shucked oysters followed by sand crab linguine.

Vince was an absolute delight, regaling her with stories from his corporate world, talking about his travels and quizzing her about her job.

'Yes,' Abigail chimed in. 'What *are* you planning on doing with your practice?'

Jacqueline smiled at the younger woman, who had watched them like a hawk all evening. *Good question.* She smiled at Nathan while she gave his thigh a firm *Now what?* squeeze.

He smiled back at her, his hand moving up her bare arm, pushing under the heavy fall of her hair to caress her nape. 'We've been talking of buying something here— haven't we, darling?' Nathan said, thinking quickly.

'Oh? So you're selling the country practice, then?' Vince asked.

'We're not sure yet. We'd like to keep Jacq's place as a holiday home. Somewhere to get away from it all.'

Jacqui smiled at him. His hand at her neck was causing tiny trills of sensation up and down her body. It was utterly distracting. Still, she was amazed at his capacity to think on his feet. No wonder he was so good in business. It was taking all her might to remember that it was all an illusion and not to let the magic of his fingers suck her into the happily-ever-after picture Nathan was faking.

'Sounds idyllic,' Abigail murmured.

'Oh, it is,' Jacqueline said, shooting the other woman her best dreamy expression.

They were interrupted by the arrival of the most decadently sinful slice of chocolate cake Jacqui had ever seen. Abigail declined her piece, and gave Jacqueline a look that said, *You're not really going to eat that, are you?* Jacqui smiled at Nathan, picked up her fork, and tucked in.

They moved inside for coffee. Nathan was pleased with how the evening had gone. More than pleased. Jacqui had slipped into her role with gusto. She'd smiled, flirted and bantered with him as if they'd never been apart. And the touching! She'd touched him constantly. His arm, his cheek, his thigh. She'd even raised her mouth in silent invitation on a few occasions. So what was a man to do?

He didn't know if Vince or Abigail were convinced, but he sure as hell was. Between her flirting and the distracting knowledge that she was starkers underneath that dress, he was going quietly mad. He ached to get her alone. To kiss her for real. Have her touch him for real. Because—whether she knew it or not—that was exactly where tonight was heading.

He made himself comfortable on a blizzard-white leather lounge chair as Abigail brought in the coffee and a laden cheese platter. Jacqui joined him, cuddling her body into his. Her breasts were squashed against his arm, her hand lay high on his thigh, and she sighed as she rested her head on his shoulder.

She crossed her legs and seductively angled the foot of her crossed leg under his closest knee, so she could rub lazy circles on his opposite calf. Nathan almost groaned aloud. The erotic caress was having a predictable effect. He'd spent most of the last few hours in a state of rock-hard readiness.

Even when the conversation moved on to the boring-as-watching-paint-dry subject of the company's float, desire still thrummed through his veins. He checked his watch, impatient to be gone. When Jacqueline yawned he seized the opportunity.

'Oh, dear—sorry,' she apologised.

'Don't be,' Vince assured her. 'No doubt this bloke's been keeping you up.'

Nathan chuckled, shifting to stand, disrupting the way her legs had entwined around his but knowing they'd be even more entwined shortly. Hopefully wrapped snugly around his waist. He pulled her up with him by the hand and looked her square in the eye. 'I think it is time to call it a night.'

Jacqui almost swooned at the look of blatant lust in Nathan's eyes, and gripped his hand to steady herself.

Oh, God. They were going to make love!

No, no, no. She looked away from the smouldering heat. This was an act—just an act. Yes, she was impossibly turned on—practically blinded by a fog of desire so thick not even a superhero with X-ray vision could see through it. But it wasn't real.

Okay, the lust was real. But their relationship wasn't. It was fake. An act. She was just doing what he'd asked of her. Her resolve to keep everything platonic between them behind closed doors still stood. She knew there were women out there who could divorce emotion from sex, and she was glad for them. Bravo to them. God, she'd kill for a bit of that now. But she knew herself too well. She couldn't. Not really. And not with Nathan.

Nathan didn't linger over the farewells, and Jacqui felt her panic increase exponentially the further they got from Vince and Abigail's apartment. They waited for the lift, and she could feel his gaze travelling over her like a caress, as if he'd licked with his tongue straight up her middle from her toes to the tip of her nose.

The lift arrived. They got in. Nathan punched a button. 'That went well,' he said, his voice rough with building desire. He could feel his circulation pulsing through every vein as each footfall took him closer to their destiny tonight.

'Yes,' she murmured, standing as far away from him as possible, her brain searching for a way out of the sticky web of desire her brilliant acting had spun them in.

Nathan watched her stare fixedly at the floor as she shrank into the corner. She was withdrawing, struggling for control. He'd seen the flare of panic in her eyes when he'd suggested they leave. But they'd passed the point of no return. This was bigger than them. Way bigger.

They rode down six floors. The lift dinged. He

gestured for her to precede him out and they walked to his apartment. Nathan unlocked the door and pushed it open for her. She walked in. He followed. The door shut.

There was a few seconds of silence where Jacqui could hear only their breath in the semi-dark. She barely registered the soft moonlight invading the apartment through the undressed windows over the screaming in her head.

Run, run, run.

But the heavy tentacles of desire were turning her bones to liquid, anchoring her to the ground, paralysing her will. She opened her mouth. She didn't want this. Well, she did. But she shouldn't. It wasn't rational.

She dragged in a breath. It was loud in the silence—like the first gasp of someone who'd crossed over briefly only to be sent back for a little longer.

'Goodnight, Nathan.'

He placed a hand on her shoulder. 'Jacq.'

Jacqui shut her eyes against the longing in his voice and the primal pull deep inside. She reached for the wall. 'Please, Nathan.'

A beat or two passed before he stepped closer, his chest skimming her back. He lifted a finger and brushed a lock of hair aside, leaving a bare portion of skin.

'You want this,' he whispered against her neck. 'We both do.'

His voice filled her head and her heart, and heat unfurled like a bud flowering beneath the sun. She whimpered. At least it sounded as if it was her. But then she was turning, powerless to resist his pull.

And his mouth was on hers, and somehow she went from being wrapped in his embrace to having her legs wrapped around his waist. Her bottom was cradled in his palms, the wall was at her back, and they were kissing and kissing like a pair of teenagers three seconds before curfew.

Except there was nothing adolescent about it. It was deep and frantic, tainted with desperation after three hours of teasing and ten years of denial. Nathan held her against the wall, his strong hands supporting her bottom, kneading it as he pushed his tongue into her mouth, groaning as her tongue joined in.

He moved, needing to get her horizontal, but she was pulling frantically at his shirt, tearing at the buttons, unbalancing him. He only made it as far as the opposite wall.

Her hands were at his fly now, and he left her mouth to bite down her neck, his own hands coming up to palm her breasts roughly. She moaned as he held her, pinned with only the thrust of his hips and his hands. He could feel the erectness of her nipples beneath the fabric of her dress.

'Need this off,' he demanded, before dipping his head and claiming her mouth again.

He steadied them and moved again, heading in the direction of his bedroom. But her hand had finally found a way into his pants, and when she palmed him his knees almost buckled and he staggered. Luckily the back of couch was there, and they tumbled awkwardly against it, her breasts squashed to his chest, her hand still firmly grasping his throbbing erection.

Nathan took advantage of her standing and grabbed fistfuls of the dress, working it upwards, exposing every inch of her naked legs and then finally—finally—her very naked *derrière*. His hands palmed the surface of her buttocks, refamiliarising themselves with their contours as he pulled her pelvis in close to his and plundered her mouth.

He gave them a squeeze and she moaned against his lips. Then she returned the favour and he lost his mind.

He dragged his mouth from hers. 'Need to see you naked. Bedroom.'

Jacqui shook her head. It had been ten years. She didn't want to wait any longer. Not a few minutes. Not even a few seconds. And she certainly didn't want to give her earlier doubt demons any time to talk her out of it.

'Later,' she said, plastering another kiss to his mouth before pulling away, turning around, leaning her elbows into the plush leather of the couch and bending forward slightly. She pushed herself into his exposed groin for good measure.

Nathan swallowed as his erection surged. Her round, naked rump wiggled enticingly, and he clutched her hips, jerking her against him.

'Jacqui—' He hadn't meant it to sound so guttural, so base, but he hadn't pictured their first time in a decade being like this.

And he'd thought about it a lot in the last few hours.

He'd pictured it slower. A leisurely exploration. Taking his time, getting to know her again.

She turned and looked at him over her shoulder. He was staring at her as if she was Aphrodite herself, his thumbs stroking her hips, making her hot, making her needy, making her want.

'Nate!' She wiggled again, feeling his erection push against her cheeks. 'I want you in me. *Now.*'

He looked at her, trying to keep a hold on his fraying self-control. 'I'm not going to last very long like this.'

Jacqui shut her eyes as a surge of pure female power intensified her desperation. 'Oh, God, Nathan. Do you think I am?'

And that was all the invitation he needed. He gripped her hips, his erection nudging her slick female entrance, and slowly eased inside her. She cried out and he leant over her, pulling her into his chest, wrapping himself around her.

'Are you okay?' he murmured in her ear.

'Of course, Nate,' she panted. 'It's incredible. You're incredible. Don't stop.'

Still, he took a moment to gather himself. The urge to bang into her, again and again, was overwhelming, almost primal. But he wanted it to last, to go on for ever. So he took it slow. Going deep, but not all the way, sensing perfectly the moment to withdraw.

At another time Jacqui might have appreciated it long and slow, but she'd been hot for him all night and she didn't want slow and steady. She didn't want him to hold back. She wanted Nate. She wanted all of him.

'Damn it, Nate,' she cursed as he pulsed into her again. '*All* of you.'

He didn't think it was possible, but he hardened even more. 'Jacq…' God, she was killing him!

'Nate! Stop being so damn respectful!' And she pushed back against him, crying out as she felt his erection sink deeper.

And he broke. *She wanted all of him?* He pulled out quickly and slammed into her, ramming himself in to the hilt. *She could have all of him.* She moaned and called his name, and he repeated the movement.

'Yes, Nate! Oh, God, yes!'

And then he didn't need any further encouragement. He reached for her breast and, encouraged by her corresponding groan, squeezed it through the fabric. His other hand reached between her legs and sought the tight round nub amongst all the slick heat. He touched it, and her guttural moan filled the entire room. He rubbed it and she sobbed.

'Nate—' She could feel herself rushing, hurtling towards inevitability, and she wanted him with her.

Her belt and her bangles tinkled with each pelvic thrust. 'Hold on, baby. I know,' he whispered.

'Nate!'

'It's okay.' His own climax was rushing forward fast. 'Let go, Jacq. I've got you.'

Jacqueline did as he asked, and the whole world ceased to exist. Just him and her as everything imploded. She was vaguely aware of him joining her, calling out her name, squeezing her so tight she thought she might asphyxiate.

But what a way to go.

The waves of pleasure seemed to go on and on for ever, buffeting her, stroking her like a thousand velvet fingers. In ten years she'd never had sex this good, and she sought through the treacle that her brain had become to remember why she'd ever walked away from this sex god.

'Nate,' she gasped.

Nathan collapsed against her back, holding her tight,

his breathing ragged, his chest exploding, trying to get everything under control. Trying to form a coherent thought. It was minutes before that was even possible. And his first thought was the realisation that, despite his spent status, he was far from done.

He pulled out, hitching up his trousers, reaching for her, swinging her into his arms.

'Where are we going?' Jacqui asked, still floating on a cloud somewhere.

'My room. For more.'

She smiled against his chest, her arms creeping up around his neck, liking his answer. Liking it very much.

Nathan lowered her to the ground gently when he reached his bed. 'Off with this,' he murmured, slowly drawing the dress up her legs again.

Jacqui didn't argue. She wanted it off as much as he did. She unclipped her belt and let it slide to the floor.

'Oh, no,' Nathan said, lifting the dress over her head and tossing it aside. He retrieved her belt. 'That stays on.'

Jacqui smiled and clipped the belt in place. The cool chains added a sense of the exotic. And then he laid her on the bed and made love to her with a thoroughness that left her speechless.

CHAPTER FIVE

AN HOUR later they were laying sated in a post-coital haze that, had they been able to bottle it, would have made them a lot of money on the party drug scene. They were staring at the ceiling, Nathan's hand trailing up and down her bare arm.

'We should have reconciled years ago,' he murmured.

Jacqui smiled. 'If I'd known the sex was going to be this good, I might have considered it.'

He chuckled, rolling himself up onto his elbow and looking down at her. 'It *was* good, wasn't it?' He trailed his finger down her stomach, tracing the decorative loops of gold adorning her waist, the coins tinkling.

She gave a half-laugh. 'Sex was never our problem, Nate. Sex we did good. It was just marriage we sucked at.'

He swirled patterns outwards to her hip. 'Why was that again?'

Jacqui sobered. *Because I was never enough for you.* 'We were just too different.'

Even in the semi-dark, with the room illuminated

only by the moonlight filtering through the partially open wooden louvres, he could see the swirl of emotion in her toffee eyes. He dropped a hard kiss on her mouth. The blood roared through his veins, his stomach muscles twisting as her arms snaked around his neck. Her nipples grazed his chest and he wanted to taste them again, hear her cry out as he laved them to tight peaks.

He pulled away, his breathing ragged. She was naked and glorious, her russet curls fanned out on his pillow, and he was surprised by the streak of possession that lanced him with sudden savage intensity.

'You're not going back to the guestroom.'

Jacqui knew she should protest. Sex hadn't been part of her reluctant bargain. A public reconciliation to pay back a debt and divorce papers to finally draw their relationship to a close. That had been the deal. But something primal was calling to her. Something too big for her to stop.

'Guest bedroom? What guest bedroom?'

Nathan rubbed his thumb against her lips, staring at them intently for long seconds. 'Good answer,' he murmured, before savaging her mouth in a blatant display of possession.

The next two weeks flew by. Between the flurry of media events heralding the float, dinner parties, and their insatiable desire keeping them awake into the wee small hours, Jacqueline was exhausted.

They slipped into a routine. Nathan worked all hours—practically all the time apart from when they were attending a function or making love behind closed doors. And she was at his beck and call. Both in and out of the bedroom. It wasn't very feminist, but she was way out of her depth in Nathan's glamorous world so it was just easier to let him plot their course.

Jacqueline found it no hardship playing Nathan's adoring wife. When they were out on display she slipped into the role effortlessly, enjoying their easy banter and the way he flirted and looked at her as if he was going to spread her on his toast the second he got her alone.

Which he did at every opportunity.

Abigail Slater was everywhere she turned in those two weeks. The younger woman clearly held a torch for Nathan, and Jacqui wondered how shrewd, savvy Vince could be so blind to it. Jacqui got the impression that, although the younger woman had backed off, she could see right through their façade and was just waiting for the moment they let down their guard, or Jacqui dropped out of the scene altogether.

It made her work a bit harder at the whole newly-reconciled-couple thing. She flirted with Nathan a little bit more when Abigail was round—smiled wider, was more tactile, laughed in a way that spoke of intimacy far greater than any words could.

She had to admit to a touch of jealousy too. The thought of Nathan with Abigail was disturbing. Actually, now she was back in his life—in his bed—again, the thought of Nathan with any woman was disturbing. Years after their split, it wasn't an emotion she had a right to. But it was there anyway.

The highlight of the fortnight was a trip to Sydney

on Nathan's private jet. He had a major business meeting with lawyers in the morning, and when he suggested she join him she jumped at the chance to tag along.

Afterwards he took her down to the water, and they climbed on board a yacht which sailed them under the Sydney Harbour Bridge, past the Opera House and around to Watsons Bay. They dined on fresh seafood and drank champagne as the sun sparkled like party lights on the surface of the harbour.

She looked at Nathan over the rim of her champagne glass. 'You look tired.'

He chuckled. 'That's because I'm sleeping with a nymphomaniac.'

Jacqui smiled. 'That's the pot calling the kettle black.' She sipped her drink.

Nathan's laughter fizzed through her blood like the champagne bubbles on her tongue.

'Seriously,' she said, leaning forward and snatching his sunglasses off his face. His usually clear green gaze looked bleary, as if he had a hangover. 'You look old.'

'Hey!' he protested, squinting as the sun stabbed into his weary eyeballs.

'Do you always keep up this insane pace? I mean, you get home long after I've gone to bed, and then…' She stopped and blushed.

'And then you keep me up for hours,' he supplied.

She ignored the way his deep baritone made it sound deliciously dirty. She'd been so swept along the last couple of weeks, trying to come to terms with her crazy new life, she hadn't realised until now—until this moment of stillness—that they hadn't actually talked about anything of consequence since that day on the beach.

'I don't think you even kept these kind of hours as a resident.'

He shrugged, retrieving his sunnies, feeling the instant relief behind his eyeballs as the lenses cut through the harsh sunlight. He made a quick dismissive gesture with his hands. 'I thrive on it.'

It occurred to her then that, apart from when they were out socialising or when he was making love to her, he just didn't seem very…content. She'd been so busy shoring up her emotional defences she hadn't been paying attention to him.

She searched his face, frustrated by her inability to see his eyes. 'But are you happy?'

Her question cut right to the centre of the persistent well of discontent that never seemed to be far from the surface, and he cursed her intuition.

'Of course,' he dismissed. 'This is the culmination of all my dreams—what I've been working towards.'

Jacqui felt a prickle of unease at his terse reply. She reached for his glasses again and pursed her lips as he moved his head to evade her grasp. 'Really? You don't come to bed and talk for hours about your day.'

'That's because I'm too busy making love to you.'

She ignored him. 'I remember when you couldn't wait to tell me about the patient you'd saved, or the baby you'd delivered, or the latest joke old Dulcie in Rehab told you.'

In the two weeks she'd been back in his world she hadn't witnessed anything that told her he actually enjoyed his work. He was about to take his company public—surely that deserved some level of conversation? Some degree of excitement?

'You're naked and in my bed, and probably only here for another few weeks. Forgive me if I see talking as overrated.'

'Nate.' She didn't bother to keep the reproach out of her voice.

He sighed and rubbed his eyes under his glasses. 'It's not medicine, Jacqui. I'm not saving people's lives. It's dry and dull and boring.'

Jacqui quirked an eyebrow. 'Your words. Not mine.'

He made an exasperated noise at the back of his throat. 'I meant it's hardly pillow talk.'

'How much actual medicine do you do these days?'

He shrugged. 'The odd high-profile client. Maybe half a day a week. The demands of the company have pretty much kept me away for the last few years.'

Jacqui shook her head, appraising his suit and tie. He looked every inch the grim businessman. 'And this is what you want?'

Nathan's mouth flattened into a thin line. 'This is the way it is.'

Hardly the same thing. 'And that's all right by you?'

Nathan tore his glasses off and threw them down on the table in disgust. 'What do you want to hear, Jacqui? Do you want to hear that I'm working every hour God sends because I'm terrified that I'm going to mess this up and end up like my old man, ruining the lives of everyone who works for TrentFertility? Do you want to hear that, yes, these last few years I've had this nagging sense of something being missing from my life?'

He paused and searched her eyes, saw the earnestness there, the compassion. He took a deep breath.

'I've got too much riding on this to pander to some airy-fairy, can't-quite-put-my-finger-on-it feeling,' he said. 'I don't have the time. My whole life has been working towards this point, Jacqui. My biggest goal is about to be realised. I swore the day Mum came to school to tell me about Dad that I would realise his dream for him. And I'm here. And pretty damn content about it too. So, can we please just drop this?'

His green gaze held her enthralled with its zeal-like intensity. Her heart broke for the teenager who'd never come to terms with a father who'd cared more about his business failures than his personal successes. Like a wife and child who loved him.

Her sudden conviction that Nathan was unfulfilled beneath his Italian suits and flashy car was absolute, but the man was forty-two and a billionaire—he didn't need a mother. She was only here for another few weeks. He needed a wife, not a conscience.

Jacqui forced a smile to her lips and lifted her champagne glass. 'Consider it dropped.'

A week later Nathan picked Jacqui up for lunch with the visiting CEO of a pharmaceutical company.

His phone rang and he answered it via his Bluetooth earpiece. Jacqui listened absently as she looked out of the window. Nathan was trying to placate somebody.

He pushed the button to end the call and turned to

her. 'I'm sorry. There's a bit of a crisis at work. I have to go in.'

Jacqueline nodded, well used to frantic calls from Vince or people at the office interrupting them. 'Please don't let me keep you from the world of high finance.'

Nathan glanced up at the sharpness of her tone and frowned. 'No, no—it's the clinic. A patient's having a bit of a…meltdown. I'm sorry. I need to see her.'

Jacqueline blinked. 'Oh.' She was momentarily speechless. 'Of course.'

Nathan changed direction and was parking in his reserved space at the Paradise Private Hospital ten minutes later.

'They have a really nice coffee shop on the ground floor,' Nathan said as he unbuckled. 'You can wait there for me.'

'Actually…would you mind if I come too?'

It had been years since she'd seen Nathan in action as a doctor. She'd seen the businessman twenty-four-seven since coming to live with him, but ever since their conversation last week she'd been wondering about the doctor more and more.

Plus, she had to admit to a certain curiosity from a purely professional standpoint. What did Nathan's clinic look like? What were his staff like? Did he have up-to-date magazines in his waiting room?

Did he still look mighty fine with a stethoscope slung around his neck?

Nathan faltered, surprised at the request. 'If you want. It might be a bit boring.'

Jacqui almost laughed at his deeply furrowed brows.

'You think lazing around your apartment all day is stimulating?'

He shook his head at her. 'Most women would kill for an apartment with that view.'

Jacqui gave him a sad smile. 'You should know by now I'm not most women.'

They entered one of his exclusive suites a minute later. A harried-looking woman, her eyes swollen and red, her belly large with child, jumped at him the second he entered the reception area.

'I'm so sorry, Nathan. I know it's irrational. I know it's stupid. But I can't lose another baby. I just can't.'

Jacqui felt her gut clench at the emotional frailty of the stranger. She was obviously distressed, but everything else about her—from her suit to her chic hairstyle, to her trendy frames—said capable, kick-ass, corporate go-getter.

Nathan placed his arm around his patient's shoulders, his hand rubbing gently. 'It's okay, Sonya. Of course you did the right thing contacting me. We'll do an ultra-sound. You'll see everything's fine.'

Jacqui watched as the woman who'd looked as if she was about to crumple to the floor a second ago responded to Nathan's assurance. She gathered herself, looking around, the colour in her cheeks heightening as she suddenly became conscious of everyone in the waiting room pretending not to notice her—of Jacqui.

'Oh, hello,' she said. 'Sorry, Nathan. Did I pull you away from something?'

'Not at all.' Nathan smiled. 'Sonya, this is Jacqueline—my...wife.'

Sonya seemed nonplussed for a moment, and then recovered. She held out her hand to Jacqui. 'Oh, I didn't realise… That is, I didn't know… Oh, dear, I'm terribly sorry. I'm afraid I'm not very eloquent these days. My IQ seems to have fallen incrementally with each week.'

Jacqui gave a half-laugh as she shook the other woman's hand, liking her instantly. 'It's okay.'

'Are you a doctor too?'

Jacqui blinked at the rapid topic-change. 'Sort of.' She laughed. 'I'm a vet.'

'Oh! I love vets. If I wasn't so happily married and—' she looked at her stomach '—so huge, I'd put the hard word on mine. He saved our darling Jock's life when he got tick paralysis.'

Jacqui kept a straight face. She didn't know this woman from Adam, but she'd bet her last cent her pre-pregnant self wouldn't have been anywhere near as forthcoming. 'Er, yes—that can be very nasty.'

Nathan blinked. He'd known Sonya for nine years. They were friends. She ran her own PR consultancy. He'd never seen her so…scatterbrained. 'Is Brian coming?' he asked.

Sonya pouted. 'No. He had to fly to Perth early this morning.'

Nathan nodded and patted her hand. 'Okay. Well, let's get one of the nurses to sit in with us while we do this, huh?'

'Oh, no—wait,' Sonya said, and turned to Jacqui. 'Do you think *you* could?'

Jacqui looked at the woman who had been a total

stranger until a minute ago. Still was, really. 'Er…' She glanced at Nathan. 'I…I suppose so. Are you sure?'

Sonya nodded happily. 'Absolutely.' She grinned manically for a few seconds, and then it faded. 'Oh…it's probably not very appropriate.' She bit her lip. 'I'm sorry. I'm really not myself these days.'

Jacqui was so taken by her frankness, by her candour, she couldn't refuse the woman. It was as if she had pregnancy-induced Tourettes. 'Don't worry about it.'

Sonya pulled her into a huge hug and Jacqui laughed at the spontaneity. She caught Nathan's frown over the other woman's shoulder. 'Unless, of course, Nathan would rather I didn't?'

Nathan shrugged. 'Fine by me.' And they all trooped into his office.

Jacqui was pleasantly surprised. She'd expected it to be in the same awful minimalist style evident in the reception area. All white on beige on cream, with expensive but indiscernible art and discreetly elegant indoor plants.

Instead it was colourful. Busy. Anne Geddes prints of babies on pumpkins and in flower pots decorated the walls. A high, wide couch with crazy-patterned sheets stood against one wall; an ultra-modern, ultra-expensive ultrasound machine stood nearby. A large toy box stood against another wall. Nathan's desk, slightly chaotic, sat in the middle.

Nathan shrugged out of his jacket and helped Sonya onto the couch as Jacqui hovered at the end. Her gaze was drawn to a large corkboard attached to the wall, and her eyes skimmed the photos pinned to it as Nathan placed his stethoscope on Sonya's belly while he waited for the machine to boot up.

The photos were amazing, and Jacqui's heart just about crashed to a stop. They were of Nathan. And babies. Lots and lots of babies. And lots of happy couples. There were so many of them they overlapped in places, and there wasn't a millimetre of cork to be seen anywhere.

In some he was in theatre greens and the babies were still wet, covered in vernix and blinking blearily at their bright new world. In others the babies were wrapped and snuggled peacefully in layers of soft cloth as he held them close, and in the rest he posed with ecstatic couples nursing their precious bundles in hospital beds or here in his office as he looked on.

Jacqui noticed a few famous couples amongst the faces. But mostly she noticed, amidst this incredible montage of his career, how indescribably happy he looked. In every single snap. How joy shone from his face as he looked down at the little lives he'd helped bring into the world. How big the grins directed at his clients. How utterly, completely, totally...content he looked.

She hadn't seen him look like that in the last few weeks at all. Not flying in his private helicopter or talking about the float or rubbing shoulders with the business elite.

Not even in bed had he been that unguarded.

Nathan chuckled, and she glanced at him. She saw it again. The look from those snaps. The snaps that told a story about a man happy with his lot. Enjoying his work. The absorption, the confidence, the ease in those photos were all there in his face right at this moment as he doctored Sonya. He was relaxed—in his element.

She watched surreptitiously as he chatted with his patient, pointing to the ultrasound screen. He laughed again, and she watched how Sonya's fears seemed to melt away like a mirage, as if they'd never existed.

Nathan leaned forward and flicked a switch and the whole room was filled with the amazing staccato rhythm of a baby's heartbeat. *Whop, whop, whop.* Fast and steady. Jacqui's skin goosed at the sweetness of the noise, the ache in her chest throbbing anew at knowing it was a joy she'd never experience.

She watched as Nathan squeezed Sonya's hand and passed her a tissue as a fresh wave of tears filled his client's eyes.

'Your little girl's doing really well,' Nathan assured her. 'Her heartbeat is strong, and she's really kicking around in there.'

Sonya nodded, blowing her nose. 'Thank you, Nathan. Thank you. So you don't think I should have an early C-section?'

'She's only just thirty-five weeks' gestation, Sonya. Let's give it a bit longer, okay?'

'Of course. Of course. I'm so sorry to have wasted your time.'

'Hey,' Nathan chided as he wiped the gel from Sonya's belly. 'If you want to come and have an ultrasound every time you're feeling a bit wobbly, that's fine. Just ring.'

Sonya half sat up, pulling her shirt down. 'Really?' She sniffled.

Nathan squeezed her hand again. 'Really. That's what we're here for.'

Sonya launched herself up and pulled Nathan into a big hug. 'You have no idea how much that means to me,' she whispered fiercely.

Jacqui watched as he laughed, gave it a few seconds, then gently extricated himself.

Sonya climbed off the couch and looked at her. 'He's the best,' she said. 'Don't let that one go—he's solid gold.'

Jacqui nodded. 'Yes ma'am.'

'I'm sorry about that,' Nathan murmured when they were alone. He turned to the machine, busying himself with storing the data and logging off. 'Sonya and Brian are old friends. They lost a baby a couple of years ago at thirty-seven weeks after years of infertility. She's just really paranoid.'

Jacqueline could well imagine why. She heard the empathy in his voice and was curiously touched. 'That's awful, Nate.'

He nodded. It had been devastating for Sonya and Brian. And for him. He wiped off the probe head, and then used a sterile wipe to disinfect it for the next client while he waited for the computer system to shut down.

Jacqui waited, crossing her arms, staring at him. Waited for him to get it. Waited for him to realise that seeing Sonya, what he'd done for her today, had been the act of a truly caring physician.

Nathan looked at her. Her toffee gaze was watching him with a startling intensity. She raised an eyebrow at him.

'What?' he asked warily.

'You were great with her.'

Nathan shrugged. 'She just needed some reassurance.'

Jacqui waited some more. 'Don't you get it, Nate?'

He sighed. He really didn't have time to play games with her. They were very late for lunch, and there was an important meeting scheduled for this afternoon.

'You were great today—relaxed. You were your old self. For the first time since I've been back.'

He was still staring at her with a vacant expression, and she could tell the cogs of his brain were already spinning on to the next thing.

'Look at you, Nate, in these pictures. You look... *giddy.*'

She pointed to one where an older baby in a pink dress and a bow in her hair was reaching out for his face. He was looking at her with such wonder—as if she'd just told him the secret of life.

Nathan looked at the picture. Looked at all the photos surrounding it. They'd been fun times. There just wasn't time to fit it all in any more.

He looked at his watch. They really needed to get to the restaurant. 'What's your point?'

'Oh, Nate, isn't it obvious? That nagging feeling you talked about at lunch the other day? It's medicine.'

How could he look at these pictures and not see that?

'Look.' She pointed to the pictures. 'It's obvious in every one of them. And just now with Sonya. This is your calling. You want to know what's missing in your life?'

She crossed the small distance between them, picked up his stethoscope and draped it gently around his neck.

'Go be a doctor again.'

CHAPTER SIX

NATHAN pulled away, recoiling from her statement. 'No.'

Jacqui nodded. 'Yes, Nate. *Yes.*'

He pulled the stethoscope off his neck and slapped it down on the examination couch. 'Don't think because you're back in my life that you suddenly know me and what I want better than I do.'

Jacqui refused to be put off. 'I've always known you better than you, Nate.'

Nathan glared at her, ignoring the truth behind her words. 'I'm exactly where I want to be,' he said, walking away from her and her unsettling gaze.

'And yet you feel empty,' she said calmly to his re-treating back. 'Isn't that what you told me in Sydney?'

'Not empty,' he denied, shrugging into his jacket. 'I said something was missing.'

He turned to face her, sitting on the edge of his desk, his photo collage framing her nicely.

She pointed backwards at a point behind her head. 'Well, look no further. I think those pictures say it all, really.'

Nathan rolled his eyes. 'I'd defy anybody to not look happy when they've just helped a new life into the world, Jacqui. Witnessing other people's emotions, sharing such an intimate moment, is bound to bring out the grinning idiot in anyone. This has nothing to do with that. I think I'm old enough to know what I want, Jacqui. Old enough to know what makes me happy.'

Jacqui sighed. How could such an intelligent, successful man be so blind to the basics? 'And you really think a fully listed company on the stock exchange is going to do it? You can't rely on external stuff to bring you the inner contentment you seek. That has to come from inside—from being totally and completely comfortable with who you are.'

Nate rubbed his eyes. 'I am.'

Jacqui raised an eyebrow at him. 'Come on, Nate. Be honest with yourself.'

Nathan gripped the edge of the desk and felt the angle of his jaw tighten involuntarily. He pushed himself off and strode towards her, holding her gaze. 'Are you calling me a liar?'

Jacqui felt a wave of goosebumps march across her skin both at his nearness and at the sinister gravelly quality of his voice. But it was no time to back down. 'A little too close to the bone?'

God, he'd forgotten how stubborn she could be. How dogged. Never letting up, never letting him hide from anything. He shook his head. 'You're like a cracked record. I command a billion-dollar company. What else should I want?'

'I remember when just being a doctor was enough.'

'No, Jacq. No. It was never enough.' Nathan placed his hands on her shoulders. 'And if *you* were honest with *yourself*, you'd admit being a doctor was never enough for me. I always wanted more.'

Jacqueline searched his face, looking for a crack, a weakness, a sign of doubt. But there was none. His strong features were unflinchingly sure. And she had to at least concede that point to him. He'd always been driven, ambitious. She'd just fallen into the trap so many women fell into—hoping love could change a man.

'And now you have more has it made you happy, Nate? It's okay to reassess, you know. To say, *Hey, I was much happier when I was eating cold spaghetti out of a tin and doing something I really loved, that really fulfilled me.*'

Nathan gave her a grudging smile. He picked up a spiral lock and rubbed it across his fingertips. 'I hate cold spaghetti.'

Jacqui covered his hand with hers, stilling the sweet torture of his fingers brushing her neck. 'It's a metaphor.'

He was looking at her with such conviction. Utterly confident that all was well in his world. And it was so tempting to melt into his arms and leave him to his delusion. After all, she was only back in his life for a few more weeks and then she need never see him again,

And maybe if she hadn't seen those photos, or witnessed the magic of him with Sonya, she'd be able to do just that. But nothing he said would persuade her that he wasn't setting himself up for a fall.

'Oh, Nate,' she sighed. He was close, and his hands in her hair and on her shoulders were so tempting. She wanted to lay her head on his chest. Skim the flat of her palms up the front of his crisp white shirt and feel the shift of muscles. But would he thank her for leaving him to his illusion? 'You're wrong.'

Nathan dropped his arms. This was getting them precisely nowhere. They were never going to agree on this. They were polar opposites. Really, they always had been.

'We have to go,' he said, turning away, striding to the door.

Jacqui felt a hundred more arguments bubble to the surface. But he was once again all business. The warm, smiling doctor who had calmed a frightened patient was gone and the cold, austere businessman was once again standing before her.

'Fine,' she murmured, and followed him out.

Later in bed that night their lovemaking bordered on punishing. Nathan had been thinking all day about what she'd said, unable to erase it from his mind. He'd had a million things he should have been doing, should have been thinking about concerning the float, but instead he'd found himself looking deep inside, examining his motives.

He hated all that psychological claptrap. He remembered it vividly from the counselling he'd had after his father's suicide.

He'd spent the afternoon roaring at anyone who'd stuck their head around his door. By the time he'd crawled into bed at one a.m. he'd been tired and irritable.

Worse than that, Jacqui had been naked, the sheet half kicked off, and, despite his wanting to shake her, his body had betrayed what he really wanted to do. Still, it had not been his intention to act on it. He was an adult, capable of restraint. But as he'd lain beside her, her female aroma filling his senses, he'd itched to touch her. And when she'd rolled away from him he'd followed her on to her side, spooning her back.

Normally he woke her leisurely—stroking her hair, tracing the graceful arc of her spine, kissing her neck. But tonight he'd been in no mood for pleasantries. He'd reached for her breast and given a guttural grunt of satisfaction as the nipple had budded in his palm. He'd already been hard, and he'd nestled his erection against her cheeks.

Jacqui had come instantly awake—Nathan's aftershave and the other scent that made him exclusively Nate combining to lance her womb with hot, savage lust. She'd turned her head awkwardly, her hand snaking into the back of his hair, pulling his lips towards her, finding his mouth, meeting his hard kiss stroke for stroke.

She'd known on some base level that he was still angry with her, and hated that she wanted him so much his approach just didn't matter. And then his hand had moved from her breast to the heat between her legs, and it really hadn't mattered.

Nathan wasn't sure how long they lay panting in the dark afterwards, staring at the ceiling. All he knew was that it seemed like an age and yet his heart still hammered madly.

'I've been thinking about what you said today.'

Jacqui's pulse, which had been tripping along, suddenly slowed, coming perilously close to stopping. 'Really?'

Nathan nodded. 'You were right.'

Jacqui shifted slightly so she could look at his face—not that she could see it properly in the night shadows, just the strong outline of his jaw. 'Really?'

'I *am* missing something.'

Jacqui lay silently, waiting for the qualifier. 'Okay…?' she said tentatively when one wasn't forthcoming.

'I've worked my butt off for years. And I haven't taken my eyes off the prize. Not once. Not even to acknowledge that a part of me wasn't that thrilled with it all. That there was something missing from my life. Let's face it, I hardly do any real medicine these days. I go to work at my corporate office and I spend all day trying to make my company the best it can be—pushing papers around, talking with accountants and lawyers, stockmarket analysts and pharmaceutical directors, government ministers. I chair executive meetings and network my butt off, but deep down…' He rubbed his jaw. 'I don't feel…fulfilled.'

And suddenly he knew what it was he'd been missing from his life these past few years. The source of the nagging sense of disquiet. It was Jacqui.

'It's you. I'm missing you.'

Everything careened to a stop around her. Her breathing, her pulse, her vision. Even the air currents ground to a halt mid-swirl. Jacqui wondered if this was what it felt like to have a stroke. She gave a hesitant laugh.

'I'm serious.' And he was. It had taken him a while to figure it out, but now he had he didn't want to waste any more time. He didn't know the logistics of it all—he just knew he didn't want to see her walk away in a few weeks. 'What do you think?'

What did she think? Oh, God! She must have really rattled him today. 'I think you're letting great sex sweep you away into nostalgia land.'

He rolled up onto his elbow. 'It isn't about the sex.'

'And,' she continued, ignoring him, hoping that she sounded calm above a pulse that was thrumming so loudly through her ears she couldn't even hear herself speak, 'when you feel you're missing something it's only natural to want to reclaim something that worked for so long.'

'It can work again. We just need to commit.'

Jacqui rolled her eyes. Typical Y-chromosome, can-do attitude. Some things just didn't work—no matter how much you wanted them to. 'You can't give me what I want.'

He nodded. 'Yes, I can.'

Jacqui looked up into his face, shadowed by the night, softening the arrogance of his statement. She raised her hand to gently cup his jaw. 'Nate, you don't even know what I want.' She wasn't sure *she* knew any more.

'Yes, I do.'

Jacqui's heart was banging madly in her chest. 'Really? What is it, Nate? What *do* I want?'

'The same thing you've always wanted, Jacq. A baby. I can give you a baby.'

Jacqui drummed her fingers on the steering wheel as her hire car ate up the miles to Serendipity the next morning. She was so angry with Nathan it sat like a molten shard of hot metal in her chest, burning like acid, cutting like diamond.

She hadn't even been able to lie with him after his preposterous announcement—had fled to the guest-room, visions of a beach baby with pudgy arms and a strawberry-blonde fringe snapping at her heels.

I can give you a baby.

Just like that. As if he could walk into his lab and engineer one for her. Which was exactly, of course, what he *could* do. But how dared he use a baby as a commodity? A bargaining chip. Waggling it in front of her nose like a carrot.

Yes, discovering her infertility, knowing she'd never hold her own baby, had been one of her greatest laments, but she wasn't about to let him manipulate her or the life of an innocent child for his own advantage. To plug some hole in his barren billionaire existence!

But as angry as she was with Nathan, she was angrier with herself. Because driving in the opposite direction, driving away from him, hurt more. More than the insult of last night. It was time to face facts. She'd fallen for him all over again.

She banged her fist against the horn a few times in sheer frustration. *Stupid! Stupid! Stupid.*

She felt the prick of tears at the back of her eyes and bit her lip to beat them away. She would not shed tears over the stupidest thing she'd ever done. She deserved to be flogged for getting herself into this predicament again.

Although, if she was going for total honesty, she had to admit that she'd never really stopped loving him in the first place. She'd wanted to. Wanted to so much she'd convinced herself it was so.

Oh, sure, if anyone had asked her if she still loved

him she would have told them yes. But in that genteel, familiar way one might reserve for a comfy old jumper or a childhood teddy bear. Not this vibrant, alive, hell-this-is-going-to-hurt kind of way.

But spending time with him, falling prey to the same old chemistry, catching glimpses of the uni student she'd fallen in love with, had freed the full-throttle version from the vault she'd triple-locked it in all those years ago.

She groaned out loud. How could she? Not only fall for her ex, but fall for the grown-up version who was even further removed from her and what she wanted and needed and believed in than he'd been the first time round.

A man who had offered her a baby in exchange for her…company. No words of love or family. Just a cut-and-dried deal for a commodity he'd suddenly decided only she could provide.

Goddamn it! She should never have invited him in to her house that night. Should have slammed the door in his face and gone back to bed. Should have known he'd be trouble. With a capital T.

Shep greeted her at the door with as much exuberance as a twelve-year-old golden retriever with ageing hips could muster. She dropped to her knees, buried her face in his long white coat and promptly burst into tears.

'Oh, Shep, I've done something totally idiotic,' she murmured.

Shep whined and licked her face and Jacqui hugged him closer.

'Come on, boy,' she said after a few minutes, pulling herself out of the mire of self-pity. 'Let's go for a walk.'

Shep wagged his tail and gave an enthusiastic bark, and Jacqui laughed, ruffling his head.

They spent a lot of time together over the next two days. In fact Jacqui had a great time catching up with everyone. Word soon got out, and people from all around the district called in to the practice for a yarn— sick animal or not.

There was something soothing about being sur- rounded by people who loved her and work that fulfilled her. The ache in her chest was still there, but she was laughing. Living.

During the day, anyway.

But there was nothing to distract her during the long hours of the night. Not even her fury at Nathan helped with the acute loneliness. It had only been a few weeks, but she'd quickly grown used to sleeping with him again. Waking next to him. Being roused in the middle of the night by his touch at her hip, his lips on her neck.

Their years apart had lulled her into complacency over the potency of the feelings Nathan could arouse. And it was a wake-up call she wished she'd never had.

Lightning cracked across the sky late Saturday after- noon, and the roiling surf pounded angry fingers against the beach as Jacqueline made sure all the windows were closed. She could see the gnarled old trees along the shoreline bending like mere saplings. They were in for a hell of a storm.

The weather had been crazy for months now, and the ground was still boggy and the creeks and rivers still swollen from the deluge the weekend Nathan had forced his way back into her life. Roads and bridges had been washed away, property damaged, stock lost. Another soaking now would add to the area's woes.

When the storm finally hit, it didn't disappoint. It unleashed its fury in a swirling, seething, growling maelstrom. Heavy rain pelted down and Jacqui, for one, was pleased to be curled up in her lounge room with a cup of tea, a good book, and Shep warming her feet.

When the knock came half an hour later she went to investigate with an eerie sense of *déjà-vu*. Shep barked from the top of the stairs, wagging his tail as she opened the door.

To a grim-faced Nathan.

Jacqui's heart gave a huge *kerthump!* Nathan was here. He looked a little haggard, but at least he was dry this time, despite the deluge.

'What is it with the weather around here? If it keeps this up the bridge's going to go under again.'

Jacqui's grip tightened on the doorknob. He'd come to chat about the weather? 'What do you want, Nathan?'

'You've been avoiding my calls.'

The urge to hurl herself into his arms warred with the desire to slap his face. 'I told you in my note I'd be back tomorrow.'

'I came to make sure.' She was wearing her red cotton gown, and he doubted much underneath it, and the desire to touch her, to pull her close, was strong. But he had erred badly the other night, and she was glaring at him as if he was the enemy. Or at least as if she was going to slam the door in his face.

'There was no need.'

He took a step forward into the house, forcing her to take a step back. 'Humour me,' he said dryly.

Shep barked, and Nathan pushed past her, bounding up the stairs to greet the dog.

'Do come in,' Jacqui muttered.

He leaned forward to receive a sloppy smooch from Shep, and his faded blue jeans pulled interestingly across his butt. Her heart contracted. She followed him up the stairs, torn between devouring him with her gaze and beating her head against the wall. She really had it bad.

'Cup of tea?' Jacqui asked, sailing past him as he made himself at home on the very couch where he had lain naked a handful of weeks ago. Shep climbed up on the chair with his old master, and placed his head along Nathan's thigh.

Jacqui glared at him. *Bloody traitor. He left us*, she wanted to say. But the truth was they'd left each other.

Nathan grimaced. 'Got anything stronger?' He had things to say that required a beverage with a little more kick to it.

She escaped to the kitchen, pleased at the respite. *What the hell was he doing here?* Her brain turned the question over and over as she fixed herself another cup of tea and grabbed a beer from the fridge left over from a dinner party months before. She took a deep breath before heading back.

Nathan looked up from petting Shep as Jacqui re-entered the room. She passed him the beer and he cracked the top, taking a long, deep swallow. He watched as she settled herself on the chair opposite, then shut his eyes briefly. The thin cotton covering her didn't immunise him against what lay beneath. She looked as good as the cool beer sliding down his throat felt. But her toffee gaze was turbulent with emotion. She looked confused, wary, and mad as hell.

'Don't look at me like that, Jacq.'

Jacqui gave a disgusted half laugh. 'Like you've lost your mind?'

Nathan guessed he deserved that. 'I owe you an explanation.'

Jacqui's eyebrows just about hit her hairline. 'You think?'

He sighed. 'You're angry.'

'Damn right I'm angry, Nathan. I mean, who do you think you are? Got a few billion dollars and you think you can buy anyone? Well, I'm not for sale, Nate.'

Nathan shook his head vehemently. 'No. It wasn't like that. The last few weeks have been great. Really, really great, and I was lying there with you and I suddenly realised that I missed you. Really missed you.'

Jacqueline slammed the mug down. 'So you offered me a *baby*?' she practically shrieked.

'Okay, yes,' he agreed, holding out his hands in a placatory gesture. 'I handled that badly. I spoke without really thinking it through. I just couldn't bear the thought of you leaving in a couple of weeks, so I guess I wanted to offer you a deal you couldn't say no to. But I have thought about it since. A lot.'

God knew, he'd been unable to think of anything else since she'd run from his bed and refused to talk to him. And when he had come home the next afternoon to an empty house he'd been devastated. 'I have missed you, Jacqui. I was just too busy in my rush to the top to admit it.'

He stopped and looked at her, knowing she'd been one of the casualties of his single-minded drive to succeed. His beautiful Jacqueline, with the crazy hair and the bangles and the big toffee eyes.

'Oh, poor Nathan. Poor little rich boy,' she said frostily. 'Do you think giving me a baby is going to appease your empty existence?'

Nathan shut his eyes—boy, was she steamed. He opened them again. 'I'm sorry. It was clumsy of me. But...' He stopped again, hoping to broach the subject more delicately this time. 'Why not, Jacq? I know you want a baby. Always have. I'm a fertility doctor with a chain of clinics worldwide. I can do this for you. There was so much I couldn't give you when we were together. But I can give you this. Let me.'

Jacqui snorted. He was acting as if it was a diamond ring or an expensive dress. He just didn't get it. He hadn't back then, and it seemed a decade and several billion dollars hadn't wised him up. 'I never wanted anything but you, Nate.'

Nathan shook his head. 'Yes, you did. You wanted a baby.'

She rubbed her brow, her bangles jangling. '*Your* baby, Nathan. Not just *a* baby. Yours.'

Nathan swallowed as his male pride swelled and rose in his chest, his throat. The thought of her belly pregnant with his child pierced his heart with a savage arrow of possession.

'It's not that I didn't want to have a child with you, Jacqui. I just wanted to wait.'

'Wait? Till what? Your first million? Billion? Till you floated your company? What? What the hell were you waiting for?' Despite herself she felt a huge well of emotion rise in her chest and tears stung her eyes. 'I was right there, Nate. For years.'

Available. Eager. Some would even have said desperate. And now, when they were estranged, nearly divorced, now he wanted a baby?

Nathan shrugged. Truthfully, he didn't know where he'd thought the end point would be. All he knew was that now he was where he'd always wanted to be—on the verge of his ultimate goal—his life had never felt emptier. Less complete. Making a career out of helping make other people's baby dreams a reality had suddenly seemed to magnify the barrenness of his own life.

'I'm ready now.'

Jacqui shook her head at his supreme arrogance. This from the man whose company was just about to go public? When would he even have the time? Was he ready, or did he just hate to lose? To have his plans thwarted?

'You want this with all your heart, do you?' she demanded. 'You want it so bad that you'd give up every penny just to hold your child in your arms?'

Jacqui could see Nathan recoil from the suggestion, the tentacles of his past holding him firmly in their grip.

'Because that's what I demand. At least if you're going to have a baby with me, that is,' she continued. 'I'm not going to take some kind of arrogant offer from a man who's going to be too busy building an empire to spend time with his kid. Or do you not want anything to do with this child at all other than providing the sperm? You're okay with being a stranger to your kid like your father was to you?'

Nathan felt her barb pierce the centre of his chest, and sucked in a breath at how deep it tore. 'Damn it, Jacqui!' he growled. He would never wish the torment of knowing it wasn't loved on an innocent child. 'Of course I want to be there for my child. And you. I want a reconciliation for real. To live together for real. I want to be a family.'

It was Jacqui's turn to feel the tear of the barb. How many years had she yearned to hear those words coming from his mouth? And he offered them up now in some half-baked, ill-thought-out plan. Because his life was empty. Because billions of dollars weren't enough.

He hadn't even mentioned love. Had he become that arrogant, that cynical, that detached he could contemplate being a family without love? It hurt. It hurt a lot.

'You're not going to use me to paper over the cracks, Nathan. And I won't let you use a child, either.'

Nathan studied her intently, his heart crashing in his chest as his grand plans slipped slowly out of his grasp. She returned his gaze unflinchingly. Her chin had a proud tilt; her toffee eyes were deceptively hard. How could she stand there, vulnerable in so many ways, and yet seem so resolute under the glare he knew had brought grown men to their knees?

More importantly, how could he convince her that it wasn't some whim? That he really wanted this?

CHAPTER SEVEN

'JACQUI—'

A loud banging on the door interrupted him. Nathan frowned as Shep roused himself half-heartedly from his slumber.

'Is it common practice to have people knocking on your door on dark and stormy nights?'

Jacqui rose, pleased with the respite from this heart-breaking conversation. 'Lately, yes.'

He preceded her down the stairs, opening the door to reveal one very soaked man holding what appeared to be another man in his arms. Beyond the stranger, a car idled, parked at a crazy angle, its lights on, its doors open.

'Jimbo? Is that you?' Jacqui asked, flying down the remaining stairs.

The man nodded. 'Think this young fella's not well, Jacqui.'

Jacqui didn't ask questions. Country men weren't prone to exaggeration. If Jim Owen thought the kid was crook then she'd bet her last cent he was right. 'Bring him through, Jimbo,' she said, leading him into the clinic with Nathan following close behind.

Jacqui took them past her reception area and into a medium-sized room that looked like a theatre to Nathan, and helped Jimbo place his load on the central table. He looked like a kid—probably not even twenty. And 'not well' was a very accurate description. He looked pale and listless. He groaned.

'Isn't that Ross Earnshaw's boy?' Jacqui frowned. She'd been to his eighteenth birthday party a few months ago.

'Yup. Jeremy,' Jimbo replied.

'What happened?' Nathan demanded, searching for the kid's carotid pulse while Jacqui applied an oxygen mask to his still, ashen face.

'He skidded off the road in front of me and rammed into a tree. Stupid kid, driving too fast for the conditions. Anyway, I helped him out, and he said he was fine. He'd been wearing a seatbelt and he hadn't banged his head. We tried to get his car back up on the road for a bit, but it was pretty boggy, and then he kind of half collapsed against me and said he had a lot of pain. I was going to drive him to the hospital at Wongaree, but a few minutes into the journey he started to look real pasty and drifted off. No mobile reception to ring an ambulance, and you were only ten minutes away.'

Jacqui absorbed the information as she switched on a monitor, ripped open the soaked shirt, and hooked Jeremy up to it. It was the first time she'd ever used it on a human.

'Jeremy? Jeremy!' she called, giving the boy a brisk sternal rub. 'Can you hear me?'

Jeremy moaned and opened his eyes, clutching at his side. 'Cold,' he murmured.

Nathan followed the path of the subcutaneous petechial haemorrhaging across the boy's belly, where the seatbelt had obviously left its mark. 'Can you remember what happened, Jeremy?' Nathan butted in.

'Accident,' he muttered. 'It hurts.'

Nathan palpated over the area Jeremy was guarding and the teenager cried out. Nathan looked at Jacqui. Was she also thinking possible splenic or other abdominal injury from the seatbelt? His gaze flicked to the monitor. Tachycardic at one hundred and twenty.

'Spleen?' Jacqui asked, their earlier argument forgotten amidst the seriousness of the drama being played out in her veterinary theatre.

'Could be.'

She pointed behind him. 'Ultrasound help?'

Nathan looked over his shoulder at the machine. It was like manna from heaven. He looked back at her. She'd secured her curls in a hasty ponytail and was chewing anxiously on her bottom lip. He smiled at her. 'You bet.'

She smiled back at him, and the adrenaline surging through his system spiked.

'Let's get a couple of IVs into him first and get him warm. We'll have a quick look with the ultrasound, and then arrange to get him the hell out of here to a primary care facility.'

Jacqui agreed with his razor-sharp assessment. 'Jimbo, can you go upstairs to my linen cupboard and grab some blankets? Nathan, I'll stick a large bore in this arm; you can do that side.'

'Don't suppose you also have a blood pressure cuff amongst that lot?' Nathan asked, indicating the monitor equipment.

''Fraid not—don't really use them on animals. But I do have a manual cuff that I bought after Timmy Marshall's grandmother had an MI in my waiting room.'

Nathan stared at her nonplussed for a moment. He'd missed out on so much of her life. Her stories. But now really wasn't the time to go there. He smiled. Despite the gravity of the situation, working with Jacqui was exhilarating. He hadn't felt this alive in a very long time.

'God bless Timmy Marshall's granny.'

Nathan inserted his IV while Jacqui retrieved the sphygmomanometer and took a quick BP.

'Ninety over forty,' she said. Borderline. She wasted no time inserting another large-bore IV into the crook of Jeremy's elbow.

Nathan whistled. 'And on a human too.'

'Shut up,' she said, her voice bordering on affection as she handed him some of the synthetic plasma expander Wongaree hospital regularly supplied her with.

Within two minutes Jeremy had two IVs running wide open and was cocooned in blankets. They fired up the ultrasound and Jacqui watched as Nathan ran the transducer through the jelly he'd squeezed on Jeremy's abdomen. She squinted at the fuzzy screen, looking for evidence of any free fluid.

'Hard to tell,' Nathan mused. 'Nothing obvious. Don't suppose you've got a CAT scanner hidden somewhere?'

Jacqui rolled her eyes. 'Sorry.' Her gaze flicked to the

monitor. 'Heart-rate settling at one hundred. He's responding well to the fluid bolus.'

Nathan placed the transducer back in its place and strode to the wall phone as Jacqui pumped up the blood pressure cuff one more time.

'One hundred systolic,' she told him.

Nathan repeated the figure to the emergency call taker and she watched surreptitiously as he gave a succinct summary of Jeremy's condition.

Nathan replaced the receiver. 'Ambulance is on its way. ETA twenty minutes.'

Jacqui hadn't realised how on edge she'd been until help was at hand. All they had to do was keep him warm, monitor him and keep his vitals stable, and then Jeremy would be whisked away.

Animals she could handle. Humans were a whole other proposition. Thank God Nathan was here.

'So he's going to be okay, then?' asked Jimbo, who had been hovering in the background.

'He's stable at the moment.' Nathan nodded.

Jeremy groaned again, and Jimbo said, 'He seems to be in a bit of pain. Surely you've got something here you can give him, Jacqui?'

Jacqui shook her head. 'We don't want to give him anything in case it masks a deterioration in his condition, Jim. When the ambulance gets here, they'll give him something.'

Nathan smiled at Jacqui's answer as Jeremy groaned one more time. He hoped the pain was coming from soft tissue damage, and not blood oozing into his abdomen from a hole somewhere.

THE BILLIONAIRE CLAIMS HIS WIFE

Jacqui took advantage of the lull to get out of her red gown and into some theatre greens. They watched Jeremy for the next fifteen minutes. He seemed settled, but with five minutes to go his heart-rate accelerated again and Nathan was concerned that his abdomen had become more tense.

Jacqui watched with growing disquiet. His vitals were slipping. Her heart-rate climbed incrementally with Jeremy's, and she prayed the ambulance was only a few minutes away. They should be able to hear the sirens any minute now.

The phone rang. Nathan snatched it off the wall. Jacqui heard the one-sided conversation with dismay. The ambulance wasn't coming.

'The bridge is under, isn't it?' she asked as Nathan replaced the receiver.

He nodded. 'And they can't send a helicopter out in this storm. I'm afraid we're stuck here for a while.'

Jacqui looked at him. She'd expected to see the same fear in his eyes that had a stranglehold on her gut, but it wasn't there. He oozed confidence, authority.

She swallowed. 'He's deteriorating.'

Nathan looked at the monitor. Heart-rate one-thirty. He raised an eyebrow at Jacqui as she finished another BP.

'Seventy systolic.'

Yes, he was deteriorating. Yes, he'd bet every one of his billions that Jeremy was haemorrhaging internally. How much blood the boy had already lost, where it was coming from and how fast, he couldn't know for sure.

'Let's run some more colloid in,' Nathan said.

It restored Jeremy's flagging circulation transiently,

but his condition continued to deteriorate as the storm continued to rage.

'What's your operative set-up here?'

Jacqui was actually trembling inside now. There was no doubt in her mind that Jeremy needed exploratory abdominal surgery—but here? In her veterinary theatre? 'I do minor ops only. The most complex I do is spaying. I have a ventilator, suction, diathermy and some basic instrument sets.'

Nathan nodded, his brain leaping ahead. 'I think we need to go in. Would you be happy to do anaesthetic and assist?'

'Sure,' she said, hoping she sounded much more confident than she felt. 'You'll have to help me with doses.'

'What have you got?'

'I use Thio for induction and Isoflurane during.'

Nathan examined Jeremy's increasingly rigid abdomen. 'Good. Let's go.'

For a second Jacqui just stared at him. But his confidence was inspiring, and she found herself responding automatically.

'Jimbo, you've done a first aid course, haven't you?'

Jimbo swallowed, looking from one to the other. 'Er, yes…'

'Good. We're going to need your help.'

Fifteen minutes later Jacqui had successfully intubated her first human since university practice sessions. She'd hooked him up to the ventilator, and was watching as Nathan made a mid-abdominal incision. Jimbo had been given a crash course in assisting a surgeon, helping Nathan prep the patient in sterile green drapes, and had been entrusted with monitoring Jeremy's blood pressure.

Nathan's hand was rock-steady as he made the incision. There wasn't a single moment of self-doubt. The only operations he'd performed in over a decade were fertility related or C-sections, but it was as if he'd never left his surgical residency.

Jacqui angled the metallic sucker to slurp away the excess blood, and he headed straight for the spleen. The number one cause for ruptured spleens was motor vehicle accidents, usually seatbelt related, and his gut told him this was Jeremy's Achilles' heel. One look at the severely ruptured organ confirmed his suspicions, and his fingers moved rapidly to do what he needed to do.

First priority was to fasten the splenic artery and achieve haemostasis, which Nathan managed in good time. He saw an almost instantaneous stabilising in Jeremy's vitals. His heart rate dropped to one hundred, his blood pressure climbed to one hundred and ten systolic, and Nathan took his first deep breath. It took him a further thirty minutes to remove the mangled spleen altogether.

'You going to see if anything else is damaged?' Jacqui asked, peering inside the abdomen.

Nathan looked down at her. 'Let's do a saline lavage, and we'll see if any blood wells up from anywhere.'

It had been a long time since Jacqui had seen Nathan in a mask, and she'd forgotten the impact of his eyes. She'd always adored them, but the green of the mask emphasised the green of his irises, and there was a glint to them that gave them an almost supernatural glow. The result was dazzling.

She dragged her gaze away and concentrated on the open abdomen. After a minute, satisfied that no further bleeding appeared to be coming from anywhere, and with Jeremy's systolic blood pressure improving all the time, Nathan closed the wound in layers. Forty-five minutes after they began, they were done.

Nathan degloved, pulled his hat off and his mask down, and swept Jacqui into a tight embrace. 'Oh, my God, Jacq!' He picked her up and swung her around, letting out a mighty whoop. 'That was amazing!'

Jacqui laughed, feeling more relief than exhilaration.

Nathan pulled back. 'We make a good team.'

Her heart contracted. She loved him more now than she ever had. 'Thanks, but I think I'll stick to animals.'

If only Nathan didn't look as happy as a pig in mud.

The chopper was finally able to land on the beach an hour later, and Nathan accompanied Jeremy back to the Gold Coast, putting an end to any hope he had of continuing their conversation.

Jacqui returned the next day too, as promised, for the lead-up to the float. Thanks to a very grateful Ross Earnshaw word had leaked out, and by the time Jacqui set foot back in Nathan's apartment it was plastered all over the news. And the press went crazy!

The story of Dr Nathan Trent, billionaire doctor, performing an emergency splenectomy on a dark and rainy night in his wife's country veterinarian surgery had captured the imagination of the nation. Jimbo and

Jeremy and the entire Serendipity community were bathed in the white-hot glare of publicity, and the story grew more grandiose every day.

Suddenly Nathan wasn't just fabulously wealthy and extraordinarily sexy, but he was an honest-to-God Aussie hero to boot. And Jacqueline was catapulted into the limelight with him.

She'd been able to keep their 'reconciliation' reasonably contained within the business community until now, but suddenly it was impossible. In the days that followed they were photographed, stalked by media whenever they stepped out of Q1, and endlessly speculated over on radio talkback and current affairs shows. Magazines and television stations wanted to interview her. She had requests for 'happy couple' pictorials from all the nation's glossies.

It made her feel like a fraud. But there was no time to think or talk as the crazy week hurtled past. No time for reflection. There was only time to keep her head above water, smile for the cameras until her face hurt, murmur appropriately vague answers to incessant questions, and pray she didn't sink like a stone to the bottom of the very murky waters they were treading.

And all the while her heart ached.

Nathan was out till late every night at his office, tending to last minute business before the big float. And she'd moved back into the guest bedroom, so the opportunity to talk to him about his insane baby proposal or what had happened in her surgery before he'd been whisked away with Jeremy in the retrieval chopper never arose.

But she knew he'd felt it again that night. The pull inside him that tugged at his soul. That demanded to be heard. She'd seen it shining in his eyes. A vibrancy. He hadn't looked as if something was missing as he had hugged her goodbye and run towards the chopper. He'd looked alive.

She suspected he welcomed this frantic week so he could avoid the topic altogether. She'd bet her last cent that underneath all his efficient businessman bluster he was running scared. Ever since she'd known him he'd been on a direct path to the top, and she knew he wouldn't welcome any feelings, no matter how vague, that rattled his gilded cage.

And then float day arrived, and TrentFertility shares were the hottest debut stock the market had seen in decades. They were snapped up like hot cakes. The recent phenomenal media exposure Nathan had attracted was better than anything he could have bought. He'd endeared himself to both the business sector and the Australian public, winning both their affection and their confidence, and they all wanted a share of him.

The security of the company he'd built up and nurtured over the last decade was most definitely assured. In the end he hadn't even needed the respectability Vince brought to the board—he'd earned the respect all by himself.

Jacqui and Nathan got home late to the apartment that night, after a celebratory dinner with the Trent-Fertility executive board. It was the first moment they'd had alone since the previous weekend.

Nathan's gaze fell on Jacqui's bags, sitting just inside the door.

'You're leaving.'

Jacqui shut her eyes as the warmth from his body behind hers, so very, very close, almost touching but not quite, wrapped her in an embrace. He'd been in his element tonight. Larger than life, filthy rich and sexier than anyone had a right to be. He'd made every other man in the restaurant fade into the background.

'Yes.'

Nathan hesitated. She was so close. If he inched forward they'd be touching. But she'd never felt further away. 'I thought you were going to stay on for another week or so?'

Jacqui opened her eyes. 'You don't need me, Nate. TrentFertility shares are an overnight success.'

To hell with the shares! She was wrong. Dead wrong. He'd always needed her. He loved her.

Hell, he loved her.

He stilled momentarily. Man! What a stupid, blind idiot he'd been! He loved her. He just hadn't realised it until her case was packed and she was set to walk out the door again. He'd been angry at himself *and* her when she'd fled to Serendipity for those few days, but now the thought of her leaving—for good—gripped him in a cold panic, chilling him to the bone.

He'd thought something was building between them again. That they'd recaptured some of their magic. But he hadn't suspected it was love. His heart crashed in his chest. Everything depended on what he said next. And he doubted, given her tense stature, that a declaration of love was the right strategy. He was likely to get it thrown back in his face. She would see it as a desperate ploy instead of what it was. The truth.

He cleared his throat. 'You were right.'

Jacqui frowned. Right about what? 'Really?'

Nathan could bear her back no longer, and gently placed his hands on her shoulders, applying enough pressure to turn her to face him. His breath caught in his throat.

God, she was beautiful. 'I miss medicine. I miss being a doctor.'

All week he'd been searching his office for the same exhilaration that he'd found during his operation to remove Jeremy's spleen. The thrill, the utter elation of helping another human being. Saving a life. The same thrill he'd always felt when catching a wet newborn or telling an infertile couple they were pregnant.

And when he hadn't found it he'd pushed himself a bit more. Stayed later, worked harder. God knew there'd been enough to keep him occupied. But no matter how long he'd sat at his desk, how many nights this week he'd crawled into bed exhausted for a few measly hours' sleep, the emptiness had persisted.

It was past time to admit defeat. Jacqui was right. He was a doctor. First and foremost a doctor. Sure, he could play at being a businessman, but it was never going to fill the gaping hole that had been steadily deepening over the years as he'd tried to be something he wasn't—tried to live his father's dream.

And if he could finally admit it to himself, he could certainly admit it to the woman he loved. The woman who had opened his eyes. Made him look into himself. Kept at him, not letting him hide inside his comfort zone.

And maybe it was the key to making her see that he had changed. That he was worth sticking around for.

Jacqui blinked, stunned by his admission. She opened her mouth to say something—anything. But nothing came out. He looked overwhelmingly hand-some in his business suit, with the knot of his tie loosened and pulled to one side. She dragged her gaze from the broadness of his shoulders, and from carnal thoughts of how good they looked without the suit.

'I realised this week at work. It's been such an intense week—full-on. And I hated it. It used to be thrilling. It used to be heady.'

Jacqui smiled. Maybe he was finally getting it. 'Like it was the other night,' she said quietly. 'With Jeremy.'

Nathan nodded. She looked so damn calm, with that I-told-you-so gleam warming her toffee gaze. It wasn't right that he should want to kiss her this badly when she'd been right and he'd been a blind fool. When she was walking away. Again.

'Like it was with Jeremy. Yes.' He accepted his judge-ment had been in error with complete humility. 'I felt energised, I knew what I was doing, and it was exciting and exhilarating. I felt…complete. I felt whole.'

Jacqui knew she should be grinning like a crazy woman. Wasn't this what she'd been saying to him all along? He'd finally given in to his destiny. But, con-trarily, she wanted him to say that *she* completed him. That *she* made him whole. As he did her.

It hurt so much inside right at that moment that she

had no idea where she dredged up the huge smile that split her face. It must have come from the deep, dark depths of her utterly joyless soul, but it arrived at the appropriate time and she was grateful.

'Oh, Nate,' she said, grasping his lapels in a familiar gesture that almost broke her heart. 'Are you sure?'

He nodded. 'I've never been surer of anything in my life. I mean, it's going to take me a while to step back from the business side of things, and I'll have to juggle both for a while until I can appoint a CEO, but I know what I want now.'

And it's not just medicine.

'That's wonderful news. So wonderful.'

She hugged him then, tight, her arms sliding beneath his jacket, her face pressed into his neck. She was desperate for his warmth, to inhale the very essence of him that made him the man she loved. He put his arms around her shoulders and hugged back, and she never wanted to leave this spot. Never.

They broke apart slightly and it was inevitable that he kissed her. In fact she wasn't sure who kissed who. All she knew was that his mouth opened wide over hers and she accommodated him. It was deep and wet and sexy. Greedy, and getting faster and harder, more desperate. And when he groaned against her lips her belly clenched as if he'd stroked her.

It was the kind of kiss that melted clothes and inhibitions as if they were trifling details. She thrust her hands into his hair and pulled him closer, deeper. Wanting all of him, needing to feel him tremble, lose control a little as she was.

Damn, the man could kiss.

Nathan felt as if he was losing his mind. How could she kiss him like this and still want to leave? She tasted like wild raspberries. She smelled like woman. Her breasts were squashed against his chest and he could feel the rub of her body against his burgeoning erection. He wanted to crush her against him, sheath himself inside her, never let her go.

He broke away, holding on to the one slim thread of sanity that was left. He searched her turbulent gaze. She was beautiful tonight. The crazy retro gown that she'd bought from a local op shop had outshone all the designer labels at the restaurant. Her crazy corkscrew curls framed her face and her lips glistened with clear stuff that emphasised their fullness and tasted like forbidden fruit.

He placed his forehead against hers. His palms cradled her face. 'Stay with me,' he groaned, his breath ragged, his pulse echoing through his head. 'I love you.'

Jacqui's head spun as she clung to his lapels. Her limbs were heavy, laden with desire, her brain was fogged with lust. She was breathing hard, trying to compute what he'd just said at the same time as wanting his lips back on hers.

He loved her? *What?* Oh, God, this was madness. All they were doing was torturing each other. It had to stop.

She took a couple of deep calming breaths and slid her hands from his lapels to grasp his wrists. 'Nate.'

'Jacq.' He could hear the huskiness as his breathing took its own time to settle.

She pulled gently on his wrists, and was gratified

when he dropped his hands and took a step back. She needed space. They both did.

'I think one revelation is enough for tonight, don't you?'

Nathan placed his hands in his trouser pockets lest he reach for her again. *Damn it!* He'd known it was too early. But what the hell? It was out there now. 'No.'

Despite herself, Jacqui felt her heartbeat trip at the utter arrogance of his statement. His unflinching green gaze looked at her with frank sexual hunger. She swallowed.

'It's been a day of highs. You've just made a big decision about the entire direction of your life, Nate. One sweeping change at a time, huh?'

The thought that he actually might love her wheedled its way past her sensibilities. She quashed it before it burgeoned out of control, before she took the two very tempting paces it would take to be back in his arms. He was mistaking desire for love. Lust for something more. He was high on the day's successes and the night's revelations and their crazy, mixed-up, tangled sexual chemistry was just confusing the issue.

After all, if he loved her as he claimed why had he said that medicine completed him? Surely if he loved her then *she* would have that honour? Be the other half of his whole? He was certainly her half. And she wouldn't take anything less. She couldn't get involved with him again knowing that his job—even the right job—meant more to him than her. She'd been down that road before.

Nathan took a moment to gather his thoughts—a little difficult when all his blood was stubbornly stuck down yonder. He'd got carried away with the moment, with that mouth. He needed to take it back a step or two.

'Come with me. I want to show you something.'

Jacqueline looked at his outstretched hand and blinked at the abrupt request. 'I have to go.'

'Please, Jacq. It won't take long.'

She shut her eyes at the way his voice sighed her nickname. His gaze was roving over her as if he had X-ray vision. Her skin tingled in the wake of those knowing green eyes. Where did he want to take her? And what did he have in mind?

She knew exactly where they'd end up if she went with him now. But she had the rest of her life to be sensible. To be alone. Tonight she needed to be with her man in the most carnal way possible. To say goodbye.

She took his hand. 'Okay.'

'What are we doing here?' she asked as Nathan pulled the car up in his space at Paradise Private Hospital ten minutes later.

Nathan's heart thudded in anticipation. This was his last ace. 'I told you. I want to show you something.'

Jacqui sat motionless for a few seconds, looking out of the window. And then he was opening her door and ushering her out, and before she knew it they were standing in the middle of his office, where she had watched him with Sonya that fateful day.

'What are we doing here?' she repeated.

Nathan shrugged. He wasn't sure why he'd brought her here—he'd just gone with his gut. Maybe he felt more comfortable with her here in a hospital, as a doctor, than he did in a business suit in his sixtieth-floor apartment. This was the man she knew him as—the man she saw underneath the billionaire veneer and through the mists of ten years' separation.

The man she'd fallen in love with.

'Just wanted to get a feel for it again, I suppose.'

He wandered around his office, his desk, touching things. He shrugged out of his jacket and discarded it on the back of his chair. He picked up his stethoscope and loved the feel of the heavy bell in the palm of his hand. He stopped in front of his examination couch and looked at the pictures on the corkboard.

All those satisfied customers, all those happy families. Couldn't he have that too? Was that too much to ask?

'I wasn't totally honest tonight, Jacq.'

Jacqueline leaned against his desk, watching the pull of white cotton across his broad back and the way his hair just brushed the collar. 'Oh?'

He turned. 'Medicine doesn't complete me.'

She frowned. *Okay.* Where was he going with this? 'Oh?' she said again, a slight squeak heightening her reply.

'I'm nothing without you.'

Despite everything, her heart leapt as if it had been prodded with a defib paddle.

'I love you. I don't think I ever stopped loving you. I don't want you to go.'

She clutched the desk and reminded herself to keep her head. One of them had to be the voice of sanity.

'I was a fool to let you walk. A fool not to see that you were the best thing that ever happened to me. I'm so very sorry I wasted a decade of our lives chasing a dream that wasn't even mine.'

Jacqui swallowed, her heart nearly blowing a hole in her chest, it was beating so forcefully. 'Nate. This is insane. It's too late. We've been apart for too long.'

'But I've never stopped thinking about you, Jacq. You were always there at the back of my head, with your bangles and your crazy hair. Why do you think I went into fertility?'

Jacqui snorted. 'Because of the squillions of dollars?'

Nathan chuckled. 'No. Plastic surgery is where the big bucks are. I went into it because of you.'

Jacqui shook her head. This whole thing was insane. She wouldn't let him sweet-talk her when she was about to go back to her life. One that she loved. 'Oh, come on, Nate. Bet if I had chronic psoriasis you wouldn't have become a dermatologist.'

He gave her a gentle smile. 'I remember all those months too, Jacq. The negative tests, the arrival of your period, the investigations. I know how much it devastated you.'

'You didn't want a baby. Not like I did.'

He nodded. 'No. But I do now. With you.'

The whole room seem to narrow down to a tunnel. One that was big enough for the two of them and nothing else. And the air was thick. Tense. Jacqui wanted to believe him, wanted to let it all go, but it just seemed too easy. And nothing between them had ever been easy.

'Why?'

Nathan held his breath for a second. He could see she was wavering. Maybe there was hope. Maybe she still loved him too. He turned back to the board and unpinned a photo at random. He walked towards her with it and handed it to her.

'There's a lot of years there on that board, a lot of babies. Other people's babies.'

He looked down at the photo he'd given her. He was standing behind a lounge chair, where a set of new parents were looking down adoringly at a swaddled infant with such rapture it seemed almost too intimate a moment to capture.

'I'm tired of nursing other people's babies, Jacq. Of helping to bring them into the world. I want my own baby. I want to see my baby growing inside the belly of the woman I love.' He stopped and placed a hand on Jacqui's stomach. 'I want to look at something that we created with that same wonder and awe, like we've just received a rare precious gift. Is it so unbelievable that I'd want to share my life with someone?'

Jacqui felt hot tears sting her eyes as she looked at the photos, felt his hand on her belly. She couldn't believe what she was hearing. The only thing she'd ever wanted more than Nathan was his child. A tear ran down her face and splashed on the photo.

'Hey.' Nathan lifted her chin gently and looked down into her blurry toffee gaze.

'It may never happen. I already have documented fertility issues. I'm older. It'll be so much harder.'

Nathan felt his heart soar. Was that a yes? Was she taking a step towards him? 'Lucky for you, I know this great fertility specialist.'

Jacqui laughed, dislodging more tears down her face.

She shut her eyes as Nathan wiped them away with his thumbs. Then she opened them again. 'I mean it, Nate.'

'So then we'll adopt, or we'll foster, or we'll get a surrogate. Whatever it takes, Jacqui. I love you. Whatever it takes. I want this.' He pointed to the photo.

Jacqui looked at it too. That was all she'd ever wanted. To be a family with the man she loved. She'd never dared hope that it was all there for the taking. 'But—'

'Shh,' Nathan interrupted, placing his fingers across her mouth, sensing her doubts. 'It's got nothing to do with misplaced nostalgia, or being on some high over the float, or the decisions I've made tonight. I don't ever want you to leave my side again. My life has been so empty without you. I just didn't realise it till you came back and filled it again.'

Jacqui looked up into his face. It was open and earnest and she believed him. Hadn't there been an emptiness in *her* life that no amount of country living had ever been able to fill?

'And I'll eat organic bacon and drink organic coffee, even though it tastes like dirt, and I'll grow to love mung beans and dress in hemp suits and worship the solstice. Whatever it takes, Jacqui.'

Jacqui laughed and sobbed at the same time. 'I don't know what to say,' she whispered.

'Oh, God, Jacq. *I love you too* would be good.'

She laughed through the tears that still shone in her eyes. 'Oh, Nate.' She leaned forward and kissed him. Once. Twice. Three times. 'Of course I love you. I don't think I ever stopped.'

Nathan kissed her back. A sweet kiss full of joy and

celebration. He broke off. 'And you want to reconcile and have babies with me?'

Jacqui sighed. 'I want to have many, many babies with you. Can we start now?'

Nathan laughed against her mouth. 'I think we should. How do you feel about office desks?'

She looked behind her. 'Well, they're kind of hard,' she said, knocking on the wood. 'But sort of kinky.'

'Kinky's good,' he said, and then forgot everything as Jacqui yanked him by the lapels and dragged him to her for a kiss that was hot and wild and exceedingly impatient.

'No. Wait,' he said, pulling back, fighting for control of his neurons as well as his breath. 'What about your practice? Shouldn't we talk about that?'

Jacqui shook her head. 'I'll sell it and buy something here. I don't care where I live any more, as long as I'm with you.'

'Oh. Good.' He grinned at her for a moment, then zeroed in on her mouth for another wild ride into bliss.

'Shep,' Jacqui said, just as Nathan's mouth brushed hers. She frowned at him. 'He can't live in a high-rise. He needs land. Rabbits to chase. Butterflies.'

'I'll get us a house,' he murmured. 'On an acreage.' He dropped a light kiss at the corner of her mouth. 'I'll stock it with rabbits. And butterflies.'

Jacqui smiled. 'See? We're already better at this the second time round.'

He grinned back at her. 'Lady, you can have whatever you want. Just don't ever leave me again, okay?'

Jacqui sobered. 'No way, Nathan Trent. You're mine. Mine for life.'

And she gave him a kiss full of love and longing and promise.

Which he returned with gusto.

* * * * *

Inherited by the Billionaire

JENNIE ADAMS

Australian author **Jennie Adams** grew up in a
rambling farmhouse surrounded by books, and by
people who loved reading them. She decided at a
young age to be a writer, but it took many years
and a lot of scenic detours before she sat down to
pen her first romance novel. Jennie has worked
in a number of careers and voluntary positions,
including transcription typist and pre-school
assistant. She is the proud mother of three
fabulous adult children and makes her home in
a small inland city in New South Wales. In her
leisure time Jennie loves long, rambling walks,
discovering new music, starting knitting projects
that she rarely finishes, chatting with friends, trips
to the movies, and new dining experiences.

Jennie loves to hear from her readers, and can be
contacted via her website at www.jennieadams.
net.

Don't miss Jennie Adams's new book,
***Australian Boss: Diamond Ring*,**
coming in February 2010 from
Mills & Boon® Romance.

Dear Reader,

Do you remember being young and in love for the first time ever? The ecstasy and agony, the deep, deep feelings and hopes and dreams, uncertainties and insecurities. Does he love me the same way? What will happen if I tell him? I want his kisses and to be with him, spend time with him... Can I trust my feelings? Can I trust his?

In real life, sometimes that first love is all too quickly gone and forgotten. For Callie Humbold, Gideon Deveraux has been hard to forget, even if he did push her away the moment she tried to confess her feelings. But she was only young, and it was just a crush.

Wasn't it?

Of course it was! Now Callie is all grown up, and in charge of a successful guesthouse on an island off Australia's Victoria coast. She has an unconventional marriage to organise for Gideon's equally unconventional aunt, and Gideon is here to try to put a stop to the marriage – and Callie's plans to go on running the guesthouse after his aunt moves off the island.

Men and their hearts keep all of us dreaming, don't they? When we find one who is guarded, or doesn't believe he knows how to give and receive deep love and yet we can see the potential in him – well, that's a story maybe best told by our Callie herself. I'll let you be the judge of Gideon's potential...

I hope you enjoy this story. Maybe it will bring back some memories of your first love, too.

Love and hugs from Australia,

Jennie

For a very special 'you'. Deeper than the
ocean, wider than the sky, more enduring
than forever. But you know that...

CHAPTER ONE

'ONCE I've touched base with my aunt and with my…'

Ward? Inherited package of trouble? The first term was outdated, and not accurate; the second was more to the point. Callie Humbold was a pert, opinionated, spunky, sweet-natured, gorgeous, annoying bundle of uncontrollable youthful femininity. She had given Gideon Deveraux more than his share of headaches in the time he'd known her and ultimately felt responsible for her.

Gideon had sent Callie to his aunt seven years ago, to give himself distance from those headaches. And for other reasons that had to do with one night out of time and a lack of control and judgement on his part. But that was old news now. He didn't know why the thought had even come to him.

Because Callie was on his mind right now, he supposed. But his focus was on the obligation he felt towards her.

He'd played an almost big-brother role to her during the time her uncle had worked as the groundskeeper on his family's outer Melbourne estate. Reid had asked him to keep an eye on the boisterous girl during her childhood.

Then Gideon had saved Reid's life, when Callie was twelve years old, and the older man had put his own unique twist on 'a life for a life' and put Callie even further into Gideon's safekeeping.

It had come as no surprise, really, when Reid had died a few years later and willed the responsibility for Callie in Gideon's direction—a moral obligation more than a legally based one.

But Gideon wouldn't have been able to leave her to her own devices when Reid Humbold died anyway. She'd barely turned eighteen, and Gideon's parents hadn't exactly been going to care about or even notice her needs.

Gideon had made promises of his own at that time. To Dianna. He'd been about to get married and thus fulfil his family's nice, tidy, unemotional expectations for carrying on the Deveraux standing in society with a wife of equally acceptable status.

'Once you've touched base with your...?' The woman at his side raised her brows with just the right amount of polite, businesslike interest.

Thirty years old, career-focused, whipcord-thin and oozing determination from her pores, Heather Stiller would be the perfect new manager at the island guest house.

'With my aunt and my ward,' Gideon finally finished. He braced his feet on the jetty and lifted his and Heather's travel bags into one hand. His yacht's skipper had already turned around the small boat Gideon had purchased to get him here and left them to it.

'Nothing much to see, Mr Deveraux. Wish I could have brought you in your usual style, in one of your *real* seagoing craft…'

Those had been the man's parting comments. And there *wasn't* a whole lot to see.

One tiny windswept island off Australia's Victoria coast. One guest house being run on that tiny island by Gideon's hippy aunt Mary—the scandal of the Deveraux family, as far as his parents were concerned, because she'd been born on 'the wrong side of the blanket'. *Not* a socially acceptable thing for the Deveraux family!

His family had refused to officially acknowledge Mary, in any way. Years ago Gideon had tried to address that fact with Mary on one of her rare visits to the family estate to see 'her favourite nephew'. Actually he was her only nephew, and she had pushed her way past his parents for those visits.

That day she'd patted his hand and told him she had the guest house to run on her wild little island. If he wanted to make her happy, she'd said, he could take it over so she was renting it from him and not his parents.

Gideon's business dealings had taken him from the status of inherited millionaire to self-made billionaire. So he'd bought the island and everything on it, set things in place to make sure Mary was safe and secure there, and then he'd got on with his own interests.

Mary had somehow drifted out of his life. And then he'd put Callie into his aunt's hands.

He should have checked on Mary more often—made the effort to come out here before now. Should maybe have checked on Callie in person, too, once she was here.

He'd been certain Mary would look after Callie, and it had seemed better for him to stay away.

Gideon gestured to the coastal track ahead. 'The guest house is only a couple of minutes' walk from here, Heather. Once I've spoken with Mary and... Callandra, I'll show you around so you can get a feel for the work you'll be doing here.'

Gideon had a wedding to attend—his aunt's. It might be nice to know something about the groom before then! And he had a new manager to instal in his aunt's island guest house—the woman now standing at his side, glancing around her in proprietorial fashion.

And Gideon had Callandra Humbold to sort out, too. Just to be sure Callie had a secure future ahead of her. He owed Reid's memory that much at least.

'It's not a very large island, is it?' The woman he'd chosen to replace his aunt Mary fell into step beside him.

A brisk wind battered at them, whipped Heather's shoulder-length brown hair about her narrow, intense face. It was February—the end of summer. Not cold here, but blustery.

Heather went on. 'I don't imagine there's much in the way of entertainment, but I can tolerate such conditions for the sake of furthering my career.'

'Yes...' Gideon wasn't really listening. His attention was fixed ahead, beyond the wild shore to the left, beyond the wild battered trees and shrubs to the right, to the guest house perched on a rise.

For all that the place hadn't made a profit for years, it appeared Mary had finally used some of his generous allowance to keep it in good order. He would put things on a better business footing now he had a non-family member to place into the management role, of course.

A figure dressed in green dungarees and a bright orange T-shirt, with a ponytail of matching orange hair, emerged from a shed carrying a bucket. She had a purposeful expression on her pixie face and she glowed with energy and vitality.

It was Callandra. But not the young girl he remembered. There was maturity in her face that hadn't been there seven years ago—a womanliness about her that was unmistakable. She'd grown up. He'd known she would have, but somehow seeing the evidence of that…

Callie scrunched up her face and examined the contents of the bucket in her hand before she squared her shoulders and started along the path. A memory of her face tipped up, the freckles across the bridge of her nose standing out as she glared at him, flashed through Gideon's mind and for a moment froze him to the spot. God, they'd had some arguments.

And then they'd stopped arguing, and somehow there'd been that night that had led to him shipping Callie out to Mary…

Not relevant, Deveraux. But he did have to talk to Callie. He had to at least know what her plans were for the future—that she *had* plans and wasn't going to be left out on a limb by Mary marrying and moving away from the island.

Gideon could ensure Callie employment here, of course. But under his new management she wouldn't have the freedom for long walks on the beach and the other ac-

tivities that seemed to be all Mary had to tell him about
Callie when he did occasionally phone in to check on her.

His aunt could be vague. Indeed, Mary hadn't even
asked Gideon to provide a replacement manager here,
or mentioned Callie's future.

Gideon felt an odd stab of something in the centre of
his chest that might have been guilt. For sending Callie
away seven years ago, and for pushing her to the back
of his mind so thoroughly once he'd done that.

'That's your ward?'

'She was, unofficially, when she was younger—yes.'
How much had Callie changed? She'd been full of
inexplicable dreams and notions back then. Did she still
have that wide-eyed outlook on life that he'd found so
touching, even when it had driven him mad?

'Would you excuse me, Heather?' Gideon wanted to
catch Callandra before she got too far away. 'Perhaps
you'd like to take a look at the grounds for a few minutes
while I speak with my—with Callie.'

The woman at his side nodded her agreement.

Gideon fixed his gaze on a retreating back with a set
of slender shoulders, the bucket swinging wildly from
her hand and wisps of carroty hair escaping the bobbing
ponytail, and picked up his pace.

Crab whispering might be an unconventional pastime,
but it was popular with the guests. If Callie Humbold
wanted to continue the fine tradition of her midnight
crab whispering tours once this weekend was over, she
needed to keep her exoskeleton friends happy between
now and then.

Which meant drawing them out to feed them, whether the guest house was abuzz with pre-wedding activity or not. Callie hefted the bucket with renewed determination.

'Callandra? Will you hold up a moment? I'd like to talk to you.'

The words, spoken in a firm, masculine, oh-so-familiar tone brought her to a standstill while her heart did all sorts of unwelcome flip-flops in her chest.

'You didn't reply to your invitation,' she said with a snap.

Great, Callie. Start with an accusation and the conversation can deteriorate from there.

Why did he always manage to make her feel either defensive or offensive? Never anything in between?

Oh? Could that be because he was always putting you on the defensive? Or, more to the point, because the last time you saw him you were deeply embarrassed because you'd naïvely tried to seduce him and he had just wanted you gone before his fiancée got there?

Yes, the whole episode had hugely embarrassed her—especially Gideon trying to gently push her away…

But that had been seven years ago. Surely he'd have forgotten all about it in the intervening time?

'I—Mary didn't think you were coming.' Callie swung around, bucket and all, to face the man who'd banished her to his aunt's island after that episode. He'd gone on to get married. And, yes, Callie had been hurt about that.

A little. Barely at all, really. And only because she'd been young and naïve and hadn't understood how he

could want only the right social ties, someone to look
good on his arm, in a way Callie, with her lack of any
kind of social *anything*, never could have done. He
hadn't wanted love. That had been the most inexplicable
part to her. And she'd come so close to offering it to him.
Well, in a young girl 'crush' sense.

The worldly prince and the foolish gardener's niece?
It might cut it as a fairy tale, but not as reality.

Callie drew a deep breath and schooled her face to
show nothing of those thoughts. They were old news
anyway.

'I wasn't expecting you.' Good. That was good. It
covered her unguarded initial response. 'That is, Mary
and I weren't expecting you—but I'm sure Mary will
be very pleased you've come for her wedding. She's not
here right now, but I'm expecting her back later today.'

'I only got the invitation yesterday.' He wrapped
long, lean fingers around slender male hips. Elbows
out, strong chin tipped upwards, dark blue eyes
watching her through dusky lashes. 'I've been overseas
on business.'

'Speaking with your Italian art buyer.' Callie nodded
her head before she could stop herself.

When he simply looked askance at her, Callie felt
compelled to explain.

'The last time you phoned you told Mary that was
what you might be doing.' Callie didn't hang on every
piece of information about Gideon. Mary just liked to
tell her the news. That was all.

'The worldwide galleries are proving to be an en-
joyable enterprise,' Gideon said, as though they were

simply one more means of occupying himself and investing his billions.

And no doubt that was exactly the case.

Callie looked up into his face. Gideon stood at six foot two inches tall. He had an entire head and most of his shoulders on her in height. His jet-black hair was a little longer than she remembered. His face, if anything, looked even more attractive than it had. The fine lines at the corners of his eyes added character, and somehow that character reflected his strength as a man.

So—fine. He was a man, and he was powerful, wealthy and influential. A man women would swoon over, and did.

Callie was equally as strong as him. The twists and turns of her life had left her with no choice *but* to be that way. Gideon sending her to Mary had simply been more of the same, and she certainly wasn't about to swoon over him right now.

Been there, done that. Had the embarrassment and rejection to prove it.

She'd been immature at the time—hadn't understood. She'd misread brotherly affection for desire and, worse, for love.

The desire she'd had a taste of, when he'd reacted without thinking. Before he'd remembered who he was with. The rest didn't even count, anyway.

Callie tipped up *her* chin. 'At least you're here. Your parents weren't "available" to attend the wedding, so you're it for Mary's family. It's a shame she won't be here very long to enjoy you. She and Mac leave for their honeymoon straight after the wedding tomorrow.'

'Where does that leave you?'

He seemed concerned about her answer. Yet it was an odd kind of question, wasn't it?

'It leaves me right here. Life as usual. Surely Mary mentioned that in her invitation?'

'My aunt didn't even manage to mention the name of her prospective groom.' Gideon chopped a hand through the air. 'Are you saying you're happy to remain here, working under the new guest house manager?'

What did he mean, the *new* guest house manager? 'I'll *be* the guest house manager.'

It had been her role for the past five years. Callie had no desire to change that now. And as for Mary omitting Mac's name from the invitation—there was only one reason Gideon's aunt would have done that.

Actually, there are forty-seven reasons, and they're all booked into the guest house for the weekend. But Mac has been completely open about all of it, and provided we keep the wedding private there won't be any problem. The family's really quite tame these days, anyway, apparently...

'Mac and Mary plan to live a low-key life after this. *Very* low key.'

As in totally out of the limelight and unnoticed.

Gideon nodded, though his expression suggested he wasn't entirely sure of the reason for her vigorous statement.

'I guess that's up to them. But about your future...' Gideon's brows drew down. 'Do we have our wires crossed somehow? Do you mean you plan to *assist* the new manager?'

'I mean I've been doing the job—'

A woman strolled through the gardens beyond Gideon. Quite a way back, because Callie had been halfway along the track that led to the cove by the time Gideon hailed her.

The new manager Gideon had mentioned? He'd already made his plans and now intended simply to put them in motion?

For the first time concern filtered through other emotions and got a chokehold on Callie.

Gideon *could* do that—get rid of her and replace her with someone else. He owned the entire island and everything on it. Callie had just assumed he'd allow her to go on running the guest house. She'd been doing a good job of it, turning better and better profits each year. She didn't want to leave.

Panic threatened. Callie tried to ignore it.

'When will my aunt be back?' Gideon rammed a hand through his hair. 'Soon, I hope? It appears I need to speak with her, about a few things.'

Yes. Mac and the family and the wedding. Callie suppressed a sigh.

Gideon started to stride back towards the guest house.

Callie wanted to keep him away from there, to wait until Mary returned and leave his aunt to sort all that out with him. But she didn't have the luxury of choice. And if they were going in, she wanted to get her words in about her job *first*.

'I don't want to leave your replacement manager jobless, Gideon, but I've had the role of manager here for five years. I've done well in it, and the guest house is more profitable than it's been for years. You can't simply push me out of the role.' Well, he could, but… 'There are fair and reasonable rules about that sort of thing.'

That was what mattered right now—ensuring her job was secure. Not memories of the past.

Yet Gideon's gaze had swung to hers, and amongst the confusion in his eyes was the memory she had thought he might not have held onto. Of that night when she'd gone to his detached apartment on the family estate and they'd kissed. Her young heart had been on her sleeve until Dianna had arrived and Gideon hadn't been able to get rid of Callie fast enough.

She hadn't known Dianna even existed as anything more than a contact in Gideon's wide circle of glitzy, upper-class associates. It showed her naïveté at that time that she would have assumed he *wasn't* with someone.

'Mary has always been the guest house manager.' Gideon stated this with a frown on his face as shields came down over his eyes, hiding his thoughts from her as he'd finally hidden them that night.

'Your aunt trained me into the position.'

Callie pushed the thoughts of the past away as best she could. It wasn't easy. Not when that brief expression in Gideon's eyes had stirred both memories and senses. Oh, how she hated that it was so!

'I know the work. Your aunt has taught me the business from the ground up. I've taken that knowledge and developed my skills further to make the guest house the most profitable and viable it's been in all the time Mary's had it. *I* achieved that, Gideon. And I want to remain here and continue in the role of guest house manager.'

What she didn't want was to revisit the past. Not in her thinking, and certainly not in a stirring of old awareness.

Her words had shocked him. That fact was in his eyes.

'But I've been propping the business up financially for years,' he said slowly.

'Apparently you've thought that to be the case, but in fact that 'prop-up' money is untouched. Your finance manager should have told you.' Callie hefted the bucket in her hands. 'Now I really have to do this job at the cove. If you'll excuse me…'

Maybe if she walked away, took care of her small task and came back, everything would have miraculously fixed itself. Callie sighed.

'I'll come with you.' He eased the bucket from her hands, glanced into it.

'There's no need. I can do this myself.' She didn't want to end up explaining her crab whispering to Gideon on top of all the other issues she had to face with him right now. Good manager material would not conduct midnight crab whisperer tours—but they worked for her, and they worked for the guest house's clientele.

Callie reached for the bucket to take it back and go on her way, ignoring the fact he would still be here when she returned from feeding her 'pets'. She needed just a few minutes' break—a chance to regroup.

'Why don't you and your…guest check in while I do this? You're lucky. Rooms twelve and eighteen are still available. They're the only ones we have left.' What else could she do but invite both of them to stay? 'Take the keys for those and I'll talk to you later—'

Instead of the bucket handle, her fingers had closed

over Gideon's hand. That contact—that simple, ordinary, shouldn't-have-done-a-thing-to-her contact—sent twinges through her that shouldn't exist.

They had to be echo twinges. Past twinges. Seven years ago twinges. They were not current twinges, because she was not going there again with that old silliness about him. It had been a crush!

'Really, Gideon. Thanks for the offer, but I need to do this by myself.'

Callie wasn't cutting and running. She simply needed to go and do this. By herself. Just for a few minutes before she came back and faced introducing him to MacKay and his family. Before she met the woman he'd brought to the island to replace her as manager of her beloved guest house.

Well, Callie wasn't giving up that position.

She regained ownership of the bucket and stomped away along the path.

CHAPTER TWO

GIDEON gave Callie the space she so clearly wanted. While he did so, he used his mobile phone to contact his finance manager. What he learned from the man was still in his mind as Callie rinsed out her bucket, stored it in the shed beside the guest house and rather reluctantly moved towards him and Heather, where they stood several feet from the guest house's open front doors.

Gideon finished his second phone call and turned to the woman who had travelled to the island with him.

'Heather, I'm afraid there's been a misunderstanding about this position.' Gideon quietly explained the situation. 'Callandra has been running the guest house herself for several years now. I didn't realise that, and I'm assured she's been doing a very good job. I can't let her go in these circumstances.'

He took a deep breath. 'I've recalled our boat. My skipper will have it here within the hour, so you can return to Melbourne with him. You'll be reimbursed for your time, and I'll arrange a meeting with you once I'm back in Melbourne myself. We'll sort out an alternative position for you.'

'Something as good as this? With the advantages of being on an island and autonomous as manager—?' The woman cut her words off, but it was clear she wasn't happy. Her gaze narrowed, and a hard expression crossed her face before she masked it behind a blank smile. 'Well, I'll hold you to that discussion.'

Callie joined them then, and he made the introductions. 'Callandra, this is Heather Stiller. Heather, meet Callandra Humbold.'

'I won't be staying.' Heather bent to retrieve her travel bag. 'In fact, I think I'd prefer to wait at the jetty— if you'll both excuse me?'

She walked away purposefully and had her mobile phone at her ear before she was halfway gone. Calling a friend to complain about her treatment, perhaps?

Gideon didn't have time to think about the woman's abrupt leavetaking. He would straighten things out with her when he returned to Melbourne.

For now, he turned to Callie. 'I just spoke with my finance manager.' How did he explain that he had ignored all reports on the guest house's progress, preferring not to let himself think about the waif of a girl who had tempted him almost beyond his commitment to marry Dianna? That marriage had foundered two years ago, but that was hardly the point.

Gideon *couldn't* explain it—other than to put that night down to an unexpected burst of sexual attraction on his part, and a sweet but childish foolishness on Callie's. Yet he still felt it now—that edge of conscious-

ness of Callie that had been birthed when she'd set out
so naïvely to try and seduce him.

Being attracted to her was the last thing he'd wanted
to feel. Back then Callie had been too young, and he'd
been about to get married. Now he was divorced. Dianna
had taken her nice tidy financial settlement and moved
in with the even tidier minor prince of a struggling prin-
cipality on the other side of the world. A social step
upwards. Given his own family's attitude, and their expectations in relation to social standing, how could he
blame Dianna for that?

After their separation Gideon had got on with his life
without much of a ripple. Callie, on the other hand, was
a ripples kind of girl. A girl who would fall madly in
love—not want to see financial statements and a family
tree back five generations before she committed herself.
Gideon wasn't a ripples man. And he'd been taught
from the cradle that financial statements, and the content
thereof, were right up there with the Holy Grail.

'The management position here is yours, Callie, for
as long as you want it and as long as it's working out.'
That was what he needed to say. Callie's secure future
was all he needed to think about. 'I only needed to
know you weren't being left out in the cold, and since
you're not—'

'I'm nicely tidied away once again?' Her words were
flippant, throwaway. The expression in her eyes before
she glanced away belied that flippancy, but then a burst
of noise came from inside the guest house and she
turned her head.

Gideon followed the direction of her gaze just in

time to see a middle-aged man step out through the front doors. He walked straight towards them.

'Callie?' The man had a deep voice, and a face that was somehow familiar to Gideon. 'Is this Mary's nephew? He's made it for the wedding after all?'

'Yes, actually. Isn't that wonderful?' Callie stepped forward with a strained smile.

Because of her conversation with Gideon? He'd let the replacement manager go. Callie's job was secure. So what was worrying her?

Gideon examined the tall, middle-aged man with blond hair and grey eyes and plenty of life stamped into the deep grooves of his face. Puzzle pieces began to click into place.

Callie paused and drew a deep breath. 'MacKay Jones, I'd like you to meet Gideon Deveraux. Gideon, this is Mary's fiancé.'

Gideon's brows snapped down. There might be more than one MacKay Jones in Australia, of course, but Gideon now understood the sense of familiarity. He'd seen this man's face splashed across the newspapers and on the TV news. It had been years ago. MacKay was the head of a well-known family—and not in a good way…

Gideon's gaze swung to Callie's face.

Her chin lifted and she directed a stare at him. One that warned him.

What? Not to ask what his aunt was doing, marrying a notorious white-collar criminal? The eldest of a family of four brothers who'd cost Australia's economy enormous amounts of money because of the crimes they'd committed? They'd got away with it over decades, until they were finally caught. They had all been incarcerated for those crimes in the 1990s. MacKay would have been behind bars for at least a decade.

And Mary wanted to *marry* this man? Marry into that history? Put herself in the hands of someone like that?

'I recognise the name.' From the corner of his eye Gideon caught movement across the guest house's garden grounds. A guest, no doubt. A MacKay guest? Were there a lot of MacKay guests here? Even more potential for trouble? 'Not that I saw it on the invitation,' Gideon murmured, while his mind examined the possibilities and he tried to comprehend why Mary would have aligned herself with this man. 'Mary hand-scribbled it on a piece of pink paper and conveniently left out—'

'Mary invited her favourite nephew to her wedding because she wanted you to be present for an occasion that means a lot to her.' MacKay Jones spoke mildly, but his eyes narrowed. 'As far as I'm concerned, that's the only fact that's relevant here.'

There was a protectiveness in this man towards his future bride that Gideon couldn't miss, and he didn't quite know what to make of that other than its meaning that if Gideon felt he needed to pull Mary out of this situation—even with his power and his money—doing so could potentially a) be difficult, and b) have ramifications. What sort of man was he dealing with?

Gideon wanted information—knowledge so he could work out how best to manage this unexpected turn of events. He hefted his travel bag in his hand.

'Perhaps I could dump this somewhere and we could have a chat, Callandra? Catch up about a few things.'

They needed to do that now even more than before. When Mary returned Gideon would need to speak with her as well. But for now, he had questions for Callie. 'In the manager's office?'

'I have responsibilities—things I need to do.'

The old familiar gleam of defiance was in Callie's eyes. A mixture of anger and…and feeling trapped, as though her power over making her own decisions was under threat. Why hadn't he seen that in her before?

'Callie—'

'There's nothing to speak about anyway, Gideon.' She glanced at MacKay Jones, and this time, despite the worry in the backs of her eyes, it was clear that she, too, felt affection for this man his aunt must obviously love.

A daughterly kind of affection.

The sort that might blind her to keeping herself safe?

'Please.' Gideon glanced at MacKay and then locked his gaze with Callie's big green eyes. 'I really don't feel I can take no for an answer on this right now.'

Callie dithered for several seconds before she finally gave in. 'Fine. It'll be a waste of time, but we'll talk. At least by doing that I can pave the way, so Mary doesn't have to—'

She stopped herself, but the same thoughts were in Gideon's mind. Mary had disappeared today in case he'd decided to show up. That way she wouldn't have to be the one to confront her nephew when he arrived and discovered just who she intended to marry.

Callie glanced at MacKay once more. 'Mac, will you keep going with the wedding preparations for me? This won't take long.'

The man hesitated. Not because he didn't want to do the work, Gideon imagined, but because he wasn't sure he wanted Callie fighting any battles on his behalf.

MacKay frowned in Gideon's direction. 'It might be better if Gideon and *I* speak.'

'Not this time.' Callie said it gently, before Gideon could say anything at all. She rested a hand on the older man's wiry arm and gently met his gaze. 'Please, Mac?'

After a moment MacKay dipped his head. 'All right. But I'll be here if you need me.'

'I know you will.' Callie touched his arm again as she passed him.

Gideon followed her as she veered not towards any office area but outside.

They got as far as the beach before he broke the silence. 'Do you have some kind of objection to speaking inside? In the office?' The sand beneath their feet made soft crunching sounds as he asked his question.

Callie shrugged one shoulder. 'Mary always says things discussed in the outdoors are easier to resolve. I thought you'd like it. *You* had a beach wedding…'

'Dianna's idea. It made her look good in the society pages.'

'I'm sorry she left you, Gideon.' Her expression held empathy, concern for him, and questions he could read as clearly as if she had spoken them aloud.

Had he managed to fall for Dianna during their marriage? Or had he still seen her as an accessory to his life and goals, nothing more?

If the former, Callie would be disappointed in him. If the latter…he wasn't sure what she would think.

She went on. 'I hope that it didn't hurt you too much when it happened?'

This much was clear. Her sincerity was obvious. The almost wounded expression that quickly came and went in the backs of her eyes was less so.

She dropped her gaze away from his. 'Sorry. I forgot for a moment that it was never about that for you. It was only about suitability.'

'That's right.' He hadn't been hurt, and yet, looking into her eyes, now he ached in ways he couldn't explain.

Callie kicked at a clump of damp sand with her foot.

He thought she murmured, 'So why did it hurt me so much at the time?' but he wasn't certain.

Gideon wondered how the conversation had turned into this territory anyway. He forced it back—because that was better for both of them. 'We need to speak about Mary and this man.'

'About a wedding that's going to make two people very much in love even happier?' Callie's chin tipped up to a challenging angle.

'Will my aunt be happy if her safety is in danger with MacKay Jones?' Maybe it hadn't been all that wise to put Callie into Mary's hands. At the time he'd thought it would be best for Callie.

It had been best. Callie was happy here. That was what mattered. Mary did check in and make sure you knew that, even if you didn't often respond to her messages.

Yes, but what about now?

'Mary adores Mac.' Callie spoke the words to Gideon with conviction. She had to make Gideon see this and accept it. The sooner the better. Yes, Mac had a criminal record. Yes, he'd done some dubious things in his past. But the Mac she and Mary knew was a wonderful man, and Gideon was going to have to accept that.

Callie searched Gideon's face and her heart ached. He didn't understand about Mac and Mary's love. *Because he's not capable of loving like that, and he was certainly never going to love a young girl like that.*

It had hurt so much when Gideon married Dianna. Callie had spent that day wandering all over the island and trying not to think about him—about how he had rejected the offer of her heart and chosen an emotionless match with Dianna instead.

Callie cut off the thoughts. They were the height of silliness anyway. She'd been a baby—hadn't known her mind, let alone her heart!

Crush. It had been a *crush*.

'MacKay Jones has spent years of his life in jail.' Gideon's brows drew down.

Callie forced her attention back to the conversation. This was about Mac and Mary, not her and Gideon. Not that there *was* any 'her and Gideon'. There never had been.

And there she went again. Thinking about things she didn't need to think about.

'Mac has spent years since then being integrated into society. Quietly, it's true, but he's a well-adjusted model citizen.'

'Maybe that's true in terms of how the public sees him, but what about his private life? Jail is a hard place, Callie. Even if he went in there a gentleman, I don't believe it would have been possible for him to remain one over that period of time.'

Enough of his concern came through that Callie softened a little and joined the dots on what Gideon wasn't saying.

'You think he might harm Mary?' This was something that had crossed Callie's mind, too—but only until she knew Mac. 'It won't happen. He adores her, and he *is* still a gentleman. In all the ways that count.'

Gideon searched her gaze for a long moment. 'I wish I could put my faith in that.'

'You can.' Callie brushed sand off the cuffs of her dungarees. They were too long, and she should probably have rolled them up a little before she started walking.

Better still, she should get back to work now, and put all these silly resurrected thoughts about Gideon right out of her mind.

'All the rest of this aside, the guest house is busy at the moment. MacKay has almost fifty of his relatives here for the wedding, and though they're all working to help prepare everything I'm still needed for all sorts of things. I don't have a lot of spare time right now. There's nothing really to discuss. The wedding is happening. End of story. And it's not your place to investigate him, either—just in case you had that in mind.'

Oh, yes, she had worked out Gideon would want to do that, and the expression in his eyes right now confirmed her suspicion.

'It's my place to protect my aunt if she needs to be protected.' Gideon sucked up a slow breath and blew it out again. 'And please tell me none of those guests are MacKay Jones's notorious brothers.'

'Of course they're his brothers. And his cousins and his uncles, and all their partners, wives and significant others. None of them are *that* notorious. Not any more, anyway.'

Callie clamped her teeth together. She lifted her face and let the sea wind blow through her hair and across her cheeks, whip at her clothing and blow some of her stress away.

'Mac's family have come from all over Australia to be here for this wedding.' That had to count for something.

'A wedding I am truly not at all convinced is in Mary's best interests—whether you feel resolved about it, or not. What is my aunt *doing*, Callandra?' His tone sharpened. 'And what were *you* thinking, to let things come to this and not tell me?'

'How do you know it was me? Just because I introduced—' She cut the words off.

'Actually, I didn't mean that, but I might have known *you'd* have brought them together. Let me guess. You picked MacKay up as a stray, somehow, and thought he needed to be loved and accepted. Next thing he and Mary were interested in each other.' He turned his head to stare out to sea, as though he might find calm in the tossing of the waves.

Callie felt more like the tossing itself. 'Mac is a nice man.' In Callie's opinion he was one of the best. 'And he's not a stray.'

Were strays so bad, anyway? *She'd* been one—handed to an uncle who hadn't been quite sure what to do with her when her mother died. 'I got talking to Mac on a tram in Melbourne one day and he offered me a coffee. Since I was meeting Mary after we did our separate shopping, I agreed.'

'I didn't know—were you in Melbourne often?'

Apparently he hadn't ever imagined her there. Callie wasn't sure how she felt about that. She had certainly thought of *him* there—had always watched and wondered if their paths would cross. Though she had refused to do anything to try to instigate that.

He'd banished her, after all. She had to have *some* pride.

'As surprising as it might be to you, I do have a social life that includes trips to Melbourne. Dates, outings.'

Mary had always insisted Callie take time off at weekends on a rotational basis for this reason. But Callie gave up on that topic now. Something told her she really didn't want to go there with Gideon, who was suddenly looking quite fierce and disapproving.

Whatever was *that* all about?

'Mary and Mac love each other.' This was what she needed to focus on. 'Whatever his past, he is a good and kind man now and as far as I'm concerned if he makes her happy that's all that matters.'

Gideon stopped on the crunchy sand, turning to face her so she had to stop, too. 'You can't tell me he's some run-of-the-mill, mild, trustworthy nice guy, Callie.'

'A conventional good guy? Does he *have* to be perfect to love Mary and be all that she needs?'

She opened her mouth to try to explain that it didn't matter. That when a man loved a woman, or a woman loved a man, it just *was*. Callie somehow *knew* this, deep inside her soul. She hadn't ever loved like that, of course. No doubt she'd merely sensed it, as a result of her observation of others—like Mary and Mac.

A little rush of emotion clogged her throat and she had to swallow it back.

You're just getting overly sentimental because there's a wedding in the air, Callie. And that's perfectly normal and to be expected.

'Mary got to know Mac. And he loves her. He's very sincere.' Callie forced the words out over that stubborn lump in her throat. It wasn't about her and Gideon. It was *not*! 'For Mary, any possible perils don't matter anyway, because she loves Mac *that much*.'

'And what about the rest of the family? How can you know *they're* all trustworthy?' Gideon's words were all about the current situation, and yet his gaze lingered on her with a focus that was about more than that.

Why did he have to do that? Look at her as though she was the only person he *wanted* to look at? It wasn't fair. Anything else aside, it didn't help her equilibrium at all!

'I'm sure MacKay and Mary are perfectly—'

'What if one of them harmed *you*?'

He bit down on the words but his gaze didn't lose its concerned, protective edge. And whether it was old-fashioned of her or not, Callie softened to the concept of him wanting to *protect* her.

That's a dangerous way to respond, Callie Humbold.

Gideon went on. 'What if they harmed you or Mary, I mean? The possibilities are endless. Attempts to extort money from the Deveraux family, bad press, bad behaviour, bad associations any of them have formed—'

'We've taken care to keep their marriage plans secret.' Callie could at least assure him of this. 'We gave most of the guest house staff this weekend off the island. The family all understand the need for discretion, and the remaining staff are completely trustworthy.' Callie hesitated. 'I assume Heather Stiller—?'

'She's gone.' On a boat back to the mainland by now. Or, if not, his skipper would collect her soon. Gideon hadn't thought to watch for the boat's arrival. 'She doesn't know the bridegroom's identity anyway.' He frowned. 'That's not the point. You're vulnerable here if anything ever—'

'It won't.' Callie hadn't found it *entirely* easy to have the MacKay brothers and all their extended family arrive *en masse*. But they seemed like reasonable people, mostly. If somewhat rough and ready at times...

No. This was all going to be fine. Mary knew what she was doing, and Callie must trust in Gideon's aunt's judgment.

Right. Callie drew a stabilising breath. 'Try to understand, Gideon, there's nothing to worry about.'

'I understand perfectly.' Gideon's face took on an implacable set. 'Mary's allowed herself to be taken in by some airy-fairy feeling that she's in love with the man and it's blinded her to everything else. That kind of attitude is dangerous.'

That was what Gideon *would* say, wasn't it? Never mind that there'd once been another person who'd thought herself in love. Never mind that Callie had softened to him moments earlier. *This* was the real Gideon. She needed to remember that.

He was kind when he rejected you, Callie. And you can't judge him for being worried now.

They'd retraced their steps along the beach during their discussion. Callie turned to Gideon. 'Promise me you'll simply enjoy this wedding—support your aunt in it and be happy for her?' Maybe if she kept emotion out of her request she would get somewhere with it. Maybe if she resolved this she would stop thinking about the rest.

But Gideon didn't give her what she needed. Instead, he shook his head. 'Callie, I can't—'

'Callie?' Mac called her name from the front steps of the guest house and the moment was fully lost. 'The decorations have been delivered for the gazebo. I got them to leave the boxes there, but there's a bit of a crisis going on in the kitchen at the moment. Do you have time to take care of the delivery?'

Callie sucked back a sigh.

'Absolutely.'

She waved Mac back with a determined smile, and turned towards the gazebo perched high above the beach on a knoll.

Before she started in that direction, she turned to the man at her side and tried one last time. 'Your promise, Gideon. If you can't give it to me, maybe you should get on a boat out of here as well.'

'I'm not leaving.' Gideon fell into step beside her as she walked towards the gazebo. 'I'm not going any-where until I've spoken with my aunt. If she needs talking out of this marriage, I'll do it. For *her* sake.' He hesitated, frowned, then added, 'And for yours. You may not be a child any more, but I still feel a sense of responsibility for your welfare.'

CHAPTER THREE

'MARY should be back quite soon, so you'll get your chance to talk to her.'

Callie flung herself into the task of unpacking the first box of supplies in the gazebo. She couldn't really be cross with Gideon when even in his immovable state he showed that he cared for her and for his aunt. It just would have been better if Mary had been here to speak with him!

'Had Mary planned for long to go into Melbourne today?' Gideon moved in to help Callie unpack as he waited for her to answer his question.

Callie turned with her hands full of ribbons and table flounces. 'Actually, it was a last-minute decision.'

'She left you holding the bag?' His voice was deep, and he couldn't help looking at her with all those bits of lace in her slender hands. Even in her practical clothes she looked feminine and...desirable.

Not a thought you should pursue, Deveraux. Callie might be all grown up now, and fair game to any man who found her attractive—and for some reason Gideon didn't like to think of *that*, either—but she was not fair game to a man who wouldn't love her.

He didn't know how to do that—love a woman. At this age, and with a marriage behind him that hadn't exactly left him devastated when it ended, Gideon figured he didn't have what it took to love truly, madly, deeply.

He was too practical for that—too determined to keep his best interests safe.

And he'd hurt Callie once already. He'd tried not to think about it, had tried to attribute that night to Callie pursuing some random teenage crush, which no doubt she had been, but in the throes of that crush she'd had her heart on her sleeve, and that was the one thing he hadn't been able to take into safekeeping for her.

If circumstances had been different...

But they hadn't been. *He* hadn't been. Something inside him ached as he thought this. Well, it was the truth.

Gideon turned his thoughts back to the conversation at hand. 'You shouldn't have been left to introduce me to Mac.'

Callie sighed, and her shoulders slumped for a moment before she straightened them and pinned a smile back on her face. 'Maybe not, but Mary doesn't like confrontations.' She started to attach the table flounces to the long tables already placed around the room.

Gideon thought about that shoulder slump and his voice softened. 'You've probably been working since dawn. At least let me help you while I'm waiting to speak with my aunt. There must be something I can do.'

He thought she would refuse his offer, but in the end she gave a single nod of her head. 'Thank you. I could do with the extra pair of hands—just not forty-seven sets of them at once, if you know what I mean. It *has* been a long couple of days, though I don't begrudge any of it for Mary.'

They got to work. Time passed, and Gideon began to tease out details about the time Callie had spent here with Mary over the years. As she started to talk more freely he got a picture of how much his aunt meant to her—and how much he had kept himself out of both their lives.

He watched Callie spread cloths over tables, and he arranged rows of chairs just so at the other end of the gazebo under her eagle eye. She folded napkins into swans, he placed cutlery with as much precision as the best of the best waiting staff. The need to ensure her future was secure and that she would be happy in it crystallised inside him.

'You'd truly be happy here without Mary? You haven't thought about how isolated you'd be, carrying on here by yourself?'

'Not isolated. We have good staff. Some of them are dear friends as well.' Callie started to buzz past him. 'I'll be fine. I appreciate your concern, but I'm all grown up now. You don't need to worry about me, Gideon.'

'I've felt responsible since the day I pulled your uncle clear and stopped that tractor from crushing him.' Gideon caught her gently by the arm and registered warm, soft flesh beneath the edge of her T-shirt. The touch of Callie that he hadn't experienced since that night…

'My uncle—' Her eyes darkened to moss-green, and her gaze slowly dropped from his eyes to his mouth and lingered there.

Just like that Gideon was back on the estate, in his apartment's living room with his arms full of her, his mind scrambling as he kissed her and forgot about his promises to Dianna and Callie's age and everything else that should have stopped him—until the doorbell rang and Dianna called his name and he and Callie sprang apart and Callie rushed outside. He'd left Dianna there and followed Callie, explained that he'd made a mistake and shouldn't have touched her, he was sorry, she just had a girlish crush...

'Your uncle?' he prompted, and told himself he must not draw her close, could not possibly want to taste her again as he had seven years ago.

'Reid... He shouldn't have made you feel responsible for me.' A soft flush filled Callie's face and made her eyes soften and darken even further. 'To say you'd inherited me because you saved his life, to *leave* me to you—even if only informally—in his will.'

Gideon *had* felt responsible. But he had never minded that. 'It doesn't—'

'Well, you're not responsible any more.' Callie drew away from him, broke the contact of his fingers circling her upper arm. 'I can look after myself now, and have done so for quite a long while.'

That should have been a matter of relief for him. So why did he feel she'd taken an emotional step away from him with her words?

Callie went on. 'As for the rest, Mac is reformed and rehabilitated, he loves Mary, and if it's Mary's choice to be with him—well, their love for each other will be all they need to be happy.' Her voice trembled just a little—just enough to let him know she wasn't as composed or calm as she wanted him to believe. 'Can't you please try to see that, Gideon?'

'It's not that I don't want to respect your point of view, but Mac—'

'You're looking at this with your head, not your heart. Your unemotional attitude about love between a man and a woman—' She broke off and bit her lip. 'I'm sorry, but you said you didn't love Dianna, and that wasn't what marriage was going to be about for you. That night…'

That night he had forgotten his commitment to Dianna completely. Until it had come back to him, saved him at the last moment from taking Callie to his bed and creating a situation they both wouldn't have been able to deal with.

Something inside Gideon stilled even as her words hit home, challenging something deep within him that he didn't want to examine; yet he couldn't stop his words. 'You don't know what I feel—what emotions are inside me.'

For the first time in his socially acceptable, upper-echelon, controlled, plotted and planned, heir to millions, owner of billions life, Gideon wondered if he was quite as certain about what he wanted as he had always believed. If he was as incapable of giving and receiving as he had believed because of his relationship with Dianna and his lack of feeling true loss when she left.

Callie chewed her lip. 'That night I embarrassed—'

'You were beautiful.' He spoke over the top of her,

out of something deep inside him that he'd pushed away for seven years. Out of a need to assure her that he had… 'I wanted you too much.'

And now he'd *said* too much.

Green eyes locked with his gaze while sparks arced between them. They were back there, but more than that they were here and now…and here and now was somehow not at all the same.

Gideon became aware of just how close they were standing, almost nose to stuck-in-the-air pert nose. His body was bowed towards hers, wanting to be close. Wanting…*her*. His mouth was halfway there already and he had no desire to stop that forward progress.

Callie's breath caught as she stared up into his eyes and Gideon thought, *Why shouldn't I?*

'Gideon. Darling boy!' His aunt's voice sounded as she rushed into the gazebo.

Callie sprang away from him as though caught in an illicit act. He'd wanted it a great deal more than he had thought he might. Just as *she* had when they had been caught, or almost, by Dianna.

Gideon wanted to tug her close again and finish that act. But Callie had a soft glow on her face, an even softer expression in her eyes as she struggled to pull herself together.

And the chorus from seven years ago came back to him: *Don't hurt her. Don't hurt her with what you don't have in you to give her. Don't take your limitations to her. She deserves so much more than that.*

He did have those limits. His relationship with Dianna, his cold, calculated choice of Dianna was proof of that. And then Dianna had moved on to a colder, more calculated choice. Ironic, really.

Gideon turned to Mary, forced his attention to her. He couldn't believe what he'd been about to do with the woman still standing so close to him. 'I'm glad to see you, Mary. You look well.'

Indeed, as Gideon finally looked at his aunt properly he saw that she was glowing.

She had a scarf over her wavy brown hair, and now she pulled it off and smiled. 'I am well, dear boy, and all the happier for seeing you.' At this statement her smile did falter slightly, before she pinned it back on with renewed determination. 'Mac said I'd find you here with Callie.'

At least the other man had sent Mary to him. The mention of MacKay's name reminded Gideon of the reason—the forty-seven reasons, in fact—he needed to speak with Mary, whether she had a glow on her or not. Whether Callie was standing beside him glowering at him in warning or not.

'Can we chat, Mary? I met your fiancé.' Gideon glanced at Callie and registered her prickly disapproval. 'Callie introduced us, and I have to say I'm a little concerned about your relationship with MacKay. How long have you known him, for example? What do you know of his life in the past, and since he…?'

'Got out of jail?' Mary shrugged her shoulders. 'Don't feel uncomfortable saying it, Gideon. I certainly don't feel any concern about Mac's history or where he is in himself now. He's a good man.'

'He could potentially be dangerous to your health and well-being, and so could his family.'

Mary's calm expression didn't waver. 'That's not how it is with Mac.' She paused, and her expression firmed. 'Give me your presence at my marriage and your good wishes. That's all I'm asking of you, Gideon. Indeed, it's all I want.'

Gideon passed a hand over the back of his head. 'I don't want you to be hurt.'

'And I won't be. You have to trust in that, Gideon. Trust it with your heart, for a change, rather than trying to see everything with your head.'

Mary glanced towards Callie and gestured at Gideon's chest. 'It's past time you started thinking with the organ housed deep inside there.'

Callie's glance met his, and he remembered wanting to kiss her.

That hadn't involved his heart. It hadn't. But it had involved him not thinking logically. He turned back to Mary. 'I prefer to stick to facts and trust in analytical judgement.'

'Oh, Gideon. You do make me sad sometimes.' Mary sighed and patted his arm, then turned to Callie and asked her how the wedding preparations were going.

End of discussion, her actions seemed to say. Did Gideon realise that for Mary this discussion *was* now over? He'd expressed his concerns. Mary had rejected them.

Callie watched Gideon chafe at Mary's change of topic as she answered his aunt's questions. In detail. With enthusiasm. Because this was Mary's 'day before the wedding' and she deserved it to be exactly what she wanted it to be.

And if answering Mary's questions helped take Callie's mind off the sadness of Gideon's stance on marriage, took the attention away from 'Gideon and Callie' and how much they weren't any part of these questions or answers, then that was a good thing. Wasn't it?

'So, I'd like you to get quite a few cuttings of that, if you could, dear. You can take Gideon to help carry it all back here.' Mary dusted her hands off, as though she had just organised something that would greatly please her.

Callie *had* listened, but just with part of her, while the rest of her remained overly aware of Gideon.

Mary wanted her to take foliage cuttings from native bushes that only grew in one place on the other side of the island. She wanted lots of those cuttings because she'd done a reading, and the cards had told her the foliage should be used to scent the gazebo for the ceremony.

Well, it would be a break from the intensity of the past moments with Gideon, Callie supposed!

Callie pinned a smile on her face. 'Of course I'll get the cuttings for you, Mary. But I can harvest them myself. I don't need help.'

'Oh, do take Gideon, Callie.' Mary waved her hand. 'I'll feel happier knowing you have company. Yes.' She cast a single repressive glance in her nephew's direction. 'That sorts everything out.'

Right. Mary didn't want to talk with Gideon any more right now, so she was foisting him off on Callie.

One glance in Gideon's direction showed that if he stayed here he *would* pursue the conversation further with Mary. Which meant Callie had no choice but to do what Mary wanted.

Callie gave in as graciously as she could. How bad could a bit more time in Gideon's company be? She glanced at the looming overcast sky, thought about the weather predictions of storms for tomorrow, and crossed her fingers behind her back.

They didn't need gale force winds and a storm that could wreak havoc over the entire island. Not on the wedding day. That was one more worry on Callie's mind. And Callie didn't need to be fixated on the thought that Gideon had been about to kiss her when Mary had interrupted them. They must both have been temporarily insane to almost allow that to happen. The possibility was a storm warning of another kind altogether!

'What replacement job will you offer Heather Stiller now she's lost the chance to manage the guest house here?'

Callie posed the question as she clipped another portion of bush and passed it to Gideon, who placed it carefully into the canvas carrier at their feet. The aroma, a lovely blend of spice and evergreen, filled the air around them.

That air was heavy with the approach of rain, and that worried Callie. She glanced at the darkening sky. 'I don't want Mary's day spoiled tomorrow. I hope it stays fine. The storm warnings haven't been great, to be honest. I'm hoping Mary hasn't been checking, otherwise she'll be worrying, too.'

'I'll find a place for Heather.' Gideon would worry about that when he got back to Melbourne. 'I have enough business enterprises that I'm sure I'll find something that will satisfy her. She joined one of my

Melbourne-based business companies about six months ago, so I don't know a huge amount about her working history, but her ambitions are obvious and her current qualifications read well.' He, too, glanced at the sky. 'It does look a bit black, but perhaps there's just some rain on the way?'

Gideon reached forward to pick a piece of greenery from Callie's shoulder. He inhaled the scent of it before he let it drift through his fingers to the ground, and then seemed to realise he was standing rather close to her and backed away a step.

Callie lowered her gaze to the secateurs in her hands. She'd liked his closeness too much. She snipped another sprig off the bush. The wind whipped at her hair and clothes and plastered Gideon's clothes against his body. He had a rather splendid body, Callie thought, and then reminded herself not to think about *things like that*.

But Callie stood there, secateurs in hand, unable to move. His gaze captured hers, and then it was all there again.

After a loaded silence, and a sigh from him that was rather like acceptance, the secateurs were taken from her grasp and dropped into the tote.

'I need to know…' His voice dipped, deepened, and his hands came up to close over her upper arms. 'Should I have sent you here seven years ago? Maybe there was some other way to protect—'

Her.

To protect her from what he'd seen as a bad thing at that time. And it would have been. Whether his feelings had been involved or not, he had been committed to

Dianna—though Callie hadn't known that until he'd told her they were engaged to be married, that they'd kept the fact low profile because he hadn't wanted media attention.

His concern touched her, softened her when she already felt too vulnerable to him. But Callie fought to give him a coherent response. Not easy with his hands on her.

All she could find was, 'I'm not that young girl.'

It sounded too open, perhaps too needy, and she didn't want him to think she *needed* him, because that insinuated something more than attraction, and that depth of feeling for him was not a place she was prepared to go. Not when she believed him incapable of loving with all his heart.

I didn't really love him. It was just a young girl's imagination, even if it felt much deeper than that at the time.

Callie forced her gaze to drop to the tote bag. 'We have enough cuttings. We should head back.'

Head back. Avoid lingering here with him. Avoid the temptation of this moment away from everyone, just the two of them, alone on an isolated stretch of the island.

Gideon let go of her and lifted the bag.

A fat drop of rain fell, then another and another, and then a deluge of it. She'd known it was coming and she'd let it creep up on her anyway.

Rather like the feelings that had driven her to Gideon's door when she was young enough and believed she loved him enough to expose herself that way. She had been so sure she could seduce him, draw his attention, and that when she had it he would somehow miraculously realise he loved her.

So silly.

'There's an empty cottage beyond the rise.' She blinked splashes of rain out of her eyes, felt the sting of the droplets against her cheeks and nose and mouth, the whip of a wind that was indeed stronger than she would have liked.

They stumbled up the small hill against the wind; against the rain that soaked them in the space of time it took them to hit the top of that rise. The cottage was just beyond it.

Callie pushed the door open, and Gideon stumbled in behind her and slapped it shut again. Their breaths sounded loud in the sudden stillness inside those four small walls.

There was no furniture. Just bare faded walls and a wooden floor. A bank of uncurtained windows to one side, what used to be a kitchenette, gutted now, in the far part of the room.

Maybe it was the sudden onset of the storm that made her glance out of those windows and feel as though they were being watched.

They stood there dripping with rain, facing each other. Gideon had set the tote bag onto the floor at his feet; all his focus was on her, and Callie forgot that odd feeling. Instead, something in his expression made her heart stutter.

'Mary,' she said. *There was something that had to be said about Mary.* Callie resisted the urge to retreat a step while her concentration shattered, but all she could do was look into blue eyes that had darkened and focused so intensely on her.

'Mary…?' He reached out his hand and wiped a drip of rain from her cheek. His fingers lingered, cupped her face.

'Mary—your aunt. She…' *Do not press into his touch. Don't do it, don't do it.*

Callie pressed. Closed her eyes and then forced them open again, hoping somehow she'd have managed to break this…whatever it was that had her standing here, unable to move away from him, wanting all sorts of inexplicable things she probably shouldn't want.

What did she mean, *probably*? She *knew* she shouldn't want those things.

'Mary is in love. With Mac.'

Callie drew a breath and his hand dropped to his side. She told herself it was all right now, but the rain outside got heavier and pounded on the roof, and in here it was filled with quiet and intimacy, and that was *not* all right.

'They've been planning this wedding for a year now. They're committed. She knows everything there is to know about Mac. Just…you know…just to reassure you about things. I should have said all that at the start. I was worried about keeping my job here. I'm glad you're going to let me do that.'

Callie forced her concentration to remain on Mary's situation, not on the intimacy of her own.

'If you investigate Mac, which you really shouldn't, your investigation won't reveal anything that will surprise Mary, because Mac has been completely up-front with her. He spent the first six months of their courtship doing his best to make her push him aside, after all his truthfulness about his past. I watched that happening.'

'I don't want to breach Mac's privacy, Callie.' Gideon's brows drew down. 'But I do have to be certain Mary will be safe.'

'I know.' Callie did know. She knew because she knew Gideon. She had cared about him all the time she'd lived with her uncle. 'Can't you take my assurance on the issue?'

He pushed back a sigh. 'The wedding is tomorrow. I'm going to contact an investigator I know and set him onto this immediately. He's discreet, and I expect to have information from him by nightfall—or early tomorrow at the least.'

'I see. Well, I guess I can't blame you for caring about her.'

'And about you.'

Water dripped down the side of his cheek as he gave a reluctant sigh. Callie's fingers twitched with the need to reach up and trace the line left by that rivulet of water.

Her heart acknowledged something. He cared about Mary—loved her. That was why he felt so concerned about his aunt. He wanted her to be happy and safe.

And don't you think maybe he felt the same way about you?

Something inside Callie softened despite herself. 'I truly believe Mary will be okay, Gid. If I didn't believe that I would have called you long ago and *asked* for help to protect her. And I believe *I'll* be quite safe, too.'

The planes and angles of his face softened as though

that diminutive use of his name had got past his defences. 'Callie—'

She did back away then, when he spoke her name in that soft, deep tone. Backed a step physically, tried to back up emotionally as well.

'It'll all be over tomorrow and you'll leave again.'

And then Callie could get on with her life and not be confused by feelings about him that she didn't want to have, hadn't wanted to admit she had, still couldn't consider she had.

'I don't want—' Gideon was at a loss as to what to say as he felt an intensity inside himself that he couldn't allow to be there, and yet it still was.

A big drip of rain splashed onto his face and dribbled down his nose. Gideon glanced upwards. 'The roof's leaking.'

'Yes. The rain is hammering down, but the wind seems to have died down, don't you think? That may be a good sign.' Callie's gaze tracked over his hair, face, chest, and came back to meet his eyes. 'You look quite bedraggled, actually. Your shirt's going to wrinkle.' She gave a half-reluctant laugh and swiped the drip from the end of his nose.

And Gideon took a really good look at her for the first time since they'd come into the shelter of the cottage. He knew they were standing in an empty room, and the place smelled musty. He had noticed those things—peripherally at least. But now he noticed Callie.

The rat's tail her ponytail had become. Her face with its freckles and not a scrap of make-up. Her milky skin and soaked orange shirt and soggy dungarees. Her big green eyes locked to his gaze.

It just welled up in him then. The same need that had hit him earlier.

'Callie.' He murmured her name, and somehow she was reaching for him, and he was reaching for her, and his lips closed over hers.

All he could register was the taste of her. The feel of soft lips beneath his, moulding to his. He couldn't force himself away from that kiss. He had to have it. He didn't know how she did that to him. Put him so far out of control so fast.

Gideon's lips on Callie's brought all kinds of emotions to the surface in her.

Her heart squeezed.

His eyelids drifted closed and he inhaled. His mouth softened against hers as the kiss went to a whole other level—one that held her spellbound, lips to his lips, as everything within her reached for this moment.

Gideon sighed his pleasure.

Callie was sensual in his arms, beautiful and…and *hungry* in a way that heated the blood in his veins as her hands shaped his shoulders, his upper arms and chest. He realised he'd crushed her close and could feel every inch of her body pressed to his.

Gideon tipped her head back and deepened the kiss. His senses took over. One hand drifted down her spine to the base of her back. The other cupped her neck, shaped the outer curves of her breasts, her waist and hips.

'God, Callie.'

The heat had washed over them so fast, so strong. As

Gideon realised that he finally made himself slow down. Enough to stop him crushing her close. Enough to ease off on a kiss that had become all the most tempting kinds of ravishment—of the woman in his arms and of his own senses.

He didn't want to lose this closeness with her. But he forced himself to draw back.

Cloudy green eyes looked into his face.

'What are we doing, Callie?'

Gideon wished he knew the answer.

CHAPTER FOUR

'I DON'T think there's going to be much more rain—'

'We should go. The rain has stopped—'

They both spoke at once, stepped back—way back.

Gideon glanced out of the windows. Anything other than looking at the kiss-softened woman he'd held so recently in his arms.

Callie did the same. Though he wondered if she registered the view outside any better than he did.

Hands dropped away. Bodies that had warmed against each other chilled back to awareness of wet, uncomfortable clothing and the musty smell of the cottage, the earthy, pine and spice scent of the foliage they had cut for Mary.

Gideon felt all this inside himself. Then Callie shivered, and he wanted to wrap her into his arms and keep her safe and secure, and kiss her again and more...

Kissing her was not smart. And 'more' was out of the question utterly. If they did that he'd want her again. And again and again and again. He wasn't stupid enough that he didn't know that. And Callie had held her heart out to him once already. He hadn't been able to take it then, and she was still a generous, giving person.

She would understand now that she wasn't *in love* with him, as she'd believed she was back then, but she was still capable of becoming emotionally attached to him. And he… He wasn't good at that. Like his parents, who had a calm but unemotional and distant relationship with each other, Gideon didn't do well at the kind of intimacy that needed to come from a soul-deep level. He'd simply never found it inside himself for a woman. If it wasn't there, it wasn't there.

'Callie, I can't— I don't have—'

'Please.' She cut one slender hand through the air. 'We let ourselves get a little carried away. I guess that's natural when we've been there once before. You know— curiosity, old history… Let's go back. There's so much still to do, and I want to check in for another weather report with the bureau.'

'Yes. That's what we should do.' Gideon picked up the canvas tote, moved to the door of the cottage and opened it, and figured the tightness in his chest was an after-effect of realising he'd gone somewhere with Callie that he shouldn't have. It *had* to be that.

'You should be looking for a nice guy. Someone your age who can give you what you need.' The words came out whether he should have let them or not. But Callie *should* try to find someone to…to love her. She deserved that. She needed that. She didn't have that. And if she had that she would be purely and simply out of bounds. Not that he should view her any differently but out of bounds now…

'I'm twenty-five. I can choose someone any age that I want.' Callie stepped past him through the door. Maybe it was the glare she cast his way, or the emergence of the sun from behind the clouds, or the fact her hair was still damp, but she seemed to glow all over…

She'd stomped quite a way from him before he tugged the door shut and followed, using his longer stride to catch up with her. She glowed. Appealed. Made him want to take her into his arms all over again. Callie did all of those things.

'For your information, I've looked for relationships.' Her words were low, and, yes, irritated. And something else he couldn't define as she turned her face away to look out to sea. 'Living on an island doesn't stop me from spending time socialising—both here and in Melbourne, and in other places when I feel like it.'

Callie couldn't look at Gideon. If she did, he might see all the feelings in her eyes. His kisses had swept her away. The landing when he'd put an end to them had been bumpy. She was too conscious of him still, and that was dangerous.

Back to the point. She enjoyed socialising and she'd done relationships. Well, she'd done dating.

There was no need to admit she'd struggled to care enough about any man to get beyond dating, to find much more than fleeting pleasure during the one or two times those relationships had gone that way.

'Anyway, *you* haven't settled into another relationship since Dianna. Not a serious one.'

'How do you—?' He broke off to help her over an old fallen tree limb.

Callie let him help her, and then took care to shift away from him again—because his touch on her was somewhat problematical to her concentration still. But she was going to take care of that!

'You're a billionaire bachelor, you have business interests that put you in the papers all the time, and your whole family is of interest to the media anyway because of your combined wealth.' She didn't add that he was also gorgeous and appealing, and of interest for those reasons as well. He had to know he was on every 'Top 100' list in existence for reasons that included his appeal as a male of the species. Instead she said, 'I doubt you'd hide any kind of significant relationship from the public eye for long.'

That was enough. And she hadn't *deliberately* followed his business interests or his attendance at this glitzy function or that one. The coverage was just there, and she noticed it.

Sure, Callandra. Whatever you say.

'I need to get back to work. Get focused on this wedding and make sure everything is done in preparation for tomorrow.' Callie picked up her pace. But she couldn't outrun her thoughts, or her consciousness of Gideon striding along at her side.

He'd kissed her, and she had felt such tenderness in her heart for him when it happened. One minute she'd been laughing, the next her heart had been cracking open and letting him most of the way in, while her senses had simply flown away at his every touch and caress.

Even if that had only been the upsurge of a long-time affection, it was dangerous. She had to retreat from that emotional position. From her awareness of him altogether. And she had to do it fast, because Gideon wasn't opening up to her in the same way.

He wasn't even capable of trusting her judgement over Mac and his family. And he wanted to throw her at the first stranger who came along and offered a nice, secure relationship.

At this sobering reminder, Callie drew a fortifying breath. 'Let's just get this wedding done, so life can go back to normal for both of us. That's what's going to be best.'

It might have been nice for her to go straight to the gazebo, put the foliage in place as Mary wanted it done. Preferably while Gideon went to the guest house and did anything that didn't involve being with her.

Instead, a group of Mac's family spilled out onto the steps of the guest house as they approached. It *had* to be Mac's three brothers, didn't it? They were life-weathered men, strong and muscular, and somewhat life-roughened.

'I see the rain caught you, Callie?'

The one named Andrew grazed his hand over his shaved head, revealing a tattooed underarm in the process. Callie particularly liked the serpent with its jaws wide open.

'Yes. I want to get a weather report. What's brought you all outside?'

'None of us can stay indoors for more than an hour at a stretch.' This comment came from Damien, the youngest of all the brothers. He gave a grin that didn't quite reach the world-weariness in his eyes. 'Been that way since jail.'

'Do the crime, do the time.' The third brother shrugged his shoulders. 'We learned—didn't we, boys?'

And on that note…

'Gideon,' she murmured, 'I'd like you to meet Mac's brothers.' She introduced each one. 'Mac's happy to have his family around him for this special time, and it's a rare opportunity. He doesn't see a whole lot of his brothers.'

She hoped Gideon understood the subtext—the fact that the Joneses didn't spend a lot of time massed in one place—but he didn't look particularly reassured.

After brief hellos, the first brother turned thick shoulders in the direction of the doors. 'Two of our wives almost came to blows over how to make the sauce for one of tomorrow's desserts. It could get ugly if we don't supervise. Better get back in there.'

They disappeared, laughing at what Callie hoped was a joke.

'I have to find out if we're still on storm alert,' she said. As far as the weather was concerned, at least. Callie wasn't sure if she should think about possible storms among the Jones family!

Callie followed the men into the guest house, and prayed that tomorrow would dawn fine and mild and the forty-seven people inside the guest house would feel equally mellow and mild.

Someone shouted from inside the kitchen, and someone else shouted back. So far her hopes weren't looking overly realistic.

Gideon's mouth tightened and he strode purposefully in that direction. 'I think I'll meet everyone else now.'

'Oh, good.' Callie forced the words out between teeth

that were inclined to want to chew her lip. 'That sounds like a great idea.' She bolted towards the office. 'I'll just check the weather while you do that.'

Hopefully Mary would be in the kitchen, and she would be able to introduce Gideon to all those lovely people—who really *were* lovely people, including Mac.

Being boisterous didn't mean they were scary.

Or anything.

Honest!

CHAPTER FIVE

THE weather warning was even more severe on the morning of the wedding. The authorities couldn't say which way it would go, and most often storms passed by the island, but the air was heavy, thick and still. Callie hoped for the best—or, if not that, for the worst to hold off at least until after the ceremony was over.

Mary looked beautiful, in a simple cream sheath dress, with multi-hued flowers in her bouquet and in her hair.

Callie stood to Mary's left and let the words of the ceremony wash over her. She'd given up all pretence of fighting off tears the moment Mac first looked into Mary's eyes and began his vows. The sound of waves on the beach wafted through the gazebo's wide-open doors as Mac continued to speak. A flash of something caught Callie's eye through those opened doors. The glint of sun on a bird's wings in the distance? She wasn't sure.

Mac caught Mary's hand and held it in his, and his voice deepened to an emotion-roughened rumble. 'And I will love and cherish you for ever, and never forget the gift you are to me. I won't ever forget, Mary.'

The celebrant smiled and nodded, and pronounced them husband and wife, and Callie surreptitiously wiped the tears from beneath her eyes. She couldn't let herself look at Gideon, who stood on Mac's other side. That would be just too difficult. It would tug at her heartstrings too much, and she didn't want to ask herself why that was.

Mary and Mac kissed, and when they broke apart the family gave a boisterous cheer of approval.

They walked down the makeshift aisle, with Mac receiving back-slaps and Mary receiving kisses on her cheek.

Callie followed, with her bridesmaid's bouquet clutched in her fingers and the rustle of pale blue silk whispering against her legs. She tried so hard to focus on those things.

Tried, but couldn't. Because her thoughts were on the man at her side, who now had her hand tucked through his arm.

'Mary looks beautiful.' Gideon's voice was rough, resigned, but tender as he watched Mary, glowing on her new husband's arm. He was still worried. That, too, sounded in his tone.

Somehow, knowing the service had moved him moved Callie, too. It softened her to him—and that was such a bad thing to have happen.

'The celebrant was good, hey, Mac?' Andrew Jones let his pride show as he addressed his brother. 'I know how to find someone who can do the job and keep quiet about it.'

Mac nodded his head. 'For Mary, it has to stay quiet. I don't want a media circus for her, so it's good to know

324 INHERITED BY THE BILLIONAIRE

this person won't talk now or later.' His voice held reserve
as well as appreciation, but he produced a smile for his
brother. 'You did well, Andrew. I do appreciate it.'

Just for a moment Gideon's expression gave away the
fact that he was on the same page with Mac when it
came to preserving Mary's privacy over this marriage.
The couple intended to keep a low profile always; Callie
had assured Gideon of that before they went their
separate ways last night.

'Mary does look beautiful, and years younger than
she is. Happiness has taken age off her.' Callie hoped
her words would shift Gideon's focus from the potential for disaster involved in this marriage.

Yes, Callie had her concerns, in certain ways. She'd
worked with Mary to ensure secrecy. She'd met Mac's
family and worried, and hoped Mary truly would be safe
amongst them. In the end she'd concluded that Mac,
despite his ways, quieter than some of the others, would
do everything necessary to ensure Mary's security—
even from his own relatives if need be.

'Are you okay now, Callie?' Gideon dipped his head
to search her face.

She nodded self-consciously. She hadn't expected
to feel raw like this when Mary said her vows and
bound herself to Mac. It wasn't because Callie feared
Mac wouldn't love Mary enough. It was because she
knew he *would*.

'I'm fine. I'm happy for Mary. She looks lovely—
glowing and happy, inside and out.'

'You look just as beautiful, Callie.' Gideon spoke the
low words and squeezed her hand.

For a moment there was a sadness in him, and Callie's heart hurt—because she was remembering another wedding day, and how she'd taken herself away to a remote part of the island and grieved alone because she simply couldn't share it.

She had pushed that grieving down so far…

'Callie?' Gideon's hand folded over hers. Shadows filled his eyes—concern for her—but he didn't understand and she was glad. She didn't *want* him to understand, because that would mean he knew…

Knew what?

That she'd…she'd cared about him back then, that was all. Simply cared about him.

Callie drew a shaken breath. And then there were people all around and the moment passed.

They rearranged chairs around tables and ate their buffet dinner in the gazebo while the sun set and darkness fell. Tiny rows of fairy lights twinkled overhead on the domed ceiling. The scent of Mary's special foliage and hundreds of flowers filled the large room.

'MacKay's relatives have done a good job with the catering. The meal was excellent.' Gideon made the observation into Callie's ear as they watched the newly married couple take to the small area set aside for dancing.

It was a conciliatory statement, and Callie treated it as such. She was relieved that he hadn't been able to read her thoughts earlier, anyway.

'Yes. I'm glad they went with the buffet idea. It kept it that little bit more informal, and allowed for a wider variety of foods.' As she spoke the words the music started. Not a bridal waltz, no—not that for Mac and Mary.

Instead they danced the Charleston. The couple had practised the dance for months, and Callie couldn't help smiling as she watched them. She observed a look of anticipatory unease on Gideon's face as he glanced her way.

'Oh, don't worry. That won't be expected of us.' Callie laid a consoling hand on his arm, the first voluntary touch she'd given him today—though not the first touch they had exchanged.

You don't want to think about that, Callandra. You haven't been noticing all those necessary touches, and the few unnecessary ones he's given you.

And you certainly haven't been affected by them.

Right. Of course she hadn't. Callie's fingers tightened against Gideon's arm, and then she drew away abruptly. The flicker of intensity in his eyes didn't help her cause. But *why* was he looking at her like that after they'd both agreed that yesterday's kiss was a mistake and they were over all that? Not that he meant he'd ever been *other* than over it. He'd just been momentarily distracted yesterday, nothing more.

What had she been talking about?

'The next dance will just be a regular one that anyone can do.' Though it *would* be expected that they'd be the next couple on the floor, before anyone else joined in.

Well, Callie could manage dancing with Gideon in front of a bunch of Mac's relatives. No problem. No drama. No big deal.

The music changed as she had those thoughts.

'I think that's our cue.' Gideon got to his feet and held out his hand.

'We haven't danced together before.' Callie placed her hand in his and got to her feet, and suddenly her heart was beating fast and she was breathless.

He took that hand in a strong clasp and led her onto the floor. He turned her into his arms. He didn't comment on her statement of the obvious, but his hands were gentle as they held her.

Callie should have been conscious of people watching them. The sounds of laughter and boisterous talk should have impinged. Yet she could only feel Gideon's hold on her, acknowledge how she relaxed into that hold, welcomed it.

She could only notice the man who held her.

There were so many sensations to notice. His hand holding hers. His other hand high in the centre of her back. The bridesmaid's dress had spaghetti straps and a not at all plunging back, but it left enough skin bare that his fingers touched her flesh. What Callie couldn't let herself notice was how right it felt to be held by him.

'Let's see if we can do this.' Gideon's low words were clearly intended to be jovial. The deep, husky tone of them somewhat put paid to that intention.

Callie imagined she murmured some appropriate assent. Once her hand rose to rest on his shoulder she could no longer focus on words. His shoulder beneath her fingers was rock-hard. She could feel the outline of bone and muscle, and when they began to dance could feel every movement of his body through that one touch, even without the sense of his fingers gripping her other hand.

Other couples joined them on the floor.

There were more dances and changes of partners over the next hour, and pieces of wedding cake and wonderful coffee, and far too much champagne flowing, but Callie never lost the memory of that first dance in Gideon's arms. Never lost her awareness of him at all.

Mac and Mary slipped away quietly, after speaking with her and Gideon briefly. Mary didn't throw her bouquet, Mac didn't throw a garter, and Callie was kind of glad about that. She didn't want to think of Gideon throwing a garter at a wedding years ago.

Mary and Mac left by special chartered boat—a pre-arranged deal to get them away after nightfall.

Somewhat similar to Gideon's arrival, except he'd told her he'd simply bought a boat to get here. Only *he* would do that!

The party went on until the early hours, and turned into somewhat of a family reunion. A very loud one.

Callie had to see the party through to the end. And Gideon chose to see it through with her.

'One more dance, folks.'

The DJ set another vinyl onto the turntable and a sweet poignant song flowed through the gazebo. The warm mellow sound of the music lent it an intimacy that Callie did her best to fight. And no, her best was not good enough.

'There's something about music played the "real" way—on a turntable, with the scratch of a needle.'

Gideon took Callie into his arms for this one last dance and told himself it was fine—because he'd made it through the evening, made it through the myriad temptations of Callie so close at his side.

Callie was more temptation than he wanted to

consider or acknowledge. He didn't know why. Except for yesterday's kiss…

But still he held her for the final dance, and his hands touched her gently because that was what she drew from him.

'Seven years ago I sent you away from me.' He murmured the words against the hair that was piled on her head in artfully arranged Titian curls. He'd sent her away for her sake. Hadn't he? 'Now I'm wondering…'

'You were getting ready to marry Dianna.' She glanced up into his eyes. 'I embarrassed myself that night—a young girl blurting things she shouldn't have.'

'I was a lot older, and I have to take my share of the blame for what happened.' He was glad to have the incident out in the open at long last. 'I could have dealt with it better at the time. But you tempted me then. You…still tempt me now.'

The music faded to silence then, and they broke apart. Maybe it was as well, because she was a lot of temptation in his arms.

People began to gather their things and head for the guest house.

'You did a wonderful job with the wedding arrangements, Callie.' Gideon's words were determinedly focused away from the two of them.

That was wise.

So why did Callie feel almost disappointed?

He went on. 'I'm glad it's over, and that it was kept quiet. Maybe if the family all leave, and Mary's happy and she and Mac keep a low profile, you'll be fine to carry on here.'

He was still worrying about her. Callie didn't want to think she glowed as a result of his words, but she probably did exactly that. Because Gideon *cared*.

Oh, she was far too soft when it came to him!

The last person finally left the gazebo. Callie let out a sigh of relief.

'It all went without a hitch. No doubt the storm that was predicted will have passed over us by morning, too. Mary and Mac are away for their honeymoon, and tomorrow everyone will make their way back to the mainland.'

'You'll be able to get back to normal.'

Did he sound as unenthusiastic at the thought of that as Callie felt?

She spoke into the silence—but not the words that were inside her head: *I wish you didn't have to go.*

'I'd better get back to the guest house—see if anyone needs anything. The clearing up in here can wait until tomorrow. I'll just shut the door on all of it for now.'

'Take a walk on the beach with me first. Give yourself a minute to wind down. You've worked hard today.'

Gideon rested a hand on her arm, and in the moment she hesitated, uncertain what to say or how to refuse what sounded like a dangerous but alluringly tension-easing idea, he pulled her the rest of the way through the doorway and closed it at their backs.

Somehow, minutes later, they were on the beach. Her strappy sandals were in her hand, his shoes and socks were in his, and the moon was above them, casting a silken glow over the sea and the island and the night.

'Are there jellyfish to avoid?' Gideon gripped her

free hand, as though he would protect her from such things if need be.

Callie let him hold her hand, and her heart pounded just because he'd done the protective thing. 'There are no jellyfish. They don't end up here, which is good.'

So that meant he could let go of her, right? She could make her own way, breathe in the sea air, centre herself after this long, busy day, and then retire to the guest house and sleep, and be ready for an early start tomorrow.

Callie didn't shift her hand.

'All the guests are leaving first thing in the morning.' The words were almost plaintive. She cleared her throat. 'I hope Mary and Mac have a wonderful honeymoon. It's their first step in a whole new future.'

'I hope they're happy, Callie.' He stopped walking. 'I do hope that. When I discovered Mac's identity I was worried. I still am. The report I got in wasn't entirely reassuring. Mac himself seems to truly have changed his outlook, to be determined to live a crime-free life, but that doesn't erase his past...'

'I know.' How could she blame him for caring when that worry came out of his concern for his aunt? When Callie herself shared much of it? 'I don't blame you, Gid. To be honest, I'll feel a little better when his family are all gone. They're a little overwhelming all at once.'

'You're the only person in my life who calls me that—Gid. The only one who ever has.' That husky tone was back in his voice again, and he turned his head to look at her in the moon-limned night. 'I think it's just as well I'll be leaving in the morning, Callandra, because I'm having trouble viewing you the way I should.'

Don't ask him. 'What way *are* you viewing me?'

'In this way.' He lifted his hand to stroke his fingers over her shoulders. 'In a way that can't stop me looking at the soft dusting of freckles across your shoulders and wanting to kiss each one.'

'You—ah—' She closed her eyes as his fingers rose to caress her cheek. 'You make freckles sound enticing. I've always viewed them as a nuisance…'

'Enticing, tempting. As tempting as this.' His fingers drifted into her hair, pulled at pins, dropped those pins onto the sand at their feet as her hair tumbled down around her shoulders. 'God, Callie. I've never seen anything as beautiful as your hair. Why do you tie it back all the time?'

Before she could answer he shook his head. 'I'm glad you tie it back. At least no one else is seeing…'

If he'd imbibed too much champagne she would have thought that was behind this loosening of his tongue— this spill of words that whispered into the night air and echoed on the roll of the waves, wending their way through her until she stood frozen, unable to resist them.

Callie couldn't remember any more why she needed to resist. Something about Gideon's negative attitude to emotional commitment, his rejection of her offer of her love seven years ago…

What was she saying? She'd had a crush on him. It hadn't been anything more than that. She certainly didn't have any deep feelings towards him now.

Yet the feelings are quite familiar, aren't they, Callie? Such longing for his arms around you, for him to hold you and do it as though he means it.

'What are we doing, Gid? Why are *you* doing this?'

The words burst from her. 'This wedding, watching Mac and Mary bind themselves together, all I could think of was when you married Dianna and I didn't want to think about you that day. You don't want—'

'I want. I…I can't help wanting.'

His mouth stopped her words, sealed to her lips, and his hands folded her in until the two of them were pressed close from chest to knee.

There was rawness in Callie's heart and in Gideon's hold—in the way his mouth moved over hers. Rawness, and a need that matched the feeling deep down inside her. And she finally acknowledged that feeling, even if it didn't have a name.

Maybe its name was simply Gideon.

And though she shouldn't think it if she wanted to protect herself—protect whatever corner of her *did* care about him because, yes, there *was* a corner of her that did—the thoughts came.

Why *shouldn't* this go wherever it wanted to go? Why *shouldn't* she let herself have whatever he wanted to share with her?

Callie had known Gideon for ever. She'd come close to making love with him once. If she wanted to have that intimacy with him now, why shouldn't she?

A thousand reasons, her mind tried to tell her. But she couldn't hear the words. She could only feel.

The hard muscle beneath his shirt. The contours of his shoulders. The breadth of his back and the male slimness of his waist. Callie closed her eyes and let her hands relearn those parts of him. Let her hands have something they had wanted for years.

She had cared for Gideon, wanted him and, yes, needed him, even. And now she made herself admit that not all of those feelings had gone away. She had thought she'd completely let go of them, of him, but her need for his touch, his arms around her, told her she hadn't.

Oh, God. Had she merely locked him away inside herself and not dealt with it at all?

But she didn't love him. She'd only *thought* she did. At that age she couldn't have known her heart anyway.

'What are you thinking, Callie?'

He kissed the tip of her nose. She could have taken it as the kind of comfort a man would offer a child. But it wasn't. The way his arms held her told her that. The deep cadence of his voice as he spoke her name told her that.

'I guess it's this.' She searched his eyes in the moonlight and her hands came up to grip his forearms. His hands clasped her waist. 'But I don't know what to do about *this*.'

His fingers tightened for a moment against her waist. 'I know what I want…'

She knew what she wanted, too. And that scared her— because she wanted him too much, and she wanted him with parts of her that had cared too much seven years ago.

'I have to go in, Gideon. I can't—I can't do this with you. It's not a good idea for either of us. It just…complicates things. You don't want me this way—not really. And I don't want the…the stress.'

How she managed to deny herself she didn't know, but she got the words out and walked away without waiting for an answer. There was only one answer anyway, and

Gideon gave it to her in his silence, in the way he remained right there on the beach as she walked away.

Callie tipped her face up and told herself this was brave of her, and smart and sensible and practical. He would go in the morning. She would stay here and get on with her work. All would be well.

It would.

Wouldn't it?

CHAPTER SIX

ALL being well didn't exactly happen.

At four a.m., the man who handled transport to and from the island had to start boating people away. Gideon called in his skipper as well, but it still took time to get everyone gone.

'You're fully confident it's safe to make this final trip now?' Callie posed the question to her regular boat skipper.

'It's safe, but I do want to get moving. I hope that third boat's skipper knew what he was doing, heading to the other side of the island the way he did. I'll radio in on him once I'm away. Don't know what he was doing, anyway. There's no one over that side. Illegal fishing, maybe? I'll see if anyone knows…' With this resolved in his mind, he went on with more urgent concerns. 'This storm—' Her skipper shook his head, glanced at the sky. 'If anything, the weather warning has failed to register the depth of this one. It's going to get the island square-on, and it's going to hit soon.'

Callie swallowed hard—because she knew she could

trust the skipper's prediction. He'd spent enough time in this area to know what he was talking about.

'Go safely.'

If illegal fishing *was* going on it would have to be reported, but now wasn't the time for her to worry about that. Callie stepped back and the two men boarded their crafts. Finally everyone was gone. Everyone but her and Gideon.

He refused to leave.

'If it's safe for you to stay, to use the storm cellar until this is over, then it's safe for me to stay with you. Either you come away with me or we both stay. I won't leave you here alone.'

'All right.' She pushed her hand through her hair. There hadn't even been time to draw it back in its usual ponytail after the couple of hours she'd slept before she'd got the emergency call to start evacuating the island. 'But you should have gone with them, Gideon— though I do appreciate your company.'

'Have you been through anything like this before?' He ignored her comment and glanced at the roughening sky.

'I haven't, but I know what has to be done. Storm shutters have to be closed over all the guest house windows, and mattresses need to be put against those windows from the inside. And all the other usual things.' There was so much else that needed doing. Cleaning out the gazebo, taking down the fairy lights… She didn't know if there would be time to do any of those things.

'Then let's move. From what the authorities have said we have two hours, tops, before this thing hits. Less if your skipper's predictions are accurate.'

His hair was uncombed, and he had beard shadow on his jaw and a determined gleam in his eyes, and Callie felt…

Safe. She felt safe in the face of the storm that was about to break over her little island, doing its best to wipe everything on it into the sea.

The guest house would stand. Well, she hoped and prayed it would. Mary had experienced two storms of this predicted severity in her time here, and both times the guest house had weathered the storm quite well.

But nothing like it had happened during Callie's tenure as manager. And Mary *had* had to rebuild the gazebo once…

'I'm glad Mary and Mac left before this came along. Knowing your aunt, she would have wanted to skip the honeymoon and stay.'

They took care of the guest house, but did only a little work in the gazebo because they didn't get their two hours. In less than that time the wind was roaring.

They'd carried the last of the supplies into the underground storm cellar, and only just managed, between the two of them, to get the door closed and barred behind them.

Gideon leaned his weight against it while Callie slid the bolts home. She had to lean in close to him to do it. Close enough to feel his body warmth. Her gaze lifted to his, locked, and she became instantly aware of the intimacy of their situation.

Two people locked in a cosy storm shelter until further notice. 'I'm…ah…I'm glad we got the breakables out of the gazebo.'

Callie stepped away from him, rubbed her hands down the sides of her jeans and tried not to think about the roaring of the wind outside or the roaring of her awareness of Gideon. Maybe fear of the elements was raising her consciousness of him.

She glanced at the overhead light in the cellar's main room and wondered how long the electricity would hold up.

'I wish we could have cleared the gazebo out completely.'

'We did what we could in the time frame.'

God, his voice was so deep.

Callie drew a shaken breath and reached for one of the baskets of leftovers they'd brought with them. He wouldn't see how her hand shook, would he?

Gideon lifted the other basket and carried it to the small kitchenette. His back muscles flexed through his cotton shirt as he moved.

Callie had pressed her hands to those muscles in the abandoned cottage during the rain. Had that only been two days ago?

He turned to face her. 'Try not to worry about what will happen next. The storm is out of our control until it's over now.'

Yes, it was—and Callie felt a little out of control, too. 'I don't think I like not being able to have my eye on what's happening on the other side of that door.' She might be safer on that side—away from the temptation within!

'I feel the same, but we'll be fine.' He half reached for her hand before he turned away, opened the basket and began to draw items out of it. 'Let's get these things into the fridge.'

Wedding food. Rich, luscious desserts, delicious pastries, and several kinds of meat and vegetables in tangy sauces. A feast for the senses.

Not a good way to think of it, Callie, given your senses appear to be overloaded with Gideon-consciousness as it is.

Callie forced a smile. 'At least we won't starve.'

She glanced at their surroundings. Felt rattled by that roar outside again. It was getting louder, rougher. Callie forced herself to think about their comfort down here. Bathroom and basic kitchen facilities, living area. All good.

'There's a bedroom with a bed in it,' she blurted—and could have winced. She rushed on to explain. 'It's a king-sized bed, so that will be fine if we need to…to sleep. There'll be tons of room.'

She was overstating the case, wasn't she? She clamped her lips shut so nothing else would blurt out.

But Gideon didn't laugh, or even smile at her verbal spill. Instead his gaze locked onto her, and his body stilled close to hers, and somehow she knew he was thinking of kissing her, of holding her.

'Callandra—'

'Movies.' She rushed the word out with a hint of poorly disguised desperation. 'We can watch movies for as long as the electricity holds out. There's a TV and DVD-player, and I know Mary left some movies down here.'

They *could* watch movies, and that would stop her

from thinking thoughts she should not think. Such as that she had never found a man to match up to Gideon...

One very short moment passed before he nodded. 'Movies are a good idea.'

Yes. Good. They both agreed.

When she didn't immediately move, he led the way to a cabinet in the corner and gestured to the selection of titles. 'Pick whatever you want to see.'

Callie chose two she hadn't watched before. One comedy, one drama. Those would be quite safe, wouldn't they? They watched the drama first. Who knew it would be a sensual drama? That just made things even worse. It even made her stop noticing most of the storm noise outside. Well, other than the crashing and banging and smashing...

When the movie ended she bolted to her feet. Anything to get off the sofa and away from the temptation to lean into Gideon's body, to snuggle up and enjoy all the warmth of him in all sorts of ways she shouldn't be thinking about when there was a storm raging outside that might well be destroying her source of income.

'I'll make hot drinks. Would you like tea or coffee? There'll be instant and teabags, at least.'

'Tea is fine.' He also stood, pushed his hands into his pockets. He had on a pair of tan trousers and a navy shirt loose over them. He scrubbed his hand over his jaw.

As he did so, something smashed against the outer door.

Callie squealed. Just slightly. Purely because that one had surprised her. 'Ah—that's really getting going now.' She blew out a breath and told herself to *get a grip*.

'It's all right.'

He wrapped her in his arms. Just drew her in and cuddled her. And it should only have been for comfort, but the moment his arms closed around her their gazes met, and then it wasn't only comfort being given and received.

His hands rubbed against her back, and his eyes warmed with delicious interest and an edge of the need that Callie felt inside herself.

She curled her hand around the back of his neck. Only that. It was all that was needed. He dipped his head, gave her what she had silently asked for: his mouth close to hers, then pressed to hers.

They kissed in counterpoint to the raging of the storm. Soft, soothing, slow kisses that eased one into the other in a lovely, mellow cadence.

The whistle of the kettle broke them apart, but Gideon's arms remained loosely around her.

'Leave it. Let it shut off.'

Oh, she wanted to do that—wanted the promise inherent in that suggestion.

'We—ah—I'm not sure if we should skip having tea.'

Callie wasn't sure if she was capable of making tea right now!

Gideon made it for them, and carried it back to the sofa for the second movie—but she couldn't have said what it was about.

Her shoulder was pressed to his. When they'd finished their drinks he played with her fingers. It was almost unconscious, so how could she be so *conscious* of such a simple touch?

'It's not simple, though, is it?'

His words made her realise she'd spoken her thought aloud. And he turned her into his arms and kissed her again. And they watched and kissed and cuddled their way through every movie Mary had brought down until it was finally nightfall. By then Callie's senses were so overwhelmed she didn't know where she began and ended any more.

But she couldn't regret what they'd done. She needed to give herself this time with Gideon.

'I must be insane, but I just…just can't stop touching you.' Gideon's eyes were ringed with the blurry edge of desire, and that was there for *her*, and it was beautiful. God, so beautiful.

Callie raised her mouth so he would kiss her again. It had to happen. It was that simple and that complicated.

The electricity cut out ten minutes after the final movie had ended. Callie only noticed because the blue screen on the TV ceased to cast its light over the planes of Gideon's face, which was angled to hers as he kissed her.

She'd lit a candle late in the day, in anticipation of this happening, so they weren't plunged into utter darkness.

'You're beautiful in this light.' His words were gravel, and they shivered over her senses like a touch. 'The candlelight makes your hair gleam.'

Her heart beat so fast and thunderously in her chest she wondered if he could see its movement.

Gideon. He'd filled a young girl's world and her dreams, and now they were here, and Callie's resistance was gone. Just gone.

He couldn't fill her world now because that would

mean she had a deep emotional attachment to him—and she wasn't prepared to have that. It would be stupid to have that. But, oh, she needed him so, and she understood now that she had to give herself to him, have him give himself to her.

Once. So she could have her answers and lay this to rest. She needed to have him. And she needed to do that accepting that he was not a man who could or ever would love her deeply. Callie needed to take what she wanted with him this once, here and now. It would be her goodbye, of sorts, so she could move on, resolved, and be free, finally, of any lingering feelings for him.

The thought saddened her, but it was also as necessary as her next breath.

'I should get the generator online.' His hands caressed her shoulders. 'I don't want to leave you.'

'We can do it together.' Callie stood on legs that felt like rubber.

Somehow they took care of that, and then she was babbling again—on about the storm and the weather and what they might find tomorrow—until Gideon laid a finger over her lips, and then she knew that there would be no staving this off. She didn't want to, anyway.

'I thought I was doing the right thing for you, Callie. When I sent you to Mary.'

It was the last thing she had expected, and it came from him with both tenderness and a self-doubt she imagined must be rare as his hands shaped her shoulders and his gaze searched hers.

She drew a shaky breath. 'I know, Gid. It *was* the best thing for me. I needed to grow up.'

'And have you?'

Callie knew what his question meant, and the answer was inside her—fully formed and ready. 'Yes. Yes, Gideon. I've grown up.'

Enough to take this night with him, this time out of time, and let it be all to her that it could be.

Tomorrow he would go. That, too, was understood. That was what she needed.

Gideon sighed into her hair, pressed a kiss against the crown of it. 'I want to kiss you now, Callie. Kiss you and not only kiss you. I…I don't want to stop.'

'I want that, too.' Oh, she did.

Callie met him halfway. Maybe a little more than halfway. And Gideon quickly took her past that point.

'God, Callie. Nothing tastes the way you do.' He sank his fingers into her hair and angled her head for better access, to deepen the kiss until their tongues tangled and every part of her was held flush against the strength of him.

The tips of his fingers brushed the nape of her neck, where the sensitive cords that felt filled with a thousand nerve-endings were all attuned to him. Callie stroked her hands up over his chest and across his shoulders, and simply held onto all that strength and focus.

And inside herself she thought, *This time we finish this.*

She had Gideon in her arms, the way she had wanted for so long.

And of course she knew what she was doing.

CHAPTER SEVEN

'CALLIE. I need—' Gideon didn't know how to express what he needed.

To make love to her. To hold her. He needed Callie in ways he didn't want to think about, because they came from a place inside him that he didn't understand, didn't trust. A place he hadn't realised still had its grip on her somehow even when he hadn't been with her.

A place that dictated things to him like, *Look after Callie. Make sure Callie stays safe. Give her the chance to grow up, become who she needs to become.*

And it also dictated, *Don't let yourself become too attached to her, because the potential is there for a great deal of hurt if you do that.*

Hurt for her, because he didn't know how to care the right way for a woman who needed more from him than desire and affection.

But…hurt for *him*? Had he been protecting himself by staying away from her?

What odd thought was that?

Callie made a soft, needy sound and stretched up to

wrap her arms around his shoulders. Her fingers dug into his back and his arms came around her tightly. There were emotions inside him that he didn't want to confront or think about, and he wasn't sure he would understand if he did but the thoughts washed through him anyway.

She is mine.

I'm going to have her.

He'd come here to make sure her future was secure. If need be, he would have rescued her. Now he forced himself to admit he'd also come here to finally give himself sight of her again.

Seven years ago they'd been on the brink of this. The barriers had been her age, his commitment to Dianna, and Callie's heart on her sleeve and his entrenched belief somewhere inside himself that he was unable to feel that way towards a woman.

But now he could hold Callie and give her everything he had inside himself. And provided she understood what was being offered...

Gideon looked into green eyes shining for him. He ran his hands the length of her arms, down over her elbows, and drew her hands into his own. He made himself warn her, so she could end this now if that was what she needed.

'You know where this is headed, Callie?'

'I know.' Her lips softened on the acknowledgement. 'I know where it's headed, and I know what it will be and what it won't be. Just this. You and me exploring this, once, so we know—so we can put our past to rest and go on in our futures with all questions answered. For those reasons, I want it—'

Want was the right word for her to use. *Want* was the word he needed to hear from her—the only word he could give her in return. She'd made a sensible case of it—put it into words as well as he possibly could have done.

So why did it leave an ache inside him as though it *wasn't* what he needed to hear?

Gideon pushed the question aside and looked down into Callie's eyes.

She squeezed his hands, and the sparkle in those green depths softened to sweet acceptance and desire as she read *his* acceptance and desire.

'Come to bed, Gideon.'

Gideon took Callie to bed. In one small part of herself Callie noticed the silence outside, knew she should be worrying about the damage out there, but all she could hear was the beat of her blood in her veins, all she could think about was her sweet need for the man who held her in his arms.

'Let me see your beautiful body.' Gideon drew the soft T-shirt over her head and tossed it aside, caught his breath as his gaze took in what he had revealed. 'All the way to your navel…'

His fingers, the palms of his hands, tracked over her breastbone, down across the cleft between the swell of her breasts in the lacy bra. Lower.

'Freckles? You're talking about my freckles?' Her words were choppy, breathless. Her hands were at his shirt, fumbling with buttons until Gideon's eyes blazed.

When the shirt was gone, he gripped her hands in his

and brought them up. As she touched his chest it
expanded on one big, long inhalation.

'Yes, I'm talking about your freckles. I wondered...'
His words trailed off and he gave his attention to exploring instead.

Her bra disappeared in a soft rustle, and gentle hands
worshipped her while those deep blue eyes held her gaze.

'Actually, they go...' She lost her focus as he unbut-
toned her jeans, pushed the zipper down and drew them
slowly, slowly down her thighs. His hands followed.

'Yes. They go...' His finger grazed the top of her
panties and he growled low in the back of his throat.
'Callie, you're so beautiful. If I'd seen you then—'

That, too, was clamped back. But she didn't mind
because she could see the rest of his statement in the
eyes that burned for her.

If they'd gone that little bit further than they actually
had seven years ago this would have happened then.
And she knew now that she wouldn't have been ready.
No matter what she might have thought or believed
back then, she would *not* have been ready for the intensity of being with Gideon this way at that age.

*Maybe you should listen to that warning, Callie.
Because how can you be so sure you're ready even now?*

Maybe she wasn't. The ache inside her chest told her
she wasn't. But there was no going back now. No matter
how she felt when this ended, Callie didn't want to—
could not—go back.

Resolve it. She had to resolve it. And yet her
emotions were not feeling closer to being resolved.
Even so, the words poured out. 'I want this moment with

you, Gid. Everything we can have in it.' And at least she managed to add, with barely a quiver to her voice at all, 'And no worries about tomorrow.'

Whether she could believe them herself or not, her words should have reassured him. She'd thought they would. Maybe the clouding of his gaze was in her imagination…

A moment later he blinked away whatever had been there. He kissed her long and deep, and his hands caressed her until all their clothes were gone and it was just Callie and Gideon on a bed in a room, loving each other, gazes locked. And whatever was there, was there.

His mouth stole sweet kisses from her lips as he loved her over and over, brought her gently and inexorably to climax. His eyes filled with need and affection for her as he also reached his fulfilment.

And Callie realised in that moment when Gideon found his release, and she found her own release, that she loved him. Really loved him. That her whole heart and all of what was inside her loved Gideon Deveraux. Not with the childish love of an eighteen-year-old, untried and uncertain of her ground, but with a mature love that sliced right through all her objections and concerns and simply yielded to what, to her heart, appeared to be completely inevitable.

She was *deeply in love* with Gideon. Oh, why hadn't she seen that coming in the way she'd felt when he'd called her name on the island two days ago? Why hadn't she understood it when it had felt so right to be kissed by him in the abandoned cottage, and again, last night on the beach?

If she'd understood, maybe she could have protected herself.

And maybe you couldn't have done a thing. You love him. You loved him seven years ago. That love stayed with you and grew up with you. How could you have hoped to stop yourself from feeling that way?

'Callie?' Gideon's hands rubbed up and down over her arms. 'Are you all right? I wasn't…I'm not usually…I don't—' He broke off, didn't seem to know how to articulate his thoughts.

That made two of them, because Callie didn't know what to say either. She had to take a great deal of care not to blurt out what was inside her. Those feelings were too intense, too strong. If she gave them to him he wouldn't be able to receive them. She had to find a way to make them go away.

Because this hadn't been about that. This had been about resolving, not *beginning*. About closing, not *opening*.

Callie shook her head and smiled as best she could through the knot of emotion and uncertainty and deep internal fear of what she had unleashed and now didn't know how to leash again.

'I'm fine. I hope you're not going to ask me to regret what just happened, though, because I won't do that.'

Later, by herself, when she faced all that this had brought about in her, then, maybe she would have to regret it. If she could bring herself to do so.

'How did you—?' He closed his eyes in a long, slow blink. When they opened again, his hands were closed around the balls of her shoulders in a tender grip.

'Come closer, Callie. Cuddle with me a while. I...I need to hold you.'

Those words, *that need*, cut through her defences as nothing else could have. And for now at least Callie had lost any ability to distance herself, to start rebuilding her walls or shoring up her defences.

She had burrowed deep into his arms before she'd realised she'd moved. He wrapped those strong arms hard around her, stroked his fingers through the tangle of her hair, and a deep sigh came from his chest.

Gideon made love to Callie twice more before they finally slept. Slow, gentle loving that seemed right for her and felt right to him. He didn't know why he needed that with her. He simply sensed it was something he must take care to give her.

They drifted into sleep in each other's arms and he felt...blessed. And more content and happy than he could remember feeling. He had never felt that way with Dianna.

All Gideon knew was that his arms didn't want to unlock from around her. That it wasn't a case of being so content he didn't want to let go. *He couldn't make himself let go.* Possessiveness, yes, there was that inside him—a great deal more of it than he had any right to feel. Caveman instincts, maybe? He'd claimed her. He wanted the world to know she was his and he was...*keeping* her.

But that was the thing.

He *wasn't* keeping her.

They had this night and nothing more. Callie herself

had made it clear that was all she expected or wanted. She'd made it clear this wasn't about her heart.

She'd made it clear this had been a goodbye for her, a way of moving on, to lay the past to rest, their questions to rest, and go forward. Maybe into a relationship with a great guy who would be everything she needed.

A chill started somewhere deep in Gideon. He drew the comforter over them and hugged Callie closer. He drifted to sleep with a thousand questions and no answers twisting through his insides, playing through the recesses of his mind.

When Gideon woke, it was to shards of sunlight streaming into the room, emptiness beside him, and none of his questions resolved. His arms felt too light, as though they weren't right because there wasn't the weight of Callie within them.

Instinct drove him out of the bed—drove him to search her out and not waste time doing it. He didn't know what he would say when he found her, only that he had to find her.

But he forced himself to take a quick shower, and then he yielded—to the instinct he understood, and the one he didn't. He sought Callie out. He wished she had stayed all night in the haven of his arms.

What kind of haven are you to her, Deveraux? You have nothing to offer her that she would need.

He didn't. Couldn't.

Could he?

No. Last night the feelings that had washed through him as he'd held her in his arms must have simply been some random kind of overload. Maybe because he'd known her so long and they had almost made love once before.

Well, he had to see Callie *now*. Talk to her. To say… Gideon didn't know what.

He slung a shirt over his trousers and made his way outside still buttoning it, because there was this sense of urgency that he couldn't explain, could only act on.

'The guest house survived with nothing worse than a couple of broken windows and some rain damage through the breaks. The gazebo is wrecked, but it's insured.'

Callie was in the garden. The area was flattened— covered in debris. She was dragging branches into a pile and focusing on it very thoroughly, so she didn't have to focus on him.

'I'll get an assessor here as quickly as I can to deal with that.'

'Those are too heavy for you.' He stepped towards her. Wanted to take her in his arms, hold her, kiss her, take her back to bed or at least for starters tell her that one night together couldn't possibly be enough.

And where had *that* thought come from? More importantly, where did he go with it? They had agreed on one encounter, and even that had perhaps not been a particularly smart idea.

He shouldn't want more. Yet he did.

Gideon reached out to help her with her burden. 'Let me—'

A crack sounded overhead and Callie gasped and leapt forward, shoved at him. And because it was so unexpected she actually managed to push him several feet. Her momentum sent her back with him.

The tree limb that smashed to the ground behind them was twice the thickness of a human torso and about twelve feet in length.

She turned her head from the sight and her arms clamped around Gideon's middle. His arms came around her while they both drew a collective breath.

'You could have been killed—'

'You just saved my life—'

They both stopped, and Callie truly realised the grip she had on him. A wash of memories from last night poured through her, and she dropped her arms and almost stumbled back as she put distance between them.

Because that distance *had to be there*. She had to protect herself—her feelings. She'd decided that when she'd woken cuddled in his arms, when her heart had been first-thing-in-the-morning vulnerable and she'd wanted so much for him to love her and want her as she loved and wanted him.

Because she did.

Making love with him had only confirmed that fact for her, even though it was completely wrong and totally unhelpful to feel that way.

So Callie had got up. She'd told herself she had to *toughen up*. As much as she could. To save herself. She had to let him go graciously or, at worst, without him seeing her feelings for him.

'Callie—?' Gideon's voice was deep, his gaze on her intent.

She wanted to read so much into his expression, but she couldn't go there. Not when she knew she loved him, and knew equally that he didn't share those feelings towards her. She'd looked into his eyes last night and wanted to see all sorts of things, but affection was exactly that—nothing more. Callie steeled her expression to guard her thoughts.

Gideon searched Callie's face, watched the emotions chase each other across her features until she became quite guarded.

His chest ached as he acknowledged *he* was the reason for that guardedness. 'I shouldn't have made love—'

'I did just save your life.' Callie said it with a determination that seemed to come from deep inside her, as though she couldn't bear to hear what he had been about to say.

'Yes, you did save my life.' He hadn't been conscious of their surroundings, only of her. Now he realised that for him they *had* made love last night—not simply gone to bed together. His emotions—well, he wasn't sure what had happened there. He knew only that protectiveness had once again risen in him as he thought how close Callie had just come to being harmed. 'You put yourself in the path of danger in the process.'

'I acted on instinct.' Her face firmed into some kind of resolution. 'Just as you must have the day you saved my uncle, when that tractor rolled and you leapt in to get him free so it didn't roll on him.'

That was true, he supposed. But... 'I don't see the significance. I simply did what I had to do.'

'You saved *his* life.' Callie shrugged her shoulders. 'Well, I just saved *yours*. By Reid's code, that means we're even. You're free of any lingering sense of responsibility you might have felt for me. I'm setting you free,

Gideon. We can end the chapter now. It's—we can be finished now.'

She was releasing him. Not only from that old feeling of obligation, but totally setting him free.

So she could move on?

Gideon's chest felt odd, and he suddenly wasn't at all sure he wanted to be released. 'Callie—?'

The phone in his pocket rang and he drew it out to shut it off. Later. The world could intrude later. Right now he needed to get to the bottom of this with Callie.

'It's Mary,' he murmured, and reached to silence the ring tone.

'She's probably heard about the storm. She'll be worried about the state of things here—and about me, I guess.' Callie waited expectantly for him to answer the call.

Gideon gave in to the inevitable. 'Deveraux.'

In fact it wasn't Mary on the phone but MacKay Jones, and the news he had to impart was serious enough and concerning enough that Gideon had Callie's arm in his grip and was moving her towards the guest house's storm shelter before the call had ended.

He barked questions into the phone, his gaze shifting left and right as he moved them, and he had Callie at the entry door to the storm cellar by the time he finally closed the phone with a snap and met her gaze.

'Inside, Callie. I'm going to get some more food and rejoin you. Lock the door until I get back, and don't open it without hearing my voice.'

Three minutes later he closed himself inside the shelter with her, drew her away from the door area and into the kitchen, put the supplies into the fridge and met her gaze.

'That's only in case we're here a long time. I doubt that will be the case. You understood most of that conversation I had with MacKay Jones?'

'Someone took photos of the wedding and leaked them to the press, and that's led to this man phoning Mac and making a threat against my life.' Callie's mouth pinched tight. 'Who is it and what kind of—?'

'It's one man with a vendetta against the Joneses.' Gideon explained what MacKay had told him. Andrew had made an enemy during his incarceration—an unstable man the police had been trying to track down for months now, for a list of recent crimes that would put him away for the rest of his life if they caught him. 'Although the media coverage of the wedding was respectful and positive. That's one good thing to have come out of this.'

'But the bad thing is this man is coming to the island?' Callie suppressed a shiver.

'Yes, but the authorities are also on their way. It's proof of his instability that he phoned MacKay to state his intentions. Maybe a part of him is ready to be caught.' Gideon closed his hands over her arms. 'You're safe here. All you need to do is stay here—wait it out.'

'With you. I'm staying here *with you*.' Callie sought his eyes with hers and her worried green gaze clung to them. 'You mustn't go out there or get involved. What I don't understand is who leaked the photos in the first place. There's no way any of Mac's family would have done it. And we took such care.'

Gideon lowered his hand until his fingers were wrapped around her wrist. 'I may know. I have my suspicions, anyway.'

Her brows drew down. 'Who?'

'Heather Stiller. She was angry at having her opportunity here taken away. I didn't like the look in her eyes at the time, but I was distracted. I didn't think about it as much as I should have, and I didn't reassure her very well either.'

'I didn't actually see her leave.' Callie drew a sharp breath. 'Did you?'

He shook his head. 'She could have stayed back, or even made her way to the guest house to discuss the matter more—caught sight of MacKay, or other family members, recognised them, and realised she had a chance to be a bit spiteful by getting their photos to the press.'

'That bounced back on her, then, if the coverage was positive.'

'If it was her, she won't be employed by any of my companies again after this.' His thumb stroked over the skin of her inner wrist.

'First the storm threat, and now this.' Callie turned her head and soft curls brushed his face and neck.

Gideon wanted to take her in his arms and bury his face and hands in that riot of colour, inhale the scent of her as he remembered...

No. No remembering. No thinking about something that had happened that shouldn't ever have happened. No longing to go there again.

'What do we do, Gideon?' Her question came from deep down, and it was maybe about more than the threat to her life.

'We wait until I'm sure you're safe.' Something inside Gideon's chest softened, tightened. 'Then I want you to come back to Melbourne with me. I'll get you a management job in one of my hotels there, where it's not isolated.'

'I can't do that. It's kind of you, but I already have a job, Gid. I don't belong with you. I belong here.'

There were barriers in her face and in her eyes. Barriers she'd put up to protect herself—not from this worrying situation, but from him.

Gideon wanted to take those barriers down and get to the woman behind them. He wanted to kiss her sense-less and make love to her until everything melted away. Everything except the two of them. He wanted to insist she let him keep her safe. He thought maybe he wanted her to let him in, and how could he want that?

'Callie—'

'We should settle in, if this is going to take a while.' She gestured towards the living area.

So practical. So determined not to show her fear or, in this moment at least, her emotions.

Does that remind you of anyone else you know, Deveraux?

But in his case he didn't have the depth of emotion to bring to her in the first place.

No? And yet the protective instincts he battled right now seemed to suggest otherwise. He'd always had those feelings for Callie. Today she'd set him free from them, said the debt was paid, but it wasn't like that. He *needed* to keep her safe—for himself. For what it did for *him*.

Gideon tried to understand what that meant.

A shout sounded outside.

Moments later his mobile phone rang. Gideon

released Callie reluctantly and answered the call. It was a short discussion, but he gave a nod of satisfaction when it ended.

'They got him, Callie. Mission accomplished. A task force is sweeping the island now, to make sure he had no accomplices, but we'll be able to leave here soon, and then we'll talk with them about what happens next. I'm still favouring taking you back to Melbourne.'

Callie wanted to argue, but other things took over. The meeting with the special task force, and phone calls with Mac and Mary, who were relieved but shaken, and determined to get back so they could check on Callie in person.

'We're organising flights to Melbourne now, Callie. We'll boat out to the island straight away from there.'

Mary's voice had been so worried that Callie had compromised, and agreed to go to Melbourne with Gideon.

For now—just to check in with Mary and Mac.

Once they were packed and on Gideon's small boat—which was a state-of-the-art small boat, Callie noted, with a measure of seafaring appreciation—Gideon took her aside quietly and met her gaze with his own.

'I'm glad it's all over, Callie, but I *will* make sure you're completely safe before you come back to the island. Even if that means employing security personnel for a time.'

'Oh, I'm sure that won't be needed—' she began, but he waved a hand.

'Whatever's necessary to keep you safe, my dear.'

The endearment washed through her, and as the silence stretched his gaze became even more serious.

'I don't know what to say to you about last night, Callie.' His voice was low, tight. Regretful and concerned, and perhaps…confused? 'There are no words. I shouldn't have let it happen and yet I did, and I'm finding it hard to regret…'

'You can regret it if you want to.' Her chin came up and she met his gaze without flinching, made herself do it. 'I said last night *I'm* not prepared to regret what we shared. There was something between us that had been there for a long time, whether you want to admit that or not. As far as I'm concerned it's a braver move to address it, do something about it, than go on trying to deny or ignore it. So…I'm glad. I'm glad we visited that. It's not the end of the world. It's happened. We can put an end to all those questions now and go our separate ways. This doesn't have to be complicated.'

'Doesn't it?' Why couldn't he believe that?

'Let's just get to Melbourne, see Mary and reassure her.' Callie turned her gaze to the land mass before them. 'Doing that is what matters now.'

CHAPTER EIGHT

'MARY—you shouldn't have interrupted your honey-moon for this. I promise you I'm quite fine.' Callie murmured the words, and a moment later she and Mary were hugging fiercely.

They were inside Gideon's Melbourne penthouse apartment. Mary and Mac had spoken with the task force before making their way here.

'I'm so glad you're safe, Callie. If I'd known what might happen—' Mary broke off on a sob.

'It's my fault. I should never have thought I could ignore my past.' Mac stepped closer to rub Mary's back with the flat of his hand.

Gideon overrode all of it. 'The threat is completely taken care of. From all accounts this man was nothing more nor less than psychotic. Your brother did nothing to aggravate him, during his term of incarceration or afterwards. The police are glad to have apprehended him, and the matter is done with now.' Gideon drew a breath. 'Most of all, Callie's safe. That's all that matters.'

Mac and Mary accepted his reassurances. Eventually.

They all spent a little time together then, before the older couple made their way to the hotel they'd booked for the night, with Callie's stern words no doubt ringing in their ears.

'You're to go back to your honeymoon in the morning!'

Gideon smiled at the thought as he watched Callie's gaze rove his home. 'What are you finding of interest, Callie?'

Callie's gaze shifted to Gideon's face and she gave a wry smile. 'I'm just impressed. It's a lovely apartment. Nicer even than the one you had on your family's estate.'

And Callie admitted it really *was*. Striking. Beautiful. And a *home*. That showed in the scatter of Gideon's things all over the place. Cufflinks tossed on the coffee table beside a pile of newspapers. Towers of hardback and paperback books.

'I like the russet and cream colour scheme.'

He shoved his hands in his pockets and glanced at his home as though seeing it through new eyes. 'I didn't realise I'd matched the colours to your—' He broke off. Shook his head.

And they were there again. That simply.

He drew a deep breath. 'I'm glad you weren't hurt today, Callie. I…I don't think I could have borne that.'

For the first time she saw the depth of his care for her and, oh, her heart ached—because what if he could really, truly care, deep down inside, in a way that matched the way she felt about him? Care even beyond his need to keep her safe? That had no doubt started when he'd felt responsible for a young girl, but she was all grown-up now.

Callie wanted to hope—and that was a truly terrifying feeling, because all her life she had stopped herself from hoping, from letting herself need others in more than the barest minimum of ways.

Yes, she had loved Gideon for a long time, but even in that she had allowed him to push her away, send her away. Deep inside she had known that by doing that she was protecting her heart.

She had to protect it now, too, because Gideon's feelings weren't the same as hers. His protectiveness was simply that.

'I need to go back. To the island. Go home.' That was what she needed to do. Go back, regroup, put these feelings behind her and hope they evaporated as time went on.

It didn't matter that they hadn't evaporated in seven years. Things had changed now. She had to move on now. Surely she *could* move on now? Callie prayed it would prove to be the case.

'You can go first thing tomorrow morning.' Gideon hesitated. 'Or stay longer—go shopping or something before you head back…'

'No. I'm fine. I need to get back.' She needed it for her sanity—and, indeed, wouldn't it be better to go right now? 'I could call Joe and ask—'

'Call him—but arrange it for morning.' Gideon's shoulders tightened beneath his shirt. 'I don't want you out at sea at night. Although at least they've contacted Heather Stiller, and we know her only interest in passing on those photos was spite.'

'I'm glad you gave her a second chance—positioned

her into another job under a very watchful senior eye.'
Callie rubbed between her brows, where the effects of
a headache had begun to take hold. 'That was kind.
From the sound of her, when you had her on speaker
phone earlier, she truly appreciated the seriousness of
what she'd done and regretted it. Almost capsizing in
the storm in that boat she hired to get her off the island
must have frightened her, too. Her time there can't have
been pleasant.'

'She's fortunate she's not in a lot more trouble.' He
watched the movement of Callie's fingers against her
brow. 'Let me get you some paracetamol for that.' He
rummaged in a high cupboard in his kitchen and came
back to her with a glass of water and two white pills.

Callie took them with a grateful nod, and then wished
she hadn't dipped her head quite so vigorously. 'Thanks.
I guess I got a little more tense today than I realised.'

'You did really well, Callie.' He glanced away. 'Why
don't you get in the hot tub for a while? Let the jets do
their thing—get rid of the stress.'

'That sounds like heaven.' The only thing she could
imagine that would be better would be to share the tub
with him. Callie's face heated as her thoughts registered.
'A nice *solitary* soak in the tub,' she articulated with
belated care, 'sounds nice.'

He took her elbow and guided her forward, down a
hallway, until they stood outside a closed door. Gideon
opened it and a bathroom was revealed. The tub was
sunk into the floor—tiled and definitely beckoning.

Gideon flicked on the jets while she stood at the top
of the room. 'There's a bathrobe on the back of the

door. Take as long as you want, Callie.' He backed out of the bathroom. 'I'll order in some dinner.'

'Thanks. I think I will enjoy a good soak.'

Callie gave in to her need for the tub, stepped fully into the room and, the moment Gideon closed the door behind himself, started to peel off her clothes.

Callie came out of his bathroom smelling of bath crystals and warm woman. She must have piled her hair on her head before she climbed in the tub, because it was mostly dry, with wispy bits that curled around her neck in damp tendrils.

Gideon's hands flexed at his sides. For a moment he wasn't sure if he'd actually stepped forward to touch those tendrils or remained where he was. The slam of desire blindsided him, and when he came back to himself his gaze was locked on Callie's face and his heart was pounding with something that was desire and emotion mixed.

'I hope I wasn't too long in there.' Callie's glance went beyond him to the Italian food on the table. Risotto *pollo*, gourmet pizza made with mozzarella cheese and sundried tomato, fresh bread rolls with rich, creamy butter…

A smile broke across her face. 'You got Italian for dinner. I haven't had it for ages.'

'I remember you used to like it.' For long moments all he could do was stare at her, while everything inside him told him to keep her here, not to let her leave. Not in the morning, not at all.

This was what was behind his sense of emptiness when he'd woken this morning in the bed they'd shared

INHERITED BY THE BILLIONAIRE

and felt the coldness of her absence so keenly. He'd developed some kind of feelings for her. Feelings that were deeper than friendship, stronger than care for someone who'd been placed in his charge.

When Callie drew a breath her mouth trembled, and he knew she wasn't unaffected by whatever had leapt to life between them just now.

'Shall we eat here at the table?' Callie brushed her hands across the thighs of her jeans, tugged the cerise blouse into place.

Gideon watched those movements and remembered her legs wrapped around him, remembered kissing his way along rows of freckles…

'We'll eat in comfort.' He growled out the words and led her into the living room.

They ate their meal and talked about nothing. And the awareness between them was a roar in his ears until they'd eaten their fill and he turned to face her.

'There's still risotto left.' She gestured towards it.

'I'm not hungry…not for more of that.' He was hungry for Callie. 'I don't want "the end" yet, Callie.' He searched her face and didn't fully know his own thoughts. Only that he needed more of her. 'Stay with me longer. Don't go back in the morning.'

If she stayed, he would lose this feeling of dread and loss that threatened to lodge somewhere deep inside him and refuse to leave.

'I can't…' She tipped her head to the side, studied his face as though she might find insight there.

'You said we'd explored something and that was the end of it,' he said. He had thought so, too—until this morning. 'But it didn't feel like an ending to me. It didn't feel like it should be that.'

At Gideon's words Callie's heart did a slow roll in her chest. 'What—what are you saying?'

'We're good together. I'm saying…we're good together.' He rammed a hand through his hair, but he didn't take his gaze from her. 'One night—we could have more than that. Cuddling and companionship, friendship and togetherness. We could keep all that.'

Under the limits of his ability to embrace it.

Because this wasn't a declaration of love. At no time had he told her he loved her—the one vital ingredient any relationship between them could not do without. But that word was missing from Gideon's vocabulary, and her feelings went deeper than the lack of that word.

The hope that had risen in her heart dissipated. 'I can't do what you're asking of me.' She turned her face away, forced her body to follow suit. 'I—I have to go to bed. I'm tired. Please excuse me.'

She walked away before he could say anything. Retired to the guest room he'd allocated to her.

And she knew she would be gone long before he rose from his own bed in the morning.

Gone back to her home and her life. Because Callie did belong somewhere. She wasn't all alone in the world.

She belonged on the island.

CHAPTER NINE

'AND if we listen very carefully we may hear them digging down into the sand.' Callie was on all fours, in jeans and bare feet and a thick fluffy jumper that had seen better days. The sand beneath her was damp and cold, the cave dark but for the light of the single torch in her hand.

Fifteen excited schoolgirls and one somewhat less excited supervising teacher crowded behind her as they made their way through the low, narrow passage that led out of the cave to the shore.

Most of her crab whispering tours fell substantially into the 'great performance, not much reality' bracket. But those who signed up for them never seemed to mind. And Callie did enjoy taking tour groups through the warren of caves, sighting the occasional crab there. No one needed to know that was because she fed them here regularly, as well as on the beach.

Yes, she enjoyed the tours, but for the past week she had struggled to find the enjoyment. It was hard to do that when she couldn't seem to focus her thoughts away from Gideon. Thanks to him sending an expert team of workers, the island was almost restored to normal after the storm. Callie's equilibrium was taking longer.

What if they *could* have been together, and he *could* have come to have deeper feelings for her? What if she'd cut and run without trying hard enough to see if that was an option? Maybe he'd have wanted to continue, and then he might have found those feelings inside him? Maybe he was capable of that…?

'Crab whispering is a rare art form,' Callie went on, while the conviction grew inside her that she *should* have done something more than back away. She should have fought for what she wanted and needed from him. 'But these exoskeleton creatures *can* be whispered out if we take enough care.'

'Is it much further until we get out?' The teacher whispered the question.

'Not far at all.' Callie hoped her distraction hadn't shown. She shone the torch around the cave and said in her best crab whisperer tone, 'There's one of our friendly creatures now.'

The crab received the gift of some of the special feed Callie had brought along. The girls giggled, as girls were wont to do. Lots of shushing followed, and then they were out on the beach. Callie shared the crab feed out, and stood back while her guests enjoyed the sight of dozens of crabs scuttling about in the moonlight on the beach.

Some of the girls started to giggle in earnest, then, and something changed in the atmosphere.

Callie followed the direction of their gazes and her heart stopped.

Gideon.

What was he doing here? And why did her heart have to melt with love for him? That wasn't fair. She felt the teacher's gaze on her, and with some part of her she heard the woman's words.

'Come along, girls. It was a wonderful tour, but I'm sure Miss Humbold would like an opportunity to…ah… to tidy up after the tour and…and so forth.'

Fifteen curious schoolgirls were hustled away.

A man and a woman were left facing each other across a stretch of beach.

Beyond Gideon, Callie could make out a small array of glass containers on the beach. But she only really had eyes for Gideon.

'Callie. I came because—'

'I'd decided to come to *you*. I'd just now decided—'

'I needed to see you.' His words came out in a low murmur. He gestured at the retreating figures of the schoolgirls and the teacher. 'I can see you're busy this weekend, but I'm hoping you can spare a few moments for me.' He hesitated, as though uncertain how to go on.

'I can spare the time.' What did he want to say? 'Why did you come, Gideon?'

It was a cry from deep inside her. Need and guardedness and a wish all rolled into one—because it appeared she couldn't stop herself from hoping after all. And where did that leave her, if she needed to protect her emotions as she had always protected them, even when she had let herself care about him?

Even when she had discovered that deep down she loved him, had fallen in love all the more with him later?

'You were crab whispering.' He said it with what she would have sworn was admiration. 'I could see how much the group enjoyed themselves.'

'Yes, I took them through the caves. It might sound like a silly concept, but the guests love it.' She forced herself to meet his gaze. '*I* love it.' At least she did when she could concentrate on it. 'Why are you here, Gideon? I heard from Mary just today. We spoke on the phone, so I know there's nothing amiss there.'

'I've talked with her recently, too. Mary and Mac sound very happy.' Gideon took a step closer to her and cleared his throat. 'I was wrong to doubt Mac and Mary's love, Callie. It *is* enough to carry them through anything.'

He searched her eyes as he spoke these words.

Callie swallowed hard. 'I'm happy for Mary and Mac—'

'I am, too. But that's not what I want to talk about.' He threw out one hand, as though he didn't know how to go on. The struggle inside him was obvious, and she wanted to help him through it. She just didn't know how to do that.

I would love him through it.

I would love him through anything—just like Mary would love Mac through anything.

'Gideon…'

'Will you come for a walk on the beach with me, Callie?'

He reached out his hand and Callie placed her hand in his. Her heart hurt so much—but how could she do anything but go with him?

They walked until they came to all those glass con-

tainers. Here, the beach was sandy and flat. They
stopped, and Gideon turned her to face him. He swallowed hard, and in the moonlight she thought she caught
a nervous expression in his eyes.

A moment later she figured she must have imagined
it because she *wanted* it to be there.

'You want to be released—you need better closure—
maybe you don't want me working in your employ? I
could find another job.'

Maybe if she said it for him they could get through
this faster, and then she could get to the part where her
heart started to heal and she got on with her life without
thinking of him every moment of every day, longing for
his arms around her every second of every endless night.

'No. You're perfect here.' He gripped her hands,
closed his eyes and inhaled. 'That's not what I want
from you, Callie. It's not why I'm here. I thought I'd be
able to tell you—that it would be easy once I was face
to face with you.' Gideon's hands squeezed hers and he
seemed so intense.

'You're scaring me.'

'That's the last thing I want to do. Can I…can I hold
you?' He leaned forward, rested his chin on the top of
her head. His lips stirred her hair, the lightest of kisses,
and then he leaned back enough to look into her eyes
once again. 'Do you feel it, too? When we touch? This
need that starts so deep inside and spreads?'

Yes. She felt it. And in those few short seconds Callie
went through so many emotions. Love, need, affection,
hope, fear.

Hope was the thing that scared her the most. Because

hope was something she had kept to the parts of her life she could control.

Even when she had loved Gideon years ago she hadn't let herself hope he would love her back. Not really. Not enough to stick around and fight for that love.

And she had walked away a second time, hadn't she?

Callie stared at this man she held in the depths of her heart, and she realised she had shown weakness by walking away like that. She should have stayed and fought for what she wanted—should have at least told him what was in her heart and what she needed from him.

What was the worst that could have happened? He would have rejected her? Been there, let that happen—not once, but twice. Well, she had decided she would go to him, and now she had that chance.

'Gideon, I want to tell you—'

'Will you let me say something first, Callie?' He squeezed her hands. 'Let me say it by showing you, and then let me say it with words? I need to do both. For this. With you.'

He stepped away, walked until he reached the first of those glass containers. He bent down and a lighter flared in the darkness. A candle came to life, and Callie realised it was inside a fluted glass cover.

Soon there were more candles lit. He stood back and Callie read the message through eyes that wanted to blur: *I love you.*

Her gaze flew to his while all her hopes and her heart leapt inside her.

'I love you and I need you, Callie. When I knew your life might be in danger everything inside me locked up

with concern for your safety. I put it down to an old protectiveness, similar to what I felt for you when you were
younger, but it was far more than that. The threat to your
life made me realise I don't want to live without you. I
want us to make this real.'

Gideon stepped back along the beach towards Callie.
God, she looked so beautiful in the moonlight, with the
flicker of the candles' glow bringing out the shine of her
hair and casting shadows and light across her pale face.

She looked beautiful and scared and confused, but
her gaze came to his and she drew a shaky breath.
'You…love me? How? How do you love me? As a
friend? As the girl you inherited from my uncle?'

'As a friend, as that girl.' Yes, as both those things.
But, oh, as so much more than that. Gideon's voice
deepened as he went on. 'As the woman I held in my
arms and loved and didn't realise I *was* loving with my
heart and my soul, not only my body.'

He took her hands in his and prayed she would be
able to accept what he wanted to give her.

'As someone I can't do without. I need you, Callie.
I love you and need you with all my heart. I asked you
to stay longer with me, but I hadn't let myself admit just
why I wanted that. I love you and need you way deep
down inside myself, in places I didn't know were
capable of such feelings. I thought I only wanted a
society wife—someone who would look good on
my arm and fulfil my family's expectations for the
Deveraux heir.'

He drew a slow breath.

'Being with Dianna proved how hollow that kind of

relationship is. All along, deep in my heart, I knew there could be so much more with you. When I held you and made love with you I *fell in love* with you. And now I know that I need you…to stay with me, to be with me, to let me love you. Not for a day or a week or a few times. For ever.'

'I want to believe you, Gideon.' Her words were low, cautious. Not fully believing.

'Then believe.' He glanced at the candles burning on the beach, spelling out his message to her. 'Believe that message and believe *me*. I had to come back—to find you and tell you. I don't…' The words were hard to say, but they needed to be said. 'I don't expect you to love me the way I love you. What I hope is that you might love me a little, and trust in that love to grow over time.'

Callie looked into Gideon's eyes and acknowledged that she wanted and needed to trust him with her heart. To trust in the feelings he had found in himself for her. And she needed to trust the love she felt for him—trust enough to give it to him, nothing held back.

'I don't have to try to grow my love for you, Gid. It's been there all these years, and it's still there—strong and sure for you.'

'Are you saying—?'

'I'm saying yes.' Oh, God. She *was*, wasn't she? 'I'm saying yes to staying. To loving and being loved by you for the rest of my life. Yes to everything you want with me.'

'Then you're marrying me. *Soon.*'

Gideon reached for her, tugged her into his arms and wrapped them right around her. He held on so tightly his fingers dug into her back, and Callie realised hers were digging into his shoulders just as much.

He kissed her so sweetly then, with such pent-up emotion, and it was the feeling in that kiss that pushed away any lingering doubt she might have had.

'I'd made up my mind to come to you, to tell you how I felt and fight for the chance to be with you and be loved by you.' She whispered the confession into his neck, and then made herself draw back and look into his eyes, so he could see all her love in her expression. 'I wanted to fight for you, Gid. For what we could have together. Fight instead of cut and run and not trust in the chance to be loved that way, to…to give love that way.'

'Because you've been alone. You haven't had family, except your uncle. When he died you were alone again, and I sent you away.'

Callie laid her fingers over his lips and smiled with all that was in her heart and soul. 'Yes, but in your way you've been just as alone. Mary was the closest you got to real family. Your parents are self-absorbed enough that I don't think they really count, and Dianna…'

'Didn't love me any more than I loved her. But I *am* capable of love, Callie.' He hesitated. 'I just needed to take it to the right person. That person…is you.'

'I'll move to Melbourne to be with you.' The words were an offering. She didn't want to be apart from him.

His fingers caught hers and squeezed. 'I'm not taking you from here, Callie. I've realised how wrong that would be. We'll make the island our base, and I'll make changes to my workload to make it work. I can pick and choose what I do. I want—'

'Yes?' She searched his gaze and found all the love and hope and openness she could ever need to see shining there for her.

'I want to be with you. I just…want you, Callie.' He stroked her cheek with his fingers. 'And maybe some babies with you one day.'

Oh, yes. Babies and Gideon and a whole life ahead of them, doing whatever made them the happiest. Callie wanted that!

'I guess we both had to come to a place where we could trust in how much we needed each other.' She received his kiss and snuggled close to him as the sea breeze rustled over them. 'It's okay to need and want and…love.'

Gideon dipped his head and kissed the tip of her nose, snuggled her closer still. 'It's more than okay.' He looked into her eyes with a question and a promise and a great deal of love. 'Do you think anyone would notice if we disappeared into the storm shelter until tomorrow? I really need to be alone with you.'

'The storm shelter seems exactly the right place to go.'

Because Callie had found her safe haven in Gideon and he had found his in her while they were there.

And so that was where they went!

millsandboon.co.uk Community

Join Us!

The Community is the perfect place to meet and chat to kindred spirits who love books and reading as much as you do, but it's also the place to:

- **Get the inside scoop from authors about their latest books**
- **Learn how to write a romance book with advice from our editors**
- **Help us to continue publishing the best in women's fiction**
- **Share your thoughts on the books we publish**
- **Befriend other users**

Forums: Interact with each other as well as authors, editors and a whole host of other users worldwide.

Blogs: Every registered community member has their own blog to tell the world what they're up to and what's on their mind.

Book Challenge: We're aiming to read 5,000 books and have joined forces with The Reading Agency in our inaugural Book Challenge.

Profile Page: Showcase yourself and keep a record of your recent community activity.

Social Networking: We've added buttons at the end of every post to share via digg, Facebook, Google, Yahoo, technorati and de.licio.us.

www.millsandboon.co.uk